Ronald K. Myers

ALMOST FREE

DOUBLE DRAGON

A DOUBLE DRAGON PAPERBACK

ISBN 978-1-78695-518-0

Double Dragon
is an imprint of
Fiction4All

Published 2021
Fiction4All
www.fiction4all.com

Cover art by Ronald K. Myers

INTRODUCTION AND DEDICATION

The only thing Freddy Crane wants to do is be free from desperate violence. To do that, he will have to find the strength and courage to go on a dangerous detour, not only through Vietnam where a five hundred dollar bounty has been placed on any ASA member captured but also through a fog-shrouded island jam-packed with fortune seekers who claim to be secret agents. To outwit a mysterious colonel who's using him, Crane, a former malnourished kid from a dilapidated town who believes everything bad thing in life had already been thrown his way must quickly find new toughness and new wisdom he never knew he possessed. Young and new to a most secret United States military intelligence unit, Crane unexpectedly reunites with his childhood friend who is now a Green Beret. But to expose the colonel they must be willing to pay with their lives. A fiercely independent French woman who is also beautiful and resourceful, delivers a terrifying message. Even before she teams up with Crane, she becomes closest to his heart. Will his hard-edged instincts, honed from years living in poverty, serve him and her as they take a desperate stand against the shadowy agents out to drive them away?

This book is dedicated to the memory of my Army Security Agency brothers for their courageous service to our county and their undying friendship to me. Clandestinely serving their country and often called "Spooks" these men had the highest IQ's in the military and were the best intelligence gathers there ever were. Formed from the Office of Strategic Services, OSS, and way before the National Security Agency, NSA, the Army Security Agency, ASA, was a form of military intelligence that operated undercover from 1945 thru 1976. Although many were not honored with awards, and were ignored, and were overlooked, and were forgotten, the ASA earned over 120 awards and over 40 foreign citations.

Much gratitude to Marine, Gary Vath, for guidance and assistances during an unprecedented fifteen-year run of the writers' group: The Slack Waters Improvisational Collective.

Also: Much gratitude to Brenda Koppel for editing and first reader assistance.

CHAPTER 1

Jogging across the parched grass of the parade field, Freddy Crane watched intellectually incapable army personnel stare at him with weird looks on their faces. But their stares didn't bother him. Before the glorious blue sky day was over, he was going to be free from the insanity.

Even though a broken nose from his boxing days made it difficult for him to breathe, he was in the best shape of his life. He never wanted to fight, but when something made him angry, he became insanely unstoppable. Although his muscular body was rock-solid, it was agile and easily responded to his every command, and his reflexes were faster than anyone he had ever fought. But it no longer mattered how physically fit or how quick he could fight off an enemy, he wouldn't be needing those skills. After customary pronouncements, his new home would be in a place where the setting sun crowned trees with gold. Except for fond memories of Piper, the girl with the marvelously deep blue almond eyes, gnawing at his heart strings, he would be free to view the world with complete detachment.

Even without Piper, his life would be far better than it had been before he enlisted in the Army Security Agency. Then he had been raised in the squalor of an oven-like shack that was so dilapidated it could have fallen over in the next wind. Many times, after being chased by cops down dirty alleys and feeling the street press through the thin soles of his shoes, he had gone to bed hungry. And when he did eat, he ate as if he were facing starvation, and many times he was.

His neighborhood had become so rundown it couldn't qualify to be a ghetto. Like other malnourished kids from dilapidated places, he never wanted to be like the barely surviving rabble shuffling around on the streets. To him they were empty people, contributing nothing, building nothing, but striving to live off the work of better men. Going from hand-out to hand-out, preferring the illusionary comfort of the familiar, they believed they were the wise ones. But when they were suddenly old and worn out with no placed to go, they wondered what had happened.

During Crane's gawky years of adolescence, he has always wanted to be like the strong men wearing custom-tailored suits who had gotten what they wanted. Now it was his turn to grab the world by the throat and shake it until it gave him what he had been too poor to have. He was always amazed at the way prosperity made people critical of all who were less prosperous. After the people had gotten a few dollars more than they needed, their ugly eyes stared at him with hatred. In a little while, not only would he be relaxing in his wooden chair, people would be giving him money, and he wouldn't be staring at anybody with hatred.

Overseas, the tension and secrecy of special operational units and their casual disregard for authority had been like running away and joining the circus, but that was before he had been ordered to an isolated island where wild winds gnarled shorelines and annihilated just about every living thing. A haven of horror with grotesque, nightmarish fog, knee-deep tundra, and whirling snow storms, Shemya, Alaska, AKA, the Rock, was a little two by four-mile afterthought of land that no man wanted to visit. For the entire year, Crane was there, it had been like being incarcerated on Alcatraz.

When Crane left the Rock, he thought the bad times were over, and he was going to return to a normal life, but when he got off the plane at Oakland, California, a raggedy horde of protestors were yammering away in preparation to harangue returning soldiers. He tried to slip past them, but they greeted him with a hail of spit, boos, hisses, and catcalls. Living in comfortable homes and miles from Vietnam, protesters, preaching peace who didn't have the guts to bravely face the cruel new life of the military, never experienced what they were protesting. Naturally it was easy for them to tell veterans how they should live. Crane didn't care what they did until a chunky protestor with a perfect Beetle haircut walked up to him, spit directly into his face, and laughed. As a natural defensive reaction, Crane lifted his hand to start cultivating hematomas on the protestor's face. But not wanting to start trouble and miss his flight home, Crane lowered his hand.

But it did no good.

The protestor defiantly stood in front of Crane and said, "You touch me, baby killer, you'll go to jail."

Crane tried to slough it off, but the protestor's certainty that his exalted station in life relieved him of any obligation to treat others decently, caused an uneasiness to build in Crane's clinched fists. "I wouldn't want to touch anything like you."

For a moment the protestor glowered at Crane, then his face beamed a mocking, full-toothed smile. "Oh, really?"

The way he had said, "Oh, really," sounded worse than any of the classic vulgarities.

To Crane, *oh really,* caused a horrid flashback of being humiliated by the self-righteous people standing in front of their gray, decrepit little shops in his decaying hometown and becoming infuriated just because, he, with a lowly status, had walked past. Mocking him and his shabby clothes, they had repeated, "Oh! Really!" over and over. And it was happening again, causing a sad wave of sentiment to roll over him. After risking his life for his country, this is what he had come back to. Wanting to just get away from it all, he waved his hand in a gesture of dismissal and turned to walk away.

But the protestor taunted again, "Oh, really!"

The abuse, the pointless hostility, and the resentment was like lighting a fuse on a stick of hate-filled dynamite.

Thinking about the brave men who had been shot, killed, tortured, and imprisoned more times that most Americans realized or cared to hear about, Crane turned back and faced the tormentor.

The contemptuous smile of the tormentor loomed large. "You touch me, you'll go to jail."

With unbelievable speed, Crane whipped his own belt from around his waist, wrapped it around the protestor's neck, lifted him into the air, and held him there. Shaking him so violently that the protestor's Beetle haircut was flapping up and down, Crane screamed into his face, "For every day I spend in jail, you'll spend three days in a hospital."

The protestor gaged and struggled for air. As he kicked and grabbed at the belt around his neck, the shiny brass buckle of Crane's belt flashed a brilliant gold into the faces of the other protestors.

The spitting, boos, hisses, and catcalls stopped.

Shocked, the protestors stared in awe.

Crane released his belt from the protestor's neck.

He slumped to the floor.

Crane walked away.

He caught his flight and made it home okay, but many times after his Vietnam involvement and the appalling airport incident, he had gotten out of bed in terror with a cold sweat on his forehead. Some men who had managed to return, used liquor or drugs to forget what they had gone through. It was a kind of deliberate bandaging of the mind, so they could ignore the hell they had suffered. If Crane wanted to get four or five hours of sleep without unwanted nightmares jarring him awake, he threw down three fingers of scotch. It would enable him to stop wondering how he came back and was trying to make believe it all didn't happen. If he drank in the bars, he would have to listen to drunken mill workers crying in their beer about how they lost their jobs, or their seniority, or how they got a strange piece of ass. If Crane re-enlisted, because of his restricted Military Occupational Specialty he would be sent back to the Rock, and it would start all over again.

But today, that wasn't going to happen. Referred to as a "Short Timer" Crane only had a short time left to serve. During the past few weeks when asked how many days he had left, he had replied that he was so short he had to sit on the edge of a razor blade to tie his shoes.

At the end of the parade field, Crane looked up. As if it were a great gateway to a heaven in the Virginia sky, the sun threw cathedral-like beams of light down through the clouds and caused him to feel as if God were welcoming him to a better life.

Off to his right, speaking harshly, the portly company commander hunched his shoulders, placed his hands on his wide hips, and with a tube of fat hanging heavily over his belt buckle, he roared, "Specialist Crane!"

The bawling voice was so loud that it hurt Crane's ears, but he was glad that intelligence counted for something in the ASA. Specialist ranks were not only created to reward personnel with higher degrees of experience and technical knowledge, they kept people with regular army ranks out of areas where they had no expertise and no top-secret crypto clearances, and this always angered the company commander.

Crane's feelings of a better life vanished. He came to an abrupt halt and unwillingly stood at attention. Since it would be his final salute, he threw back his shoulders, lifted his hand to his forehead, and prepared to give the captain the crispest salute that he'd ever offered anyone. As he held the salute, he stared his contempt directly at the flamboyant company commander walking toward him.

Unlike the regular army personnel, where most decisions were made for those who followed the way of least resistance and had become part of a rigidly bureaucratized and conventional force, special operations soldiers of the ASA were carefully selected and specially trained and possessed unique skills for missions the conventional armies could not conduct, and most officers didn't trust special operations soldiers. Understandably, they didn't appreciate people they couldn't control. The company commander wasn't special forces qualified, wasn't airborne qualified, had no combat time, and his face had tapering features of a rat. If weren't for high-level bureaucratic inanities, he would never have been promoted to captain. Being one of those officers who must feel themselves superior, and their ranks gives them that opportunity, he haphazardly returned Crane's salute. "Crane! Where do you think you're going?"

Crane did not give his planned crispest salute. He only dropped his hand.

The captain's disparagements were frequently venomous. Earlier this morning, after he had amused himself with verbal cuts at Crane, he had freely flaunted his authority and ordered Crane to get a haircut. Not wanting anything to interfere with his discharge, Crane had gotten the haircut and figured it would be the last army haircut he would ever be ordered to get. "No disrespect, sir. But may I remind you that I'm getting discharged today?"

The captain's face screwed up with excruciating irritability and through the folds of fat around his eyes, he cast an ugly stare in Crane's direction. "I've seen your kind before," he said and grunted. "You may get out, but you'll be back."

For a moment, Crane felt sorry for the captain. Just because he was stuck in a rut of army life and had no other place to go, he believed Crane was, too. The captain was like most men who ended up on the bad end of a deal. The way Crane saw it, if the captain stayed in a rut, it was his own fault. Every time a man got up in the morning, he started his life over. Everybody didn't have to stay in a pattern. They could always follow another path. And that was just what Crane was going to do. Today, he wasn't going to let anything bother him.

He smiled at the captain. "If I were intellectually incapable, I might consider coming back but I won't."

Hatred blazed in the captain's eyes. "You not smart enough to be out there on your own. If you think the world is fair, you have been seriously misinformed."

Evidently the captain didn't know what Crane had done before he joined the army or what he had done in the army, and he wasn't going to waste time telling him.

"Life might not be fair," Crane shot back. "But it's all we got."

As if the captain were making sure he was going to force Crane to do one of the most important things in the world before he was discharged, he puffed up with importance. But his fat belly swelled into his shirt. The strain placed on the buttons caused his shirt to wrinkle at each button, and the sight caused Crane to recall rule one for every OCS candidate: Make sure the people you are commanding respect you. If they like you, that's okay. But if they don't, fear will do. Crane had no respect for this officer, and the officer knew it.

So…like a typical officer who had their show of superiority ruined, the captain tried to use fear by yelling at the top of his voice, "Didn't I tell you to get a haircut this morning?"

Crane relaxed his stance and ran his hand through his black hair. "I did, sir."

As if he had just run a marathon and was trying to catch his breath, the two hundred fifty-pound coronary waiting to happen, huffed in three great drafts of air. Then he assumed an aggressive stance and continued to shout, "It's not good enough. Get another haircut!" He pulled a dirty white handkerchief from his back pocket and mopped his head. "Get another haircut," he repeated. "And report back to me."

When Crane had been with special operations group, SOG, its top-secret world had its own unspoken code brought on by danger, duty, and loyalty. Even if the team leader was outranked, he was God. He was the first man off the helicopter, and unlike the captain, he had never led by force of rank or intimidation, but by example. Crane could argue with the captain and show him he couldn't push him around, but he figured the captain was a born subordinate. Not too smart and unimaginative. Crane didn't want to lower himself to the captain's level. And he had no intention of getting another haircut or reporting back to anyone who had not seen or done what he had done. Once again, the captain had affirmed many of the ASA men's definition of the regular army: Leading the unwilling to do the unnecessary.

Figuring it would be his final fawning response, Crane snapped to rigid attention. "Yes, sir!" In his most fake and enthusiastic manner, he issued a brisk salute. Then in exemplary fashion, he performed a perfect about face and energetically walked away.

Walking toward the windowless operations building, he cursed under his breath. In the regular army, if soldiers in combat couldn't follow a simple order, others would be killed. So, there was a need and proper place for foolish orders to be strictly obeyed. But the Army Security Agency, ASA, needed the services of nonconformists for sensitive work. At times, the work was so secret that few officers knew the men or what they did. The ASA needed men that the regular military regime annoyed. The ASA needed men who thought for themselves and didn't go by the book. Crane was not only a free thinker, he was what the ASA wanted. He had never adapted to the spit and polish of the regular army.

In the ASA, he had served with innovators and imaginative people who wanted to try something new and challenging. In the field, it didn't matter what rank a person was, they were treated according to their abilities. Because most ASA men had chafed at the rigidity of the regular army, it had always given ASA people a bad time.

After passing though security at the entrance to the steel-reinforced, four-foot-thick-cement-walled operations building, Crane walked through a windowless, narrow hall of locked doors that concealed soundproof, windowless rooms. In this super secure area, special people worked on projects they could not discuss. Crane didn't know if it were a curse or a gift, but he had a pretty good idea what every person behind those doors had done, was doing, or was going to do.

At the end of the hall, he unlocked the green combination lock on a gray steel door and entered his former room of operations. Inside, he stood in front of Sergeant Joe Gillette's desk and told him of his plan.

Gillette was a slender man with a friendly mouth and eyes that smiled easily, but a look of discomfort had formed on his brow. "Do you believe your cockamamie plan will work?"

In the past, this negative talk may have bothered Crane, but he was getting out. Nothing could bother him now. "Sure, it will," he said with more confidence than he had had during his past four years. "All I need to do is earn enough money to buy a piece of land."

Gillette smiled his all-knowing smile. "The people you have associated with have died at an unusually high rate. What makes you believe you 'll live long enough to do it?"

Recalling what had happened in Shemya, Vietnam, and Japan, Crane shrugged. "Things that happened were not my fault."

Gillette held up a reassuring hand. "I know, I know. Actually, what you've done makes the rest of the agency look incompetent, almost irrelevant."

Crane didn't feel he had done anything great. "Anybody could've done it, "he said. "The only thing I did was been in the wrong place at the right time and do the right thing."

Shaking his head, Gillette's face flushed with discomfort. "I wouldn't say that. But I'm sure you realize that most of the stinking lousy sons of bitches don't give a rat's ass about your special warfare training and devotion to your country that you were physically and mentally tough enough to endure."

"I know that," Crane answered with a sigh. "But what about all the radios and other advanced equipment I've used or worked on? Shouldn't that count for something?

"Don't kid yourself," Gillette said with distress. "All the equipment you worked on, or operated, is so far advanced or classified, your expertise is useless in a civilian society. You may have done better if you had run away and joined the circus."

"With all the clowns around here, it feels like I did join the circus."

Gillette's eyes lifted in a curious, speculative glance. "I know what you mean, Crane. Good luck on getting a decent job."

"Thanks for the advice. But I've turned the unexpected into a victory many times. I can make my own luck."

Gillette gave Crane a reassuring nod. "I hope you can."

"And besides, as a civilian" — Crane smiled big — "if I don't like a job, I can quit. I can even have a Border collie."

Even though the practice of using a subject's first name as much as possible unnerved a person being questioned and caused him to relax and make mistakes, Crane never did like the military practice of people being called by their last names. He lifted his finger to make a point. "And people will call me by my first name."

Gillette lifted an eyebrow. "It doesn't really matter what people call you. You have an uncanny knack of barging into things that could get you killed. If you're going to make it in the civilian world, you'll need an assembly line, manufacturing luck twenty-four hours a day."

"After I get out, all that will change."

Staying seated, Gillette used his feet to push his wheeled office chair and rolled to the next desk. "I wouldn't bet on it." He leafed through a stack of papers, pulled a page from the center, glanced at it, and held it toward Crane. "Here's a request from a new special operations unit." He ran his finger across the page. "Your expertise is just what they need." A big smile spread under his mustache.

"They claim it's not safe when you're loose." He pointed to a line on the paper. "Look here. There is an opening for a mission code named Tinkerville. They want you to re-enlist."

Well, that would not be new, Crane was going to say, but before the words were out of his mouth, a dull pain thudded in his chest. "Tell them to get some other sucker."

Gillette's eyes sparkled with mischief. "What's the problem? Don't you like all the hot babes, the cool gunplay, driving fast cars, and opening fat envelops full of money?"

Although some people would like to believe the ASA was like that, Crane's four years of service had proven it was not. But it didn't matter what Sergeant Gillette or anyone said or promised, Crane had made up his mind to be an observer. If his signature ended up on any re-enlistment document, he would not be able to view life with complete detachment. He laughed, reached out, grasp Gillette's hand in a secure, caring grip, and shook it. In the ASA there was not as much bull about rank than there was in the regular army. Officers and Sergeants were often called by their first names. There was a spirt of community as well as a sense of individual worth. Crane addressed Sergeant Gillette by his diminutive. "Sorry, Joe, I'm going to go back to a bourgeois lifestyle. I'll leave all the hot babes for you."

"Gee thanks," Joe said and winked at Crane. "I already have to fight them off with a stick, and you want to send more my way."

Crane shook his head and smiled. "It was nice working together, but I gotta cut and run."

"Don't be in such a hurry," Gillette said, and Crane detected disappointment.

Gillette leaned his head crookedly against the back of his chair. "Crane, you know there could be a mistake?" As if in jest, he grinned. "Maybe they've made a clerical error, and you won't be discharged." He straightened his head and shrugged. "Of course, in a few years, when brought to the attention of the proper authorities, it will eventually be rectified. You'll get to go home, but you'll have to take a dangerous detour."

"That's impossible," Crane said with a tinge of disappointment in his voice. "The ASA is more highly evolved than that."

Gillette chuckled. "I almost had you going." He stood up and extended his hand. "It was a pleasure working with someone who knows what the hell they're doing."

"It was easy," Crane said, shaking Gillette's hand. "I had your help."

Smiling, Gillette nodded, but he seemed to be holding back a tear.

Crane unclasped Gillette's hand and turned to go, but Gillette held his hand fast.

"Old soldiers tell you to put the entire experience behind you," he said. "Consider it gone. Always remember the chasm between people who have gone through what you have and those who haven't, is wider than the Pacific Ocean, and it is not to be crossed."

He released Crane's hand.

With a tear in his eye, Crane nodded and turned to go.

Gillette touched him on the shoulder.

Crane turned back.

There was anguish in Gillette's face, but he talked sternly. "Crane, if you get rich, there will be a lot of people out there trying to take it from you. Don't fall into their rivers of nonsense. It isn't always their fault, but it's the way they live. If you know that, you 'll always give yourself an edge. You may never need that edge, but if you do, it will make your life a lot easier. Learn to depend on nobody but yourself. He who can stand alone is the strongest. If you expect nothing from people, you will never be disappointed."

To keep from choking with emotion, Crane held his breath, tightened his face, and said, "Thanks, Joe."

Gillette gestured to the door. "Be careful out there. Sometimes they can be worse than Sergeant Mullin."

With his non-helpful, down-right rude, and rotten attitude, Sergeant Mullin seemed to be highly motivated and specially trained to irritate, aggravate, and infuriate people. Out of jealousy, he had manipulated the paperwork of a special operations soldier he didn't like, so his award of The Medal of Honor was downgraded to a Silver Star. Crane tried to replace the choking feeling of emotion with humor. "If Mullin entered an asshole contest, he's be the winner."

"He's not the brightest bulb in the basket, but people like him can make a hard road for you."

"Why is he always giving me a hard time?"

"There could be a lot of reasons. One reason could be that he doesn't have the top-secret clearance, the people supposedly working under him have, and when a lower ranking ASA man tells him he doesn't have the need to know, it irritates him."

Crane nodded in agreement. "I've watched a lot of NCOs do that."

"Get used to it. The better you do in the world the more bad things people will say about you. Or people could be like Mullin who hates something he doesn't understand or anything different. But he's not doing anything new."

"What are you talking about?"

"In World War II, the predecessor of ASA was known as the Overseas Strategic Service, and it had to continuously fight for its existence. If it weren't for President Roosevelt, it is unlikely that the OSS would have been created."

Crane gave Joe an encouraging nod. "If the idiotic half-wittedness would have succeeded, the United States would have been in for a bitter awakenment."

"They were awakened all right," Gillette said. "After Roosevelt died, MacArthur saw an OSS briefer wearing argyle socks with his uniform. The socks got MacArthur so riled up that he didn't allow the OSS to operate in his theater." He lifted one finger and smiled. "Naturally, he lost his final battle."

Cranc let out a deep pained exhale. "What happened in the past doesn't really matter. I won't be fighting any more battles. In fact, I won't be fighting at all. I'm going home."

CHAPTER 2

Seconds after Crane had been honorably discharged, he was looking forward to being a civilian again and being addressed by his first name.

His Chevy pickup truck with the shrouded headlights, set in visored fenders that accented a classic egg crate grille was waiting. All he had to do was step on the running board, hop in, shift the Chevy into gear, and tromp on the gas. The small block, two hundred sixty-five cubic-inch, overhead valve engine that waited under the hood would take him home. Excited to finally be free, he sprinted across the parade field. Feeling something was wrong, he suddenly stopped.

Out of habit, he stood still and breathed shallow. Listening for any sound, watching for any motion, searching for any suspicious odor, he locked all his senses on full alert. When he was satisfied it was safe, he glanced back at the barracks and started running, again. Although the barracks had been a better place than where he had grown up, he felt like he was leaving an amusement park.

Just before he got to his truck, a man with the look of an idiot condemned to a mental institution was standing to his right with his arms defiantly folded across his chest. It was the dreaded Sergeant Mullin. While his mean eyes flashed enjoyment, he opened his ugly mouth and yelled at Crane, "Hey! You black-headed bastard. Where the hell you running to?"

Mullin was a typical tyrant-type sergeant with a hard, rat-like face who believed he had unlimited power and authority, and he had always harassed Crane. People like Mullin didn't have enough brains to go on special operations missions, and they thought they were important, but were not. To keep up the illusion that they were important, the few on the base huddled together in cliques and lived in unhappy packs. From the way Mullin boasted that he could kill someone, Crane believed Mullin would never be able to do it. Saying he was willing to do it and then backing it up with a trigger pull against a human being were two very different things. Not everybody could do it without hesitating or thinking about it first. And the least bit of hesitation would allow the enemy to make the first killing move. If Mullin were sent on a special operations mission or got out of the military, he would not be able to hide his ignorance behind his rank.

Crane had always wanted to tell Mullin that if he wanted to gamble with the lives of others, he should include himself in the game. And Mullin's hair was the color of diarrhea which fit his turd-head personality. But Mullin outranked Crane. So Crane was forced to take most of whatever Mullin dished out.

But this time, Crane wasn't going to waste his time with a loser like Mullin. He kept on running.

Just as he was about to run past him, Mullin let a crude laugh escape from his rat-like face, lifted his foot, and kicked at the side of Crane's knee. Crane saw it coming. He jerked his leg away. Mullin's boot hit Crane's knee, but it wasn't a direct hit. Crane stumbled but caught his balance. If Mullin would have made a direct hit, Crane's knee could have been displaced.

To let Mullin know he couldn't be pushed around, Crane thrust his jaw out defiantly and unleased a string of pent up profanity. "Hey! You bigmouth, goddamn, stinkin', lousy son-of-a-bithin' shit head. What the hell's the matter with your dip-shit brain?"

Instant surprise flashed from Mullin's bronzed face, and his small reptilian eyes opened wide with alarm. "What did you say?"

"You heard me the first time. Quit trying to use brains you don't have."

With his muscles budging under his uniform shirt, Mullin's cold, tombstone-like eyes bored into Crane's very soul. "You can't talk to me like that." He snarled and pointed to the stripes on his arm. "I outrank you."

Crane took off his uniform shirt, threw it on the ground, and pointed to his own bare arm. There were no stripes there. "Nice try, bigmouth. I outrank you. I'm a civilian."

"I don't care what you are," Mullin flared back. "You have one last briefing."

Crane looked right into Mullin's eyes and held his stare. "Hey! Rat Face! Just in case you haven't been informed, your hierarchy of ignorance over me is finished. I'm not going to your bullshit briefing." He turned to go. "I'm outta here."

Mullin glanced appraisingly at the supple muscles on Crane's bare arm. "I don't care how strong you think you are. All you top-secret-cleared assholes think you're better than everybody else. I'm here to tell you, you've been a lone wolf too long."

Crane turned back and smiled. "The only reason we act sanctimoniously is because we are."

Livid with hatred, Mullin clinched his fists and stared at Crane's shirt laying on the ground. "Pick it up."

Crane leaned back, spread his arms out to the sides, and assumed a nonchalant attitude. "I only wear clothing suited to the activity in which I am engaged." He pointed to Mullin's uniform. "I see you're wearing your clown costume?"

As if confused, Mullin paused. "I'm no goddamn clown."

"Maybe you're a garbage man. After all, your army's a refuge for the refuse."

Livid with indignation, Mullin puffed up his chest. "I don't have to take that kind of shit off of you."

Crane couldn't help it. He laughed with amazement. "What kind of shit would you like to take?"

In quizzical disbelief, Mullin stared at Crane. "The army's no place for individualists." With his face purpling with anger, he jerked his finger at Crane's shirt. "Pick up the shirt, turn around, and go to that debriefing."

Crane flashed an ear-to-ear mocking smile. "What if I don't pick it up?"

"I'll kick your ass all over this field."

Crane felt his eyes narrow, but he couldn't help but laugh.

A puzzled look filled Mullin's face. "What's so funny?"

"You're so uncoordinated that if you fell and tried to hit the ground, you'd miss."

"You're going to that goddamn debriefing if I have to drag you there." Mullin reached out and grabbed Crane's wrist. Crane simply held out his thumb and twisted his wrist free.

Mullin grabbed for his wrist, again. Crane jerked it out of his reach. "I never did anything to you. Why do you keep harassing me?"

"Because young snots like you are ruining the Army." Mullin's face filled with pitiless intensity. "You made E-5 in eighteen months. It took me twelve years."

"It's not my fault you begged to stay in the states because you were afraid you might get shot at."

Mullin flared up angrily. "I'm not a beggar."

"You're afraid to get out because you're afraid they'll put locks on garbage cans, and you'll have nothing to eat"

The cut about eating out of garbage cans must not have registered in Mullin's limited mind. He only replied, "I'm not afraid of anything."

"Maybe you're too ignorant to be afraid. Why don't you go back to where you lousy ancestors come from?"

"All right, smart ass." Mullin's mouth curled into a vehement sneer. "You're on."

"No disrespect, Sergeant," Crane said and grinned. "But your elephant mouth is overloading your canary ass."

Mulling took a boxer's stance and lifted his fists. "Shut that smart mouth and show me what you got."

With his fists held high, Mullin's legs were wide open.

Shaking his head at Mullin's stupidity, Crane said, "Your sight's too slow to see what I can do." As if he were going to punch Mullin, Crane lifted his fist and reared back. Mullin reached out and tried to block a punch that never came. At that instant, Crane gracefully lowered his level, took one long step, and wrapped his arms around Mullin's legs. Then he hooked his foot over Mullin's ankles and pushed with his shoulders. Immediately Mullin's fists harmlessly flailed the air. He thumped onto his back. Crane jumped up and looked down at him.

Mullin's face turned red and filled with rage. "When I get up, you're a dead man."

The low ugly sound of Mullin's voice that scared others didn't bother Crane. He defiantly lifted his chin, looked to his right, and yawned as if bored. "I'm standin' here."

Mullin rolled over and got to his hands and knees. Crane could have reared back and kicked him right in the jaw. It would have shut his mouth for a long while, but Crane only wanted to put him in temporary discomfort. He jumped on Mullin's back, threw his legs around his thick gut stomach, formed a figure-four by placing the top on his foot under his own knee, and arched his hips into Mullin's back. This created tremendous pressure on Mullin's spine. In instant pain, he let out a squeal. Crane relaxed the hip pressure, reached under Mullin's arms, and placed him in a full nelson.

Mullin whined like a baby and gasp for air.

Using the full nelson, Crane put pressure on the back of Mullin's head.

Snot flew from Mullin's nose. He quit whining long enough to say, "Let me go!"

"Say you're a dumb, scared-ass beggar."

"Screw you."

Crane leaned back and arched his hips into Mullin's back and held them there. "Say it."

In severe pain, Mullin groaned. "No."

Crane arched the figure four, more. As the move placed extreme pressure on Mullin's stomach and spine, Crane used the full nelson and put more pressure on the back of Mullin's head. His mouth flopped open and his body went flaccid.

With steady controlled fury, Crane let up on the pressure. "Say it!"

Gasping, wordlessly and begging for oxygen, Mullin managed to squeak out, "No!"

This time, Crane applied even more pressure.

Mullin screamed. "Stop! I'll say it."

Crane let up the pressure.

"I'm a dumb, scared-ass beggar."

"Louder." Crane put the pressure back on.

Mullin bellowed, "I'm a dumb, scared-ass beggar."

"Say it again, louder."

"I'm a dumb, scared-ass beggar." This time he screamed so loud that the heads of people on the other side of the parade field turned to see what the ruckus was.

Crane got off Mullin's back and stood next to him.

Seeing people at the side of the parade field, watching, Mullin yelled, "You're not going to make an ass out of me."

"Don't have to," Crane said with delight. "You've been an ass for years."

Mullin jumped to his feet and charged toward Crane.

Crane sidestepped. With a lifting uppercut, he caught Mullin in the stomach. The force stood him on his toes, and a whoosh of air escaped from his mouth. Before he could react, Crane hit him with a right cross to the chest. Mullin wheezed once, crumpled to the ground, and lay still.

He was out.

A military police jeep grumbled along the gravel drive next to the parade field and stopped a few feet from Crane. Four MPs, military police, displaying threatening attitudes, crowded around and stared at Mullin's hideous figure.

One of the MPs stepped in front of Crane and pointed to Mullin. "Even though he deserved it, we should throw you in jail."

Crane unclenched his fists and deliberately assumed an expression of impassive calm. "I don't know what's the matter with him. He fell down. When I tried to help him up, he tried to punch me.

So, I jumped on his back to keep him harmless until you could get here."

The MP looked at Crane and smiled a disbelieving smile. "Nice story, Crane, but we have special orders. You're not going anywhere until you're debriefed."

Crane put his uniform shirt back on, and took one last look at a now whimpering Mullin.

Dumbfounded, Mullin looked up. He had walked onto the parade field with the intention of asserting his authority. But now he was on his knees, visibly conscious of his inferiority.

"Hey, Mullin," Crane said, "It wasn't nice knowin' you."

As if he were going to attack, Mullin's jaw muscles drew tight with anger, but he only leaned forward in a helpless heap.

Crane turned to the MP. "I have been discharged. Why can't you just let me go home?"

"You're out but we're still in. We have to follow orders." The MP reached around his back and pulled out a pair of hand cuffs. "Sorry, Crane. We have some silver bracelets for you."

Crane turned and complied.

The MP clicked the handcuffs onto Crane's wrists. "Get in the jeep."

Crane placed his cuffed hands on the side of the Jeep and turned back toward Mullin. "I don't know why you're so mad at me. I saved your life yesterday."

Mullin's forehead wrinkled with confusion. "What the hell are you talking about?"

"I killed a shit-eaten dog."

While Mullin cussed and the MPs held back laughter, Crane hopped into the jeep and went with the MPs.

CHAPTER 3

Although the MPs dropped Crane off at the Noncommissioned Officers' Club and drove away, Crane knew where he had to go. Once inside the club, he stepped into an elevator with a bullet-proof, red backlit control panel. The glowing red numbers indicated that the elevator serviced a basement floor and a number one floor. He pushed the button to go to the basement floor. The clanking elevator slowly descended to the lower level. The clanking sent sharp pains into his ears, but the clanking was one of many security features. Every time the elevator descended, the clanking began. It was to alert Security that the elevator was descending, and it should be checked for unauthorized personnel.

Before the elevator stopped, Crane used the toe of his shoe and pushed a flexible panel that covered a switch a foot off the floor. When the clanking stopped, the elevator stopped, but the main door stayed securely closed, and a secret back door slid open. Behind a steel gate with bars painted yellow, a familiar guard with a tight face and high cheek bones stood at parade rest, or in civilian terms, a sidewalk superintendent's stance. With his legs apart, his eyes squinting, and his mouth thoughtful, he studied Crane's face. When he glanced at the handcuffs on Crane's wrists he grimaced and shook his head. "Guess you're not going home today."

Trying to keep an upbeat attitude, Crane smiled at him. "I wouldn't bet on it."

The guard nodded and typed a code on a numbers pad on the wall. A small room with an air lock that helped keep out unwanted contaminants that could harm sensitive equipment, opened with a soft hiss.

The guard stepped through.

Crane followed.

Once the door was closed, as a precaution against unwanted contaminants being on those who entered, a shower of air blew on Crane and the guard.

On the other side of the room, the guard unlocked the securing handle to a gate that blocked a set of double doors, and pushed the locking lever to the side. Then he relaxed a bit, put his shoulder behind a steel bar, and pushed the gate open. When he pulled the steel bar back. The double doors opened.

They stepped through and the guard escorted Crane down a narrow hall and stopped at a locked, lead-lined door.

The guard rapped twice on the door. As the lock buzzed, the door opened. Crane stepped into the sterile white confines of a room that boasted two metal folding chairs, one steel desk, and a bare light bulb with a tin shade hanging from the ceiling.

It looked like a scene from an old gangster movie was going to be used to intimidate him, but Crane thought it at best, childish. He shot the guard a quick, hard look. "What kind of Micky Mouse set-up is this?"

The guard stared at Crane. "I'm only following orders." He ushered Crane to a chair. "Have a seat." He grinned wickedly. "The colonel will be with you shortly."

Wondering if the guard would act that way if he had ever felt what it was like to hold his hand on somebody's belly so his guts would stay in until a medic got there, Crane sat down.

After the guard walked out the door and locked it behind him, Crane stood up. Forcing his handcuffed wrists as low as he could get them, he backed his hips through the circle of his arms. Then lifting one leg at a time and pulling his knee against his chest, he stepped over his hand-cuffed hands and got them in front of him. Then he pressed his tongue against two of his teeth that had been capped. The teeth opened. He pressed again. The lock pick that had been implanted in his tooth swung out. He bared his teeth and went to work on the handcuffs. In fewer than ten seconds, he had the handcuffs open.

He set the handcuffs on the desk, and just as he sat back down, the door opened. A full-bird colonel with his shoulder flashing the ASA's embroidered insignia of an American eagle's leg with a lightning bolt clutched in its talons, walked to the desk and stopped. Then he planted his feet in a wide stance. When he dropped his hands to his side, a stupidly serene look of being drugged or cataclysmically wounded filled his ancient face. His eyes had the terrible weary stubbornness officers had when they thought they were always right. Not only did he smell like a body that had set too long before embalming, an aura of death seemed to surround him.

Special operations units, Crane had served with, usually consisted of a cocky group with a laid-back sense of confidence, and everyone had a specialized skill. They served in places on their own with no chain of command disrupting proven operational techniques. Officers didn't have to manage specialists, and specialists weren't afraid to tell officers a better way to run a mission. They rarely began a sentence with, "I."

Just the way the colonel stood, told Crane that the man did not operate like a special operations unit officer who would accept constructive criticism. Many times, a know-it-all officer with the rapport abilities of Attila the Hun had bungled infiltration. When that type of officer continued his bull-headed ways, he became more of a threat than the enemy. Crane would not be able to stand working with this man for longer than fifteen minutes. In fact, just to feel the thrill of hard punch landing, he had the urge to punch him right in the face. More than ever, Crane was glad he was out of the Army.

Out of habit, Crane raised his hand to salute, but because he had been discharged, he figured he was no longer obligated to salute anyone. He dropped his salute.

Without looking up, the colonel haphazardly returned a salute Crane had not given and sank into his chair.

With a whisky, rasping throat, the colonel began, "Specialist, Crane, what we have to say to each other is for our ears only. What you say and what you hear, when you leave, leave it here."

Knowing what he was about to ask, Crane interrupted. "With all due respect, Colonel, I just got discharged. I don't have to accept another assignment." To rub it in, he smiled directly into the colonel's face. "I'm a civilian now. We don't have to use that tauro-scatological anymore. Call me, Crane."

Even though Crane was sure the colonel didn't know tauro-scatological meant bullshit, anger flashed in his face. "I'll call you what I ..." His voice trailed off.

Crane had detected smugness and a self-adoration in the colonel's voice. He had a reputation for being a choleric man, given to sudden bursts of fury, and he hated being thwarted, even when the other person was right and he was wrong. An additional insane asylum qualifying attribute was that he was impatient with anyone who disagreed with him. Like most regular army officers, he didn't like being told what to do, especially by someone below his rank.

Crane could feel the colonel itching to get on his case, turn into a nut house thing, scream in his ear, accuse him of stealing the handcuffs that he had set on the desk, or order him to do some asinine thing, so he could show Crane who was in charge here. Since he was getting out, whatever the colonel said or did wouldn't' bother Crane. He decided to regard the colonel's forthcoming outburst as a form of amusement.

But the colonel didn't turn into a nut house thing. For a second, he grimaced, then smiled like they were old friends. Using the higher than the person you are trying to sell something to as an advantage, the colonel stood and Crane sat. Expecting Crane to sit properly in his seat and look to him for direction, the colonel was all set to orate, gesture, walk about, spin on his heels, shake his head in disbelief, and smile in paternal approbation. He was both the director and the star of this little amphitheater production.

The stage was set.

He began. “It’s not that simple, Crane. You signed the Official Secrets Act. Even though you may not be officially in the Army Security Agency, you are still an element of the special operations unit. It took us two years to run your ultra-top secret, your top secret, and your secret crypto security clearance. It’s not our fault that you have an unexplained ability to ferret out information we never dreamed existed. We have added so many letters behind your clearance rating that we had to start another line.”

Staring at the colonel’s chest, devoid of medals, because they might give people an inkling of where he had been, Crane stood up. “It doesn’t matter how many clearances I have or how desperate you’re going to say my country needs me.” He looked at his watch. “Over twenty minutes ago, I became a civilian. I already quit! You don’t have to run your little amphitheater production past me.” He turned to go. “Let me out!”

Almost unruffled by Crane’s abrupt action, the colonel threw his head back, to emphasize the grandeur of his sternocleidomastoid muscles and nonchalantly waved his hand. "Sit back down, son. You owe us."

"Owe you?" I served my enlistment. You can't sit there waving a banner of what I owe you or anybody else. Legally you have to let me out. Law is not a creature of the few. It exists for all. I am not swayed by your threats. I'm going home!"

"You want us to enforce law?" The colonel stiffened and puffed up his chest. "I'm sure I don't have to remind you what the penalty is for assaulting a superior officer." As if he had just noticed them, the colonel looked critically at the handcuffs setting on the desk. His voice became harsh and authoritative. "You may have gotten out of those, but after we declare you a deserter, you'll never get out of maximum security at the prison at Leavenworth."

Smiling, Crane arrogantly replied, "There isn't a mark on him."

The colonel relaxed. His voice took on a forced friendly tone. "We knew you wanted to settle a score with Mullin. We set that little bullshit skirmish up. If you sit here a few minutes, we won't court-martial you."

"I'm a civilian. You can't use your military law and court-martial me."

"Just because you have been discharged from the regular army, it doesn't give you the right to hit a senior officer. You're now assigned to the reserves." He lifted his hand and pointed at Crane. "You still have to serve the last two years of your six-year obligation."

Going to reserve meeting once a month would be easier than staying in the Army. Crane wasn't worried. "I'll go to the reserve meetings for two years." He smiled a big sunny smile directly into the colonel's face. "Then I'll be out for good. And besides, I'm not qualified for another mission."

For a moment, the colonel looked at Crane in an uncomprehending daze. "I am bemused by your attitude. You have a propensity for language-learning and Phase Six training." Again, he looked at the handcuffs setting on the desk. "You didn't have any trouble getting out of those. Instances like that indicate the high predictive value of what your abilities are."

Crane waved his hands at the handcuffs. "Anybody could have gotten out of those tin bracelets. Just because someone else does something, it doesn't mean you can predict what I can or will do."

With a fierce glare in his eyes, the colonel stared at Crane like a man who seemed to know him as someone he wasn't. "I'm not going to say you're right or wrong." He raised one finger. "However, predictive is not fortune telling. It is the term psychologists use when they speak of the predictive value of psychological tests. I'm sure you're familiar with Rorschach ink-blot test."

Crane had taken many tests, including the Rorschach test, but not wanting to cooperate, he shrugged. "I'm a high school dropout. How would I know what kind of tests I took?"

The colonel made a face but continued. "Before two hundred aviation cadets began training, they were given ink-blot tests. Interpretation of the tests showed that six in the group were emotionally unfit for the life of a pilot. However all two hundred cadets were permitted to continue the course. At the end of the course the six cadets that had been designated as unfit had dropped out for physiological reasons." The colonel stared at Crane. "Are you still going to tell me you are not qualified for another mission?"

"I don't care what some ink-blot test says. Let me out."

"There are superior and inferior people in the world." The colonel jerked his finger at Crane. "You are one of the few superior people. It is your sacred duty to lead, enlighten, and defend the inferior ones."

Although ASA people had IQs of 140 or better, Crane knew the colonel was using a snow job to persuade him to reenlist. But he wasn't falling for it.

The colonel gave Crane that we-got-cha look he hated. "Whether you like it or not, you're one of a few who were culled from those who scored in the top ten percent of our aptitude tests. Having a high IQ and qualifying for both top secret and crypto security clearances, you would have to agree that you are in a rather exclusive group." A warm smile softened his got-cha look. "Your security clearances and your indefinite travel restrictions make it possible for us to extend your active duty status until the end of your natural life. You are still ours, twenty-three hours and forty-five minutes a day. The fifteen minutes you have left are to shower, shave, and go to the latrine."

An indent on the side of the colonel's crew-cut skull and his drooping cloudy eye indicated that he may have had a brain injury, and the military had made an unimportant job for him so he could spend a few months playing a futile re-enlistment army game with people getting out so he could qualify for a higher pension.

Crane decided to try something. If the colonel were mentally deficient and Crane claimed he suffered from a nervous disorder brought on by the exhaustion and the stress of combat, he might be able to end this threat. The first time he had seen a Viet Cong, the puffed face of the VC had been swollen and out of shape. When the VC had looked at Crane, Crane felt the shock of the VC's eyes, and the hatred in them seemed to burn into his very soul. Although he believed such a nervous disorder was psychopathic nonsense, he was going to try it anyway.

He sat down, and like a whining weakling, he held out his empty hands to pantomime his helplessness. "I don't know if I can function anymore, Colonel. I keep seeing those VC in my sleep."

The colonel paused but his expression did not change.

Peeking between his fingers, Crane thought his childish prank had worked, but this man was smarter than the average colonel. With the sureness of a sniper aiming his rifle at a bull's-eye, he calmly went on. "I would imagine that more people than you are going through the same sort of feelings, but they *are* mentally unstable."

Crane lifted his head and snarled. "What makes you think I'm not mentally unstable?"

"None of your conditions are a psychosis. They are all neuroses or mild personality disorders that will not necessarily interfere with what we want you to do."

Crane sizzled with resentment. "That's not true and you know it."

"Okay, you got me." The colonel shrugged. "Actually, the real reason is simple to explain. Your ability to laugh at other people's tragedies because they were nothing compared to the social inequities of your underprivileged childhood showed that you were mentally unstable before you enlisted." Smiling, he flashed Crane a look of great confidence. "And besides, you have to be crazy to try an amateurish prank like claiming a nervous disorder. It will never earn you a transfer to a psychiatric ward. Your intelligence has allowed you to gain dominance over any psychosis you may have had or ever will have."

He was right. Growing up in an environment three grades below a slum area, Crane was often forced to fight for a stale slice of bread. This and other horrible experiences had caused many things that bothered other people, of better upbringings, to be of little significance to him. But he was sure the colonel didn't know about his search for Al Capone's gold vault, when, at an early age, he had seen death first hand and realized that most people cannot accept absurdities of the mind and end up calling anything they don't understand, anything they don't like, or anything they can't accept, fake or insane. As far as Crane was concerned, fake or insane were just two of the convenient words people used when they didn't want to take the trouble to evaluate an uncommon situation.

Crane kept trying to get out of the mission. "I may have been mentally unstable, but I never had to kill anyone."

As if he had three aces showing in a card game and was about to flip over the fourth, the colonel pulled a large manila envelope from under the desk. He opened it and carefully slid out a red-striped-bordered folder and shook it at Crane. "Your dossier, shows that you may not have directly killed anyone before coming into the agency, but when you and your buddies were chasing after a gold vault, you pushed a man off a moving railroad car, and the wheels cut him into pieces." The colonel lifted one finger. "And you were close enough to a lethal shot to a man's head to get bone splinters in your face."

At that time in Crane's young life, the instant flash of gunfire that had killed a man, for no reason, and the man falling under the steel wheels of the railroad car, had caused Crane to be sick with nausea and fear. And it had caused something to come into his life he had never known before: the dark shadow of senseless hate. For months, he could not understand it.

He couldn't believe anyone but himself and his buddies, Neal, Rafferty, and Blondie, would reveal anything about the shootings and murders that had happened when they were searching for the vault. Someone else must have informed the colonel. But that didn't mean Crane had to re-enlist. He arrogantly leaned back. "I don't care what you know. I'm not re-enlisting."

The colonel raised his voice. "The hell you're not."

Crane was tired of being nice. "You sound like a shit salesman with a sample in your mouth."

The colonel dropped the folder and jumped up so fast that the backs of his legs hit his chair. It shot back and crashed into the wall. "You can't talk to me like that!" he roared. Lunging for Crane, he thrust his upper body across the desk.

Crane didn't get scared or excited. He only waited for the colonel's next move. If he scrambled over the desk and came at him, Crane was sure he could place him in temporary discomfort. But the colonel didn't scramble over the desk. He stayed leaned over and shouted, "If you don't re-enlist, we'll send you to Leavenworth, if and when, you get out, we'll make your life miserable." He pulled his upper body back from over the desk. Standing, he removed a number of pages from the dossier and waved them at Crane. "We have propaganda pamphlets all ready to go. All of your work prospects will dry up. We'll make it so your friends will shield themselves from you. Before we're finished, people will look at you in a different way. Trouble will not only come looking for you, it will find you."

Crane defiantly looked right into the colonel's face. "Judging by what *your kind* pulled off in Nam, you would be rotten enough to do that?"

Hatred blazed in the colonel's eyes, but he didn't lunge back across the desk. He retrieved his chair, set it behind the desk, and sat down. "What do you mean, what *my kind* pulled off?"

"People like you started the war in Vietnam."

"The colonel was silent for a few seconds. Then he jumped up. "Damn you! He slammed the red-striped-bordered folder onto the desk. "What makes you think you know anything?"

Crane snapped back, "I know your special operation units performed hit-and-run raids against North Vietnam's coastline, in July of 1964."

"That wasn't me." The colonel violently shook his head. "That's not possible. Congress didn't give President Johnson power to deal with attacks on United States forces until August seventh."

"You're telling me that your Nasty boats' hit-and-run raids in North Vietnam didn't happen?"

In a show of defiance, the colonel sat down, leaned back, and folded his arms across his chest. "I have no knowledge of what the CIA does or doesn't do. As far as I'm concerned, the war was started by newspapers, so they could sell more newspapers."

Crane knew the colonel was lying. The CIA acquired Norwegian-boats and called them Nastys which was short for *Nasty-class PTF, Patrol Type, Fast,* and the colonel's special operations unit commandos used them. The colonel knew the boats were acquired by the CIA, therefore, he knew what they had done.

Crane stood up and pointed at the colonel. "Do I have to remind you that your sea commandos demolished five targets in North Vietnam, then two more, and then launched its biggest assault on radar sites."

The colonel leaned forward and bared his teeth in a grimace of ferocious hate. "Stay where you are."

"No doubt you have secured the area," Crane stated with a feeling of excruciating discomfort. "I can't go anywhere. But don't think you can change the truth by turning into a nut house thing."

The colonel's face turned sick. He turned away. When he turned back toward Crane his demeanor had changed. "Oh yes, I remember now," he said in a most pleasant voice. "The assaults were praised as well executed and highly successful, with secondary explosions."

"You failed to mention that they were so far north that they were closer to Haiphong than to Danang."

"It doesn't matter where they were. We're at war, you know."

"We weren't at war then, but you started it."

"Okay bright boy, sit down and tell me how I started a war with a few hit-and-runs."

Crane sat down and sneered. "Days after your Nasty boat crews went into North Vietnam, they were in Danang, taking it easy. When the North Vietnamese PT boats came down to get even, they attracted the U.S. destroyer *Maddox*, which became known as the Tonkin Gulf incident."

"So?"

"So, hell. It doesn't matter that President Lyndon Johnson didn't refer to your special operation unit raids in North Vietnam, but warned Hanoi that another high-seas attack would have dire consequences, and the destroyer *Turner Joy* was sent to reinforce the *Maddox.*"

"A little action always helps the situation." The colonel's brow furrowed. "We're not here to talk about the war. We're here to talk about what you will find out if you don't re-enlist."

"I don't want to find out anything," Crane said. "Let me go home."

"Why would you want to go home to some kinda shit-hook neighborhood and end up doing stupid things?"

Crane couldn't believe the colonel had stooped to the level of bringing up Crane's childhood milieu. Patagonia was the other-side-of-the-tracks place, but after what he had been through, life in Patagonia would seem as relaxed as a summer resort. He would rather be there than in the Army. He gave the colonel an unconcerned shrug. "It doesn't matter what Patagonia was like or what it has become. I should get what I want, once in a while. Let me out."

"What's the rush? You should be eager to stay." The colonel closed his good eye and squinted through his drooping cloudy eye. "After all," he said in mocking amusement, "The agency's not just a job. It's an adventure."

Crane felt like he had stepped on the business end of a rake, hidden in a pile of classified information, and the handle had flown up and smacked him right in his unsuspecting face. He didn't know how the colonel had found out about the gold vault, his friends and he had found and lost, and there was always an outside chance that he would be able to find the vault again. He didn't want to go into details with the colonel about the vault or anything else. Just the thought of re-enlisting caused his entire body to ache. and a deep pain pressed inside his chest.

"I don't care what you do. I'm out and I'm staying out."

"Maybe we can make a deal."

This aroused Crane's curiosity. "Start talkin'."

"How about we let you do one thing to Mullin?"

"So you can throw me in jail?"

"Not really. Just consider it a re-enlistment bonus"

Wanting to vent his frustration for Mullin's constant harassment, Crane almost immediately said, yes, but a pain in his chest would not let the word out of his mouth. It wasn't only a pain because he realized his enlistment was not over. It was a renewed pain he had endured before. Much of it had started when his trust in mankind had fled. Then his instincts had sharpened to a fine edge, where, just a look, a nod, or a person's gait could tell him if the person could be trusted.

Chasing Capone's vault at a young age, he had learned to be an animal when he had to be. But that had been a fight that should have made him wealthy. Unfortunately, he and his friends had been used for the profit of others. If he could help it, he wasn't going to let something like that happen again. Just the thought of it happening, again, kept him in constant fear and caused him to always be on the alert.

Crane was sick of it all. In jest, Gillette had said, "You'll be going home, but you'll have to take a dangerous detour." Now what Gillette had said had become truth.

Resigning that his civilized civilian life had temporarily come to an end and knowing he could be placed on the express for Leavenworth, Crane felt like he had been stabbed. Trying to suppress the pain his chest, he cringed and became irritated at himself for the self-pity he'd been indulging in the last few months. He had sacrificed some, but others had sacrificed far more. And who wouldn't want a chance to get back at Mullin?

The colonel was getting impatient. "Due to the fact that your re-enlistment is critical to a long and healthy life, you could be receiving a ten-thousand-dollar Variable Reenlistment Bonus."

"I've have been told those are never paid."

"Paid or not, you're still going to reenlist."

Accepting the fact that whatever happened he would lose, Crane shrugged despairingly. "When do I start, and where do I go?"

With scornful satisfaction, the colonel grinned brazenly. "You bought your ticket. Take your ride."

CHAPTER 4

As if the colonel were celebrating, he pulled a cigar from his breast pocket. Apparently attempting to break the officer and enlisted man's formal atmosphere and lower himself to the level of Crane's lower rank and put him at ease, the colonel placed his feet on the desk, leaned back, and lit up the cigar. Suddenly his voice rose. "You want to know where to go and when to start?"

"Yes, I would like to know," Crane admitted grudgingly.

Displaying a cool, measuring look, the colonel looked directly at him. "As you may know, anyone who entertains the notion of letting it be known that he is associated with the ASA's highly classified functions is advised to act as if he is oblivious of their very existence. So you see, it's not that simple."

The colonel's casual actions and tone infuriated Crane, but as silence commanded the room, he waited for him to continue.

The colonel took a long drag on his cigar. As if he had all the time in the world, he blew a series of smoke rings at the ceiling. "Do you know anything about railroads?"

Instead of answering right away, Crane thought about when he was just a kid playing along the Shenango River. When he was thirteen, he had hopped a boxcar. When it went hurtling out of Patagonia, it was the first taste of freedom he'd had in his life. At that time, he thought the railroad was the greatest of mankind's inventions. After that, he and his gang used to sneak along the railroad tracks and latch onto cars of slow-moving freight trains. Crane knew the cars that trailed behind those powerful diesel locomotives were dirty, and the grab irons had sun dried paint that would cut into his hands. He knew the various horn signals used by the locomotive engineers, such as two longs, one short, and one long was for a railroad crossing, and he knew the various names of freight cars. So they could pose as maintenance crews during surveillance missions, Agency operators had been sent to airports to learn aircraft repair, baggage handling, and cabin cleaning, but Crane didn't know any who had been sent to a railroad.

With a blue haze of cigar smoke encircling the colonel's head, he repeated his question. "Do you know anything about railroads?"

"Nothing that would be of interest to a special operations unit."

The colonel gave him a cold, intent look. "We may not need you after all."

At first, because of the colonel's clouded eye, Crane didn't recognize the look. When he did, it was the same sneaky look carnival people flashed when they were about to take a gullible person's money in a rigged game of chance. As the colonel continued, his sneaky look faded, and his demeanor became arrogant. "If we need you, we may have to send you to the top of the hill."

When Crane had been at the top of the hill, he had trained for only what was necessary to complete his mission, and the information coming from the training was too much for most human brains to absorb. It had been said that one week at the top of the hill was equivalent to two months of real life. But he had done it with ease. In the few months he had been there, his mind had developed into a special operations frame of mind. Not just anyone with a high IQ could become a special operations operator. A special ops person had to have a mind-set to finish a mission no matter what the dangers were.

The top of the hill was located somewhere, not far from CIA headquarters in Langley, Virginia. There, a single dirt road led to a windowless installation hidden by pine trees on top of a small mountain. Two, four meter-high, chain link fences, topped with circles of razor wire, laced with electronic sensors and hidden cameras, stretched more than twelve miles around the facility. No animal larger than a squirrel could move across the land without being monitored by motion doctors, heat sensors, microphones, and cameras that provided a continuous stream of data to a computer for analysis.

If an intruder somehow made it over one fence, he was confronted by the second fence. In addition to cameras recording every movement, twenty-four hours a day, drivers in gray patrol cars, cruised the perimeter, watching for anyone or anything straying near the training center. Most people who had lived in the area were unaware of the installation's presence. And the few who knew of it, figured it was some sort of maximum-security prison with inmates so deranged and violent that packs of

German Shepherds patrolled the area between the fences, and were trained to grab an escapee's throat and rip it out.

Inside the fences, tall banks of earth provided protection and insulation that hid pistol, submachine gun, shotgun, and demolition ranges. Behind one of the banks of earth, commandos walked a jungle lane, ran through obstacle courses, and fired at targets that sprung up without warning. A little further into the compound, snipers practiced dropping targets from as far as seven hundred meters away. Also hidden, were special ops men firing bullets from fast cars, or getting shot at from the fast cars. The strip of road, used to practice driving maneuvers, was also hidden from outside eyes. Little was known about how the top of the hill unit actually worked. It was one of the most secretive special operations units ever created.

Here, special ops people used an advanced "practical shooting stance" and practiced "rapid aim fire" shooting in rooms filled with pop-up moving robots. This practical shooting stance of twisting their bodies and firing over their braced right arms acted like a rifle butt and steadied the weapon hand. This stance not only made the operator less of a target, it enabled him to be ready to spring for cover.

More advanced rooms contained things the public never knew existed. One of Crane's favorites were the three-dimensional holograms of the enemy that were flashed on walls and ceilings. Bullet traps absorbed and marked the rounds fired.

Every day, commandos fired over five hundred rounds.

In one of the halls, long boards with seventy different locks and handcuffs waited for operators to practice picking them.

Self-contained, the compound had a cafeteria and bedrooms, where operators, training for an isolated mission, could sleep. On a four-story-high climbing wall, mountain teams practiced scaling and rappelling from cliffs. An Olympic-sized swimming pool, steam bath, handball courts, a fully equipped gymnasium, a weight room, and a tall swimming tank, for drown-proofing exercises, kept the operators in superb physical shape.

But the training wasn't all physical. To gain information from unsuspecting sources, Crane was taught how to get along with people, how to notice their mannerisms, how to spot the tricks of expressions and gestures that indicated they were lying, uncertain, or afraid.

One lesson in observation that surprised Crane was when he was told to go to a window and look out. After he had stood looking out for a minute, he was called away from the window and asked how many buildings were across the street, what color they were, and how many windows. When he didn't know, he was told not to just look out the window, but to learn to see, and to remember. After that, rarely a day passed when he was not suddenly called on to describe what he had just seen. It would be the clothing of a man, how many boards were on a platform, the location of articles the hall, or just about anything that could be of value in a mission.

The top of the hill only accepted men who had the sort of faith that could move mountains and build pyramids. It could train dying men to perform tasks with smiles on their lips. And they could pull their own weight and others', too.

The first time Crane had trained at the top of the hill, security had been so strict that he had been blindfolded and dropped off at the front gate. An armed guard had taken the blindfold off. Then under camera surveillance, and with the stoned-faced, non-talkative guard standing next to him, he waited for an hour to gain entrance. Inside, when he used the bathroom, guards watched as he sat on the toilet. At the top of the hill, security was no joke.

Crane had been given an identification coin that all personnel at the top of the hill carried. "Anything, any time, any place, and anyhow," had been stamped on the coin.

Although he had not taken all the training, and the coin would mean nothing to people who had not taken the training, it had made him feel he was part of an elite group.

The colonel waved his hand in a dismissing gesture.

Confused, Crane asked, "Does that mean I can go home?"

"You can go home, but you're still in the Army. If we need you, we'll let you know. If you don't hear from us, you can go back to your useless life in Patagonia."

CHAPTER 5

After Crane left the colonel, he walked under trays of fluorescent lights hanging from the high ceiling that shone on the walls that had been painted with something he hated: a government-work-green color. Glad he would never have to look at those walls and look at the ugly paint, he walked toward the exit door to cross over the parade field and go home, but a seemingly harmless chubby young officer came down the hall twirling his cap on the end of his finger. Crane smiled at him, and even though the officer's face had the look that said he didn't want Crane anywhere near him, the officer smiled back. "Getting out today?"

In reluctant admiration of the officer's phony good mood, Crane only nodded.

When Crane got close to the exit door, as if he were an event that would cause people to stop and stare, Mullin stood with his feet spaced solidly apart and his fists resting on his hips. The very look of the building, Mullin's strict posture, his military uniform, and the sergeant strips sewn on his arm, should have proclaimed the gravity and all-powerfulness of army rules. But having been included in a surge of collective talent of the ASA that had the highest IQ's in the military, in which Mullin had never been a part of, Crane wasn't buying it. As he approached, Mullin held his head at a self-satisfied angle, thrust out his hand, and clamped onto the cold steel lever of the door and blocked Crane. Crane stopped five feet from him.

The hard bronze of Mullin's face tightened. "So you didn't get out," he said, and his voice rang loud. "Now you're all mine. You're gonna start acting like a soldier."

To boost their anonymity, Crane and other agency men were taught how to dress, act, and move as if they were not in the army, and most important, how to assimilate as people in the countries their missions sent them to. Apparently Mullin didn't have the intellectual abilities to qualify for a class on the basic principles of the process.

"Even though you're a dip shit with less than modest intelligence," Crane replied. trying to stay calm. "I'm sure you will gladly step aside."

Mullin flared up. "You'll act like a soldier. Stand at attention! You'll go around when I tell you to."

For a moment, Crane considered bringing up more of what he knew confused Mullin's amazing facile mind. But a pent-up reaction caused his blood instantly turned to fire. "Like hell I will," he shot back.

His reply stunned Mullin. He just stood there. All body movements stopped.

Crane bent over, grabbed the rug Mullin was standing on, and yanked it. Mullin lifted his left foot, but his right foot turned sideways, snapped, and flew out from under him. He went crashing to the hard floor.

Before he could get up Crane shot his left hand out and forced his fingers down inside the front of Mullin's collar. Closing his fist, Crane bent his knuckles forcefully against Mullin's Adam's apple. Gagging and gasping, his eyes bulged, and his hands wildly fought to rip Crane's fist away. Crane pulled him close and quietly said, "Just wanted to show you that I've taken it easy on you for the last time. "He jerked Mulling forward one more time and let him fall to the floor. As he lay there, with his face stupid with shock, Crane looked down at him. "Because of your ignorance, men die. Why don't you get out?"

Unaccustomed to pain, Mullin held his right foot and whined, "You broke my foot. I'm a professional. My country needs me. What am I going to do?"

Mullin's professional claim reminded Crane of H. G. Well's un-discerning generalization many ASA men cited: "The professional military mind is by necessity an inferior and unimaginative mind. No man of high intellectual calling would willingly imprison his gifts in such a calling."

"Sorry about that," Crane said, feigning an apology. Get that right foot or yours cut off. I know some people that have lost their left foot. I'll give you their addresses. If you stay in touch with them, you can save money on shoes."

Mullin started to open his mouth to speak, but a look of complete confusion disfigured his face.

When Crane walked past Mullin, he held up his arm for protection and weakly sunk with humility.

Crane placed his hand on the door and looked back. "So much for the bright chatter."

Just before Crane walked through the door, Mullin dropped his arm. Sitting on the floor and shaking his fist he yelled, "You're going to Leavenworth for this."

Crane walked out the door, crossed the parade field, hopped into his Chevy truck, and drove away.

Instead of going to the top of the hill, Crane was sent to Ferrona Yard, the Erie Railroad switching yard in Sharon, Pennsylvania. Without filling out an application or being interviewed, management had somehow arranged for him to be awarded the job as bill box clerk, working steady midnight turn. He had no idea what a clerk's job had to do with a mission that would be of any importance to the security of the country. But he figured he was about to find out.

CHAPTER 6

Driving under the riveted steel I-beams that supported the Clark Street Bridge, Freddy Crane peered through the wrap-around windshield of his 1955 Chevy pickup and glanced to where the water concealed a meter-wide underground concrete storm culvert that emptied into the Shenango River. He knew his stainless-steel chamber was still hidden there. Thinking about the counterfeit money in the chamber gave him a bad feeling, and at times it had made him sick. But he hoped the chamber still contained his savings and a weird sphere that had fallen out of Al Capone's Vault.

When Crane slowed for the railroad tracks, the familiar crossing watchman's dirty-white railroad shanty appeared on the right and caused Crane's mind to flood with fond childhood memories of swimming in the river and sneaking into the Ferrona switching yard of the Erie Railroad.

Beyond three railroad tracks, the crossing watchman got up from his wooden bench he had been sitting on, grabbed his octagonal-shaped white sign with black letters that spelled "Stop" and walked to the center of the crossing. Wearing, red suspenders, a cotton shirt, and baggy pants with a red spotted bandanna hanging from the back pocket, the man projected the persona of a rodeo clown. He adjusted his gray and white striped railroader's hat so that it tilted at an angle and held up the sign.

Crane tramped on the brakes of his pickup truck, took the four-speed transmission out of gear, and waited for the approaching train.

Laboriously pulling the cars, two maroon locomotive engines with yellow stripes running the full length of their sides thumped past the front of the truck and continued on down the tracks. Loaded with just about everything, the cars following behind increased speed. In a great dazzle and rumble, reefer cars hauling meat, ice cream, cheese, and frozen dinners, whipped past. Then gondola cars, laden with concrete pipe and construction steel, thumped over the crossing. A few empty automobile transport cars, rattling steel racks, breezed past. Three slat-sided cars, carrying livestock, lumbered past, too. Black tank cars full of chemicals, oil, gasoline, or ammonia, slid quietly over the rails and followed.

Crane looked to his left. Upriver, a boy was sitting on a log that extended out over the water. Another boy was standing on the log behind the boy that was sitting with a fishing pole in his hands. Apparently checking his bait, the boy lifted his baited hook just above the surface of the water. Without warning, a large mouth bass leaped clean out of the water and grabbed the baited hook. As the pole bowed over almost to the handle on the pole, the boy behind him pointed and shrieked with joy. Before the sitting boy could pull the huge bass to the shore, it wiggled off the hook and splashed into the water. Crane recalled the same thing happening to him at just about the same place on the river. It would be something the boys would talk about for the rest of their lives.

After the dull-red caboose clattered past, the crossing guard turned and went back to his little wooden bench. Crane shifted the transmission into low gear, let out the clutch, drove across two sets of tracks, and turned left.

Driving on railroad property and not being subject to being arrested for trespassing gave Crane a sense of freedom. Just as it had done when he was a kid, the railroad switching yard seemed as inviting and as much fun as a toy train set. As he neared the clapboard-sided yard office, the aroma of creosote from the railroad ties, rusty railroad cars, oily switches, and diesel fumes, mingled with the night air. It had been years since he had been there, but an unmistakable railroad atmosphere still filled the yard.

As a clerk, he soon learned how to run teletypes, line up trains, weigh cars, make up switching lists, take over for the yard master, and among other things, write time slips. Handing off the bills of lading and grabbing new ones at the same time as the little red caboose whipped past, required a bit of skill. If he didn't use one hand to hand off the bills so that the conductor could grab them on the fly and at the same time catch the new bills with his other hand, when the train stopped, he would have to walk a mile to the end of the yard and give the bills to the conductor.

The work wasn't as demanding or as difficult as what he had done in the agency, but the fact that he had mastered the job quickly must have caught someone's attention. After three months, he was interviewed for a claim agent's position. It paid twice as much as he was making as a clerk. Since he hadn't been sent to the top of the hill, he was sure the colonel and the special operations unit, didn't need him. They were finally going to let him get on with his civilian life. Now he could begin to look for land to fulfill his dream.

A week before he was to start the claim agent position, he was outside in the cold of night carrying a lantern and checking cars in the dark switching yard. After he had written down the number of a box car, like a derelict in a large city, a bent-over figure of a hobo came from around the end of the car. Ragged clothes, thick enough to ward off the cold in dark alleyways, covered his lanky body. Heavy soled boots, with laces tied in knots, covered his feet. A wool-knit cap sat on his head and covered the top of his down-focused eyes. He seemed to be avoiding the world in which he could not compete and looked like he found Crane's presence intimidating. His grimy hands clutched a greasy cloth satchel that he held close to his chest. He seemed to be telling the cruel world that the satchel was his, all his.

Being in the Army Security Agency for four years, the training had been something Crane had lived, breathed, and had nightmares about, and he thought he was through with it. But watching the man, he realized he wasn't. Although the man looked to be an ordinary tramp looking for a box car to hop into, Crane's training took over. Intently watching the man's face, he searched for a glance, a twitch of the man's lips, or an almost imperceptible nod that would tell him if the man was more than a tramp.

To Crane's surprise, the man simply extended his hand in friendship. "Ready for a trip?"

From the sound of the man's voice, Crane had a suspicion that the man had been sent from the agency. He reached out and grasped the man's extended hand. It was soft. This man had never grabbed onto a moving railroad car in his life. He was not a violent man, and he was not a hobo or part of the hobo jungle. A tramp at his age would have come up through the violent and hostile ranks or the hobo world. He would not have soft hands.

The man looked right then left. "I don't have much time. We tried to contact you through satellite feed but didn't receive a reply."

"When I got out, I destroyed my radio."

"I'm only here to tell you that you will be receiving a message."

"How? I just told you I destroyed my radio."

"You'll get it over the phone line."

The man had gone through a lot of trouble just to contact him, and now the man was telling him he would send a message over the phone. It didn't make sense. "If you're going to send it over the phone line, then why are you here?"

"It's a sensitive situation. We had to make sure only you got the message."

"I thought I was out for good," Crane protested. "Why me?"

"They think you know something you shouldn't know. It frightens them. Take the assignment but be careful." The man turned to go but turned back. "Your friends will think you're crazy to give up a high-paying job. So the army is going to pay you a ten-thousand-dollar re-enlistment bonus."

Before Crane could reply, the fake tramp turned and disappeared into the dark of the yard.

Back in the yard office, while Crane wondered if the ten-thousand-dollar re-enlistment bonus was real, the black phone on his desk rang. He picked up the receiver. "Ferrona Yard."

Instead of someone wanting a switching order or the arrogant clerk at Sharon Steel wanting the stock report showing how many cars of coke, scrap, or coal were available, the all too familiar click of Morse code greeted Crane's ear.

After he tapped on the mouthpiece and sent a question mark, signifying, "Do you have anything for me?" a message containing several strings of five-digit numbers were sent back to him. After he deciphered the code in his head, it revealed he had to contact the top of the hill. He nonchalantly tapped *di-di-di-dah-dit*, which meant understood. Morse code on the other end sent *di-di-di-dah-di-dah*, which meant end of message. He would have to build a radio.

***

With knowledge that the higher the frequency the shorter the antenna, Crane changed the area on a variable compactor, scrounged a few crystals, and transformed a store-bought radio into a receiver for high frequency signals. After he built a dish antenna that resembled a little upside-down umbrella on a mixed drink, he recalled October 4,

1957. That was when Russia had launched the first satellite called Sputnik.

Crane's rare ability to sniff out covert procedures and just plain common sense had revealed something about Sputnik that seemed impossible. The little dish antenna on the radio he had built could only pick up high frequency signals. Because these signals didn't bounce like lower radio frequencies but traveled in a straight line, without a satellite to bounce them off, the dish antenna would only be capable of sending or receiving signals within a 100-kilometer radius. For the United States to have such an advanced satellite feed and covertly bounce high frequencies around the world, common sense would dictate that the United States had satellites orbiting the earth way before Sputnik. But that little gem could never be public knowledge.

What made the United States' addition of a satellite program to the telemetry system, even more successful, was the unauthorized addition of a transmitter that could be tapped to find any and all data that any satellite had sent or received.

Before Sputnik had been launched, the Unites States Space program had been grossly underfunded. Politicians and people declared it was a waste to throw money into space, saying, "After all, there was nothing there."

This negative attitude made it prudent to keep satellites, the United States had orbiting the earth, a secret.

After the big hullabaloo of Russia being the first country to launch a satellite, the perception of the United States being a technological superpower and the Soviet Union being a backward country stopped. The American public's practice of believing they were first in everything in the world, and had come in second, had not only embarrassed them, it had triggered an integral part of the Cold War: The Space Race.

Longing to be the biggest and best country in the world, again, the American people rallied and got behind their elected representatives. Their efforts enabled the space race to begin, which generously provided the funds to win a race the United States had already won. When the budget for NASA was increased by five hundred percent, new political, military, technological, and scientific developments happened. The new technologies, the race had created, made it possible to educate and employ thousands of people. Although the space race had been used to control the masses, it turned out to be a wise investment.

Crane's radio was far more advanced than the Russian Sputnik radio that had transmitted on a frequency of twenty megacycles and only sent a "beep, beep" sound each time it rounded the earth. Crane's radio had a secure satellite feed. Messages were sent at a high speed, and the feed was further encoded with Morse code ciphers.

After he had used the radio to contact the top of the hill, he received coded ciphers. When he decoded the message, it confirmed that the special operations unit was sending him to the top of the hill. He wasn't going to be a claim agent for the railroad. The problem was that he needed to earn enough money to buy his land. Being a claim agent, he could earn the money in half the time it would take working his bill-box clerk job. To have a chance of getting the claim agent job after he finished the assignment, he would have to give the yardmaster a good reason for quitting. The given reason: He had re-enlisted. Friends and family knew he didn't want to re-enlist. So… to make his phony enlistment seem real, the story that he was to receive a ten-thousand-dollar re-enlistment bonus was circulated.

After he took a final anguished look at the yard office and its promise of an easy future, under the pretense of re-enlisting for the ten-thousand-dollar bonus, he traveled to the top of the hill.

CHAPTER 7

This time, at the top of the hill, Crane was given training he never dreamed existed. He even learned how to juggle and throw steel ball bearings.

Almost every day, one of the instructors would come in, present something new, and say, "Here's another toy that may add a little zest to your mission."

After Crane completed training at the top of the hill, he returned to the Army Security Agency base in Virginia. When he went into the briefing room, the colonel's face was drained of color. With his cloudy and drooping eye closed, he stared at Crane with his good eye, and there was no friendliness in that eye. It was deathly and a cloudy blue. It looked to be an eye of an angry man who never laughed.

The colonel leaned forward. "We want you to find a man who is important to us."

Crane had assumed the colonel wanted him to look for a physical object which wouldn't be very life threatening. But when humans were the object of a search, things could get complicated and dangerous. Now that he would have to find a human being, a trapped feeling of terror surged throughout his body. He wasn't ready to look for anyone. He let out a startled gasp. "Who?"

The colonel stood up and took a threatening posture. "You know him!" He bellowed so loudly that the sinews in his neck bulged to the size of small ropes. He turned from the table and jerked his finger at Crane. “Stay here!” He jerked himself to a standing position, walked to the door, opened it, went out, and slammed the door behind him.

Ignoring the colonel’s attempt to intimidate him, Crane leaned back in his chair, placed his hands behind his head, and tried to figure out who the person was the colonel said he knew.

Although the man had been with Crane before he entered the agency, and they were best friends, Crane had sworn never to mention the man’s name or recall the events that the man had perpetrated, the man he recalled was Specialist Seven, Neal McCord.

Before Neal had joined the army, he had fought a series of bareknuckle fights and won them all. Although he stood a head taller than most people, he could hear and sense things. He was more alive in the jungle than any normal human being. Being beside Neal was like having a dog that could talk. Although he didn’t wear the typical boonie hat with the floppy brim like other Green Berets, a short-brimmed Brixton gain fedora, with a pheasant feather tucked into the black band, covered his slicked-back hair, and he claimed that when he was wearing the hat nothing ever happened to him. His athletic frame, and the fact they he almost never blinked, made him more imposing than other soldiers, and the bayonet scar that bisected his left cheek added to what war had made him: a dangerous man.

Most men are creatures of habit. Their practices of living, sooner or later, become a pattern. Once that pattern is known, it is easy to find the man. Neal was not a creature of habit. He rarely yawned, said, or did, a common place thing. He never wore any of the many medals he had earned. He felt medals were like little signs that read, "Make Me Feel Important." Although he never admitted it, he was important. He would be difficult to find.

Recruited from an Army's Special Forces Group known for its guerrilla tactics, Neal became an integral cog in the machinery of the Central Intelligence Agency's highly secretive Special Activities Division, known as SAD. Even though Crane was not part of that group, his ability to be in the wrong place at the right time and discover something highly classified, had happened when he unwillingly hooked up with Neal in Vietnam.

Due to bad weather, Crane's flight from the island of Shemya, Alaska, was diverted to Tokyo Japan. Waiting for a flight at the airport, for three days, other veterans and he, had slept in chairs, on hard benches, on the cement floors, read paperback books, played cards, and did anything to pass the time.

For fear of missing a flight, Crane hadn't taken the time to shave. His wrinkled uniform, the dark circles under his eyes, and the growth of beard on his face, made him look like a homeless person.

When a flight finally became available, it was on a C-130 load master.

With a three-day growth of beard, he stood in line to board the flight. Before anyone was permitted to board, a captain called the soldiers to attention and informed them that the plane was making a stopover at the Tan Son Nhuyt Air Base in Vietnam to pick up bodies, and if anybody didn't want to go, they didn't have to.

During combat, many soldiers were hesitant to touch or grab any part of a dead GI. When it was necessary to grab the deceased man's hand, wrist, arm, or leg, and transport it to a collection point, the soldiers would freeze up. Yelling profanity usually motivated them to pull or carry the bodies, and after transferring a few dead bodies, the men's minds seemed to go numb enough to enable them to handle dead men without hesitation.

At collection points, if the body bags were seen, they tended to give away the massive state of a body collecting operation and lower morale. So medics kept body bags away from general view. After bodies were placed in plain, unpainted, aluminum transfer cases, most soldiers were still reluctant to touch or grab the cases. When it came time to volunteer to load cases onto planes, or fly with the cases, most soldiers backed away. Crane knew the bodies were going to be unloaded at Clark Air force base in the Philippines and then reloaded and flown to Travis Air Force Base in California.

He boarded the plane.

After the C-130 had landed a few miles northwest of Saigon, at the Tan Son Nhuyt facility, Crane looked toward the small white stucco headquarters near the flight line. The 224th Army Security Agency Battalion (Aviation) was there. But on the west side of the air base, the 509th Radio Research Group had initially established its headquarters. Its containment area was named

Davis Station in honor of Specialist Four James T. Davis, who had been the first American soldier killed in the Vietnam War, on December 22, 1961. Arriving in-country on a civilian passport in the summer of 1961 Davis was officially not there.

And officially the 509th and the 224th did not exist. Their undercover designation was Airborne Radio Research Unit, ARRU. To pass the time, Crane would have liked to have gone into the buildings and see if any of his agency friends were there, but entrance was on a need to know basis only, so he wasn't getting in there. And he didn't want to stand around for hours while the bodies were loaded. Keeping the thought in his head that dead people can't hurt you, he volunteered to help load the aluminum cases that held bodies onto the C-130 load master.

As he was pushing the second case onto the plane, the case tilted upward. The lid clicked open. The ice that had been placed in the case to help keep the body from decomposing had melted in the heat. A gush of water poured a morbid shower of bloody, death-smelling liquid onto his head and drenched his entire being. After visibly holding in a laugh, a man whose name tag read "Kane" walked up to Crane and stopped. They were just about the same height and build. But Kane was dressed in a hodgepodge of uniforms and civilian clothes.

Crane knew the reason Kane could dress as he did: In Special Forces, the line between officers and NCOs was blurred. Easy camaraderie based on ability, not rank, and the mutual respect of professionals replaced the rigid hierarchy of the line units. Small teams made the Army's conventional "You ain't paid to think" obsolete. Officers may have been team leaders, but when it was time to move out, everyone grabbed a load and started moving.

Although Kane's appearance looked out of place, something about him caught Crane's instant attention. Under Kane's black hair, his unshaven face looked familiar. While trying not to breathe in the terrible odor of the bloody water that had drenched his body, Crane thought Kane and he could pass for twins.

Kane lifted his hand in a halting motion. "Don't get too close," he said and backed away. "I know how rank that stuff is." He turned. "Follow me. I'll get you a change of clothes."

Trying not to throw up from the death stench that covered his body, Crane followed. He ended up in a barracks shower room, washing off the stench with his Class A uniform and shoes still on. After he kicked his shoes off and undressed, he handed Kane his wrung-out uniform. When he did, the identification coin that all personnel at the top of the hill carried fell to the floor.

Kane picked it up. Out loud, he read what had been stamped on the coin, "Anything, any time, any place, and anyhow." With a surprised look in his eyes, Kane smiled at Crane in recognition.

Crane smiled back. "I won't be needing that anymore."

A look of mischief beamed from Kane's face. "You never know."

When Crane stood under the shower spray trying to wash the death stench out of his mouth, Kane grabbed his hand. “You don’t have time to do that.” He handed Crane a set of camouflage fatigue pants.” Dry off and put these on. I’ll try to find a top.”

While Crane dried off, Kane rummaged around in his duffel bag, until he stood up and held out an olive drab Vietnam ripstop fatigue shirt. “Take this,” he said. “It’s my old one I wore before I made Spec/6.”

Crane slipped the ripshirt on. It had ample pockets to carry equipment and the sleeves had his rank insignia of Specialist/5, but he would have to remove the Special Forces shoulder sleeve insignia. What he liked about the ripshirt was that the shirttail didn’t have to be tucked in. When Kane handed him a canvas belt that had black brass female and male connections at the front, and a place for a pistol, Crane said, “I’m going state-side. I won’t need that.”

Kane smiled and patted Crane on the back. “Think of it as a souvenir. And besides, you’re out of uniform without it.” He pointed to the shoulder sleeve insignia. Crane glanced at the arrowhead-shaped patch with a dagger slashed with three lightning bolts with an arch of letters across the top that read “AIRBORNE”. He wasn’t airborne-qualified and was considered a “leg”. Although, like Special Forces soldiers, he had a high degree of self-confidence that sometimes verged on arrogance, he wasn’t qualified to wear the Special Forces insignia. It bothered him, but his plan to buy land and create a job where people knocked on his door and gave him money was waiting. He wasn't going to let an insignia stop him from going home. He reached for his knife to cut the threads and remove the patch.

"You don't have time to take that off," Kane said and handed Crane a green beret. The beret had the red patch with the Special Forces' pin with its proud motto. *De Oppresso Liber,* To Free the Oppressed.

Only men who had qualified for combat ready status could wear the full red flash. Others wore a unit identification bar, known as the candy stripe. Crane didn't qualify to wear either.

"I can't wear that."

"How about this?" Kane handed him a tiger boonie hat with floppy brims. "If you don't wear something, you'll miss your flight. I just got my jumping off orders, too."

Crane took the hat and placed it on his head.

"Looks good," Kane said. "I wouldn't want to miss my flight, either." He looked at Crane's bare feet. "They won't let you on without your shoes, but they don't match the fatigues." He bent over and took off his boots. "Here, take these."

The boots were not the usual army issue spit-shined Corcoran jump boots the airborne units wore. These boots were mountain boots, with thick cleated soles and brass eyelets. Made by cobblers, the ugly, heavy boots consisted of double uppers which rendered them warm in snow and ice, and if oiled with goose grease, were waterproof. They were the most practical field boot for a cold climate.

Kane threw a pair of thick socks at Crane's feet. "You might need these."

Wondering what this type of boot and the thick socks were doing in Vietnam, Crane slipped the socks and boots on and clinched the pistol belt around his waist. When they walked outside, Crane tried to get the putrid corpse odor out of his nostrils by sucking in deep drafts of the humid air and forcing it out. But the odor stayed.

After Kane took Crane's wet uniform and hung it on a wire for the hot sun to dry, he turned toward Crane. "I don't think it'll be dry before your plane takes off."

That's okay," Crane said and shrugged. "I only got a few months to serve in the states. I'll get by with what I have in my duffle bag."

Kane looked at the ASA patch on the shoulder of Crane's uniform. "I wouldn't be too sure of that, ASA man. Those psych war longhairs can't be trusted. They can always call you back, say it's in the interest of international security."

"I have my orders. They have to let me out."

"It doesn't matter what kind of paper-work you have. You're ASA. There will be no log. There will be no reference to your military record. The words are still in your head, aren't they?"

Crane didn't admit it, but the words were still there: Top Secret, Eyes Only, Confidential, Maximum Clearance Required, Authorization to be Accompanied by Access Code, and the red and white striped folders.

"Actually," Kane continued, "they will try to flatter you, say that you have been chosen by men who make important decisions. They'll say that you are more reliable than the people around you, and that you are about to make the most remarkable intelligence coup in a hundred years. If that doesn't work, they might just order you to stay in."

"I'm not that important or that smart."

"I wouldn't bet on it. They always skim off the best people and put them into one elite unit. Don't let them buffalo you."

Believing what Kane had told him would never apply to him, Crane nodded. "Thanks for the info, but I could use something to get the death smell out of my lungs."

Kane smiled an ear-to-ear smile, reached into his ripshirt pockets, and pulled out two cans of warm beer. "Sometimes this works."

After they had sucked in huge gulps of the warm beer, Kane playfully punched Crane in the arm. "You have to check in. This time, don't volunteer for anything."

"What if they volunteer me?"

"When they get near you, just make a show of supervising without actually doing anything. You'll be okay."

Crane finished the beer and went to check in.

CHAPTER 8

While Crane was standing in line, waiting to get onto the C-130, a man walked up to him and talked behind his back. "Nice try, Kane, but you're going to have to make one last detour."

Being that his last name was Crane, Crane figured the man had just mispronounced his name and needed help with a container or something another GI wouldn't touch. "Make it quick," he said without turning around. "I'm going home."

The man reached over and placed his huge strong hand on Crane's shoulder. "You're going with us." He yanked Crane out of the line.

Crane turned. The first thing he noticed was the short-brimmed Brixton gain fedora, with a pheasant feather tucked into the black band on the man's head. Then for the first time, he looked into the face of the man. It was his old friend, Neal McCord.

Neal, Rafferty, and Crane had been through hard times together. They were like brothers. Rafferty was a jokester who looked upon his life as his particular bailiwick, and he usually spent most of his time looking for and finding the bright side of every situation. He would be a welcome sight. Crane scanned the area behind Neal. No red-headed Rafferty was there to brighten the day.

Neal smiled his magnificent smile, and showed a charming display of pleasure at the sight of Crane. He extended his hand for a warm handshake. "It took you long enough to recognize me."

Crane grasped Neal's hand and shaking it, he looked beyond him. "Where's Rafferty?"

Neal let loose of Crane's hand. "Knowing him," Neal replied and swung his hand into the air, "he's probably somewhere out beyond the rim of the world."

Hoping Rafferty was near, Crane looked around and asked, "Is he here?"

In his ever-suave voice Neal said. "Can't say."

Crane nodded but he couldn't believe how much his old friend, Neal had changed. Although he still had an engaging smile that could sell toothpaste, his face had a rugged no nonsense look of a combat hardened veteran. As a tear formed in the corner of Crane's eye, he reached to shake his Neal's hand again.

Neal reached to shake Crane's hand again, too, but didn't shake it. Instead, he wrapped Crane in a welcoming embrace. Fighting back tears of joy, Neal let loose of Crane and stood back. "Crane! What the hell are you doing here?"

"Going home. You going home, too?"

Neal's smiling face faded and took on a serious look. "Not for a while. But I'm glad you're going..."

Stopping mid-sentence, Neal's eyes scanned Kane's name tag on Crane's chest. That look Neal always got when his mind had cooked up something new, appeared on his face.

The fact that Special Forces men were known for their abilities to scrounge things that were impossible for other soldiers to have, and they had abilities to adapt and survive in nonsurvivable situations that were unbelievable, was nothing new to Neal.

In the years that Crane had known Neal, sometimes it seemed as if Neal were half boy, half man. At times, he acted insane, but he wasn't mentally ill. For those who didn't know him, he could become a delusion, a phantom, or a mirage. It seemed as if he could be everywhere at the same time. With an incandescent personality, he rarely whined about everyday things. Back then, shambling in Neal's shadow was like hanging onto the shirttail of a mad man racing on the edge of a cliff as if it were a four-lane highway, racing toward the exciting land of some magical city. Once caught up in Neal's freewheeling ways, Crane had grown up fast. When Neal had been around, sleeping or nodding off from boredom was never an option. Neal's looks had changed, and Crane wondered if Neal had changed. But he didn't have to wonder long.

Neal placed his arm around Crane's shoulder and attacked him with a great, passionate soul that only a conman could have, saying, "Before you get out, it looks like, we've going on another adventure?"

"What are you talking about? I'm going back to the states."

Neal seemed confused. "Aren't you working Special Window?"

As if he had just been struck, Crane jerked in surprise. He hoped Neal wasn't talking about the special window unavailable to conventional units. It was directed by a permanent but unacknowledged

NSA liaison officer. Special Window had the highest signal intercept priority in southeast Asia. NSA assets, including the ASA, had satellite and isolated listening stations that had tuned their antennas for the slightest word about the identities of the moles that had penetrated the security of SOG units.

The ASA had been brought in to monitor SOG radios and phones for breaches in security. But it was discovered that because they would be the ones who would die, SOG men were already careful about encrypting and disclosing nothing on the radio. So the breach wasn't there. When Danang, Kontum and Bqan Me Thuot were monitored, the Vietnamese in those places had little access to operational data. And SOG's top-secret documents were stamped "NOFORN," which meant No Foreign Dissemination, which included South Vietnamese. So there should have been little likelihood of compromise there.

But when Saigon was monitored, it was found that each morning, a SOG liaison at SOG headquarters picked up an envelope at reports or "sitreps" which included SOG men's future grid locations and delivered it to an ARVN major across town. When the liaison found out what was in the envelope, he couldn't believe it contained U.S. team's situations. The ARVN major was giving information to the NVA, North Vietnamese Regulars, just as fast the liaison was.

When asked why ARVN had to know? The reply was that this wasn't our country and the South Vietnamese were our counterparts and all that kind of political crap. The ARVN access could have been cut off, but it was claimed that it would cause an overnight flap that would escalate to President Nguyen Van Thieu and draw in the ambassador, General Abrams, and perhaps the White House.

But the real reason the NVA were given the locations of SOG landings was that if a few SOG people landed in an LZ that the NVA didn't know about, there would be no NVA soldiers dispatched to greet them. By telling the NVA of the SOG landings, it became a successful "economy move". The known landings pulled away tens of thousands of NVA from the battlefields of South Vietnam for rear security duty in Laos and Cambodia. At one point, SOG teams in Laos were tying down six hundred NVA defenders, or about one NVA battalion per SOG recon man in the field. When SOG people found this out, they started misleading the ARVN, and Crane thought that had solved the problem.

But it looked like SOG was still being compromised, and Neal was probably thinking Crane was on assignment to help find out why.

The colonel's statement, "The Army's not just a job. It's an adventure," invaded Crane's mind and made him yearn to go home. But just as he had done when he had been with Neal before, he didn't want to show any weakness. In jest, searching for bullet wounds, he felt his own body. "I haven't been shot, yet. I rather get out of here alive.

Acting as if getting shot at was an everyday thing, Neal shrugged. "We got to do this while we can. And besides, what else have you got to do while you're waiting on your flight? Come on, man." Referring to the top of the hill coin, he said, "Anything, any time, any place, and anyhow. Let's do it."

Crane's face edged into a grin. "How about we talk about it over a few beers?"

For a moment Neal's eyes lit up. "I'd like to do just that," he said and frowned. "But we could end up in the hot sun. If our veins are floating in alcohol there is a good chance of dehydration."

In the past, when someone got on the wrong side of Neal, his mood could change rapidly. He was usually welcomed anywhere he went, but his rebellious attitude could become something apart from the known properties of a normal human being. The slightest touch in the wrong place or an authoritative tone of voice would throw him into a rage. Crane only wanted to go home. If Neal caused a ruckus Crane would miss his plane. But if he could do what Neal wanted before the plane departed, Crane figured it would be okay. When Neal made love with a girl, it was said that they generated so much excitement that people ran for tornado cellars. Maybe Neal's adventure would be nothing more than going to a place they could have a little fun.

"You think we have time to do this thing before my plane leaves?"

Neal's faced beamed with delight. "No problem. We'll be back in plenty of time."

"What are we going to do."

Neal walked Crane off to the side and talked low. "I need you to do a little favor for a buddy of ours. He's a radio operator who needs to go home early."

Nothing was more sacrosanct than a Green Beret needing a helping hand, but being Neal's friend, and remembering the many things that had happen when he had gone with Neal in the past, Crane wasn't too keen on the idea.

"I don't' know," he said. "Every time we set out to do something, it always ends up being a big deal or we barely survive being killed."

Neal leaned back and turned his palms up. "Come on, Crane. Back then, we didn't know what we were doing."

"Even if we know what we're doing, we could still get killed. Have you forgotten? This *is* Vietnam?"

"Nharm, sharm, those days are gone. I've reconnoitered the place. Before anybody knows we're there, we'll be in and out."

"What if my plane leaves before we get back?"

"You'll just catch another flight, and we'll have time to have a few drinks and relive old times together."

Crane was curious about what had happened to Neal since they had gotten cheated out Al Capone's vault. It would be nice to sit and talk for a while. But if Neal was like his old self, anything could happen. "That sounds like a great idea. But I don't know."

"And, besides," Neal added. "What else have you got to do? Wish your life away?"

Crane had heard that before, and it made him leery. "Your silver tong isn't going to work this time. It was nice seein' ya, but I'm going home."

Neal tilted his head toward a Huey setting a ways from them. "Since you have your mind made up, before you go, how would you like to take a ride on that?"

Interested, Crane looked toward the Huey.

Tail numbers had been removed, and U.S. markings had been painted over with camouflage paint that covered the entire craft. Even the rocket pods had been painted, and a crude image of a green hornet had been stenciled on the tail. Crane knew it belonged to the Green Hornets, which was the code name for the United States Air Force Huey units of the Twentieth Special Operations Squadron, which flew SOG missions into Cambodia. This Green Hornet isn't like regular army Hueys. This was an F-Model Huey.

"Are you sure about that?" Crane asked. "I've head those were designed to haul toilet paper to missile silos in North Dakota."

"That's what they would like the VC to believe." He swung his arm in an ark. "Come on, I'll give you a tour."

As they stepped toward the Huey, Neal pointed to the turbine on top of the roof. That thing's fragile, and it's a pain in the ass to maintain. But it'll get you in and out of a hot landing zone faster than any Army Huey."

"Even if it's faster," Crane pointed out. "If those nineteen, and twenty-year-old pilots can't fly it, you're not getting out of anywhere."

"We don't have that problem. Only career majors and lieutenant colonels in their thirties and forties fly these things."

"What kind of fire power do these things have?"

"Get inside. You'll love it."

Inside Neal held his hand on one of the miniguns.

Crane had heard about these guns. They were designated M134 and had six electric-powered Gatling-style rotating barrels that spit out 308 rifle caliber bullets instead of the bigger shells used by the autocannon, ATO.

"Best damned gun system over here," Neal said, and as if he were going to fire the minigun, he stepped behind it. "While two gunners man these things, the pilots can keep looking where they're going." He gestured to the other minigun. "These babies can spit out six thousand-rounds a-minute, but they work better when they spit out four thousand." He turned the gun toward the front of the Huey. "We can blast them comin' in." He swung the gun so that it was pointing outside. "We can blast them during the approach." He swung the gun toward the rear. "And!" He lifter one finger. "When we're leaving, we can shoot backwards "

"What if it jams?"

"We got that covered, too. "When a Cobra gunship's minigun jams, it goes home for repair. If a Green Hornet minigun jams, we just put on an asbestos glove, spin the barrel around, and clear it. In ten seconds, we're right back firing."

"This thing has some good firepower, but I'd rather be on a plane heading home."

Neal lifted his wrist and looked at his watch. "You still got time. Let's sit up front."

They stepped to the front of the Huey. Neal gestured to the pilot's seat. "Sit down, relax."

Neal had always been good at operating machinery, cars, and anything mechanical. Crane figured Neal was going to show him how to fly the Huey. But he didn't.

Instead, he stood and peered through the windshield and talked low. "Okay, Crane, now that we're in here where nobody can hear us, I can tell you the real reason you have to go with me."

Expecting another wild tale, Neal was famous for, Crane nodded. "Let it rip."

"I'm sure you remember what caused all the trouble we had when we were searching for Capone's vault."

"Nobody could ever forget that. Because there was so much money to be had, people came out of nowhere, and not one could be trusted."

"Neal lifted his hands and a helpless look filled his face. "Well, old buddy, pal of mine. We're in a similar situation." He turned and looked over his shoulder. No one was in the Huey. He continued. "You already know that knowing some things can become a hazard."

Crane had already discovered things he wasn't supposed to know, and those things had put him in danger. "We've both been down that road many times."

"Good, I didn't want to saddle you with the burden of knowing what it is, but I have come onto something that is worth so much money that it is like the vault. I can't trust anybody."

"What about your men?"

"If there wasn't so much money involved, all the team members would be okay. But I just don't know. I do know I can't trust two of them, but I'll tell those two that we need them to use radio direction finding units from different areas to pinpoint what we are looking for. Then I'll have them parachute out. With you along, we still can do the job."

"We?" Crane questioned. He didn't like the idea of going into a combat zone with people he didn't know. Some men would freeze under pressure. Some would make bad decisions that would get them and their buddies killed. One never knew how people would rect. Some would find calm in the heat of battle and would be able to outthink the enemy and save themselves in seeming impossible situations. The only test that determined if a person was safe to go into battle with, was being shot at with live ammunition. While he searched his mind for a good excuse to get out of going, the faint odor of a truck spraying DDT wafted into his face. He didn't want to be anywhere near DDT. He figured that if he went with Neal he would probably be covered with the stuff. "If I don't have to go," he said. "I'd rather not."

"Come on." Neal placed his arm around Crane's shoulder. "You have to go. We're an unbeatable team."

"I'd like to go," Crane lied. "But that Agent Orange makes me itch, and if I go, you'll feel like you're babysitting me. Your buddies are better trained than I am. You don't need me tagging along."

Neal dropped his arm from Crane's shoulder and looked him directly in the face. As if he were about to cry, he said, "In the past, our coordinates have been given to the NVA before we landed."

Crane nodded. "I got wind of that, but I thought it had been fixed."

"Maybe and maybe not. But I've got that problem solved for us, and the other men on my team should be all right, but I can't be absolutely sure. You and Rafferty are the only people I can trust." He grinned. "And Rafferty's not here."

Neal was right. When they had been chasing Capone's vault, the only people they could trust were themselves.

"Where we're going there isn't any Agent Orange," Neal said and sighed. "The main reason I want you with me is that what we're looking for might have something to do with Capone's vault." He squinted one eye. "And our radio security problem is serious. I scrounged two KY-38 secure voice systems. Each one weighs fifty pounds and is big as a shopping bag. All you'll have to do is patch a PRC-25 radio to it."

Crane knew that the KY-38 could keep communications safe, but its weight and bulk would slow a person down. He had used speech privacy devices much smaller and lighter than the KY-38. "Don't you have anything lighter?"

"It's the best I could get on short notice." Neal turned his eyes full upon Crane. There was something searching in his eyes. "If you think about it for a minute, you'll know the other reason why."

Right away, Crane realized that the smaller devices were far too advanced and classified to be taken into the jungle where they could be lost or captured. Even the Special Forces weren't always given the best equipment.

"Just about anybody can run a KY-39. Why me?"

"We can't call on the army for help. We're not supposed to be here. And you have enough experience to know the subtle difference between surfing and the real signal."

Surfing was the practice of transmitting alongside a real station's frequency to capture listeners who mistakenly believed they had tuned to the real station, and although Crane could easily tell the difference, he didn't want to carry the heavy speech privacy device.

"Who's going to carry it?"

"You will, but you won't have to carry it far."

Crane had not agreed to go with Neal. "I won't have to carry it at all," he said. "I might distract the other guys in your unit. They've fought together long enough that they instinctively know each other's moves. Sorry, Neal. I'm going home."

Neal looked dejected. "I figured it would be like old times. Just you and me, kid." His face looked a little gray, but the old hard light was there. "If you don't want to do it" — he smiled his famous smile — "it'll be okay. But no matter what, we'll always be friends."

Once again, Neal had managed to grab Crane's heart strings. Lasting friendships are forged with adversity and trust. He and Neal had been through life and death situations before. Crane couldn't abandon his friend when he needed him most. And it sure as hell couldn't be as bad as the past experiences. Crane had been to the top of the hill twice, and Neal was not only a Green Beret, he was part of a highly secretive and covert special operations group. He should know what he was doing. If what Neal wanted Crane to do, had something to do with Capone's vault, that could mean a lot of money. And a lot of money would enable Crane to buy land a whole lot faster than any other way he knew of.

Crane shrugged. "It sounds okay, but I don't need any trouble."

Neal pointed to the short-brimmed Brixton gain fedora, with a pheasant feather tucked into the black band he was wearing. "Remember when I wear this, nothing happens to me. So nothing will happen to you."

Crane stood up. "I guess a couple of hours won't matter."

With a look of relief in his face, Neal stood up, gave Crane a bear hug, and affectionately patted him on the back. "All right, Crane. It'll be just like old times."

After looking around again to make sure no one was watching, Neal stood at Crane's side. "I know you're ASA," he said and lifted one finger. "And,

Kane said you have the coin. I know you can operate radios, but have you ever been sterile?"

Crane had been sterile before. It was when he wore no rank or unit insignia, and to keep them untraceable, his uniform and weapons had been made in Asia. He replied, "I've done that." He pointed to his ankle. Under his pants leg, strapped to his ankle, was an unmarked, untraceable V-42 stiletto. A six-inch-bladed knife designed in Okinawa and manufactured clandestinely in Japan. "I still have the knife they gave me."

"Good," Neal said. "At the meeting, we'll pick up extra things we'll need. But from now on, when we're with somebody, because I'm the team leader, you'll refer to me by my code number, One-Zero."

Crane was familiar with the SOG's code numbers. Code number One-Zero, was a SOG's most prestigious title. Any man appointed a One-Zero had proven his judgment under life-and-death situations. The One-Zero had to outwit everything a numerically superior foe could throw at his team. One-Zeros were held in respect that verged on awe.

Crane also knew that the assistant team leader was the One-One, and their radio operator was One-Two.

"Am I going to be called One-Two?"

"You're a fast learner, One-Two. But your personal radio code name is Clarabelle Clown. Mine is Capone."

After what Capone's vault had put them through and was still putting them through, Capone was a fitting personal radio code for Neal.

Feeling the shyster side of Neal, Crane remembered that a way to defeat a careful enemy was to keep his plans from developing. Since Neal was a conniver and his methods were shrewd and careful, Crane knew Neal wanted Crane to take Kane's place for a reason. He smiled at Neal. "It figures. Are you still going to tell me that you want me to take Kane's place just because he wants to go home early?"

Neal turned his head as if he were afraid someone had heard the question. "Never could get much past you." He chuckled. "Actually, Kane isn't due to go home for a couple of weeks. An assigned radio clerk has the hots for a Vietnamese woman that I don't trust. He can transmit messages to Hanoi and certain NVA commands instantly. Our mission is much too important to have a whole company of NVA waiting for us when we land.

Crane knew about the EC-47 planes droning over Laos to eavesdrop on enemy radios. They had state-of-the art NSA intercept gear, and SOG's Leghorn's system could scan hundreds of NVA and other frequencies per second and snatch out any signal they wanted.

"Are you sure about that?"

Neal took a quick intake of breath and tensed. "I better be sure. Do you know something I don't?"

"After SOG's Leghorn system intercepts your landing zone location, are you sure they won't send it to the clerk?"

Neal relaxed. "When it comes over the KY-38, we hope they won't be able to understand it. By the time they record it and unscramble it, we should be back here drinking beer."

"Wouldn't it be easier to eliminate the clerk?"

"We would, but we've been feeding him false information."

Crane recalled that if an enemy's plan became disturbed or frustrated, he would be inclined to become enraged. And that would be an opening to be exploited. When false information placed the NVA in danger, they would trace it back to the clerk. Then the VC would eliminate him. Neal had figured a way to outmaneuver the clerk.

Realizing the simplicity of it all, Crane broke into triumphant laughter. "Let him eat what he sows."

"And you probably already know the most important reason why you have to go and Kane has to stay here."

At first, Crane thought it was because the most dangerous part of any mission was the last part. During the final few days or hours, a person's brain and body starts winding down. This causes a person to make mistakes that will get him killed, but then the real reason came to him. "Kane has to stay here and man the other KY-38."

"That's right. We're radioing all our coordinates for any extraction through the KY-38. When Kane gets them, to keep that clerk from getting them, Kane will walk to the Huey crew and give them the coordinates."

"That's going to take a while. I thought you said we'd be in and out."

"When they don't know we're coming, we're always in and out. And this time, You and Kane will make sure of that." He placed his hand on Crane's shoulder. "As long as the team doesn't find out you're not Kane until we get there, this little mission will be a snap." He looked at the mountain boots Crane was wearing. "You'll have to get rid of those. Before the meeting, I get you something better."

Crane hoped Neal was right about the mission being a snap. But in the back of his mind, Crane knew what Neal said, and what usually happened, always ended up with a different outcome. He gave Neal a questioning look.

Neal flashed an innocent look. "What?"

"Do you think our plan will work?"

"You seem to forget that I can turn anything into a selling point."

Nodding Crane remembered how Neal had jokingly said that if he wanted to sell a house with a leaking roof, all he had to do was say it was a safety feature in case of fire. In other words, if there was a way to do something, he would find a way.

CHAPTER 9

With team members watching for security threats, the pre-mission meeting was held in the empty bay of a C-130 Loadmaster. To keep from being recognized, Crane kept the floppy brim of the tiger boonie hat low and kept looking down. And it helped that the sleeve insignia on his ripshirt was Special Forces. So far, the deception was working. When he looked at the other nine people's stripes on their Vietnam ripstop fatigue shirts, none had ranks below Specialist Seven. There were no *Yards*, Montagnards, South Vietnamese hill tribesmen that were heavily recited as mercenaries for SOG teams. And there were no officers, no privates, or first-timers in this team. This had to be a serious mission. There were no "kids".

Crane knew the men around him were experts whose specialized knowledge far eclipsed his. Being with this many specialists with critical specialties caused Crane to feel out of place. He was sure he would only be with them until the trivial radio task Neal needed him to help with was done.

Neal threw a ripshirt at Crane.

Crane caught it.

Not only was it devoid of stripes, patches, or badges, it was reversible. for concealment in darkness, one side was black, and the other side was olive green. Crane wondered what to do with it.

Neal and the others took off their ripshirts and replaced them with ripshirts also devoid of stripes patches or badges. Senior leaders of the regular army believed basic training, tactics, leadership, organizational principles, and strategy that had won America's wars in the past was more than adequate for Vietnam. They were strongly against Special Warfare, Special Forces, and elite military organizations that did not conform to their antiquated methods.

While at Fort Devens, Crane remembered seeing men with ripshirts like the one Neal had just tossed his way. Those men had not worn green berets, and their shirts had no identifying patches or other insignias. As the men marched to school, other soldiers, ignorant of who the men were, jeered and catcalled at what they thought were "new recruits". The insults drew no response, but by the cocky, swaggering way the men marched, Crane knew they were Special Forces. Even though the regular army would consider him out of uniform, Crane gladly changed his ripshirt, too.

When he watched Neal and the others doing a last-minute check of their gear, he did the same. But he was amazed. Each man had three "Toe Popper" mines, U.S. M14 antipersonnel mines, made of plastic, that were small and fast to conceal, and were used as counter tracker devices. A CAR-15 submachine gun, an advanced version of the M-16 rifle, but this one had a folding stock and the barrel had been shortened. Crane picked up SOG's most popular handgun: The High Standard HDM, a semiautomatic pistol equipped with an internal suppressor that cut noise ninety percent. The weapon had been adopted by the OSS, Office of

Strategic Services during World War II. Full metal jacket 22 caliber bullets made the gun very effective. Even though Crane thought the barrel was too long, he liked it. The gear also included twenty-one magazines, a handgun, and an assortment of full-size and mini grenades that were about the size of golf balls.

Although the guns had been acquired clandestinely so a serial number check would lead nowhere, Crane wasn't happy that he was going to be carrying all that equipment. But he understood why every item he was going to carry had to be deliberately positioned. Reload magazines would be on his left, and grenades would be on his right. To get an accurate reading, his compass had to be on his left. That way he could extend his arm away from a steel weapon and get an accurate reading without taking his right hand off the weapon. Reload magazines were positioned so that even if he were moving, without looking, he could drop an empty magazine with one hand, pull a full one with the other hand, then slam it into his CAR-15 and slap the bolt release with his left palm and continue firing. When he had practiced it at the top of the hill, he had done it in fewer than three seconds.

When he took a close look at the grenades, he noticed that the pins had been straightened and wrapped with tape. That way if he couldn't use one of his arms, he could use his good arm and pull the pin with his teeth. All the gear had been muffled with tape or rubber bands so it wouldn't rattle, clank, or make noise. Unlike the regular army groups, this special operation group had practical lifesaving rules, lessons, and reasons for everything they did.

When Neal handed each man five PRC-25 FM radios, Crane remembered about the hundreds of Guard-tuned radios that the VC had captured. To prevent aircraft from wandering into the falling bombs, before each Arc Light bombing, a warning was broadcast on the emergency Guard frequency of 243.00 megahertz. Pilots could plot the impact point within a mile, but by using the captured radios, the NVA could, too.

Crane asked, "Why do we need five radios?"

"They're just little deterrents," Neal explained. "We'll drop them at various points. Some are packed with plastic explosive. When the VC turn them on, a detonator sets the explosive off. That little surprise keeps the VC from using captured American radios, but some of the radios have hidden homing transponders that makes it possible for the user to be tracked electronically."

Crane, Neal, and the other members of the team, turned in their dog tags, military ID cards, and money, including coins. And if they had U.S. cigarettes, they replaced them with Asian brands. That way, if they were killed and their bodies captured, the U.S. government could deny their identities.

Usually missions like this began at dusk. That way, the enemy would have no daylight left to dispatch a reaction force or trackers. And it would give the team a full night's head start, but Neal said it wasn't necessary, and that he liked to see the scenery on the way in.

And nobody questioned it. To be a leader, Neal had to always make everybody believe, including the bad guys that he was absolutely in charge of a situation. And just like the old days when he had been with Crane and Rafferty, he *was* in charge.

Right before they left for the chopper, to make absolutely sure they were carrying nothing attributable to the United States, they opened their rucksacks and emptied their pockets for a final inspection. After they painted their faces with camouflage paint, Neal threw Crane a roll of olive-drab ordnance tape.

Crane didn't want to ask Neal what it was for, but he gave Neal a questioning look.

Neal looked to the others. "It's bad enough having mosquitoes creeping into our ears and noses. If you don't want blood sucking leeches and pinching crabs crawling up your crotch, make sure not to leave any openings.

They all wrapped the tape snugly around the tops of their jungle boots

As they walked toward the Green-Hornet-stenciled Huey, Crane knew the people in it were very good at what they did. He and Neal would have to put on a believable show.

All of a sudden, Neal was in a real hurry, and Crane figured he wasn't moving fast enough. "Okay, okay." He adjusted the rucksack on his back and quickened his pace. "I'm going."

Crouched down and half running and half being dragged, Neal led Crane under the thundering Huey's rotating blades that could liquefy a skull. With the rotor wash blowing all around them, Neal threw him onto the alloy aluminum floor. Crane didn't know what the normal load of the Huey was, but there were ten people aboard.

What two of the specialists had just checked and placed into their pockets, caught Crane's interest: A new kind of miniature short-range radio direction finding units. Although Crane had worked with DF, radio direction-finding equipment operators, called "Duffys" for their MOS-05D designation, he had never seen DF units that small. The bigger ones he had seen were PRC-10 DF units mounted on jeeps. The smallest ones he had seen had an eight-inch circle that had to be hand held and maneuvered to tune in on a signal. These new units had a circle, the size of a quarter, directly attached to the unit.

Sitting, he slid onto the floor until his legs were hanging over the side. Then he flexed to jump out. The chop of the helicopter's spinning blades increased in speed. It was getting ready to take off. Beginning the acting job, he and Neal had rehearsed, referring to the short time Kane had left to serve in Nam, he shouted, "I'm too short to go. Let me off."

Neal grabbed his shoulder and held him secure. "Take it easy, Kane. You're not going anywhere."

With Neal pretending to keep him from jumping off, the Huey lifted off.

As it roared skyward, the pilot turned his helmeted head and looked through his dark visor toward Crane. The floor slanted. Crane felt himself sliding off the edge. The Pilot made the helicopter circle. Watching the centrifugal force from the maneuver keeping Crane from sliding out of the door, the others laughed.

"It figures," Crane whispered to himself. "Somebody always has to mess with the new guy." And he wondered if the pilot knew what he and Neal were doing.

Crane had never flown in a Huey before, especially with an open door and his feet hanging over the edge of the floor. Feeling as if he were going to slide out the door, he grasped at the floor. Over the loud thudding of the helicopter blades, he shouted to be heard and looked to Neal for help.

Neal looked down at him.

Crane instantly felt Neal's energy dominating the inside of the Huey. He quit shouting.

Neal yelled at him, "Quit foolin' around, Kane."

The Huey leveled out. Crane took a deep tremulous breath, sat up, and looked outside. From horizon to horizon, all he could see was rolling, jungled hills, wild rivers, and a few water falls. Then the Huey banked left and flew into a narrow valley, hidden from the sun by a crumbling rock ridge. If the Huey flew too high, it could become an easy target for a lucky shot with an RPG or a SAM. Fly too low, a canyon could take it out. Figuring they could dodge a mountain more easily than a missile, pilots usually stayed low.

Neal took a pistol from his vest and examined it. The High Standard, H-D, semi-automatic pistol had a magazine that held ten 22-caliber long-rifle bullets. The barrel had a suppressor that eliminated muzzle flash and achieved a ninety percent noise reduction. This enabled a target to be disabled with one, near silent, well-placed shot. And usually avoided a conventional fusillade that usually erupted after an audible shot was fired.

Neal cleared the pistol and tested its action. Then he loaded it with a magazine, placed it in his ankle holster, and looked down at Crane. "The joke's over now, Kane." He pointed to a utility belt festooned with spare magazines of ammunition. "We have a short mission, but you might need those."

Neal threw a tactical vest at Crane's feet. It had pouches for at least twelve CAR-15 magazines. The bullets inside were pretty standard issue, but the ballistic tips were designed to expand on impact, increasing trauma to the target. On each side, additional pockets held the golf ball-sized mini grenades. Each weighed just 3.5 ounces and when detonated they spewed over four hundred deadly fragments. The best thing about the golf ball-sized grenades was that they could be thrown a long way, and ten could be carried in a single shirt pocket. And two smoke grenades completed the collection. The vest even had a medical bag with needles, tubing, and a plastic bag filled with intravenous solution that he could administer to a wounded buddy or himself. The IV solution could quickly replace fluids in a wounded operator and keep him from going into shock. In a pinch, it could be used as an emergency source of water. However, inserting an IV could be somewhat dangerous. Unsterile conditions could cause infection, but was a small risk compared to a catheter shear. Because the needle inserted into the vein was encased in a plastic catheter, it could be broken by the needle. Once the catheter was in place, the needle would be pulled out of the catheter. When an inexperienced handler probed for the vein, but didn't tap it, after puncturing the arm, and pulled the needle out of the catheter and pushed the needle back in to hunt for the vein, if the catheter had been in the vein all along, the catheter would break. The broken off sliver could travel up the vein and cause a stroke. If an air bubble in the IV tubing that ran from the IV bag was more than an inch long and made its way into the vein, it could cause an air embolism that would result in a stroke.

Although he had done it at the top of the hill, Crane hoped nobody would get shot or injured badly enough that he would have to mess around with an IV tube. He leaned over and lifted the hefty vest.

It weighed almost twenty pounds.

Grimacing visibly, he hesitated.

Neal noticed. "Get that vest on, and check your rucksack."

Crane didn't like the thought of wearing the heavy vest, lugging the heavy rucksack around the jungle, or carrying the fifty-pound KY-38 secure voice system, but to keep up the ruse, he did as he was told.

Signaling that the Huey would reach the jumping off point in three minutes, Neal held up three fingers. Everyone nodded, their faces expressionless. All of a sudden, the weather became hazardous, forcing the pilot to weave between thunderheads and sunbeams. For a few fearful moments, he managed to avoid the sporadic ground fire from a fifty-caliber machine gun by tilting the Huey and weaving, but the fifty rounds kept on coming.

After the Huey leveled out and the sporadic ground fire was left behind, Neal looped a strap, connected to a radio, over Crane's neck, slammed a CAR-15 into his chest, and threw an ankle holster at his feet.

Holding the CAR-15 and feeling the confidence-inspiring heft of it in his arms, caused Crane to think about the Special Forces.

The charisma and glamour which surrounded the extraordinary Special Forces men came directly and naturally from the type of men Special Forces attracted and also from the offbeat missions they performed. The fantastically experienced bunch of rough individuals never apologized to anyone for the wars they had fought or the things they had to do. They were tough, intensively trained, proud, and competent specialist, not only in guerrilla warfare, but counter insurgency, too. They stayed with the Forces because they enjoyed each other's company and didn't care much for anyone else's.

Crane wasn't comfortable being out of his league. But he figured they would be in and out. Then he and Neal would be flown back to the base where they would relax with the assistance of liquid relaxing agents and talk about old times.

To keep the others pacified, Crane picked up the ankle holster that held his H-D suppressed pistol and strapped to his right ankle. As he did, he noticed a stack of MT-IX airfoil parachutes. He glanced over at the door gunners. With a short mission, a CAR-15 in his hands, and the fact that they would be in and out, he felt safe. After all, the Huey could land just about anywhere.

At times, Neal could be a jokester. He turned toward Crane. “Crane, strap on one of those airfoil parachutes, jump out of the helicopter, and glide eight or ten miles.”

Crane stood up and flared his arms like an eagle. “What?”

CHAPTER 10

In an effort to help keep things believable, Crane turned toward Neal and pointed to one of the parachutes Neal had just told him to strap on. "That one?"

Neal put his head back against the side of the Huey and laughed. "Don't sweat it, short timer. You won't be jumping out this time."

Kane was a short-timer. Crane thought about telling Neal that he was so short that he could walk under the space under a closed door. But he didn't know if Kane had that kind of a sense of humor, and he didn't want to talk too much as the others may recognize that his voice was not Kane's. He didn't say anything.

The two men with the short-range direction-finding units stood up, strapped parachutes on, and sat back down.

These were the men Neal couldn't trust. He turned to them. "It's time."

The specialist standing in the door looked at Neal and jokingly said, "Don't forget to come back and pick us up."

"Another ride has been arranged," Neal said. "When we're done, send the message. They should be overhead in about forty-five minutes."

The specialist nodded. His buddy and he leaped out the door. As they soared with their backs arched, arms and feet spread out wide in the "frog" position, one of the jumpers reached his right hand over to check the position of his rip cord. When he did, his body dipped to the right and he spun clockwise. To stable out, he placed his right arm back even with his left. When the jumpers were almost out of sight, they pulled their rip cords, the canopies inflated, and they sailed away.

Now, Neal wouldn't have to worry about the two men he didn't trust. Feeling comfort that the Huey would land on the ground and he wouldn't have to parachute out, Crane breathed a sigh of relief, but it was too soon. He remembered mines and booby traps usually filled landing areas.

The landing area could be a slash-and-burn area that looked like an old logging clear-cut created from logging. Laotian tribesmen had practiced the primitive agricultural technique of downing trees and burning them to fortify the soil with the ashes. They grew crops there until the nutrients in the soil were exhausted. Then they moved on and did it again. At various stages of regrowth, some of these patchworks of clearings stretched across the land. And many times, these LZs were covered by human surveillance. They were dangerous places.

Crane wished they would not land in a slash-and-burn area. He figured it would be safer to land in a hole in the jungle. And he hoped the miniguns would be enough firepower to handle any force they met. If the miniguns couldn't do that, Crane and the team could run, call for air support, and be evacuated by another helicopter. Maybe even use a STABO rig. An emergency extraction rig, also called "strings" or a McGuire rig that had a special web gear that converted to a harness that was attached to a rope lowered through the treetops from a hovering helicopter.

Ten minutes later, the Huey landed in a slash-and-burn area. With the wind from the Huey's rotors whipping the leaves of the upper tree branches wildly around, two team members, carrying plastic bottles filled with a liquid, jumped out of the Huey. While one man placed three transistor radios in a circle on the ground, the other man poured a bottle of the liquid into a half-filled wide mouthed bottle. Then he quickly poured the combined liquid over the ground around the radios, dropped the bottle, and slid back into the Huey.

After the Huey was clear of the slash-and-burn LZ, Crane realized that it had been a fake insertion to draw the enemy away from the real LZ. Dummy landings were as dangerous as the real ones, and this one had been made more dangerous, but this time the danger had been directed at the enemy. The liquid that had been mixed and poured on the ground was one of SOG's most sophisticated weapons: A by-product of NASA rocket fuel research, the unique liquid explosive called, Astrolite, was not publicly known. It was a binary explosive consisting of hydrazinium perchlorate and nitrate. Anything soaked with it had the remarkable property of becoming a liquid land mine. Astrolite made of perchlorate was the most powerful, and once mixed, it was so unstable that the person had to use it right away or get rid of it. And that was just what the men had done. As the Huey hovered at a safe distance, four VC walked into the area.

When they stepped on the saturated ground to pick up the radios, Boom!

Minutes later, Crane's wish to not land in a slash-and-burn area came true. The Huey made a rough landing in hole. When he waited for Neal to tell him get out of the chopper, Neal simply lifted his leg and shoved him out the door. The backwash from the Huey's blades whipped the boonie hat from his head, and in an instant, it was gone.

Crane looked up at Neal. Standing in the Huey, Neal threw back his head and laughed.

Crane knew he was in for another wild ride. He wanted to say, "Thanks a lot, buddy, old pal of mine." But the prospect of doing something new and exciting caused a high from the old days to surge through his body. He was about to follow a mad man. It would be like racing on the edge of a cliff as if it were a four-lane highway. In other times when Neal had done something like this, there was nothing to do but hang on for the ride. With a feeling of déjà vu, Crane grinned back at Neal.

As if it were as light as a sack of straw, Neal picked up the fifty-pound, KY-38 secure voice system, and jumped out of the Huey.

Before Crane knew what was happening, the Huey was lifting off, and the heat of the juggle enveloped his entire body. Steam rose up from the ground into a silver haze, and he felt like he was standing in a furnace with someone spraying a mist of hot water on him. Dark stains of perspiration were already spreading out from the armpits of the team members' rip shirts. The temperature had to be over ninety-nine degrees.

Crane was in excellent physical shape, but he knew he was not in the high level of physical condition of a Special Forces animal. He didn't have the conditioning to be humping the heavy rucksack and the KY-38 around the hot and humid jungle. He was already sweating. Not wanting to be exposed to enemy fire, and watching Neal carry the KY-38, he found new strength. He grabbed the rucksack and ran with the others toward the cover of the jungle. At the length of two football fields from the landing zone, the eight-man team ended up in a brush-shrouded depression.

Neal set the KY-38 on the ground and pulled out a light-amplifying pocketscope that had been hanging around his neck. The little pocketscope made it possible for him to see the faint image of Viet Cong hiding in the brush, that he couldn't see with his naked eye. He searched right, then left. While two men cradled sniper rifles in their arms, the other four men with silenced CAR-15 submachine guns slung across their chests, adjusted some sort of electronic devices, hanging at their sides.

Pointing to the radio at Crane's side, Neal looked to Crane. "Anybody close?"

Sitting on the ground, Crane knew there was a good chance that the VC had seen them. They had eyes that had been searching their country since they were babies. They would see a puff of smoke, or a mite of dirt that most people wouldn't see. With sweat dripping from his forehead, Crane adjusted the ankle holster. He didn't answer about anybody being close, but waited for Neal to begin the charade.

Doing what he said he was going to, Neal squatted with an athletic casualness. With fake concern filling his rugged face, he turned his attention toward Crane. "What happened to your scar, Kane? You're left-handed. Why do you have that holster on your right ankle?"

With the charade beginning, Crane rumbled to life. "It's like I tried to tell you before. I'm not the person you think I am. I'm not Kane. I'm Crane."

As if begging for divine intervention, Neal raised his hands to the sky. "I don't believe it. Kane's body may have been spent, but his mind's still sharp."

Crane pulled his pants leg down over the holster and continued the act. "I don't believe it either."

Confused, one of the other men bent over and looked into Crane's unshaven face. "Damn, he does look like Kane." Irate that an infiltrator could be kneeling right in front of him, he took a hold of the sleeve on Crane's ripshirt and yanked it. "Before you put this on, you were wearing Kane's shirt. How did you get it?"

Crane shrugged off the man's hand. "Unloading bodies, I got showered with body water. Kane told me my uniform wouldn't be dry in time to catch my flight home. So, he gave me his."

Neal grabbed his own face in agony and disbelief. "Kane told me he was going to do it." A huge smile spread across his face. "But I didn't believe him."

As if Crane were the enemy, another man took a defensive stance. "Do what, Neal?"

"Kane only had three days until jump off time. As we have seen happen many times, a lot of men are so excited about leaving that when they go on their last mission, they let their guards down and get killed. Kane already had his shipping out orders, but wasn't scheduled to leave for three days. He said if he were sent on another mission he would sneak past that bunch of bumbling Neanderthals, hop on a plane, and get out of there."

Faking realization, Crane said, "That's why Kane gave me his uniform and tried to give me his green beret with the red patch." He turned toward Neal. "And that's why you grabbed me out of line?"

Shaking his head, Neal said, "When I saw you standing in line, and saw Kane's name tag, our shoulder sleeve insignia, and his old rank, I thought you were Kane trying to leave early. I didn't want him to get in trouble for going AWOL. So. . . I yanked *you* out of line and threw *you* into the Huey." He studied Crane's face. "You look so much like him…" His voice trailed off.

Even though, Special Force's and ASA's lineage could be traced back to the Overseas Strategic Service of World War II, OSS, back then, because both elite groups had been hybrids with strong political and intelligence flavor, the regular army tried to steer clear of them. But after FDR died, that changed. The regular army's basic misunderstanding of what the groups really did, led it to believe that they were nothing unique. Many in the regular establishment, believed the OSS were a bunch of screwballs, or worse.

Coming from the slum neighborhood of Patagonia, Crane and Neal hadn't been the usual fresh-faced kids whose youth made them loud and arrogant. Even back then, they were quite inventive, and although they had come from the wrong side of the tracks, people didn't consider them unique, either. Crane figured the Green Berets and he shared more than a common historical bond.

"If it helps," Crane said and pointed to his own chest. "I'm ASA."

All of a sudden, the teams' attitude toward Crane seemed standoffish. But he figured they were only exhibiting a natural combat-driven reluctance to develop attachments to a doomed person.

One of the men let out a laugh. "A trained ASA diddy bopper?" he questioned and turned toward the others. "Oh, my God." He looked to the sky. "A trained diddy bopper just rolled out of our chopper. Christmas has come early."

Another man butted in. "They could train a monkey to do his job."

A diddy bopper was an ASA man whose primary mission was to take Morse code. Crane's training went beyond being a diddy bopper, and what he really did was highly classified. He didn't reply.

The sniper grunted a laugh. "Anyone who would join the ASA must be a lunatic or on their way to becoming one."

Looking in his direction, Crane squinted one eye. “I believe you’re on to something, but what am I doing here?”

Neal’s jaw tightened. “Whether you like it or not, you’re part or our reaction force.”

Crane remembered something about a reaction force from his advanced Viet Cong village training days at Fort Devens. A reaction force’s mission is usually to respond to something unexpected and as soon as possible. Being in an unorganized rush, it was usually impossible to respond without something getting fouled up worse than it was. The old army acronym, SNAFU: Situation normal, all fouled up, applied. If that happened it wouldn’t matter how many mortars, machine guns, explosives, radios, or ankle pistols they had, there would be problems. In the past, when Neal was around, problems erupted many times. Crane hoped it wasn’t going to happen again.

ASA’s mission was intercepting and sifting through mountains of clandestine communications and electronic intelligence data, gathered by listening in on enemies for the civilian-run National Security Agency. Regular army personnel with no knowledge of the mission, believed real soldiers paraded around in formations and risk their lives in combat, while ASA personnel sat inside secure buildings playing with radar and radios. Envious of the seemingly easy duty, and not knowing that an agency’s communication center was always the first place bombed or attacked, the army combatants referred to agency people as "Tit-less WACS," a derogatory label referring to the former Women's Army Corps.

One of the snipers stepped up and spoke as if Crane weren't there. "Who's going to baby sit this tit-less WAC?"

Neal turned toward the others. "If what Kane pulled off gets out, they'll break him in rank." Still pretending he didn't know Crane, Neal looked at him. "You *are* an agency man, aren't you?"

Crane nodded. "I told you I was."

"Have you been in long enough to keep your mouth shut?"

Crane had already passed the surveillance routine where he had been exposed to low-level and high-level classified material. If he had made one slip, security personnel would have found out. He would have been gone. After a while, keeping secrets had become a way of life.

He gave Neal a thoughtful, calculating look. "Not only have I been though the routine, I realize if an intelligent person wants to survive in a foreign country, he cannot play by army rules."

A look of approval formed on Neal's face. "We're on the same page. But you don't owe us anything."

Crane wasn't surprised that after he had no choice, Neal was pretending to allow him to quit. But then again, any Green Beret who needed his help, made him feel important. "If you need help, just say so."

"We owe Kane big time," Neal said and looked to the others. "He's probably at Clark Air Force Base" — he pointed to Crane — "wearing this man's uniform, waiting until his orders are valid. But if we play along, nothing will happen to him."

"Nothing will happen to Kane," Crane said. "But they'll think I went AWOL or deserted. What's going to happen to me?"

"You can tell the truth. Say you missed the plane because body water fell on you, and they threw you off the plane because you smelled too bad. Kane will make it home alive. He'll keep his rank. And no one will be the wiser."

Even though Crane kept using the sleeve of his shirt to wipe sweat beads from his forehead, because he had lost his boonie hat, some of the camouflage paint kept running into his eyes. The thought of dying in the jungle and having his body encased in an aluminum transfer case surrounded with putrid ice water made him shudder. "If I want to live through this," he said, "I'll have to play along. But what do I do now?"

Neal and the others took black bandannas from their pockets and placed them around their heads. Then Neal handed Crane a black bandanna. "You can't see with sweat running into your eyes. Put this on."

With sweat trickling down his stomach and between his shoulder blades, Crane folded the bandanna, placed the center of it over his forehead, and tied the ends in the back of his sweaty head.

Neal continued. "If the VC are sending Morse code, we can plot their radio to within two hundred meters. One-Two bailed out. I can only take eight words a minute. Can you take it faster?"

One-Two was the code name for a U.S. Special Forces SOG recon team radio operator. To throw back what the man had said before, Crane wanted to say that a monkey could be trained to take eight words a minute, but he didn't. "I'm not a ditty bopper whizz," he said. But I can take about twenty-two words a minute."

"That's two better than him."

"Get the radio out." Neal nudged the strap on Crane's shoulder that was holding the radio. "Check for VC on the air."

Crane opened the protective flap of the radio. Although not a KL-43 encryption device, it had controls similar to a radio he was familiar with: An R390 receiver but much smaller, and it had a transmitter. He turned and looked to Neal. "Have your frequency calibrations been altered?"

Neal smiled down on him and turned toward the others. "This kid's good."

VC had learned to impersonate soldier's voices so well that when a daily code word wasn't changed, they used the code word and were freely let into perimeters, where they easily killed unsuspecting GIs. If someone used the frequencies indicated on the dial of an altered transmitter, they would be on the wrong frequency. A message sent using an altered transmitter would not get through. In addition, the frequency was changed for every transmission. If lost or captured the altered transmitter would have no cryptic value.

Crane wondered what the devices that the four men had were used for. He pointed to one of the devices. "Is that a radio, too?"

The man and the other three men exchanged uneasy glances. Then one of the men smiled. "It's a bullshit detector."

With the knowledge that the man wasn't going to let him know what the devise was for, Crane knelt down, set the radio on the ground, placed his finger on the standby switch, and clamped the headset over his ears. "I'll see if I can find the frequency."

While four men stood, back-to-back and scanned the jungle, the others knelt over Crane and Neal in a tight circle. To Crane's relief, the radio's receiver had a preset frequency. He turned the standby switch to on. After a soft crackle, the radio emitted a disharmony of spoons clinking.

Neal looked to Crane. "Do you have a signal?"

Intently listening to the Morse code sent by telegraph key, Crane nodded. "Got one, but it's pretty weak."

Neal motioned to the two men with radios jammed against their ears, and pointed to the frequency indicator on the radio. "Get a fix."

Crane realized Neal had told the two men to contact the two team members who had jumped out of the Huey to tune their directional finders to the frequency the VC's were transmitting on. Intercepting the frequency from three locations and pinpointing where it was coming from would provide three reference points. Where the three lines of signal-travel crossed, would be the "fix" or location of the VC's transmitter. Usually three bearings were used, but two would also work. A weak signal could mean that the VC were not within two hundred meters.

Although the clinking was different from the smooth twenty words a minute Russian code, Crane was accustomed to taking, this code speed was irregular and coming over at only about five-words a minute. Using a pencil and notebook that was next to the radio, he copied some words, but they were in Vietnamese.

After he had copied the words "*ok ok, ok,*" the operator sent the number 20:00 which meant Zulu time. From intelligence derived from his past experience of intercepting radio transmissions, Crane knew the man sending this slow Morse was having a difficult time. The stress of trying to send code without a decent working knowledge created terrific headaches. Crane hoped the VC operator had one. Crane figured that 20:00 Zulu time would be minus nine hours or 1:00 p.m. Vietnam time. If he were correct, the VC would stay silent until their reporting time came around again, and the time of the next transmission would be 1:00 p.m., or in military parlance 1300.

The time the VC had been on the air was short. Crane figured that the signal had presented too short of a burst to get a fix. Hoping the men with the radios had advanced equipment, he asked, "Did you get a fix?"

Both men shook their heads. One said, "It didn't last long enough."

The other said, "The signal was too weak."

"Good," Neal said. "The weak signal should mean the main force isn't close. We might run into a few VCs, but before the main force knows we're here, we should be in and out."

As Crane sat on the ground with his head lowered listening to the radio, Neal and the others looked down at him with expectation. Crane looked up. "I can't guarantee anything, but it should be an hour before the next transmission. If your partners that jumped out are close enough, maybe we can get a fix, then."

"Ah, hell." Neal said and scanned the jungle which consisted of nipa palm and other tropical maritime trees and shrubs in dense masses. "Even if we can't get a fix and find exactly where they are, we've made it through tougher places than this. But it doesn't matter. Before they know we're here, we'll be in and out."

To Crane's right, the team member sniper fingered the red lenses scope on his rifle and tilted his head to the side. "I guess we're far enough into country that 'If it moves, shoot the SOB applies."

"Affirmative," Neal said. But use common sense. We don't want to end up shooting each other."

The practice of fragging was shooting incompetent American officers to save lives. The sniper looked to Neal and said, "Don't worry about it. You're not fragg material."

Referring to arrogant, know-it-all officers fresh out of ninety days of officer school who thought they knew it all, the man next to Neal said, "Yeah, you're not a ninety-day wonder."

They all nodded.

Neal reached into his vest. "Speaking of ninety-day wonders." He pulled out a handful of various officer pins. "Gentleman, what kind of officer do you want to be today?"

One man held out his hand. "I'll be a captain."

Neal tossed him captain's bars.

After he had passed various officer pins to everyone but Crane he stepped to Crane. "Only one left. Looks like you're the general today." He pinned a general's star on Crane's collar.

"Crane looked up in bewilderment. "Why the pins?"

"If we, by some very unlikely chance, get captured, the NVR will think they really got some important prisoners, and our chances of them not killing us will be greatly improved."

Surprised, Crane turned his eyes toward Neal. "What do you mean, greatly improved? Don't they shoot officers first?"

Neal placed his hand on Crane's shoulder. "Usually, but don't pin on the rank unless you are captured. He pointed to the KY-38 secure voice system. "Sorry you can't come with us, but if we have to get out in a hurry that thing will just slow us down. You'll have to stay here and guard it."

Crane knew he hadn't been trained like a Green Beret. If he had been, he would be infused with an awareness that he was going to trust his life to the other members of the team, and his survival would be depended as much on them as on himself. Each man knew that he was responsible not only for the success of his part of the mission, but of the lives of the other members of the team. And Crane hadn't been with the team long enough to be able to tell who was near simply by the odor, as distinctive to a man as his fingerprints or his voice or his walk. In short, Crane knew he hadn't been trained enough to go with them. If he did tag along, not only would he be like some rich kid, at a snot-ass school who thought he knew everything but knew nothing, he would endanger the mission and all their lives.

Crane acted like he couldn't believe Neal wasn't going to take him on the mission. But he knew he had to stay and man the KL-43 encryption device. "That's just great," he said sarcastically.

Gesturing to Crane's tactical vest, Neal said, "Your grenades and your CAR-15 should be enough, but..." He held out a 12-guage shotgun. "Just in case, take this."

"Aren't those supposed to be illegal?"

As if proud of the fact, Neal lifted his chin in an amplified arrogant manner. "We carry any weapon we want."

Crane took the shotgun.

Neal gave him a reassuring look. "You should be all right. An angel should be on your shoulder. Monitor the radio. If the VC signal gets stronger, watch out."

"What if you don't come back?"

"If you think you need help, don't holler out. And do not try to use regular frequencies to call the helicopter. If you do, the VC will put a directional finder on your ass. They'll know we're here. If we're not back in an hour, forget about us. Use the KY-38. Tell the guy on the other end," he said, referring to Kane, "to tune his transmitter to AFRN.

He'll cut into the regular Armed Forces Radio Network. People will be listening. Just whisper into the handset, 'Happy Birthday, Clarabelle Clown.' A Huey will be at the landing hole in about an hour."

He reached into Crane's vest, took out a purple smoke grenade and rolled it toward Crane's feet. When you hear the chopper, if it doesn't see you, set this off. Stay low. Getting out in under fifteen minutes is you best chance. After thirty minutes your chances fall, but you should still be able to make it out." He turned to go but turned back. "And whatever you do, after you send the message make sure you destroy the KY-38. And do not use the radio to call the Huey."

Normally a helicopter would simply be notified by radio, but if this signal was intercepted the NVA would come in droves. And even is the NVA didn't come, Crane figured manipulation was being used to alter the Special Forces' normal signature of their radio nets and procedures. These false traffic levels and controlled breaches of security denied the VC a true picture of their true intentions. If he used the radio to call the helicopter, it could cause the false traffic pattern to become known. Then the radio deceptions would fail.

He picked up the smoke grenade and nodded.

Neal straightened up, wiped the sweat off his face, and pulled a small device out of his pocket. He lifted a cover and pushed the side of the devise. Crane had never seen a TV screen that small. As he watched the devise, red numbers and letters streamed across the little screen. In a few seconds the numbers stopped and the screen turned green. Neal closed the device, placed it back into his pocket, and looked toward his men. "We only got one shot at this. If you find some, make sure the container is tight."

Crane wanted to ask Neal why the container had to be tight, but before he could ask, Neal jerked his head toward the jungle. "Saddle up."

His entourage gave him a thumbs-up.

With their rucksacks on their backs, they all held their CAR-15's ready to fire and walked into the jungle.

CHAPTER 11

Now that Neal and the others had trudged off into the jungle, Crane sat on his rucksack and checked the destruction fuse on the KY-38. Semtex, a small block of extremely difficult to detect plastic explosive was in place, and the ten-second timer pencils were ready to be activated.

Trying to push down his terror, he inhaled the aroma of the jungle. A breeze stirred leaves, and the scent of forest blossoms, damp soil, and green life filled the air, but he never felt so useless.

Wondering what Neal meant by, "Make sure the container's tight," Crane sat down on a large root of a bush and covered himself with leaf-filled branches, grass, and anything he could, but the hot rays of a merciless sun shone through. If he would have had a sleeping bag to block the rays or a mosquito net, he would have been much more comfortable. Being on Shemya Alaska for a year had cause his body to acclimatize to cold. The humid heat of the jungle was soaking into his very soul and draining his energy. Although he hadn't done any physical work, he felt utterly exhausted, and his sweat-dampen clothes steamed in the sun. He had to get to a cooler place. If any VC were around, they wouldn't be expecting him down among them, and he knew how to move through the vegetation.

Pulling the KY-38 behind him, he crawled through a stretch of underbrush. Satisfied that he was well concealed, he studied the CAR-15 rifle.

At the top of the hill, he had practiced with CAR 15, but that had been years ago. When he had been on the island of Shemya, he had target practiced with a Heckler & Kock, P-13, 9mm automatic pistol, but he had done his six-month qualification with an M-14 rifle. He had heard many horror stories about the M-16 jamming and sending bullets out as if they were peas from a pea shooter, but this wasn't an M-16, it was a CAR-15. It was a much better weapon. He did his best to re-familiarize himself with it. But from crawling through the underbrush, scratches and cuts covered his hands. When he moved his fingers, it was a painful effort. After twenty minutes, he didn't know if his painful fingers would impair his ability to pull the trigger on the CAR-15 and hit the target. But he was positive he could hit any target with the shotgun. When the odor or rice and sweat wafted into his face, he knew might have to use the shotgun.

He checked the radio patched into the KY-38. An ear-piercing squeal came from the radio's headset. It was a high-powered radio frequency, electronically jamming the signal. Twenty minutes passed. In forty minutes, an hour would have passed, and he would have to send the message. But if the jammer was still jamming signals, he wouldn't be able to use the radio and the KY-38 to send the Happy Birthday signal, and the jammer's pitch was changing slowly. It wasn't coming from an airborne source. It had to be coming from someplace on the ground. Concealed in the branches and grass, he strained his eyes and searched for movement. Although a couple of mosquitos were busy trying to getting a fill-up from his cheek, he didn't move and held his breath for any sound.

There was none.

A sinister stripe of lightning announced the severity of an advancing storm. Like a gray curtain, a monsoon, in the form of silver rods of rain came and blocked his vision, but the mosquitos were gone. As if on cue, faint gunshots and exploding mortars came from somewhere deep in the jungle. He turned the radio off, took two grenades from the rucksack and set them on the rucksack where he could easily grab them. When he looked up, he could hardly see what was five meters away: three VC in the mist. Dressed in wet, black pajamas, they wore conical straw hats to keep the rain off their faces, and had rolls of rice slung over their shoulders.

Crane felt a terror he'd never felt before. And it caused his hands and knees to spasmed so bad that he thought if the VC came closer, he wouldn't be able to move away or fight them. Barely breathing and sitting perfectly still, he watched and waited.

After peering into the jungle, one VC set his AK-47 assault rifle and some sort of equipment that could be a jammer, on the ground. Then he turned his back and began to urinate. The other two VC leaned their AK-47s against a tree, ran into a bank of reeds at least six feet tall, and faded into the downpour.

In the states, Crane had seen hard rains before. They had come down hard and fast, but only lasted a few minutes. This Vietnam rain didn't stop. He was completely soaking wet. Vietnam's monsoon season last from May to September, and it felt like the torrential downpour wasn't going to stop until September.

Holding the shotgun at his side, Crane held his breath. A snake curled off a branch and placed its fanged head right next to his face. The spasms in his hands and knees immediately vanished. Knowing that a scared person can't think right, he fought the urge not to be afraid. Just as he had done many times with wasps, called yellow jackets, he didn't move. He concentrated and created a threatening aura. The snake slithered away.

After the VC finished urinating, as if he were taking a shower, he raised his face to the sky, closed his eyes, and let the rain rinse his clothes and body. While he stood there, the rain stopped. As the lush, green foliage dripped with moisture from the rain, and the humidity became too thick to allow it to evaporate, the VC turned and looked directly to where Crane was hidden. Although dried blood had flowed down the VC's arm that was missing skin and showed muscle, his tiny rotten teeth were barred in a psychotic smile.

He knew Crane was there.

With his shrill voice mounting to a hysterical pitch, the VC made a desperate attempt to reach his rifle. With the grass and branches avalanching off his body, Crane stood up, whipped the shotgun around, and squeezed the trigger. The VC took the full charge in the stomach. He gave a grunt and bent over. With his head hitting first, he thumped onto the ground and rolled over. He was facing the sky, again. But this time, his dead glazed eyes were wide open. Crane's feeling that he hadn't been trained enough had just been reaffirmed: If he would have used his High Standard HDM, semiautomatic pistol equipped with an internal suppressor that cuts noise ninety percent, it wouldn't have made as loud a sound as the shotgun had. And he would have avoided the possible fusillade that usually erupts after an audible shot is fired. A fusillade hadn't happened, but if more VC, other than the two somewhere in front of him, happened to be in proximity, the sound more than likely had alerted them.

Before Crane's mind could process the horror of the sight, the rain started again, and the other two VC jumped out of the reeds and desperately plunged toward their rifles. With rain sluicing down through the trees, Crane fired the shotgun at them. One moaned in agony, dropped, and crumpled like a half-filled leather sack of mail. As if he were invincible, the other VC stood for an instant and pulled the trigger on his rifle.

Whack! A bullet came so close to Crane's head that he felt the sting of gunpowder on his cheek. He wanted to fire again, but the shotgun was empty. The VC's next shot wouldn't miss.

Now trapped with the stink of blood and death filling his nostrils, to perhaps live a few more seconds, Crane tried to distract the VC by waving his hand skyward.

The VC didn't waver.

Figuring this was the end of his life, Crane felt his face turn mournful.

But a voice from out of the Jungle yelled, "Happy Fourth of July!"

The VC looked to where the voice had come from. A noisy whoosh, like a Roman candle, rushed toward him. He gasped for breath and choked on a blood-filled mouth. His knees buckled. Like a jointed puppet that was being manipulated from above and its strings had been suddenly cut, the VC rag dolled and crumpled to the ground. With the odor of cordite and uncertainty filling the air, Crane figured what had killed the VC: One of the new toys he had used at the top of the hill: a Gyrojet pistol, that shoots a thumb-size 13mm mini rocket. Propelled by solid fuel that gushes from two little canted holes in the base of a steel and plastic pistol, the mini rocket from the Gyrojet pistol, had flew into the VC like a fifty-caliber machine gun slug and had blown the VC's stomach wide open. It was a grisly sight, made worse by the repugnant odor of human guts. The foul smell triggered Crane's gag reflex. It had been hours since having any chow. Other than some water he had drunk from his canteen a few minutes earlier, his stomach was empty. After regurgitating foamy water, dry heaves climaxed with hydrochloric acid burning his throat, and caused him to cough, choke, and gasp for air. But he didn't have time to be sick. He lowered the shotgun and picked up the CAR-15.

Behind him a shot rang out, then another. Knowing the VC knew where he was hiding, he picked up the grenades and threw them. Before they exploded, he leaped from his hiding place, hit the ground rolling, came to a stop, and stayed there until the grenades went off. Then he came up with the CAR-15 at his shoulder. The first thing he saw in front of the CAR-15's barrel was a VC. He pulled the trigger. Absorbing a burst of bullets, the VC faltered, stumbled, and sprawled out. Crane didn't know where they were, but the excited voices of VC filled the damp air.

In a spatter of bullets, Crane ran into the brush, stopped, and crouched down. When the VC's voices neared, he stood up and ran out of the brush. A meter from the brush, he slipped on the wet mud. His CAR-15 and he hit the ground sliding. Almost as soon as he hit, he was up and ducking into a thick stand of greasewood. He froze in place. But shouts and yells of VC were behind him. He moved on. The VC had fanned out. They were working toward him. There were probably VC in front of him, too. Studying the terrain, he felt trapped. There were more grenades and toe popper mines in his rucksack, but it was where he had been hiding. He couldn't get to it. If he were wounded and needed the IV solution to quickly replace fluids and keep him from going into shock, he wouldn't have that, either. He needed an escape, but there wasn't any. They were moving in. If he ran, before he could run a dozen steps, he would be picked off. He would have to stay and fight. He checked the CAR-15. When he had fallen, mud had jammed into the barrel.

Another VC had come up from behind and stood staring at Crane. His hideous, haunting gaze caused Crane's nape-hairs to stiffen. The man had two grotesque holes in his face that resembled a pig's snout. The disfigurement could have been a birth defect, but it was more likely that his nose had been cut off because he had violated an ancient tribal law such as lying or stealing. The very sight of him caused Crane to stare back in awe. Wearing the look of a pig and being an outcast, the man had no doubt been teased, taunted, and called a pig. For him, killing an American would be easy. And the pig had his gun sights aimed right at Crane's head. Crane knew he would never be able to reach down, grab his ankle pistol, and swing it up in time to shoot the pig before he shot him. He grimaced for the head shot that would end his life.

An almost silent whack sound came from his left.

The side of the pig's head exploded into a spray of blood, filled with bone fragments and tissue. The pig's brain turned off so abruptly that his hands leaped off his AK-47 and made it appear as if it were suspended in midair.

The gruesome sight caused Crane to realize he was the one who should be slumped on the ground, his sphincter and bladder relaxing, waste and urine emptying from his dead body. But instead, someone had saved his life. Expecting to see Neal and the others, he looked to where the whack sound had come from. The area was void of any motion. Whoever had saved his life had disappeared into the jungle. Crane remembered that during the last-minute-check no one had had a Gyrojet pistol. He wondered if the person that saved his life had been the angel Neal said should be on his shoulder.

Crane pulled the magazine out of his CAR-15, cleared the mud from the barrel, and slapped in another magazine. Then he waited for more VC to attack. But none came. If more VC did come, they would see and smell the bodies. Tromping in mud that sucked at his boots, Crane dragged the dead VC far enough into the brush that he couldn't smell them. For a moment he wondered who the dead men were. He could have gone into their pockets and found out. But like other people in his situation, he didn't really want to know who they were. When the dead were anonymous, it was easier to be impersonal. He didn't know what religion, if any, the dead men had practiced, but he silently said a vague prayer to whatever God, Buddha, or other mysterious power that really ruled the earth. When he began to conceal the bodies, a gold pin fell from one of the bodies. Crane cursed. The gold pin was a Seal Trident pin, often called "The Budweiser" because it resembled the Budweiser beer logo. One of the dead VCs had killed a Navy Seal and had taken his trident pin. The VC had to be exceptionally trained and able to do that. Being way out of his league, Crane wondered why he was still alive.

When he checked the VC's equipment that looked like a jammer, he found an on off switch. He turned his radio on and turned the jammer off. The radio worked. When the hour was up, he would be able to send the happy birthday message through the KY-38. He turned the radio off and waited.

With the adrenaline rush from staying alive fading, Crane began to have trouble making sense of what had just happen. And then it dawned on him. The constant sweating from the heat was making him dizzy. If he were a Green Beret, his responses to the Nam's environment would have been automatic, but he was not a Green Beret, so his response had not been automatic. He reached into his pocket and pulled out salt tables in a small plastic container. He chewed on the plastic until he got to the salt tablets. Salt tablets had been a constant unvarying part of a soldier's life in Nam, and now he was using them and feeling the acridity burning his gums.

Although he knew it was a matter of his life or the VCs' lives, he still felt for the dead men. He believed that if the military hadn't used its limited military mind, cluttered with images of big battles, front lines, and a century and a half of military victories, and interfered with the Green Beret's efforts in Vietnam, there would have been no need to have regular American soldiers to fight in the war.

His reasoning being that each man in a twelve-man Special Forces "A Team", spoke a foreign language and was highly trained in at least one of five specific areas: light and heavy weapons, demolitions, medical aid, communications, intelligence, and operations. When one A Team was inserted into an area of operations, it could form the nucleus of a three hundred to four-hundred-man battalion of local troops, and the Green Berets had been able to instruct as well as assist in combat.

It didn't matter who or what had started the war, or who or what could have ended the war, Crane continually tried to convince himself that the killing of the VC was nothing more than the correction of an error because the great Creator never intended people like that to be on the earth. He needed to rest and think things out, but there was no safe place he could relax. In the jungle, not a single resourceful girlfriend was waiting around a bend in the path to hide him. And his other buddy Rafferty, was somewhere back in the states. Until Neal and the others came back, he was on his own. And they might never come back. Crane knew he had to always give his adversary as much credit as possible and give them every benefit of the doubt, and at all times. If he did, maybe, just maybe, he would live. Underestimate the adversary's qualities for one second, on any point, and you might die for it.

As Crane crouched and waited, instinct shot a small charge of adrenaline through his sweating body and augmented his Indian's natural stealth. More than an hour had already passed. No more VC came, but neither had Neal or his men. Crane wanted to wait a little longer. If they didn't come back and he sent the message, and the Huey didn't come back, he would have to find a way back to the base. But he was afraid he might end up in southeast Cambodia close to Fishhook, which was one of SOG's most dangerous cross-border targets and was a major North Vietnamese Army base area that usually housed two or three enemy divisions.

Crane thought about what would have happened if he had been killed. When an ASA man had been the first man to be killed in Vietnam, little information had been given out. As the man had operated a jeep-based PRC-10 short-range direction-finding unit to locate VC transmitters that were only a few miles away, Viet Cong ambushed him on a road outside of Saigon. Since radio wave propagation in Vietnam required that DF equipment be very close to the transmitter, after the ASA Man's death, the agency ditched the jeep and used a DF platform on a single engine aircraft that flew low and slow, and had room for only a few people. Within days, ASA people in the unit were calling it TWA, an acronym for Teeny Weeny Airlines.

ASA people who were operators or involved in intelligence collection flew over enemy territory several times a week and were in much more danger than regular soldiers. The VC offered a one hundred thousand piaster bounty, about five hundred dollars American money, for any ASA member captured. Night raids sometimes got them a clerk or a mechanic, but rumor had it that never anyone who knew anything really sensitive had been caught. Crane didn't know if any ASA members had been caught, but he didn't want to be the first. If he did get killed, and the army found his body, he would not be reported as killed in action. The agency would deny that he had been a covert operative in the wrong place at the wrong time. They would probably report that he had been killed in a helicopter training accident or something, and his death would be announced to the people in somber tones. His buddies back home would never know what had actually happened. Some ASA enlisted staff's actual M.O.S.'s, Military Occupational Specialties, were classified. In the Army's general records, they were listed under the bogus M.O.S. of "General Duties." The sad truth was that while an enlisted man's various specialties were recognized within the ASA, the man's expertise was often not known or given any consideration outside of the ASA and the NSA.

Crane wasn't even supposed to be in Vietnam. The Vietnam Service Medal would not be posted on his records. Just like other agency personnel that the Russians had shot down near the Russian Kamchatka Peninsula, the disguising of his death would be a matter of national security. About the only recognition he would get would be a black star. Every time a special operations person died, the agency added another black stat on the north wall of the lobby at the top of the hill, and only top of the hill personnel viewed that. After three hours, Neal and the others hadn't returned. Feeling a monumental case of survivor's guilt coming on, Crane reluctantly turned the radio and the KY-38 on and whispered to Kane, "Send the Happy Birthday, Clarabelle Clown message."

Carrying the KY-38 Crane walked toward the landing hole. Before he got there, he noticed a four-foot wide hole that had been scooped out of a hillside. He remembered being told that these were listening holes. If someone dug a hole and sat beside it, even before they heard a chopper, they would feel the vibrations out of the hole. And it would provide some protection if the VC decided to lob in an 82mm mortar. He sat next to the hole.

An hour and a half later, it was raining, again. Sitting next to the hole, he felt the vibrations of the chopper. Then the faint thudding of the helicopter blades, shredding the damp air, met his waiting ears. He set the ten-second timer pencils in the KY-38 so they would ignite the plastic explosive Semtex.

Then he ran behind a tree and waited.

After the Semtex exploded and destroyed the KY-38, he hunched against the rain. The ground was soft and spongy and mines were everywhere. After he managed to avoid the mines, he slopped through mud and danced around a spider web of shallow creeks until he was on solid ground. Then he ran to the landing hole and set off the purple smoke grenade.

By using different colors of grenades, American troops could provide air forces a color-specific target and avoid enemy ambush. But if the enemy used the same color, the Huey could be lured into an ambush.

While Crane waited, he hoped the VC hadn't used purple for a false flag on this pilot before. If they had used purple, and the pilot of the Huey felt he was being drawn into an ambush, he might not land.

As the Huey neared the ground, Crane ran for it.

As if disappointed that he was only picking up one man, the pilot shook his head. When Crane was five meters from the door, ducking under the beat of the rotor wash, shots zinged over his head and thunked into the side of the Huey.

CHAPTER 12

When Crane was almost at the door of the Huey, the chainsaw sound of the minigun's six barrels whirred to life, spinning and spitting three thousand rounds per minute. All around him, the chain saw-like noise of the weapon resonated into the jungle, and bullets buzzed through the air. Some hit something and sparked. Others flew everywhere. With flames spurting from the rotating miniguns, the gunner in the Huey strained against his tether and sent streams of bullets over Crane's head. The streams churned the ground behind Crane, ripped into the jungle, and tore tree branches and foliage to shreds.

The enemy stopped firing.

Crane made it to the open door of the Huey.

A hand reached down and jerked him in. The Huey lifted, and glad to be alive but disappointed because Neal and his team had not made it back, Crane dreaded a sad trip back to the base.

The Huey rose a few meters, hovered, and dropped back down.

Neal's men were running toward the door.

The gunner blasted the area to the left of them.

They easily made it to the door.

As the last man was helped aboard, over the rotor noise of the helicopter, the gunner yelled, "How much did you find?"

The man who had carried one of the devices, he had said was a bullshit detector, shook his bleeding head and shouted back, "Radioactive pieces were all over the place. It's a good thing he didn't detonate the sphere." He patted a container strapped to his side. "We found all the pieces, but we're past five rems."

The sniper reached up, placed his hand over the man's mouth, and pointed to Crane.

The man shut up.

Apparently, Crane wasn't supposed to know radioactive, dirty-bombs were being used to poison or make soldiers sick. But he did know about the HALO drops, which were high altitude, low opening, skydiving SOG platoons and companies, code named Hatchet Force, that dropped behind enemy lines for precision delivery of SDAM, Special Atomic Demolition munitions, also called "suitcase nukes".

A rem was a unit for measuring absorbed doses of radiation, equivalent to one roentgen of x-rays or gamma rays: Roentgen, Equivalent in, Man. Five rems were the maximum safe amount of radiation a person could be exposed to in a period of one year.

While Crane had been on Shemya Island, radiation from the Long Shot nuclear test and the Boeing RC-135 reconnaissance aircraft, called Rivet Ball that had radar so powerful it could make steam come off the Bering Sea, had contributed to giving him a dose rate way above five rems. At the time, the radiation exposure had caused his hair to fall out and his throat to become sore. He wondered if he had been exposed again, but now he knew why Neal had advised his men to make sure the containers were tight. They were radiation containers.

The agency's habit of compartmenting their operations so that only those with a need-to-know had access to information, would make it impossible for Crane to find out how much more radiation he had been exposed to.

The sniper kneeling between the back of the pilot and the copilot's seats paused and fixed his eyes on the man with a bleeding head. "Are you all right?"

Wiping the blood from his face with the sleeve of his ripshirt, the man nodded. "It's only a head wound. Even a bloody nose looks a lot worse than it really is."

The gunner changed the subject. "Where's Neal?"

The sniper only shook his head.

It was understood that Neal hadn't made it.

The chopper lifted off and tilted left. As it gained altitude, Crane watched the ground below grow smaller. But then the ground began to grow larger. They were descending and he saw the reason why. Neal was standing at the edge of a clearing. The minigun began banging bullets into the foliage behind him. The Huey landed without getting hit with gunfire. Neal jumped in and they were headed home, again. The sad ride was off.

On the welcome chopper ride back, the physical and mental challenges, the danger, and the risking of one's life for the high principle of fighting an armed enemy slightly excited Crane. But killing two VC and seeing one cut open with a Gyrojet piston, created a festering open wound of doubt about the whole thing called war.

Crane was glad the mission was over. But when he looked out the door of the Huey he stiffened. "Look at that!"

Neal glanced out, then grabbed the handles of the minigun. "We got trouble."

Below, off to the side of a paddy field that stretched to infinity, a burning cart with a broken wheel, blocked a road that crossed the area. The cart was blocking a bus full of screaming people.

A man stepped off the bus and held up his hands. With the staccato beat of the helicopter blades drowning out the distinctive crack of an AK-47, the man's surrendering gesture was rewarded with a stream of bullets through the head. He crumpled to the ground. Screaming, three girls ran from the bus. Two of their screams were cut short with rifle fire. With her face stark-white and her teeth biting her lower lip, the other girl fell to the side and was crawling away.

Neal let loose of the minigun and leaned toward the pilot. "I know that girl. Take us down."

One of his men waved his hand in a dismissive gesture. "We can't go down." He pointed to the canisters of radiation.

A pleading look flashed from Neal's face. "You can spare me."

Nodding, the man jumped up, manned the minigun, and looked to Crane.

Crane figured jumping out of a perfectly good helicopter wouldn't help the people below. If they got close, the bullets would go through the flimsy sides and floor of the Huey. And he remembered what Neal had told him years ago: "Always play the percentages. Never be enticed into a life and death situation when you're angry, and don't ever risk your life or the lives of others because of sympathy."

Wondering why Neal was going against what he had told him, Crane just stared at Neal and said, "By the time we get there, they'll all be dead."

With a desperation filled face, Neal slung pouches of magazines into his rucksack. "We have to try."

"What do you want me to do?"

"Do whatever you want."

The pilot shook his head. "I'd have to be crazy to land there."

"All you have to do is drop me off," Neal said with immediacy in his voice. "Then get out." He clipped seven grenades to his belt, stuck some signaling flares into his ripshirt pockets, and picked up his CAR-15.

Crane looked down. Smoke from the burning cart flowed into the jungle, and heavy rifle fire shattered the windows on the bus. Several people rushed out the back and side doors. Three men were immediately mowed down, and three women ran into the reeds. Two girls managed to crawl under the bus, but one crawled out from under and stood up. Before she could run into the reeds, three VC jumped up and cut her down. While a VC waited for the other girl to come out from under the bus, the other two VC ran after the three women who had run into the reeds. All somebody had to do was eliminate the VC waiting for the girl under the bus, and she would be safe.

Neal's team member was shooting at the VC with the minigun, but they were returning fire. And the Huey was going down fast.

As the Huey hovered just above the burning cart, with the cover of smoke Neal jumped to the ground and started running away from the bus.

Crane wanted to save the girl under the bus, and with the situation inducing a form of madness, he almost jumped. But at the last second, he slid back into the Huey.

A new series of shots came in. A bullet zinged past his head and hit the pilot in the hand. The pilot jerked and looked through a gruesome splotch of blood on the windshield. For just a moment, the Huey turned sideways. Bullets ripped into the floor, causing it to become alive with metal confetti. Crane tried to stop himself from sliding. But he slid out the door. Bathed in the stench of gunpowder and burnt flesh, his boots hit the ground. Kicking dust into a swirling storm of dirt and debris, the Huey roared to full power, lifted, and turned toward the bus.

Crane had wondered why Neal had run away from the bus. When he looked up, he found out why.

Hovering above the bus, the pilot spun the Huey in a 360-degree pedal turn. Forming a circular wall of fire around the bus., both miniguns shot streams of bullets straight down. The VC weren't getting out of that, and that was why Neal had run away from the bus.

To his amazement, Crane was standing in a path clear of VCs. When he looked down, he knew why. Right next to his feet, a sparse layer of reeds covered a deep pit. Sharp feces-coated Punji sticks were sticking up at the bottom of the pit.

Suddenly he was surrounded by NVRs, North Vietnamese Regulars. For a moment, he thought of what his crazy red-headed friend Rafferty would have said in a situation like this: *I want to surround them from the inside.* That's one thing he liked about Rafferty. He always saw the bright side.

Although it would have been an ignorant thing to say, when Crane looked into the pit, he found a way he could surround them from the inside. Thankful he was wearing Vietnam boots with the steel plate inside the sole to protect him from punji sticks, he lay on the ground, belly first, and let his legs slip down the side of the pit. After he kicked over the punji sticks and slowly slid into a standing position, he could hear the NVA. They had to be awfully close to the pit. He reached into his vest, pulled out the ten mini grenades, and set them in a line. Then one by one he pulled the rings. As hard and as fast as he could, in directions all around him, he threw the golf ball size grenades out of the pit. When they exploded above the approaching NVA's heads, over four thousand fragments filled the air. Screams from the green uniformed NVA sounded like they were being attacked by stinging bees. While the NVA were wondering what had hit them, Crane carefully lifted the spoon from a hand grenade and waited two seconds. Then he lobbed it out of the pit. In a high arc, the grenade airburst above the NVA. Then he threw three more. The sounds of the advancing NVA ceased.

He slowly lifted his head up out of the pit and looked around. NVA bodies were all around the pit, but there were no more coming.

When he crawled out of the pit and stood up, a sense of shock and fear propelled him toward the bus. For a moment, he wondered why he and Neal always ended up in situations like this. Instead of risking his life in some steamy place, he could be sitting on his porch, listening to a radio. He had just gotten out of a life and death situation, and here he was in one again. And this time he had nothing left to defend himself with except the pistol he had strapped to his ankle. And he wasn't even sure it was loaded.

CHAPTER 13

After the heavy rifle fire dwindled to a few random shots, Crane circled around the reeds and ran toward the bus. When he got to the bus, he dropped to one knee and looked under the bus. The girl hiding there, turned her head in his direction. A look of hope beamed from her mud-spattered face.

Signaling for her to keep quiet, Crane placed his finger to his lips.

She nodded.

Searching for other survivors, Crane rose to his feet, placed one foot on the step of the bus, and looked inside. Hot fetid air and the odor of overripe fruit, sweaty bodies, opium, and death blasted him in the face. There were no survivors. The VC who had been waiting for the girl on the other side of the bus, walked around the bus, stopped, and looked directly into Crane's eyes. Crane grabbed the pistol from his ankle holster and fired. The bullet hit the VC right in the nose. He lifted his hand to grab where his nose used to be but his hand dropped. His body crumpled to the side into a lifeless heap. Needing something better than his 22 caliber pistol, Crane bent over the VC's body. A bulled buzzed past Crane's shoulder and hit the side of the bus. As if he had been hit, he fell to the ground and grabbed the AK-47 from the VC he'd shot. Just when he was getting to his feet, another VC came around the corner of the bus. Crane swung the AK-47 around and hit the trigger.

Nothing.

Tapping the magazine in his pocket, the VC smiled a devious smile.

Crane reared up, swung the butt of the unloaded AK-47 around, and gave the VC a thunderous shot to the jaw.

The jaw broke.

To Crane's surprise, the VC looked like he enjoyed it. And he had reason to. He reached behind his head and slid a sword from the center of his back. Holding the sword high, he wiggled his fingers in a come-here gesture.

Crane became what he had been trained to be. Balanced and poised, he moved with the quickness of a dancer, his footwork smooth and precise. Using the AK-47, he easily blocked or avoided each lunge or swish from the sword. When the VC tried to plunge the sword into Crane's chest, just in time, he used the AK-47 and hit the sword downward. It sliced into the VC's thigh. Blood from a severed artery, squirting a foot into the air, demonstrated that the sword was razor sharp. But the VC wouldn't quit. Crane counterattacked with ease, feinting with one end of the AK-47 and swinging with the other. When he swung the butt of the AK-47 around and down, a sickening crack came for the VC's head. This time, fighting for balance, the VC tottered. Gasping for breath, his face twisted. With his sword sliding from his fingers, he wilted to the ground.

He let out one last painful moan.

The blood from the severed artery made one last feeble squirt.

He went limp.

Crane bent over, and took a magazine from the VC's body and slammed it into the AK-47. Looking under the bus and motioning for the girl to come out, he hollered, *"Lai dai"*, Come here! She crawled toward him. When they were face-to-face, she lifted her blood-covered hand and pointed to the door of the bus. Badly frightened, she wanted to get back on the bus.

Crane shook his head. "It's not safe. Come with me."

She responded instantly to the urgency in his voice. They crawled a few feet, then rose to crouching position, took a few cautious steps, and ran for their lives.

A ways from the bus, they plunged into a great bank of reeds, and searching for booby traps, they cautiously followed a muddy stream. After traveling twenty feet, Crane stopped, squatted down, and listened. The only thing he heard was a bird flush about thirty feet ahead. Wondering what had caused it to spook, he eased up from his squatting position to get a better look. When he did, his feet sunk into the soft mud. And he was glad they did. If he had been a wee bit higher, he wouldn't have seen what was off to his left. A trip wire wrapped around the branch of a bush. The wire ran parallel to the ground and ended in the open end of a tin can with a grenade inside. The trip wire was attached to the grenade that had had the safety pin removed. Still inside the can, the spoon of the grenade was held in place. If he had moved forward and pulled the trip wire, the grenade would have been pulled out of the can and the spoon would have been released. The grenade would have detonated. Crane would never again have to worry about going back to the Rock. After he gradually pried his feet from the sucking mud, he disconnected the trip wire. Then he freed the girl from the mud, and they continued down the widening stream until they stopped at little island and stared at its sunny side. Under the blistering sun, corpses on the shore were beginning to stink and turn black in the heat, but three grenades were lying next to one of the corpses. Checking first to make sure they weren't bobby-trapped, Crane picked up the grenades, and she and he quickly moved on. With the girl and the corpses behind him, Crane pushed reeds aside and forced his way through the water and mud. When he had plowed into a dark pool, he wanted to catch his breath and figure out what to do next. On the side of the pool next to a hooch, a menagerie of ducks, dogs, and pigs, and a group of what seemed to be placid women and children watched him.

"Ong co so linh My khong?" Crane asked. Are you afraid of American soldiers?"

Suddenly the eyes of a filthy young woman, in ragged clothing, grew wide and the children and woman ran into the forest. Two VC were waiting on the other side of the pool. Crane wondered what he was doing here. He had no business being here. He wasn't here for medals or a need to be some kind of hero. He wasn't ready for anything like this. Ten meters away, he could see the VC's young faces.

They raised their AK-47's.

Crane raised the AK-47 he had taken from the VC, but he couldn't bring himself to fire on the boys. He braced for the onslaught of the bullets that would end his life. Neal appeared in the reeds on Crane's right. Firing from the hip, Neal blasted both of the boys until they fell into the water. Shaking his head in disbelief, Cane felt pity for the young lives that had ended, but the boy's deaths seemed to have no effect on Neal. "They were just boys, but they were dangerous boys." He stepped back into the reeds and motioned for Crane and the girl to follow.

Sloshing through the water, Crane and the girl rushed to where Neal had last been seen. When they got there, he was gone. But he had left a trail of broken grass that ran through a stretch of head-high elephant grass.

Crane looked to the girl. There was a flicker of hope in her eyes.

They took two steps.

A bullet whined past Crane's right ear.

He looked toward a hill on his right. Five NVRs that looked younger than the two boys who had just been shot, were sneaking around his right flank. He grabbed the girl's hand, held her secure, and watched. Apparently not wanting to be seen, the NVRs dropped to the wet ground and crawled under a clump of broken reeds that were at the bottom of the hill. Crane and the girl quickly made their way to the top of the hill and looked down at the NVRs. They were still under the clump of broken reeds. This time, boys or not, Crane felt no pity. He rolled the three grenades down the hill. As he and the girl slid down the other side of the rain-slicked hillside, the grenades went off, but one NVR had made it to the top of the hill, and he was sliding right behind Crane. From a sitting position, Crane turned half around and shot. The man was so close that Crane was splattered with blood. At the bottom, near a muddy stretch of water, Crane and the girl cautiously stood up. Using stepping-stones, they avoided the muddy water and worked their way through a spreading fan of weed-choked brush that led to a stream that emptied into an old bombed-out section of land that looked like a miniature canyon. All around the section, thick vegetation, mangrove roots, nipa palm trees, bushes, elephant grass, and muck created a tangled maze. The section was narrow and high walled. Parts of it were choked with brush, mud, and broken rocks, and only a small stream, running with alkaline water, offered a way out.

Working their way through the section, they jerked their feet from feet six inches of sucking mud. Each step was a struggle and the buzzing, biting mosquitos made it worse. It was then that Crane really smelled the jungle. It had the odor of decomposing nipa palm. The odor of wet and rot. The repulsive odor of Vietnam. When they were about to step out of the miniature canyon, automatic fire erupted. Just before a hail of bullets cut the reeds in front of them, Crane pulled the girl down beside him.

Crouched next to him, fighting for breath, the girl's chest was heaving. Her black hair hung well below her shoulders and was accented by her white blood-spattered headband. The broad, black leather belt, wrapped around her small waist, highlighted her red dress that clung to her firm and shapely body.

When the firing stopped, they stood up. With prickly stems and branches grasping at their legs, they ran until they were on the edge of a paddy field. Here, a curtain of reeds gave them a little concealment and Crane figured if the NVA couldn't hear or see them, the girl and he could get a little rest. Crouched over, he kept his eyes moving, and searched the area for signs of movement. All was quiet except for their breathing and their heartbeats. And those sounded loud. Before he could catch his breath, gunfire echoed from the depths of the reeds. He snapped his head around in the direction of the fire. Bullets tore into the reeds. Several whizzed past the girl and blasted the reeds next him completely off. What little concealment they had had been cut in half. As he and the girl crouched in muddy water up to their waists, he held his hand against the glare of the sun and looked for a safe way out.

There was none.

But the mosquitoes had dissipated.

Neal sprang up out of the stream, water cascading off his body and clothes. Firing quick bursts into the reeds, as coolly as though he were on a target range, Neal stepped forward and yelled over his shoulder. "Get going. I'll follow."

For a moment, Crane was amazed at Neal's total confidence and ease with his surroundings. He seemed to be in his element. Not only did he seemed to be at home, he held a M18A1 Claymore in his hand. A 1.5-pound block of C-4 plastic explosive. Ninety percent RDX, except for the nasty nukes, the Claymore was the most powerful portable explosive known to man. Setting on its unfolded scissor legs stuck in the dirt, upon detonation it will blast seven hundred ball bearings over a sixty-degree arc for a distance of fifty meters at a height of one to two meters. It's like a huge sawed-off shotgun.

No matter who was giving orders, Neal was the person you'd listen to. Neal was who you would follow. And it was Neal who you would depend on to lead you through the chaos and back to safety. And Neal had told them to get going.

Crane didn't know if he could make it without Neal's guidance. But he didn't have time to think about it. He and the girl plowed across a pool of stagnant water, crashed through the reeds and kept on moving. When they reached an open spot, the welcome sound of a Huey's blades chopping the air met his ears. As the girl's hand tightened in his, Crane waved. The Huey descended and hovered only long enough for him and the girl to leap in. As the Huey lifted into the air, Crane searched the ground below. An anthill swirl of soldiers was pouring in the direction of where the girl and he had just been, and two tracking dogs were leading them. A little further on, head-high elephant grass covered a wide valley floor. Because Neal had left a trail that could be easily tracked, the grass was a dangerous place to be. But when the dogs lowered their noses to the ground to get the scent of Neal's trail, they stopped and howled in pain. Neal had spread CS tear gas powder over the trail. There was no sign of him. But it could be a good thing. Not only could he find things on a trail and tell exactly what they meant, he could melt into just about any landscape.

But he hadn't melted. He was standing in slash-and-burn area, and NVR were closing in all around him. He took out the five FM radios and placed them in a neat circle. Then he planted toe poppers around the radios, and ran into the thickest, thorniest foliage he could find. The Huey pilot must have known what Neal was doing. To attract the VC, he hovered above the slash-and-burn area and played a crescendo of chopper music.

Two minutes later, twenty NVRs walked into the slash-and-burn area and stepped on the toe poppers. The resulting explosions didn't kill the NVRs but they had slowed their pursuit.

About three football fields from the clearing, Neal was standing in a hole too small for the Huey to descend and pick him up. He was waiting to be extracted with a McGuire rig, or "string" as it was called. It was a one hundred-foot rope with a six-foot loop at the end and a padded canvas seat. It resembled a playground swing. Once Neal was in it, the pilot would hover vertically until Neal was above the jungle canopy. Then he would fly away.

The Huey made another 360-degree pedal turn. With both miniguns shooting straight down, the bullets formed a circular wall of fire all around Neal. Then the pilot held the Huey at a steady treetop hover. One of Neal's men lay on the floor.

Peering down, and using an intercom to direct the pilot, he snaked the rope down through the trees. Neal climbed into the seat. The man told the pilot to lift. Because the rope could get snarled in the trees or a sudden barrage of fire could threaten the aircraft, it would be dangerous for a few seconds.

When Neal was just about to clear the tops of the trees, a dozen mortar tubes coughed rounds as fast as they could be dropped. Shells flew viciously all around him, and slugs from VC firing from the hole slapped through the thin aluminum skin of the Huey. For a moment, it looked like Neal had been caught on the top of the tallest tree. What was understood by everybody was that if you got in to trouble with a string, it would have to be cut. That was the only way the aircraft would fly free. It didn't matter if anyone was on the end of the string or not. If you had to cut the ropes in order to save the Huey, you cut the ropes.

Just as the man lifted the knife to cut the rope, the Claymore went off. Seven hundred, one eighth-inch steel balls blasted outward in an arc of sixty degrees, at a velocity of 3.900 feet per second, disintegrating just about everything in front of it. Firing from the hole stopped. Neal sprang free of the tree. The man using the intercom excitedly motioned for the pilot to fly away, and with the miniguns firing at the NVR, a mortar round flew up and nicked the rope.

It twanged.

It looked like it was going to hold.

But it didn't.

Forty feet below, Neal fell into the treetops. He crashed through foliage, bounced violently between branches, and then into the thick foliage that swallowed him.

Since Crane had known him, Neal had lived like there was no tomorrow. The human body falls at a speed close to one hundred twenty-five miles an hour, or a thousand feet every five seconds. This time, for Neal, it looked like there would be no tomorrow.

Low on fuel and ammunition, the Huey headed home.

Crane wanted to know if the girl thought Neal would be all right. He looked to the girl and asked if she understood him. *"Qng hieu toi duoc khong?"*

The girl didn't answer. Didn't smile. Suddenly tears and sorrow covered her face."

Crane reached out his hand to hers, wrapped her fingers in his, and as the gravity began to deepen in his voice, he lied. "He'll make it."

The girl only tightened here grip on his hand.

On the way back, crouched securely between two crew members the girl didn't speak. As if hypnotized, she only stared out the chopper door.

CHAPTER 14

Back at the Tan Son Nhuyt facility, the girl straightened her tangled hair, tied it back with a velvet bow, and smiled at Crane. "I must look a mess."

But she didn't look a mess. Although speckled with mud, her black hair still shone like silk, and the simple red shift she wore outlined the most graceful body Crane had ever seen. She wasn't tall, but she had an aggressive stance, and she reminded Crane of a princess whose crown had been taken away and no matter what she had to do, she was going to get it back. Her forehead wasn't wrinkled but projected held in pain. Through magnificent almond blue eyes set in a lovely Asian face, she stared at Crane and asked, "What are you doing here?" Her voice was low, and it caused something within Crane to quiver. For a moment, he couldn't speak.

Apparently thinking Crane couldn't understand English, she tried French. *"Th ne me comprends pas bien?"* You do not understand me well?

Crane still couldn't speak.

She spoke French again. *"Quelle mouche t' piqué?"* What's eating you?

Crane began to answer, but the eloquent way she spoke French had caused his mouth to hang open in a speechless gape.

As if she were going to run away, she turned.

Crane quickly got his voice back. "Wait! I do understand you."

She turned back.

Crane asked, "Are you Neal's girl?"

As tears formed at the corner of her moist eyes, she questioned, "Neal dead?"

Although Neal had an almost zero chance of surviving the fall and making it through the mass of NVAs, somehow Crane felt Neal was still alive. He turned to the girl. "Neal's made it through tougher situations than falling through a couple of tree branches."

With hope in her eyes the girl looked up at Crane. "Are you sure?"

Crane wasn't sure of anything, but he didn't want the girl to suffer more pain than she had already been through. "I'd bet my life on it."

Her face lit up with a warm glow, but she shook her head reprovingly. "I would like to be Neal's girl, but he is a many-girl man."

Crane wasn't surprised that the girl had said Neal was a many-girl man. Neal was remarkable to behold, strong jawed, and vibrating with physical energy, but he never stayed in one place long enough to have a steady girlfriend. He may not even remember her. "Does he know you?"

"Neal knows me very well, GI. He rescued me." Without warning, as she relived the holocaust she had endured, tears began to stream down her cheeks.

Crane reached out, drew her close, and held her until her tears stopped.

After she wiped the tears away, she looked down at the ground. "When I met Neal, my village had been burned to the ground, my family taken away. I had nothing."

Nothing, burned in Crane's brain. He had come from a place of poverty, and although it was not very comfortable, at times, he had always had a place to sleep and could usually scrounge something to eat. Compared to this woman, he realized how fortunate he had been. He had never been reduced to having nothing.

"You actually had nothing at all?"

Her face took on a stern look. "Nothing!" Then she reverted to French. "*Ça, c'est le comble?*" That's the last straw. She laughed but not in good humor. "I was so mad it made me want to kill myself and be done with it all. Neal told me, 'If you are mad, fight what makes you mad. If you still want to die, then kill yourself tomorrow. Today, you can do some good for somebody else.'"

When her almond eyes looked at him, his heart turned over. He had, never, anywhere, seen so stunning a girl. Wild and free, she was as uninhibited as an animal. He couldn't help it. He fell instantly and gloriously in love.

With a deep desire to find out everything about her, he said, "I never got your name."

At first, she looked surprised. Then she tilted her head in a cute slant and replied, "Jacqueline, but you can call me Piper." She held out her hand.

With what they had just survived still fresh in his mind, Crane grasped her hand. "I wish it had been a pleasure to meet you."

As if hanging on for dear life, she gripped his hand and held it tight. "If you hadn't come along when you did, I wouldn't be alive."

"If it weren't for Neal, we would both be shaking hands with the devil."

"Neal helped me many times," she said and cringed as if stabbed. "Are you sure he is still alive?"

Crane forced a smile. "I just know he's still alive."

Piper looked tired but her great mane of dark hair accented her bright eyes. "I do, too. Neal has what you Americans call comeback ability. He is a most unusual man." She paused, then said, "You're a most unusual man, too."

"We were just lucky. But we can't be lucky all the time."

In a tragic tone, she spoke French. "*Ainsi va la guerre.*" So goes war.

When she turned her head, two marvelously deep blue almond eyes shone up at him. "*Ả quoi penses-tu, Crane*?" What are you thinking?

The look in her almond eyes touched something way down inside Crane. "You're very lovely. After we get cleaned up, could we go somewhere to eat?"

With her face flushing as if she were facing one of the agonizing decisions of a lifetime, for a few moments, she didn't answer but then nodded slowly.

Crane figured she was hesitant because it was difficult to trust anybody in a time of war. But he was all smiles. "Piper, it would be a pleasure."

After they cleaned themselves up and changed clothes, Crane couldn't help but notice that she was a slim, lovely girl. Her scared eyes, no longer scared, had become soft and deep blue. Her black hair shone with a sheen of healthy blue, and the orchid-colored scarf over her shoulders was like a mist tinged by the elegant light of dawn. She looked like a delicate flower that the wind could blow away, and there was quick, bubbling laughter in her.

With a stripe of soft orange sunset fingering through the clouds, Piper and Crane were in a taxi, crawling through incredible traffic on their way to the city close to Tan Son Nhuyt Air Base: Saigon. On the outskirts of Saigon, pedestrians, cars, bicycles, and pedicabs blasted horns and yelled. Even in wartime life went on. Finally in Saigon, they trudged along the sidewalk in silence, although many signs were in Vietnamese, Crane was surprised how the buildings and streets resembled the streets and buildings of towns in America, but the people were different.

Peasants stooped by age and work, tottered past carrying bags of fruit and things Crane didn't recognize. Buzzing motorbikes passed people pedaling bicycles. Two men walked the street hand-in-hand. Some GIs thought this was because they were gay, but it was only an ordinary mark of friendship common in many Asian countries. Vietnamese women walking past wore their national dress of long trousers under a long-sleeved tunic slit from hem to waist. Further on, under roofs of the buildings of a market, a variety of things were for sale. Fish squid, eels, and snails in baskets were presented. Brassware, jade, cloth, and hundreds of other items were displayed. The collective odors of seashells, spices, and peppers, created an oriental odor unlike any Crane had ever experienced. After they walked past a place where wild animals and snakes were for sale they walked into a French Colonial restaurant from the old days. With white table cloths, linen napkins, silverware, and candles on the tables, it was a haven from the war.

A Vietnamese waitress greeted them at the door. Speaking fluent French, she asked Crane something.

Crane knew the waitress was speaking French, but the subdued rattle of dishes made it difficult for him to make out all the words. He looked to Piper. "What did she say?"

"Would you like to sit at the bar or go to a table."

Although the restaurant's windows were wooden louvered and totally open for air to circulate, he wanted to please Piper. "What would you like to do?"

"Sit at a table and have a bottle of champagne."

"That's a good idea. Let's celebrate being alive. Tell her to bring a bottle of Dom Perignon."

She did.

The waitress led them to a corner table on the outside veranda, seated them at a table in a warmly lit, pleasant place, and smiled. "Your champagne will be here directly."

Piper sat down. Like the lady she was, she crossed one leg over the other. As she looked at Crane, her almond eyes lost their hurt look and reached across the table and into Crane's heart. He realized she had much more than other girls who were pretty, knew it, and it was their only asset.

"Now that you have washed up," she said, "you look very handsome."

Crane leaned across the table and softly said, "You're the most beautiful person I have ever met."

"Thank you. Are you a regular soldier?"

"Actually, no, but for some reason I always get caught in situations like the one we just got out of."

Her eyes became direct and sincere. "The Good Lord, Jesus, Buda, or whatever supreme being you believe in, never gives you anything you are not ready for."

For a moment, Crane's face flushed. "I never thought of it that way. But it seems to be true."

After they ordered, they talked some more, but Crane was so deliriously happy that he could hardly remember what he had just eaten for dinner. When the girl behind the bar placed the arm of a record player on a 45 RPM record, the romantic song from 1959, *This I Swear*, by the Skyliners, flowed into air. As if in a dream, Piper and Crane glided inside and danced. She was very graceful in his arms. She was a woman no man could look at and ever be the same. A warm feeling, he had never experienced before, entered his heart, and it seemed that they had become one. They held each other and slowly danced for what seemed hours, and the smell of her perfume reminded him of the country and his plan to sit on his porch and have people hand him money. When they went back to the table and talked, he became amazed that he had never had a conversation with anyone like the one he had with her.

After they finished the second bottle of champagne, Crane sat back and exhaled a great breath of air. "You know, we should be up there in the reeds?"

She nodded.

He reached for her hand and urged her to her feet. "One way or another, life goes on."

She turned her face toward him. "I'll remember that."

In the shadows, they embraced and he gently kissed her.

At a hotel, Crane couldn't read the name of, without a word, the person at the desk, handed her a key to a room. They walked down a hallway covered with red carpet and stopped at the door of the room. With his heart leaping with apprehension, Crane unlocked the door and opened it. He stood aside then followed her in.

As she stood next to the bed, she had an undefined magnetism and a defiant confidence about herself, palpable even from across the room.

Crane waltzed to her and wrapped his arm around her waist. "Are you sure about this?"

She came into his arm as if she belonged there. "Life is for the living. Let's live it to the fullest." She brushed the dark hair from her face. With dreamy eyes and eager lips, she stood on her tip toes. Gentle as a soft whisper, she kissed him. "Give me a few moments, then come in."

***

Afterwards, Crane lay propped up against pillows, smiling. It had been the most wonderful experience of his entire life, and now she slept quietly beside him.

When she awoke, she quickly dressed. “I can’t stay here.”

“Why not?”

“Your army and the VC want to know where Neal is.”

“What’s so important about Neal?”

“He knows things he should not know.”

“Like what?”

“I can’t tell you.”

“Is that why the VC didn’t shoot you when you were under the bus?”

“There is a big reward for my capture. But I have to be alive.”

Outside, voices began calling.

“Sorry, Crane. I must leave, now!”

Before Crane could say goodbye, she leaned back, swept her arm grandly. “Try not to die.” Then she said in French. “*Ala prochaine.*” Until next time.

Like a wraith, she slipped from his arms to the deep shadow near the wall, then into the blackness of the hall, and was gone.

Just after Crane had just gotten dressed, he lay down on the bed. He had planned to take a little rest and be on his way. But before he knew it, he was asleep and dreaming about Piper. She was on Shemya, standing in front of the Rivet Amber Plane with the tiger teeth. A man with muscular arms had both hands on a huge gun and had it aimed at Piper.

Piper held an opened briefcase full of money. Before the man could shoot and take the money, from out of midair, Boozer the Malamute Husky dog of Shemya, leaped over her head and was headed for the gun.

Before Crane could find out what happened, Bam! A big man with powerful shoulders and a long sharp knife came crashing through the door and jerked him wide awake. Immediately mad, Crane jumped up off the bed and faced the man. As the man stood in front of Crane, from behind, another man's arm slid around Crane's neck, but the man had too much forward momentum. With his left hand, Crane reached up and grabbed the man's hand. With his right hand, he reached back and grabbed the man's elbow. It was a quick move that Crane had rehearsed many times. He secured his grip, and using the man's impetus, he dropped to one knee and whipped the man over his shoulder. The man went flying, slammed into the powerful shouldered man, and crashed into the table in front of Crane. As if they were toothpicks, the legs on the table collapsed, and the man lay still.

Being on his knees, Crane grabbed the legs of the man with the knife who had been standing in front of him and jerked hard.

The man's head hit the soft stomach of the man on the floor.

It made a squishing sound.

The other man jumped up, kicked the broken table, and clawed at his hip for a gun.

The move not only caused the man's face to automatically come forward, like it wanted to be punched, it left it open for an unblocked punch. Using the momentum of jumping up and with everything on it but his Chevy pickup truck, Crane threw a right uppercut. Crack! It slammed into the man's jaw with so much force, it echoed down the hall. The man fell onto his back, rolled over, and rose to his hands and knees. Now it was Crane's turn to be behind. Using the wrestling move, called a figure-four, he had used on Mullin, he jumped on the man's back, wrapped his legs around the man's waist, and leaned back. The extreme pressure on the man's spine cause him to drop to the floor. Keeping pressure on the man's spine, Crane reached under the man's arm and placed his hand on the crown of the man's head. This gave him leverage and made it easy to pry the man's arm to the front and force the back of his head flat to the floor and jam his chin into his chest. With the man groaning in pain and struggling to breathe, Crane lifted the arm and then gathered the other arm and pulled them together. Before, Crane could finish the move the man's shoulder bone popped out of socket.

The man let out a whining yelp.

All the life went out of him.

Suddenly as if it were a delayed reaction the other man screamed in pain. When Crane looked at him, his face was filled with terror, and he held his blood-soaked hands over his abdomen. At first, Crane thought the man was holding a cauliflower against his stomach. When the odor hit him, he realized the man had fallen against the sharp knife the other man had been holding. It had split his stomach wide open. Judging by the odor, the knife had also perforated them man’s liver, and the blue-white mass was the man’s intestines. It explained the squishing sound.

Crane recalled what he had been told at the top of the hill during a difficult practice. “What you learn and do here today, someday may save your life. And it had.

Crane finally caught a flight back to the states and was assigned to the base in Virginia, but he never found out what had been so important about Neal finding radiation in Vietnam, and he didn’t know if Neal were still alive. Now that he was with the colonel, he was sure he was going to find out.

CHAPTER 15

Thinking about how he missed Piper and how people in combat want to survive and pass their genes on to the next generation, Crane stared at the colonel's steel desk in front of him. Although he had previously been a participant in killing, it still made him sick. If Neal were still alive and the colonel forced Crane to find him, there would be more killing.

The faint click of the lock on the briefing door being unlocked caught Crane's ear. The door snicked open. The colonel stepped back into the room and sat down. Crane couldn't believe it. The sides of the colonel's head had been buzzed white with electric hair clippers. He had stepped out to get something Crane hated: a white-wall haircut. Crane figured the haircut and the colonel's arrogant ways showed that he was a hungry man. Hungry for all the things he thought he deserved. From past experiences Crane know that when opportunity knocked, a hungry man, eaten by envy and dislike, would become a dangerous man, and Crane didn't want to have anything to do with him. As if his voice were coming out of a fog, the colonel repeated what he had said before he had gone for the haircut. "We want you to find a man who is important to us. Do you know him?"

Startled out of a stupor caused by the prospect of working with the colonel, Crane jerked his head toward him and replied, "Yeah, I know him. We went on an unplanned mission in Vietnam. While a man who looked like me took my place on the plane and hightailed it out of Nam, I went on a recovery mission for some sensitive items."

"We have no idea how you have managed to stay alive this long," the colonel said and chuckled. "But you have a gift for doing things like that. We couldn't have planned your little escapade if we wanted to."

"Neal ended up missing in action and is probably dead. So I don't consider almost getting killed a gift. But what's the deal on the radiation?"

With a wave of his hand, the colonel dismissed the question. "In the intelligence business, you have to accept that you never have the complete picture. You'll have to learn to deal with the facts at hand, and do your best to do your duty?"

"I know that. If Neal is alive, he will leave no more of a trace than the morning mist, and the sun disperses that. If I'm going to find him, I'll need all the information I can get."

The warmth seeped from the colonel's face and his expression hardened. "Neal McCord is a moron with a wild streak a foot wide. He's like a hormone-crazed ape in a zoo. Neal McCord *is not* the man I'm talking about."

Caught off guard, Crane's breath caught in his throat. "Who are you talking about?"

"The man from Shemya is not dead. He's sitting someplace out there like he's on vacation. We'd like for you to renew your acquaintance with him."

The last time Crane had seen the man from Shemya, he had marveled at the strength of the man.

He wasn't bulky, but his shoulders were compact and hard looking, and it seemed that the man had discovered something that scared him so bad that he had risked his life to get away and died in the process.

For some reason, the Corcoran jump boots the Special Forces man, named Kane, had given Crane that had the double uppers that made them warm in snow and ice, suddenly bothered him. Could Kane have been on Shemya, or had he returned from some other cold climate?

Crane put the thought of the boots out of his mind and looked to the colonel. "Life expectancy is only a few minutes in the Bering Sea. How could the man survive in that cold water?"

"Apparently, the man is more difficult to kill than an ordinary mortal." The colonel's eyes lowered. "The man escaped in a Russian submarine. For the lack of a better name, we'll call him Shemya Stan." He looked directly at Crane. "Stan's at it again. He has the E-Brite."

As if he hadn't heard him correctly, Crane stared at the colonel. "He has what?"

"E-Brite, the code name for a special sphere of an unknown metal, the size of a golf ball."

"How did he get that?"

Before you ran into Stan, he was in a special operations group. He volunteered for an airborne cross-border operation against North Vietnamese installations and movements into Laos, Cambodia, and on up into North Vietnam."

Crane knew the Russians had closed science cities, called *naukograds*. One was named

Arzamas-16, and was the home of the Soviet Union's first nuclear weapons design. The U.S. Intelligence community called it the Russian Los Alamos. How far and where those science cities extended was highly classified. Crane couldn't tell the colonel anything about them.

Feigning ignorance, he said, "I don't remember Laos or Cambodia having anything to do with nuclear research."

"Until Stan went into Laos and got a canister of nuclear grade plutonium from a Sergeant Major Burke, neither did we. Somehow Burke got it from the Hue University reactor and managed to have it placed it into the E-Brite sphere."

Crane was well aware of the tremendously long half-life of radioactive material. "That's bad stuff he's playing with."

"You're right about that." The colonel held up his hand. "But there's more. Burke thinks because he has the E-Brite, it's his, and he made a deal with Shemya Stan to sell it. When the North Vietnamese helicopter landed to pick it up, Stan had a surprise for them. He had set up a cache of mortar rounds and booby-trapped them with a bunch of Claymore mines."

"What did he do? Ask for more money?"

"Not really. Instead of going through with the deal and handing over the sphere, Stan almost destroyed the sphere and the people after it. He blew the cache up in their faces."

"That much explosive should have destroyed the sphere and scattered radiation all over the place."

"Actually, it couldn't. The only way the E-Brite sphere can be destroyed is with an adequate nuclear detonation. It's made of some sort of weird metal. You may be surprised to know the basic ingredient, exotic alloy steel, used in E-Brite, was produced in your hometown, at a steel mill called Sharon Steel."

Crane had a feeling that something wasn't right. If the sphere could only be destroyed with a nuclear detonation, Stan had to be pretty stupid not to know about it. But Crane didn't care about that, and he didn't care if the alloy steel had been made in his hometown. He was worried that he may have been exposed to more radiation than allowable. He asked, "Can this E-Brite sphere shield radiation inside it?"

"Only if it's sealed properly. Usually, heavy steel is required to contain the detonation of conventional nuclear explosives long enough to enable its force to trigger the plutonium, but this new *light-weight* metal is strong enough to contain the initial detonation long enough for the irreversible nuclear reaction to begin."

"Was the radioactive mix Neal found scattered all around the jungle caused by a weak container?"

"We really don't know where the radiation came from. If the sphere had not been defective, there would have been a nuclear detonation."

"What's the big deal? A sphere as small as golf ball wouldn't cause much of an explosion."

"Have you heard of Big Ivan?"

Crane was familiar with Tsar Bomba. Tsar Bomba, AKA Big Ivan, was the most powerful nuclear bomb ever detonated. Set of by the Russians on October 30, 1961, it weighed twenty-seven tons and had a blast yield of fifty megatons. It was four thousand times more powerful than the bomb dropped on Hiroshima. The fireball measured five miles in diameter and had climbed fourteen miles high before its mushroom cloud flattened.

Crane sat forward in his chair. "I've heard of it. Tell me more."

"If the E-Brite had detonated," the colonel said, "there would be no need for Agent Orange, and you wouldn't have to search for Stan. North and South Vietnam and Stan would have been vaporized and turned into radioactive dust. An E-Brite detonation would have made Big Ivan look like a firecracker."

Now Crane knew Neal and his specialists hadn't just gathered low-grade radiation from a dirty bomb. They might have gathered the high-powered radiation from a failed nuclear bomb. That was one reason only ten specialists were sent to investigate the failed bomb, instead of the usual twelve-man team. Another reason was that the fewer people that knew about the E-Brite the fewer chances it would be compromised.

"No one in his right mind would want to be around that kind of radiation," Crane said. "Shemya Stan should have gotten rid of the E-Brite sphere by now."

"Not really. He's holding it for the highest bidder. He might have a girlfriend with him in Japan. She could be the go between."

Funded by the government's "black budget" the agencies had unlimited funds for all kinds of highly classified projects that weren't under the control of the Army. Within the agency, it was almost common knowledge that NSA had computers light years ahead of the twenty-foot-long computer, called HAL 9000, the public had been shown. And those futuristic computers, combined with a Tricor III Wideband Receiver/Recorder, were capable of monitoring nearly every wireless transmission in the world, and NSA had spent the last two decades compiling the most complete list of encryption techniques ever assembled.

Although the general public would never know it, finding who had really killed JFK had not been a problem. At the time the shots that killed Kennedy were fired, Oswald was standing in front of the Book Depository Building, but a man was on the roof, and a man was in the storm drain, and another on the grassy knoll. Using the same procedures, finding Shemya Stan could be done without much trouble, Crane breathed a sigh of relief.

"You know where Shemya Stan is," he said. "And you know his contact. Just go and pick him up. Can I leave now?"

"If we can't find the E-Brite, all the information in the world is useless." The colonel pointed to the eight-by-ten photograph of Shemya Stan. "This is what your man looks like. We don't think he has, but he may have had extensive plastic surgery. Since you saved his life, you're probably the only person he is not afraid of."

"I don't care who he's afraid of or not afraid of." Crane looked to the door, then looked to the colonel. Giving him a threatening stare, Crane jumped to his feet. "The deal's off. Let me out of this place."

For a moment, anger seemed to seethe inside the colonel, but he kept his voice calm and even. "You know better than that, Crane. You can't let sentimentality cloud your professional judgment. By necessity, the work we do must be unemotional."

At times on Shemya, the isolation had caused Crane to become unemotional. Many men there had become so detached they called the unruffled state of mind GAFF, and acronym for give a flying fuck.

"I was one of the gaffest men on the Rock," Crane said. "You can't tell me a thing about being unemotional." He took a step toward the door. "I'd have to be crazy to stay in your stinkin' Army."

A sly look radiated from the colonel's face. "Crazy? We could always send you back to Shemya."

As if someone were about to slice open a healing wound in Crane's heart, a foreboding feeling crawled into his very soul. The abrupt threat of being sent back to Shemya poured into his mind, and like the clinging gray mist that shrouded Shemya, it stayed there and made it impossible for him to speak. His knees became weak. He sat back down.

By design, Shemya was not identified on all maps or globes, and was not listed in encyclopedias or most sources of geographic information. In short, Shemya did not exist.

The two miles by four miles Aleutian Island of Shemya was eighteen hundred miles from Anchorage, Alaska, and the Kamchatka peninsula of Russia was much closer.

Called "The Rock", grass did not grow on Shemya, and the winds and the waves on Shemya were huge. During World War II, more people were lost to bad weather than at the hands of the enemy.

While on Shemya, Crane had never experienced such a quick change in the weather. In a few hours, it could snow or rain, or the wind would blow the snow off the island and expose knee-deep brown tundra. Then it could start snowing again. "The Rock" was not kind to the weak or injured. It was impossible for anyone to gauge the wind strength by how much a tree moved. Trees did not grow on Shemya, but inhabitants boasted of a woman behind every tree.

Crane wondered if there might still be a little pine tree on Shemya. When he had been stationed there, a Specialist Wego had placed a little pine tree in a blue Maxwell House coffee can and hand-carried it across the United States, on buses, trains, and planes until he landed in Anchorage where he jumped on a plane and continued to carry the tree for another eighteen hundred miles. When he finally landed on Shemya, he planted the tree in a fenced-off, restricted area. Although it wasn't big enough for a woman to stand behind, and was soon covered with a sprinkling of snow, Shemya finally had a tree.

Shemya also had a lovable malamute husky named Boozer that loved knockwurst soaked in beer. Being the mascot of the United States Air Force Security Service, Boozer went just about anywhere on the island he wanted. The very next day, after the tree had been planted, Boozer, managed to get inside the restricted area. Although the snow on the tree sparkled with a million tiny flecks of diamond-like snow, Boozer peed on it. It died but was left standing next to sign that read, Shemya National Forest.

The sun rarely shone on the little dead tree. It could not. A permanent low-pressure system caused the island to be constantly cloaked in a cotton-thick, cold fog. At times, wind whipped across the island at ninety to one hundred ten miles an hour. With wind shrieking across the essentially featureless island, Shemya held the state wind record of one hundred thirty-nine miles per hour.

And to make it even worse, Shemya had the worst combination of winds and precipitation a person could find. And every year, at least seventy-five inches of snow tumbled onto the tiny island. Although the mean temperature was somewhere between thirty-six and forty-one degrees, it would fall well below zero.

In the summer months, about twenty percent of the time, landing conditions for aircraft were below the required minimum of a two-hundred-foot ceiling, and a half-mile of visibility.

Heavy wind and snow caused whiteout conditions so intense that when soldiers stationed on Shemya were within a few meters away from buildings or vehicles, they had leaned against the wind, plodded along, and found themselves totally disorientated. Stanchions with guide ropes were connected to all buildings, so in whiteouts and fog, personnel could get around Shemya's facilities without getting blown off the island. If this were not discouraging enough, the jukebox in the NCO club had only two songs. "A Taste of Honey" by Herb Albert and the Tijuana Brass, and Buck Owen's "Tiger by the Tail."

When soldiers drank too many cans of year-old beer that had a strong taste of rust and took deep drags from old cigarettes that had an odor of burnt straw, they shoveled coins into the jukebox slot. Then, for hours, the same two songs would be repeatedly blasted into patrons' ears. When the jukebox wasn't playing, soldiers would attempt to amuse themselves with a pinball machine that had no flippers and no glass. Since no pinball machines, manufactured before 1947 had flippers, the machine on Shemya had to have been left over from World War II. Like many of the World War II remnants on Shemya, the pinball machine was not operational. Island friend, Jim Keener, probably described it best when he said, "Shemya's not the end of the world, but you can see it from here."

ASA people who had made it through the many months of grueling training at Fort Devens, Massachusetts were believed to have had an easier, more interesting and more comfortable life than people in the regular army. Because of security involved, weird working hours, being called to duty at any time of the day or night, and the need to know, the ASA organization did not fall under the normal "chain of command". Most of the nuisance inspections, formations, parades, barracks life, and other irksome military traditions could not be followed without jeopardizing cryptanalysis.

Although cryptanalysis, the process or skill of enciphering and deciphering of messages in secret code, was usually what the ASA was all about, on the island of Shemya, the missions were a little different. While snow, wind, fog, sleet, and rain, filled with low-level radiation from a nuclear bomb test, controlled the environment outside, men with top secret and crypto security clearances sat behind fortress-like walls, manning radio, radar, and electronic transmissions centers, picking up weak signals originating deep in the Soviet Union. Or they boarded expensive C-135s and flew unauthorized missions across the tip of the Kamchatka peninsula, hot on the trails of Intercontinental Ballistic Missiles that were headed for the test range on Kamchatka, but often strayed off course and came close to Shemya.

In 1960, U-2 pilot, Francis Gary Powers had been shot down above Soviet air space, and a big deal had been made of it, but not many people knew it wasn't the only incident. The cold war wasn't always cold. Starting in 1961 over three hundred and six intercepts of Soviet intruders had been made. Not including Europe, the memorial at NSA headquarters, Fort Meade, Maryland, listed the names of one hundred fifty-two cryptologists killed as a result of hostile action.

Most intelligent people with any common sense would not place themselves in danger behind enemy lines or do dangerous clandestine work unless they were forced to. However, when a person with something to hide was threatened with exposure, he would usually accept any mission. Anything and everything had been used to get reluctant men to do the dangerous clandestine work. Crane had never been in prison, but the isolated island of Shemya was probably worse. The threat of another year-long banishment to Shemya would get just about any ASA man to do what the man in charged wanted him to do. And the colonel was using that threat on him.

When Crane didn't answer the colonel's question, the colonel spoke with labored exasperation. "You're not dumb enough to think you are expendable." Then he raised his voice. "Do you want me to send you back to Shemya?"

Waiting for the pain in his chest to subside, Crane still found it hard to speak. He held up his hand and managed to whisper, "Wait a minute."

Thinking about when his knack for being in the wrong place at the wrong time had begun, the nuclear test called Long Shot flashed in his mind. While he had been waiting for the weather to clear enough to allow a flight to fly him from Amchitka Island to Shemya Island, he stumbled upon the workings of a plan to steal nuclear bomb secrets. Being a lowly private first class, waiting for an upgrading letter to be added to his security clearance, he didn't have authorization to do much more than guard duty or K.P.

On a rare semi-clear day, he sat hidden in the tundra. He was glad it wasn't one of those days where screeching wind exceeded one hundred miles an hour and propelled snow pellets with enough force to sand blast a person's exposed face and cause waves to crash the shore and roar like an angry God. With spaces in the tundra letting little swords of light dance on his shoulder, he held binoculars to his eyes and searched the sea for playful seals and occasionally turned toward the island looking for an Alaskan blue fox. But the last time he turned he didn't see a blue fox. He saw Shemya Stan. He was walking along the shore carrying a fishing pole. Stan looked to be Japanese. But it wasn't odd that he could be Japanese. In the ASA, linguists of varied nationalities and races, called, Monterey Marys, translated many languages.

Crane had been warned that still water freezes at thirty-two degrees Fahrenheit. But moving water can be many degrees below freezing. Since the water surrounding Amchitka and Shemya was in a constant state of motion, it was truly icy water that could freeze a man to death. And it would be a quick death. There would be fifteen to twenty minutes of painful gasping, and then the man would become giddy and blank out.

When the body's normal temperature of ninety-eight point six degrees dropped, hypothermia happened. With a body temperature of about ninety-three degrees, a person experienced amnesia and slurred his speech. Around ninety-one degrees, a stupor set in. At eighty-seven degrees, not only did the person stop shivering, his heart could stop beating. When near the water, people on the island were ordered to always have a buddy with them. It was odd that Stan was alone.

Crane crouched down, held the binoculars to his eyes, and watched. Magnified with the binoculars, Stan looked familiar, but Crane couldn't remember where he had seen him. Stan looked all around. Then he reached into a bag, the color of brown tundra, and pulled out a green glass ball, the color of a Coke-bottle. Crane had seen these balls before. The Japanese and the Russian vessels that were supposed to be fishing, used these balls as floats for fishing nets. The balls would occasionally break from the nets and wash up on the beach. Being beer-bottle brown or Coke-bottle green, it was believed that Japanese made their floats from glass from old coke and beer bottles they had melted. In various places along the shore, what appeared to be small green stones that looked like Alaskan jade, were actually broken Coke bottle glass, worn smooth by constantly being tumbled by the never-ending waves of water that battered the island.

A few fishermen may have been on the Soviet trawlers that sometimes sat off Amchitka and Shemya, but the real crew belonged to the Radio-Technical Forces and the Russian Committee of State Security, also known at the KGB.

Dirty-white over rust-red, Russian trawlers, engaged in the futile pretense of fishing, often deployed nets for a short while, but the extra bracing supplied by their antenna arrays made it clear they were really engaged in listening.

A small net made from burlap string contained the ball that Stan held in his hand. Looking around, he tied the net onto the end of the fishing line. Showing the signs of a typical amateur fisherman, he ran along the beach, and through clinging strands of mist, he flung the fishing pole over his shoulder, and cast the ball across the rough water. Before the ball could slow and fall into the water, the fishing reel back-lashed, bird-nested, and stopped solid. The glass ball plinked off the end of the fishing line and plopped into the water. Stan watched the ball float out to sea. Shaking his head, he placed the pole over his shoulder and walked away.

But Crane stayed where he was. With the binoculars, he watched the glass ball. It made a huge ark, and the evenly spaced rolling waves washed it back to shore. Crane walked to shore and picked it up. It was only a glass ball. He couldn't figure out why Stan had used a fishing pole to cast it into the sea.

Crane knew what hours the glass-ball-casting Stan was working and was going to ask him about the green ball, but the next day Crane was on a plane going to AFJOG, the Air Force Joint Operations Group located on Shemya.

Perpetually cloaked in thick fog, just about any time would have been a good time to sneak classified information off Shemya Island. After the one hundred ninety kiloton underground, nuclear test called "Long Shot" had been detonated on Amchitka and vented radiation into the air over

Shemya, when feasible, personnel were kept inside for twelve days, and to combat the long-term effects of radioactive Iodine 131, they were given non-radioactive iodine-laced milk to drink, but were told it was blueberry milk. A few more people who had been on Amchitka just before the Long Shot event were flown to Shemya. Stan was one of them.

***

Weeks later, a rare fogless day greeted Shemya Island. Hidden from view, and taking advantage of what would be the only clear-sky day on the island of the long year that he would be stationed there, Crane sat in the tundra looking through his binoculars, searching for seals or blue fox.

High-stepping with swimming fins to avoid tripping, Stan came to the beach and hooked up another glass ball to the fishing line. But this time, he didn't cast it. Instead, he searched the sea.

Then it appeared.

If Crane hadn't been concentrating on what Stan was looking for, he would have missed it: The periscope of a submarine briefly breaking the surface of the Bering Sea.

Stan waved once and cast the ball far out into the sea. Then a scuba diver, clad in a black wet suit, surfaced and swam toward the ball.

Behind Crane, a man popped up out of the tundra and tried to run down the steep cliff-like shore. He fell. He must have twisted his ankle or something. When he tried to get up, his leg collapsed under him. Holding the fishing pole, Stan did not turn or look back. Either the crashing waves blocked the tumbling man's sounds, or Stan was concentrating on the scuba diver. Carefully, but quickly, Crane made his way down the incline and stopped at the fallen man. The man shouted at Crane. "That's ball's classified! Don't let that diver get it."

Like an alert warning "Classified" flashed in Crane's brain. Classified meant that that classified material in the ball could be detrimental to national security. Crane rushed toward Stan. Just as the diver was about to grab the ball, Crane yanked the pole from Stan's hands, and cranking the reel as fast as he could, he ran away from the beach. As the ball skied across the surface of the sea, Crane stopped, turned, and continued to crank the reel for all it had. The ball skittered up onto the shore. Stan looked toward the fallen man then at Crane. In an immediate rush, Stan ran into the frigid water and began to swim away. In a few seconds his breath was taken away. His arms seemed to lock up. He went under.

Crane frantically scan the sea for the scuba diver.

There was no sign of him.

Crane couldn't let Stan drown.

Running the numbers to avoid hypothermia through his brain, Crane stepped toward the water. If the water was fifty-nine degrees or fewer, he could stay in it for ten minutes. Sixty to sixty-five degrees, he could stay fifteen minutes, above sixty-five, twenty minutes. A man wouldn't necessarily die in cold water — not quickly at least — yet the misery and discomfort of being not just cold, but cold and wet, could drive a normal man insane.

But Crane had never been considered normal.

Ignoring the frigid water, he dropped the fishing pole and sloshed toward Stan. When the water reached above his knees, it was difficult to run, but he charged forward. When the water was up to his quickly heaving chest, it was so cold, it stung. Just as it had done when he and his boyhood buddies had jumped into the ice-coated waters of the Shenango River and swam a few stuttering strokes just to be the first kids swimming in the New Year, his breath came in short gasps. He was going to turn and go back to shore, but a foamy white wave knocked him down. Stan's leg bumped him on the hip. He stood up, reached down, and pulled Stan to shallow water. His face was as white as the foam, and it seemed to be drained of blood. Clinching his fists to control his shivering, Stan looked like a ghost. As they stood there, with small chops of water slapping them, Stan coughed up water and seemed to get his breath back.

When Stan looked up, his Japanese eyes and the features of his face caused Crane to remember where he had seen him before. He was one of the men who had picked up Al Capone's gold vault.

With his breath steaming in the frosty air, the man on shore motioned for Crane to bring Stan to shore.

Crane took two steps and turned toward Stan. With his breath issuing fog with every word, he asked, "Do you remember me? The Vault?"

Although there was a slight sign of recognition in Stan's face, he didn't answer. He seemed to see something Crane hadn't seen. He turned his white body away, dove under the water, and swam out to sea. Crane wondered if Stan was some sort of lunatic that wanted to drown himself.

After an orange pickup truck from the flight line arrived on the road above, Crane was shivering, but he managed to walk to shore and direct the two men from the truck to the fallen man.

While they attended to him, Crane asked if he would be needed when they reported Stan's death to the base commander. One of the men stood up, placed a blanket over Crane's shaking shoulders, and took him off to the side.

"Just like your mission," he softly said. "Many of our operational techniques are classified. As a special operations unit, we are not under the command authority of the base commander. We report directly to SAD."

"Sad?" Crane asked.

The man looked at Crane as if he had an addled mind. "Yes, *SAD*, Special Activities Division."

While the man went back to the fallen man, Crane walked to the glass ball and picked it up. He removed a cork. Inside he found a roll of film and three sheets of folded paper. When he unfolded the sheets, the top and bottom had been stamped: TOP SECRET WINDMILL. Windmill was a code name for the nuclear event called Long Shot. The pages and the film were top-secret documents about Long Shot.

When he was halfway through reading the third page of the documents, the security people jerked them from his hands so fast it startled him. His inquiring eyes reading classified information had caused the first letter to be placed on the end of his top-secret crypto security clearance.

CHAPTER 16

At the Army Security Agency base in Virginia, under the bare light bulb with a tin shade hanging from the ceiling, Crane slumped over the colonel's desk, lost in thought.

As if he were going to examine it, the colonel lifted the folder from the desk. Instead, Whap! He slammed it down.

The sudden sound jerked Crane back to the present. He sat up straight and stared at the colonel's menacing figure. Defensively raising his hand, Crane said, "If I would have known what Shemya Stan was doing, I might have let him drown."

"It would have made matters easier," the colonel said, and his teeth gleamed in a smile. "But I don't think he would have drowned. The scuba diver that rescued him had an extra regulator. Stan may have gotten a little chilly, but he breathed easily all the way to the warm submarine."

"At least he didn't get the classified information or the film."

The colonel shook his head in astonishment. "We never considered that he would place it into a glass ball and cast it into the sea, but it wouldn't have mattered. Just to catch the person or persons he was delivering it to, we planted phony information and made it easy for him to get."

Crane knew the colonel was lying about the information not being classified. The colonel's ignorant technique of trying to feed him international hogwash made Crane want to grab him by the scruff on the neck and throw him across the room.

Instead, Crane suppressed his anger, but his voice came out in a low, steely tone. "The documents did show Long Shot was not contained," he said. "Hard rock at the bottom of the shaft and water turning into steam caused the containment cage to break. There was no way radiation could have stayed underground. It spewed a radioactive plume into the air."

"So what?" the colonel said with an arrogant tilt to his head. "It didn't go anywhere."

Crane clinched his fists and felt his mouth tighten. "Where do you get your information? The permanent low-pressure system caused the wind to take radiation to Shemya. It rained down on us and then headed toward Russia. That's why we had to drink purple milk."

The colonel's eyes opened wide. "We'll never admit to that."

"And you'll never admit that the milk, we were told was blueberry milk, was actually laced with non-radioactive iodine."

"What are you worried about. Iodine-131 has a radioactive decay half-life of about eight days. You drank the milk for twelve days. After your thyroid had been saturated with non-radioactive iodine, it absorbed very little of the radioactive Iodine-131."

"Just like Agent Orange, radiation causes cancer and diseases, and there were more kinds or radiation than Iodine-131. If I get cancer, what am I supposed to do? Just pretend it didn't happen?"

"That's exactly what I would suggest. The Russian test ban treaty of 1962 forbids all nuclear fallout to fall on Russian territory. If the Russians knew Long Shot vented and the cloud went over the Kamchatka Peninsula, the treaty would be broken. Then the Russians would start setting off their gigantic bombs again. Radiation would travel all over the world. The world doesn't need radiation with a half-life of six hundred eighty-five billion years falling from the sky." He lifted his eyes and appeared to study Crane. "And just think what would happen to the Alaskan fishing industry. If they think Alaskan fish or Alaskan crab is full of radiation, people are not going to buy or eat it. Only an idiot would let the truth be known and set off an international hullabaloo."

"I get your point, but what kind of international hogwash are you going to tell the people who get sick from it."

The colonel waved his hand down. "Nobody got blown to hell in a mushroom cloud. Low level radiation has the same effects as pesticides. We'll say they got it from a spilled shipment of Agent Orange. They'll never know the difference."

Knowing there was very little he could do about being exposed to radiation, Crane gave a submissive shrug. "It figures."

"So," the colonel said and paused. "We want you to do this one last job for us."

The colonel had already tried to lie to Crane. Crane didn't want to do anything for him. He stood up. "Let me out of here. Get an officer to do it."

"It amazes me that you'd say that. From your experience, you must have learned that the noncommissioned officers of the ASA are more capable than most officers that are over them."

Crane was surprised that an officer would admit that. He sat back down. "How did you figure that one out?"

"Trial and error." For a moment, the colonel stared at the floor and then looked up. "Again, it's based on the need to know. And why should an officer have an interest in something he will have nothing to do with, except write a phony report?"

Crane remembered officers shirking the responsibilities of critical actions by pushing them down to the lowest feasible level. Usually the lowest level of those executing a plan would be noncommissioned officers, but it made sense. The ones going on a mission were the ones who knew their own capabilities and limitations, and they were the ones who would live or die by their own plan, and it was usually a good plan. But Crane felt he didn't have experience in planning much of anything that had to do with the Army.

"You've got the wrong man," he persisted. "I'm not qualified to go after Stan."

"A railroad may be involved. You have experience there."

Crane reluctantly nodded. "Only a few months."

Angered by Crane's few-months ploy, the colonel raised his voice. "Stan has the E-Brite sphere. We want it. You saved his life. You will get the sphere and turn him, too."

"Stan knows a lot of things. His protection lies in what he knows. He's not going to tell me a damn thing."

"Stan knows a great deal. Perhaps too much." As if in thought, the colonel stared at the desk. "It's either that or our government is frustrated by its own ineffectual attempts to locate him."

"So what? He still won't tell me or you anything."

"After we inject him with everything from scopolamine to triple amytal, we'll know everything he has ever done. With the threat of blackmail, he'll gladly serve as a double agent for us."

Crane had heard of the various hypnotic drugs, such as scopolamine and thiopental sodium which was also known as sodium pentothal. They were very effective in inducing a person under questioning to talk without inhibition. If he could persuade Stan to go to Fairfax, and if he could get him into a room, the drugs would save a lot of time and effort. In a few days, Crane would be on his way home. He turned his eyes toward the colonel. "How can I get him to turn?"

"Confront him with the facts. He's guilty of espionage against the United States, Russia, and Cambodia. We'll find out who his KGB contact is. Then you can give him the times and places of his meetings before he goes to them. A few phony photos of him passing secrets would help, too."

"What if he decides to get asylum from the Russians?"

The colonel's face took on a puzzled look. "Stan blew up a Russian helicopter. I don't think he wants to give up his Western lifestyle to spend his life in a Russian prison camp."

Crane held up his hand in a halting gesture. "Wait a second. Didn't you tell me Stan blew up a North Vietnamese helicopter landed to pick it up the E-Brite?"

As if caught in a lie, the colonel hesitated, then waved his hand to the side. "It was a Russian helicopter with North Vietnamese markings."

"Actually, it doesn't matter what kind of helicopter it was. It doesn't mean he'll come back here."

"The helicopter incident may not be enough to persuade Stan to come back, but you can tell him he has three choices. He can spend the rest of his life in United States prison as a traitor. He can spend it in a Russian prison camp for espionage and murder. Or, at our expense, he can cooperate with us and quietly spend the remainder of his life somewhere safe."

"I hope you don't want me to go to Shemya to find him."

The colonel smiled. "You won't find Stan on Shemya."

Even though he wouldn't be going to Shemya, Crane still tried to get out of the assignment. "How many times do I have to tell you? I'm not qualified. I'm not an officer."

The colonel gave Crane an academic look devoid of all emotion. "You don't have to be an officer to know what you're doing. Your general test scores show you have an intelligence score above genius."

Although Crane actually had a high IQ, he never considered himself above average intelligence. He figured the colonel was inflating his self-esteem to make it easier to trap him into doing something he didn't want to do. "Those tests have multiple choices. You get points for just signing your name."

"I think you're the best man for the job."

"I'm only a Specialist Five. If you consult your staff, they'll tell you to find someone of higher rank."

"We already sent three officers. They all failed, and the powers to be want to send more. But I'll tell you one sure thing. If you mess this mission up, we both hang"

Crane had no idea who to contact, but he tried a weak bluff. "If they want an officer, I'll go to someone in higher authority."

"You can, but I'm still within my legal authority. When congress institutionalized the CIA in 1947, the Act included a statute that permits extraordinary action on the part of the agency in times of national crisis."

"This is not a national crisis."

"I'm sure you'll agree that people will always kill to maintain power. I believe the possibility of some lame-brained dictator getting hold of an atomic bomb as small as a golf ball *is* a national crisis." As if he had Crane securely trapped, he heaved a sigh of contentment. "But even if it is not a national crisis, what has happened to you is so unlikely no one of higher authority will believe a thing you say?"

Crane opened his mouth to protest, but the colonel lifted his hand a few inches above the desk. It was the gesture of an officer accustomed to demanding attention. "People do not report back through normal channels. They report directly to me."

Crane had never thought about it that way. The colonel was right. No one in high authority would give a lowly Specialist Five an appointment to talk, and if by some remote chance, they did, they would slough it off as some kook making up a deranged story to get out of the army on a mental discharge.

Crane did not want to go back to Shemya, and he knew when the other player had the winning hand, it was best to throw down the cards and start another hand. All of a sudden, the possibility of finding Stan seemed incredible and unreal, but it had become a call of exceeding allurement. He would be going to Japan. He didn't know how, but he would convince Stan to go to Fairfax.

He turned to go.

"Wait!" The colonel lifted one finger.

Crane turned back.

"What we said and what you heard, when you leave, leave it here."

CHAPTER 17

On the first day of May, Crane stood on a busy street in downtown Tokyo, Japan. With his jacket collar turned up to ward off a cool spring wind, he tried to hail a cab to get back to Tachikawa Air Force Base. He had just been to Camp Drake to see an Army Security Agency friend who had shown him an official report that had been printed on a teletype:

CONFIDENTIAL HANDLE COMIT CHANNELS ONLY

BETWEEN ANCHORAGE AND TACHIKAWA AIRFORCE BASE, PACIFIC FLYING TIGER INCIDENT. RADAR VISUAL CONFIRMATION. THREE RED OVAL OBJECTS VISIBLE OUT CABIN WINDOW, PACED AIRCRAFT FOR THIRTY MINUTES, TWO HUNDRED FEET TO ONE THOUSNAD FEED DIAMETER, FIVE-MILE DISTANCE. OBJECTS WERE TRACKED BY RADAR AND SIGHTED VISUALLY FOR THIRTY MINUTES, FOUR EXPERICNED MALE MILITARY WITNESSED THREE RED OVAL OBJECTS, ABOUT SIX HUNDRED FEET ACROSS, ON THE OCEAN. NO SOUND.WAS HEARD.

CONFIDENTIAL HANDLE COMIT CHANNELS ONLY

After Crane and his friend had talked for about thirty minutes and wondered if the report could be real, a warning had been received from headquarters signaling an impending operational mission. Crane's friend was on alert. It was imperative that he be at his duty station in fewer than five minutes.

With little working knowledge of Japanese language and no idea which way to go, Crane was left to find his way back to Tachikawa Airforce Base in time to catch his flight to Chitose and sign in at the Kuma Station military base.

Although Japanese cabs stopped, when he tried to tell the drivers where he wanted to go, shaking their heads, they waved their hands in a negative gesture and drove away. When he showed his green military identification card to give them an idea that he wanted to go to a military base, the response was immediate and a definite "No!" To make matters worse, he had to go to the bathroom.

He searched the street for something familiar. When he looked up, a sign with red enameled wooden letters of Japanese characters, called *Kanji,* was to his right. Below that, on a separate sign, the English word "BAR" stood out. He hurried to the sign and stopped beneath it. In front of him, various colors of plastic beads on long strings curtained the entrance. He pushed the beads aside and went in. Inside, the entire bar was the size of three pickup trucks placed end to end.

A girl who had been sitting on a small stool behind the little bar stood up. For a moment, Crane was taken aback. Clear dark almond-shaped eyes accented her clear face which was haloed by silky black hair that cascaded over her petite shoulders. Her supple body matched her small hips and her small breasts didn't distract from an inner beauty and friendliness that radiated and filled the bar with a welcoming atmosphere.

With much hast and urgency, Crane said, "Do you have a restroom?"

The girl gave him a puzzled look.

Crane tried again. "Bathroom?"

The girl pointed to the back of the bar. "*Benjo*?"

At the back of the bar, a sign above a sliding door read, toilet. Squeezing past the narrow space behind the bar stools, Crane hastened to the end of the bar and slid the door to the side. Inside, a narrow wooden board served as a seat on which a person sat with their rear end hanging over a rectangular opening. There was no hole cut in a board similar to an outhouse staring at him like a big dark eye. There were no commodes, no sinks, no soap dispensers, or a worn bar of soap, no running water, and no paper towels. It was like having an outhouse in the bar. After he spent a minute sending a pent-up stream of urine into the dark pit, he stepped back into the bar and slid the door closed. Standing at the end of the bar, waiting, the girl reached into an aluminum electric heating cabinet, pulled out a white washcloth rolled into a neat cylinder, placed it on a small bamboo tray, and presented it to him.

"*Oshibori?*" she questioned.

Remembering his top of the hill training, Crane realized that the girl was offering him a sterilized washcloth commonly offered to customers in Japanese restaurants and bars and used to clean one's hands before eating or after going to the toilet. He had been told that *oshiboris* were usually hot in winter and cold in summer, and this one was pleasantly warm.

He took the *oshibori* off the bamboo tray and wiped his hands.

Speaking Japanese and smiling a welcoming smile, the girl asked him something.

He didn't understand what she was saying, but he wanted to stay for a while. Maybe sample the exquisite combination of good Japanese food and a cold beer. After all, the first Japanese words he had learned had been, *Beer do wah, ikura des' ka?* How much is a beer?

But he couldn't have a beer. He had to get back to Tachikawa base to catch his flight. He handed the girl the *oshibori*, saying one of the few Japanese words he knew, "*Domo arigato*," which meant thank you, and he gave her a one-hundred-yen bill and walked out the door. Since three hundred sixty yen was equivalent to one American dollar, he had actually given her thirty-eight cents.

While he stood outside on the sidewalk, wondering how he was going to get back to the base, a caravan of Japanese Army trucks, transporting soldiers with red stars on their olive-drab hats, drove past. One truck seemed to stall and stopped right next to Crane. Face-to-face with a Japanese soldier sitting in the passenger side of the turck, Crane's heart jumped his in chest. The red star and the Japanese man's face with slanted eyes flashed memories of the Viet Cong that had almost killed him. He told himself to calm down. After all, the United States wasn't at war with Japan. Hoping to find someone who could speak English, he turned from the soldier and began to walk.

Searching the buildings for a sign that read bus, or taxi, he noticed a man who looked to be American. Hoping the man spoke English, he started toward the man. The man pulled a pistol fitted with a silencer and aimed it at him. Three English words filled the air: "Go after him!"

Crane expected to hear the "thup!" sound of the silencer, but the man didn't shoot. Making a smaller target, Crane lowered his level and ran in a zigzagging pattern until he was behind a bus in front of a store having a grand opening. Yellow triangular flags, above parked bicycles and motorcycles, announced the opening of the store, and various bamboo furniture and freshly woven baskets sat in front of a long stand filled with flowers. Crane stopped to see if the man with the gun had followed. The dull "thup!" of a gun being shot echoed from the sides of the buildings.

Crane took off running. As he looked back, the man with the gun crashed into a man with a camera. The man fell into a row of motorcycles. He only knocked over one motorcycle, but his camera clattered onto the street. The pursuer didn't stop. The silencer on the pistol meant that if the man was shooting at Crane, Crane might not be able to hear all the shots. To make himself a smaller target, he lowered his head and leaned forward. As if he were bowed against a strong wind, he ran faster.

A ways down the street, Crane looked up. A Japanese man wearing a white shirt, carrying a black briefcase was right in front of him. Veering around the man, Crane charged across an intersection. Before he made it across the street, a red Nissan truck beeped its horn and came right at him. He jumped out of its way, but a rush of air from another fast-moving truck traveled across his back. On the other side of the intersection, he zipped past three brightly-painted buildings, turned a corner, and found himself in a produce market. Here, market porters carried wooden crates or pushed hand carts. An unpainted, wooden shelter, kept the sun off worn wooden bins and boxes of strange looking lettuce, melons, and assorted vegetables, Crane had never seen before, and became a backdrop for the noise of Japanese people dressed in beige and dark clothing huddled in the center isle of the market.

Crane turned away from the huddle, slipped into a dirt alley cluttered with wooden crates, and hid behind a lone stack of crates. When he peered through the slats, there was no sign of the men. He wondered why they were after him. Forcing his mind to function as if it were a finely tuned instrument, he tried to find an answer. But being in a strange place and unexpectantly being shot at, caused him to be too keyed up to think right. Trying to relax, he walked around the crates and continued on down the street.

A block later, instead of looking back and signaling his pursuers that he was watching for them, Crane ducked under a colorful sign that read "Pachinko Palace" and went in.

Inside, plinking, ringing, clanging rows of machines that resembled upright colorful pin ball machines, decorated all three walls. Lines of people used their left hands to push handfuls of little chrome balls, they had paid for, into mouth-like openings on the machines. With their right hands, people were flicking handles that propelled the balls up and around a metal track where they spun until they came down, hitting various pins and wheels that scored points and caused more chrome balls to fall into a small shelf with a catch pocket at the bottom of the machine. The amount of balls they won determined the level of the prize they would win.

Crane didn't have time to buy balls and try to win more, he was too busy keeping an eye out for his pursuers. He bent his knees until he was the height of the black-haired Japanese people and pretended to be studying a machine. The two men with the guns stopped outside at the right end of the entrance. Deep in conversation, they looked worried. One man clenched his fist and his voice rose. Crane hoped someone had seen the gun and called the police. Resisting the urge to break into a run, he slowly weaved around people playing the machines, but he couldn't shake the feeling that everyone in the place was watching him. Just as he made it to the left side of the entrance, the two men turned to watch something down the cement telephone-pole-lined sidewalk. With their backs turned toward him, Crane slipped out of the entrance and hugged the side of the store fronts until he came to an alley and ducked into it.

At the other end of the alley, from around a corner, like a pack of huge sprawling mad dogs, a mob of Japanese people came waving a Japanese flag and pointing at him. He didn't know what was happening, but it looked like he was going to be the brunt of a mob's hatred.

While training at the top of the hill, to find out whether an operator would actually kill people in a showdown, he and other operators had gone through shoot-no-shoot exercises. Mostly because of his experiences chasing after Capone's vault, if Crane needed to, he could kill. For a moment, he thought that if he had a weapon, he could take the "practical shooting stance." Using "rapid aim fire" shooting, he would mow the whole mob down. But no one in the mob seemed to be armed. He wasn't in Nam. He was in a friendly foreign country. If he did something like that in plain sight, he could cause an international crisis. He would go to jail.

He ran a block down the street. To his relief, a phone booth sat on the sidewalk next to a cement telephone pole. He stopped, stepped inside, and picked up the receiver. All the numbers were in k*anji,* and the coin slots only took Japanese money. It was such a letdown, to keep from panicking, he laughed at his predicament and stepped outside. The mob was still headed his way. Shouts came in bursts from a hand-held bull horn. Were the shouts warnings or exhortations to the crowd?

Crane didn't know.

Today, was his first day in Japan.

There was so much he didn't know.

He tried to hail another cab.

The cab didn't stop.

The mob began to shout, pick up speed, and rush in his direction. He felt like he was in the eye of a human hurricane, watching a maelstrom, a force of nature with the power to tear him apart. The crowd quickened. They were closer now, and one man in a fraying blue shirt pointed an angry finger at him.

Crane was ready to run, but when he looked to his left, as if on command, another mob with desperate eyes all turned toward him. When the mobs were twenty feet from him, he tried to hail a cab, again. One white and yellow cab slowed but zipped past and headed for the mob. The mob opened and let the cab through. On a street, now devoid of all automobiles, a blue 1958 Chevrolet pulled next to him and stopped.

With a look of concern, a man inside the Chevy leaned over and rolled down the passenger side window. "Do you need a lift?"

"Yes, sir!" Crane said, opened the door, and hoped in.

Behind the steering wheel, a heavy man bulging in a loud blue suit shook his head. "It's May Day. What are you doing off the base?"

"I'm trying to get back to Tachikawa Air Base."

As the man leaned into a sharp turn, Crane twisted in the seat and looked back at the mob. They had stopped. Standing on a wooden box, the leader was making some sort of a speech.

Crane turned back toward the driver. “If that mob would have gotten me, I don’t think I’d be alive.”

The man smiled. “If they would have killed you, I would still have picked you up.”

“Why would you do that?”

“I’m the mortician for the base.” He chuckled at Crane’s declining fear. “No very many people go off base on May Day.”

“Why not?”

“Japanese workers take the day off. Labor unions organize rallies and demonstrations. It’s a pretty big deal. In Japanese corporate culture, taking weekdays off for personal pleasure is frowned upon. Going off base is not off-limits. It’s only a courtesy the base commander gives the locals. I don’t think they would have hurt you, but with demonstrations and drinking, there is always the possibility of trouble.”

While the mortician drove Crane back to the base, so he wouldn’t be scared by his ignorance of failing to communicate with the Japanese people, he vowed to learn the Japanese language as quickly as he could.

He caught his flight without further incident.

Flying over Chitose, a city in northern Hokkaido, Japan, he looked down from the window of the airplane. Below, red, orange, blue, green, and yellow rooftops stretched over the city. Some roofs had little tin chimneys with spinning ventilators. Crane tried to convince himself that the men who had shot at him was just some kind of nut house thing. But for the moment, he wanted to know what was under those colorful tin roofs.

CHAPTER 18

Crane landed at the Chitose Airport and took a cab to Kuma Station. After getting squared away enough to do army duties, to familiarize himself with downtown Chitose, he jumped on a bus that took him there.

Right after he stepped off the bus, he felt the tightness he always felt when appearing for the first time in a strange place. His eyes slanted down the street. With his every sense alert for trouble, he studied each building. There were no tall structures, and most of them were made of wood. And he found out what was under those colorful roofs. Along both sides of the narrow street, more bars than he could count were crammed together in long lines and displayed various hand-painted signs that seemed to stare at each other. Although Chitose was almost a bilingual town, it looked to be a rough place. Being shot at in Tokyo, he was afraid it could happen again, and here.

After he had gone into a few bars, he was amazed how many were only about a car length wide and four car lengths long. Some had just enough room for patrons to lean against the wall and squeeze past GIs sitting on the small bar stools.

Crane walked into Bar Cherry and sat at a corner table. Away from the general babble of the bar, he listened to Stephen Wolf's hit song "The Pusher" blaring from the jukebox, and the pleasant odor of beer and buttered toast, sprinkled with salt, fill the air. After the jukebox had eaten all the yen the GI's had slipped into it and the bar became quiet, Crane didn't have much to talk about. Most intelligence work, even when pedestrian, was dull. Even though the routines of digging for facts, reading newspapers, reports, scientific journals, and gathering information from a wide variety of sources wasn't too exciting, he couldn't talk about it. And he couldn't talk about what was done at the Kuma Station military base, either. And he definitely couldn't say anything about his real mission.

Through small talk he discovered Lake Shikostsu was a caldera lake located in the south-west part of Hokkaido. He didn't know what a caldera was. When he asked, he was told that a caldera was a volcanic feature formed when a volcano collapse into itself. And it made sense. Three volcanoes surrounded Lake Shikostsu. Mount Eniwa, to the north and Mount Fuppushi and Mount Tarumae to the south, and it was the second deepest lake in Japan. Many years ago, when the land between the volcanoes had subsided, the caldera had formed in the Holocene. It hadn't taken long for Crane to decide that the lake could provide some knowledge he could use in his plan to have people drive up to his front door and give him money. In addition, his converted radio, with the little upside-down umbrella-like antenna, had sent a signal. A man resembling Shemya Stan had been seen diving in the lake.

Crane would have to go there.

As thc flare of a red dawn glinted off the sides of bars in downtown Chitose, Crane walked through a smoke-shrouded alley. Before he came out the other end, a whipping sound cracked the crisp air. On the main street, sunlight fell through the many overhead signs and dappled light and shadow across the weary face of a skinny Japanese junk man. He controlled a wooden, two-wheeled wagon loaded high with heavy scrap metal. A leather harness held a small, dirty-white dog on the end of a rope that was tied to the front of the wagon. The wagon was clearly a burden for the little dog. As the dog strained to pull the heavy load, its bloody paws gained no traction on the pavement. Each time the dog stopped, the man yelled and lashed it with a whip. When the dog did not pull, the man pushed the wagon until the dog began pulling again.

Although it hurt his heart, Crane watched this cruel process being repeated until the junk man and the wagon lumbered into an alley and out of sight.

At the bus stop, a Japanese boy, dressed in a full baseball uniform stood at the edge of the yellow dirt field, waving a baseball bat. He was waiting for the sun to brighten the day and his friends to come and play ball. With his head back and his fists clinched, another player came running down the street. Apparently, the Japanese took baseball seriously.

After Crane stepped into a bus, fifty miles later, he was at Lake Shikostsu. A visitor's center, campgrounds, and tourist's facilities adorned the shore of the clear lake and gave off a vacation feeling. Blue fishing boats with long poles sticking out of them, had been pulled up onto the shore, waiting to be rowed out into the deep and used to catch red salmon, called *chippu.*

After renting a row boat and a fishing pole, Crane rowed the boat a ways out onto the lake and dipped his arm into the clear water. He couldn't believe how cold it was. The same deep water that made Lake Shikostsu warm in winter so that it never froze, made it cold in summer. Although he had one of the toys from the top of the hill: a puff-pak, a little rubber breathing mask with its own air supply that was good for seven minutes, he was glad he wasn't going for a swim.

As if the lake were whispering to him, a voice directed his eyes to the deserted shore at a bend in the lake. Bending and stepping out of a boat, a dark form, with the shadow of its big hat shielding its eyes, caught his attention. Thinking it could be a poor Japanese pheasant, like the one with the dog struggling to pull the overloaded junk wagon, Crane cupped one hand to the side of his face to cut the glare and watched. High-stepping with fins to avoid tripping, as he had done on Shemya, there was no doubt the man was Stan.

Stan stepped to the front of a boat, pushed it into the water, and hopped in. Not wanting Stan to see him, Crane grabbed the fishing pole and flipped the line into the water. While he watched Stan through the small mirror he had placed on the reel of the pole, he pretended to focusing on catching a *chippu*.

Stan rowed the boat away from shore, turned left, rowed fifty meters, and dropped anchor. After looking over the side on the boat, he removed his shirt and dropped into the water. When his finned feet slipped beneath the surface Crane jerked the fishing line out of the water, threw the pole into the boat, and rowed toward Stan's empty boat. When Crane was five meters from Stan's boat, Stan surfaced. A golf-ball size E-Brite sphere was in his hand. Without looking up, he reached over the side of the boat and laid the sphere onto the seat. Then he lifted himself into the boat. After he had taken off his fins and flopped them onto the bottom of the boat, he looked up.

Crane's boat glided next to his.

Their eyes met. Stan's head snapped in the direction of the sphere on the seat.

If Crane were fast enough, he could grab the sphere. He stood up to jump into Stan's boat. Holding onto the side of his boat, Stan lifted his foot and gave Crane's boat a mighty heave. As if a rug had been yanked out from under him, Crane tumbled sideways and splashed into the water. The initial shock of the cold water took his breath away, but he managed to tread water and watch Stan.

With a look of satisfaction, Stan grabbed the sphere and stuffed it into his wet pants pocket. Crane dove under water and swam to the back of Stan's boat. As Stan stood at the front of his boat and searched for Crane where he had entered the water, Crane tipped the boat to one side. Stan shifted his body and kept his balance. For a split second, Crane jerked the boat the opposite way. Stan tried to compensate by leaning the other way, but Crane jerked the boat in the original direction.

Stan hadn't anticipated that.

Ker-splash! He toppled into the water.

Instead of getting back into his boat and trying to out row Crane, Stan swam for the shore. If he continued to dive under the water and change directions, it would be tough to try and follow him in a row boat. And, on one of those dives, he could hide the sphere on the bottom where Crane could never find it.

Crane swam after him.

Stan rolled to his back. With his face contorted with confusion, he looked toward Crane. Crane guessed Stan never had anyone swim after him as fast as he had. Although the water was cold, he easily kept up with Stan. The problem was that he couldn't out swim the stamina of Stan and Stan couldn't out swim him.

It was a standoff. When Stan stopped, Crane stopped. In a final effort, Crane cut all the mental stops and swam with all his might. It seemed to be too much for Stan. He faltered and began to sink below the surface. Crane caught him around the neck and arm and tried to tow him to the boat. But Stan had only been playing possum. He struggled free and managed to grab Crane by the neck. Then he decided to take Crane down into the icy depths. With an average depth of two hundred sixty-five meters and a maximum depth of three hundred sixty-three meters, a thermocline in this cold lake was very possible.

Usually marked by a layer of cloud-like water, the temperature gradient across a thermocline layer would be abrupt. Going through this icy layer without a wet suit and a hood over his forehead would cause Crane's head to ache like an ice-cream headache, and as if he were being pulled to the dark depths by the devil himself, his body would rapidly descend to the bottom.

Stan must have figured that if he took Crane into the thermocline and let him free, he would be forced to swim up. Then, while he tried to get warm on the surface, Stan would hide the sphere.

Although Crane had his puff-pak, a cold dread crawled into his chest, and it felt like it was going to squeeze the life-giving air out of his lungs. Logic had lost its power. His quest to get the sphere and go home and Stan wanting to keep it from him, became a contest of wills. And it was a contest Crane wasn't prepared to lose.

He figured if they both sank to the bottom, he could use his puff pack, but Stan's lungs would cause him to feel purged of air, and that he was going to drown. He would be forced to swim to the surface with the sphere.

When they passed through the cloudy layer of a thermocline, they began to quickly descend. The water rapidly grew cold and dark, but having experienced such dark in the deep waters of the Shenango River, Crane was immune to the cloistering effect of the black depths. Stan immediately took his arm from around Crane's neck. Crane twisted around and wrapped both his hands around Stan's waist. The cold water began to give Crane a headache, but when he held his forehead next to Stan's body the headache stopped. As they descended further into the icy depths they didn't kick or make one motion to stop their rapid decent.

Stan had to be thinking, what sort of lunatic goes into the dark and drowns himself? But Crane laughed to himself. His puff-pak was good for seven minutes, and he hadn't taken a breath from it, yet. Just as his head began to ache, again, Stan kicked his legs. Finally, he wanted to swim to the surface. Crane released his grip from around Stan's waist and pushed him away. Stan swam for the surface far above, and Crane followed.

After Crane ascended above the thermocline into clear water, he took a few breaths from his puff-pack and looked up. Way above him, striving to burst through the surface and gasp that first breath of air, Stan frantically kicked and stroked upward toward the light.

While Crane leisurely swam for the surface, Stan broke the surface, swam a few strokes, and curled up. His muscles seemed to be cramping from the cold water. As the oxygen in his blood had dwindled, lactic acid had built up. His cold body quivered and seemed to spasm. He began to sink.

With long powerful strokes, Crane had learned to use in the strong currents of the floods of the Shenango River, he scooped huge strokes with his arms and quickly swam to the surface. Making sure Stan's face would be out of the water, he grabbed him around the neck and shoulder. As he towed him to shore, Stan sagged in his arms. Although Stan was breathing, he was blue. Crane picked him up, and while he carried him to shore, his weight was barely noticeable to Crane's adrenaline-filled muscles. He lay Stan on the shore to start artificial respiration, and joked, "This is getting to be a habit." Before he could do anything, Stan rolled over and smacked a strong hand on Crane's chest.

Surprised, Crane jerked back. Stan jumped up. Making sure it was still there, he slapped the outline of the E-Brite sphere in his wet pocket and ran toward Mount Tarumae and vanished into the low foliage.

Crane searched for him, but it was as if Stan had vanished into thin air. Crane would have continued to search, but he had been chasing Stan for three days. He had to report back to Kuma Station military base and play army, again. He was tired, but he couldn't give the people at the base the real reason why. In order to maintain the pretense of fellowship with other soldiers, he told them he had been shacked up with a beautiful Japanese woman. But they assumed he had been on a three-day drunk, and he couldn't convince them otherwise.

CHAPTER 19

On an August evening, a week after he had lost Stan at Lake Shikostsu, Crane walked down a street in downtown Chitose. When he turned into a dirt alley, the odor of dampness and kerosene lamps that lighted the windows of old brown shacks hovered in the air. To his left, the shadow of a man standing behind a curtain of beads that hung in the entrance of the bar called "Eiko Bar", stretched across the hard-packed dirt. For a moment, Crane thought the shadow could be Stan's. But it wasn't. It was a small, jowly man with a mustache.

Crane stopped at the entrance to the bar and listened. Inside, someone using a cajoling tone of charm and flattery, praised a sergeant. After the man stopped talking, he swept the beads of the bar entrance aside and walked into the alley. A few meters away, he ran into another man, and his brilliant humility changed. He condemned the sergeant as a fool and a moron. The man's instant deceit reminded Crane of how difficult it was to find a person he could trust.

As he watched the men swagger down the alleyway, the echoing of un-rhythmic whacking of hammers met his ears. He followed the sound to the end of the alley, stopped at an empty lot, and stared. Off to the far side of the lot, Japanese people were building a high wooden scaffold. Since construction was always going on in Chitose, Crane figured it was just another scaffold for a future bar.

After he checked five bars and found no sign of Stan, he walked back to the lot. The wooden scaffold had been built. Musicians and singers in bright kimonos were gathered on top of it.

As if he were searching for something on the foot-hammered black ground, an old wheezing Japanese man walked hunched over, looking down. When he stopped, he straightened up, lifted his head, and squinted at the musicians.

Crane walked up to the man and offered him a drink from his flask of black label, Johnny Walker scotch he had hidden under his belt. The man took a huge swallow. Unaccustomed to high-priced scotch, the man's eyes bulged for a moment. Then he smiled a satisfied smile, breathed in a non-wheezing breath, bowed, and said, "*Domo arigato*," Thank you.

Using his broken Japanese, Crane asked the man what the musicians were doing.

The man pointed to the platform. "*Yagura*," he said and explained that the platform was for the bandstand of the musicians and singers of the *Obon* music. It was the beginning of the Bon Festival.

Crane figured it was some sort of neighborhood dance, and decided to hang around.

Bon dance people wearing light cotton kimonos, called *yukata*, began to gather on the lot. When drums, as loud as thunder, began, Bon dancers lined up in a circle around the high wooden *yagura*. Other instruments chimed in, and the dancers proceeded in a clockwise circle. At certain times, they changed direction and proceeded counter-clockwise. After a while, they faced the *yagura* and moved towards it and away from it.

As the dance went on, Crane stopped GI's on their way to bars and asked them about the dance. The first GI said, "Oh that's the dance of the dead." And he went his merry way toward Eiko's bar.

The next GI Crane stopped was a linguist. As if presenting a new stage act, he waved his hand toward the dancers. "This is the Citizen's Bon-Odori Dance Festival. It's also called Bon Dance. It's a Japanese Buddhist custom." As he paused, a look of mischief filled his face. "Are you afraid of ghosts?"

"No, why?"

With a smug know-it all expression beaming from his face, the linguist leaned back. "This Bon dance is a dance of joy, where the spirits of Japanese's dead ancestors are welcomed, and their sacrifices are honored and appreciated. Some GI's have seen ghosts."

Already wise to the linguist's flimsy effort to make a game of a new GI, Crane nervously looked around and faked fear. "If I see *obake,* I'm outta here."

Apparently, the linguist wasn't sure if Crane was joking, but his ability to use the Japanese word for ghost, *obake,* or supernatural beings who have taken on a temporary transformation, caused the smug expression on the linguist's face to fall. "Hey, you're pretty smart for a new guy."

As Crane looked behind the linguist, at the right side of the high wooden *yagura,* he glimpsed a slouch hat that shadowed the face of Shemya Stan.

It was as if he were deliberately waiting on Crane. It was as if he wanted to be seen.

"Not smart enough," Crane hastily told the linguist. "I gotta go." He turned and headed toward Stan.

As Stan stood there, Crane tried to nonchalantly work his way around the left side of the *yagura.* When he was five meters from Stan, the lowering sun began to redden the evening. Stan turned and stared in Crane's direction. Crane wondered if Stan was one of the men who had shot at him in Tokyo. He felt a sense of dread and tension rise in his head, but figured he would try one of Neal's old tricks.

Usually when someone greets people with a big smile and open arms, they believe they should know the person greeting them. Then while they try and remember the greeter's name, they start trivial talk. Crane smiled his best smile, held out his arms, and walked toward Stan.

"Stan, Stan the man," he said with great excitement in his voice. "Nice to see you again, Stan. Remember all the fun we used to have?"

Stan stood still, his eyes searching Crane's face. Now Stan was one meter away from him. Crane held out his hand in friendship. Stan lifted his hand to shake. Before Crane could grasp it, Stan's eyes glinted with recognition. He bolted away from the *yagura* and into the multitude of dancers. Crane tried to follow, but the dancers had formed lines and were moving toward the *yagura.* Stan zipped left and ran along the first line of dancers, and then he made a sharp right and ran down the alley.

Crane chased him for what felt like miles. Alleyway after alleyway, he continued to run after him. Even when Crane's legs were aching for a rest, he chased Stan down Main Street. When Crane stopped for a breather, Stan kept on running. Right after Crane had caught his second wind, Stan ran back to the *yagura,* squeezed along the second line of dancers, stopped, and turned toward him. With a big smile on his face, he waved goodbye, and took off running, again.

In the waning light of the red setting sun, Crane was right behind Stan. Then, bright blue stutter-flashes from camera flashbulbs flared into Crane's wide-open eyes. As if he were one of the sprits being welcomed back to the land of the living and against the backdrop of a red sky, Stan vanished in a brilliant flash of purple light.

CHAPTER 20

A few days after Stan had eluded Crane with a setting sun spilling rose light thought the sky Crane walked past four kimono-clad ladies and headed for the Chitose River Bridge. As he walked into the approaching night, a pack of ASA men walked in front of him. When they got to the bridge, their drunken uproar carried back to Crane until they weaved across the bridge, turned right, staggered down concrete steps next the water, and stepped into Aki's Bar.

Before Crane got to the bridge, he looked toward the river. A gleam appeared in the distance. As he walked toward the gleam, wild grass screened lights glowing on the water. When he walked closer, candle-lit, colorful lanterns, called *Toro Nagashi*, signaling the Bon Festival's end, were slowly floating down the river.

While Crane walked to the edge of the riverbank for a better look, on the other side of the river, a ghost-like mist rose from the grass to a height of three meters. At the water's edge, upriver, the flickering of a stationary green light caught Crane's interest. He had to see what it was.

As he walked along the river and neared the light, he discovered the flickering light was coming from a small paper lantern snagged on the branch of a small bush. The candle inside the lantern had tilted to one side. He crouched down, straightened the candle, and freed the little lantern. Glowing steady and bright green, it gracefully floated down the Chitose River where it would flow through the city and then enter the Ishikari Plain.

Crouching down and watching the lantern, Crane became aware of how quiet it had become. Noise from the drums of the bon dance had ceased. Birds no longer sang, and voices of drunken GI's had gone silent. The slight tinkle from a small stream tumbling over rocks angling its way to the river was a pleasing change. Speckled with the lights of colorful paper lanterns, the river gave off an aura of peace and happiness of another world and symbolically signaled the ancestral spirit's return to the world of the dead.

Crane was about to standup, but foot falls on his left caught his attention. He stayed crouched down and peered through the flimsy screen of foliage on a little bush. About five meters away, Stan walked to the edge of the water, lit a candle in a yellow lantern, and gently placed it in the water. With a smoldering stub of a cigarette poised in front of his lips, he watched the lantern float away. After looking around, he pulled a golf ball size sphere from his pocket and placed it under a rock.

Crane couldn't believe it was going to be that easy. All he would have to do was wait for Stan to go away, go over to the rock, pick up the E-Brite sphere, and be on his way back home.

Stan jolted and seemed to vanish into the darkness. Crane scanned the dark area around the riverbank. Except for a small dark roll in the land, a ways from the rock, everything looked okay. He walked over, lifted the rock, and picked up the golf-ball size sphere. As he examined it, he realized that he had another sphere exactly like the one he was holding in his hand. He was amazed how a bad thing had worked out in his favor.

As a teenager, because he had lost his passbook, the local bank had cheated him out of twenty-three dollars in savings he had deposited. He was so mad he decided he would be his own bank. In high school metal shop, he crafted a stainless-steel curved chamber. Thirty centimeters long, the curved chamber looked to be part of an underwater steel-reinforced, concrete storm drain pipe that was hidden underwater and emptied into the Shenango River. After three days of swimming three meters down to the pipe, holding his breath, and hand drilling the bolt holes into the concrete pipe, he finally bolted his chamber onto the curved side of the pipe. A strip of rubber sealed the tiny sliding door at the bottom of the chamber and created an air lock. No matter how furious the raging Shenango River became or how high it rose, the airlock always stayed dry. Even if a person found the chamber and suspected it contained something of value, they would never be able to hold their breath long enough to figure out how to open the little trap door. Although he had to swim down to deposit money or valuables, the bank never again cheated him out of money.

And now, in his hand he held the twin to the sphere he had placed in his chamber. When Stan, and the men he had been with, picked up Capone's vault, the sphere had been on the bed of the truck. At the time, even though it had fallen out of Capone's vault, Crane didn't think the sphere had any significance, and the expectation of getting seventy-eight thousand dollars was more important than a little sphere. He had placed the sphere in his pocket, and in the excitement of becoming wealthy, he had not told anyone about it. When he had swum down and placed two hundred thousand dollars into the chamber, he had placed the sphere in there, too.

He had often wondered if he had placed the sphere in his chamber because of something his ear had picked up in Stan's voice, or it had been one of those feelings. Now he was glad he had placed the sphere in the chamber. He wasn't sure, but if people suspected he had a sphere, they would keep him alive until they forced him to reveal where it was.

He turned to walk away from the river. Suddenly, like a shadow in the mist, the small dark roll in the land sprang up.

It was Stan.

Crane's top of the hill training echoed in his mind. "Give someone what they are looking for and their defenses go away. Stay low and the target probably won't see you." Not only had Crane let his defenses fade, he had forgotten that most people are used to vertical targets. He should not have been looking for somebody standing upright.

Stan came toward Crane. Tensing for a fight, Crane bent over and got ready to grasp the throwing knife he had strapped to the side of his leg.

The top of the hill had taught him two methods of using a knife. When a person rushed forward, the knife was held in front of oneself. Holding the knife point upward, the stab would be an upward thrust. Once the blade was in, it could be turned. That would be the end of the victim's heart and life.

The second method, used to wipe out a sentry, was sneaking up from behind. Stabbing in the back would be easy. But if one were going to take the body away without a trace of blood, a stab in behind the collarbone would cause most of the blood to flow into the lungs, and there would very little blood. But both methods would give the sentry time to raise an alarm. To prevent this, the voice box had to be cut. And a throat was tougher than people thought. A slit wouldn't be enough. The point of the knife directed at the voice box which was under the chin and an inch or two below the ear, would create the maximum damage in minimum time.

In training, Crane had practiced the moves on life-like mannequins and had gone over them in his mind hundreds of times. He had gotten used to every detail of its horrid aspects and had reached a state of detachment that is born of habit. If he had to, he would disable Stan's voice box.

When he was three meters away, Stan held up his hand in a halting gesture. "I don't want to fight you, Crane."

Expecting a trick, Crane stayed bent over and wary. "Why not?"

Stan lowered his hand. His voice sounded friendly, but his eyes were cautious. "Because, you're a tricky little bastard. And I think we have something in common."

"Like what?"

"Wherever we go, chaos follows."

Crane looked for a flicker of motion, a facial tick, an eye expression, or any body-language that would indicate Stan had a weapon. He saw none. He took his hand away from the knife and straightened up. Staying ready to drop down and leg-sweep Stan's legs out from under him, Crane guardedly stepped close.

Stan bowed his head and held his palms downward. "Take it easy, Crane. If I were going to hurt you, I would have already done it."

He had a good point, but Crane still wasn't buying it. "How do I know you didn't place the E-Brite there for an agent to pick up?"

"Dah!" As if he wanted to make Crane laugh, Stan's mouth hung slack in an idiot's gape. "What makes you think I wasn't watching you?"

He had Crane again. Watching him, Stan could have eliminated him at any time. "Okay," Crane said. "If you were watching me, why were you doing it?"

"I need your help, but after our little fiasco at Lake Shikostsu, I knew I couldn't approach you unless I could find a way to make you trust me enough to not give my location away." He tilted his head toward the sphere in Crane's hand. "Why do you think I let you have the E-Brite?"

"I don't know. A person would have to be crazy to try to hide this thing here."

"Crazy?" Stan questioned. "With your intellectual reasoning, I find it hard to believe you are acting like you cannot accept the absurdities of the mind."

Crane had an idea what Stan was getting at, but he had not run into anyone who had agreed with his inner most thoughts about the use of the word crazy. "Are you saying that words like crazy are convenient labels that mentally limited people use to describe anything they don't understand?"

As if he had been in the darkness with some kind of knowledge-searching lantern and had finally found someone else who was able to explore the far reaches of the mind, Stan's face beamed amazement.

"I would have to agree," he said. "Crazy is one of the words sometimes used by lazy and limited minds."

Suddenly Crane felt a friendship with Stan, sort of like, when a person comes upon a strange dog and immediately knows it won't bite. But he was still leery. If he started to care about Stan, he would expose the feelings in his heart to a potential wound. If he didn't make Stan a friend and Stan got killed, Crane would avoid the pain of his death.

Crane looked at the E-Brite in his hand. "What do we do now?"

Stan didn't answer right away.

Watching the colorful lanterns float down the Chitose River, Crane stood silent, biding his time until Stan was ready to speak.

"You have two choices," Stan began. "You can take the E-Brite, go home, and get on with your life. Or, you can join up with me."

Crane wasn't ready for another incident like the one he had had in Vietnam. "I'm just a Spec/5," he said. "I'm not qualified to join you."

"Maybe it's my duty to society to take on an apprentice." Stan smiled in Crane's direction. "How else are you going to learn?"

Crane was sick of learning and committing things to memory because they were classified, and he didn't want to be exposed to pain if Stan were suddenly eliminated. He stared into the water. It reminded him of his plan. Somewhere back in the states, his cabin with his money-making porch was waiting to be built. There, he wouldn't have to worry about a friend living through a single day. "What if I don't want to join up with you?"

"If you don't, I won't stop you from going home," Stan said, but a glint formed in his eye. "Before you make up your mind, let me buy you a beer and tell you how it really is."

Instead of going to a bar, they walked to a small grocery store where Stan bought two huge brown bottles of Sapporo beer. They walked back to the river and sat next to the bush where Crane had crouched down. Using two hands, they sipped beer from the enormous bottles and watched a string of yellow and orange lanterns lazily making their way down the Chitose River.

After they drank enough so the bottles could be comfortably lifted with one hand, Stan began. "You don't actually know what the colonel is going to do with the E-Brite, do you?"

"He claims he is going to keep it out of the hands of people who want to blow up the world."

"Your colonel doesn't make a very good poster boy for the benefits of civilization." As if in thought, Stan held his bottle of beer in front of his mouth but didn't drink. "He doesn't care if the bad guys keep building missiles and setting off high-energy nuclear warheads until the little kid's bones are filled with strontium 90 and cows crap uranium." He took a drink and flashed Crane a slanted grin. "Did he tell you he plans to reproduce the E-Brite and sell it to every country in the world?"

"Excuse the label, but isn't that crazy?"

Stan answered smoothly. "Your great colonel believes that if all countries have the nuclear bomb, it will mean the end of all wars."

"You lost me."

"He believes in MAD, Mutual Assured Destruction. If all the countries of the world have the bomb, the retaliation effect would be the total destruction of the world, and all the countries would be afraid to use it. When all the weak countries have E-Brite, other countries will be forced to accept them as an equal world order."

"If there weren't so many mentally deficient leaders, his idea might have merit."

"Not really." Stan took a sip of beer. "Einstein knew if there were no means to make war, mankind would create them. When asked what kind of weapons the last men of earth would use if they survived a nuclear holocaust, he said, 'Clubs.'" Stan's eyebrows above his slanted eyes went up. "It doesn't matter if the bomb comes from a Russian missile or a little spear in a person's hand, it will still kill all of us."

From somewhere upriver the sound of car doors clunking and driving away traveled across the water.

Stan held his bottle of beer in one hand and waved his other hand around. "And your colonel believes more. He told me there are millions of people being born every week. That's too many mouths to feed. They are gnawing the planet into a wasteland. Our technology can't keep pace with need." He turned his head and met Crane's brown eyes. "The colonel actually laughed, said, 'Don't be overcome with apocalyptic fear. If a few countries use the E-Brite and a few hundred thousand worthless people are killed, so what? I'll still be alive, and the planet will be saved.'"

"The colonel's just a little cog in a big wheel," Crane said and studied the E-Brite sphere in his hand. "How is he going to get a hold of this E-Brite without someone else in the government knowing he has it?"

"Simple, he'll have you send it by diplomatic pouch. Under the need to know, he'll be the only person who will have access to it."

"But I'll know."

"Only if he lets you live." Stan held up one finger. "Nothing can be predicted with accuracy. When one thing goes wrong, all plans fall apart. People like you and I can always screw everything up for people like the colonel, and remember, you're only a Spec/5." He shrugged and took a sip of beer. "Who's going to miss you?"

Crane looked at the bottle in his hand. For some reason, Plato's "Only the dead have seen the last of war," entered his mind. No matter what countries did or said, sooner or later there would be another war, and the E-Brite wouldn't make it very pretty.

"I understand what you're saying," he said. "But if I join up with you, I'll be AWOL."

Stan flashed Crane an all-knowing smile. "I spent hours plowing through your background. The agency has perfected a magic mathematical formula called the upper confidence limit. It's used for weighing confidence against the potential for failure and they get cranky when they are not allowed to apply it. And they applied it to you. Not only do you know things others are not privileged to know, you're special, a real untouchable. Special Activities Division doesn't allow anyone to mess with you. Actually, they have been led to believe you are searching for a portable cipher scrambling machine similar to Japan's purple machine."

Crane felt his forehead wrinkle with bafflement. "That's news to me."

"You're in the army and you're not in the Army. You do not actually exist as being in Chitose. It's a weird situation. If you go AWOL, the Kuma Station's military police might pick you up, but they'll be notified that you were on temporary duty."

"If I'm not officially in the Army, then what about the reserve meetings back in the states that I am supposed to be going to for two years? Won't they wonder why I'm not there?"

"You have been assigned to a reserve unit in Missouri. When your reserve unit is over one hundred miles away, you do not have to attend meetings. As far as they're concerned, you're in New York, working for the Erie Railroad as a claim agent."

"This doesn't' seem possible. I'm no great brain. They went to a lot of trouble to get me here and find you. I still say they could have used someone else."

Stan waved his hand down. "No way. You are the only person who could ever get close to me."

"Because I saved your life?"

"Maybe, and maybe it's because we both know Neal."

Crane looked at him in astonishment. "Do you remember Neal from when you got the vault?"

"Not only that, we have been together for a while. We're on the same team."

Crane's brain snapped to attention. "What?"

"As you know, when you're on Neal's team you're in for a wild ride."

"That's a fact I have lived. But I haven't been trained as well as you Neal have been trained. To keep the colonel from seeing what I'm doing, I'll have to walk low enough to walk under a snake."

A smile formed on Stan's face. "It isn't that bad. This town's full of spooks and spies, but most will never suspect a humble Spec/5 of being in on something as big as this. In addition, the colonel believes he has you convinced that I'm on the wrong side, and that you'll do what he considers is the right thing."

Crane knew that given time anybody could become a part of any system. He wasn't going to let anyone make him part of a phony system. "I don't always do what I'm expected to do."

"The colonel doesn't really know that," Stan said. "In addition to having the ability to find things nobody else can find, he believes you are one of the many who, for the good of the country, will blindly do what you're told to do, even if it's wrong."

"The colonel's got the wrong person," Crane said. "Way back in junior high school, for the good of the school, the kids in our run-down neighborhood won the championship. The next year, when it came time to be picked for varsity, rich kids who had trouble standing upright were picked for the team, and all of us slum kids were cut."

A little bright-red paper lantern snagged on a strand of grass on the shore. Stan extended the toe of his shoe and pushed the lantern back into the slow-moving current. "Did you ever stop to think you weren't any good."

"Sure did. But we had a kid that was a Golden Gloves Boxing champion. Another kid could run faster than anybody on the team. Three kids were extremely strong. We were all coordinated, and because we swam in the strong currents of the Shenango river and just about lived in the woods, when other players were exhausted, laying around on the field, we weren't even breathing hard."

"Why do you think they cut you?"

"We were different. Our warmups were the other kid's workouts." Crane frowned at the unpleasant memory. "Most people don't read the local hometown paper or watch a certain TV channel because they're looking for facts or something different. They do it because it validates what they already believe. It seems people don't have the brain capacity to accept new things. They couldn't accept the fact that kids from the slums could continually win football games."

Stan watched the red lantern float away. "I'm glad they did cut you from the team."

For a moment, Crane was confused. "What?"

A sly smile formed of Stan's lips. "If they wouldn't have cut you, you wouldn't be here. You would have become some spoiled high school jock that got sucked into a familiar system the common people believe is freedom."

Crane gave his head a vigorous shake. "I don't understand what you're saying."

"Teachers and professionals are at the mercy of those in charge of their salaries. They are not self-reliant. Actual free people are self-reliant. They work for themselves and pay themselves according to their own intelligence. Free people don't have to spend their lives joining unions and begging for wages. They have enough common sense to control their own lives."

A beat from one of the bon dance drums echoed into the night.

Looking toward the sound, Stan tensed for action. "Probably a drunken GI playing around." He relaxed and raised a finger. "In in other countries, there are a lot of things you can't do. In America, you have the freedom to control your life."

Crane didn't' want to admit it, but Stan was right. In many countries, Crane would not be able to own land or even begin his plan to have people drive up to his cabin and give him money. Without the freedom to place his plan into action, there was not much incentive to go on living.

He gave a resigned sigh. "I guess you're right. The sooner I can get back to the states the better."

"So…" Stan said and paused. "Regardless of what the colonel is going to do with it, you're taking the E-Brite and going home?"

"Why not? I don't think the colonel is the only person in charge of the E-Brite. And besides, if it's so important to keep it out of his hands, why can't we get more people to help?"

Stan gave Crane an appraising stare. "I'll let you answer your own question."

Crane thought for a moment. There were elements in the regular army that hated the Army Security Agency. In order to brush the agency people aside and keep them out of the fight, the regular army would seize any opportunity to make the agency look unnecessary. The regular army had many egos to feed, and not enough operations to satisfy their voracious appetites for unearned glory and undeserved recognition. In a special operator's world, bureaucratic bungling and narrow-minded military strategy, used for combat, did not work. Crane's own experience had shown that when it came to questioning a procedure or an order, a few agency people were not smarter that the average person. They hated the agency just as much as they hated the army, and that kind of attitude could compromise a mission. Once in a while they'd show a flash of intelligence, but it was usually self-serving or malicious. They were like the person in Eiko's Bar who had used a cajoling tone of charm and flattery to praise a sergeant and then walked down the street and condemned the sergeant as a fool and a moron. They'd talk to you with up-front affability and agree something was wrong, but in the end, they still surrendered to the antiquated procedure of doing what they were told to do. The colonel would tell them what to do, and they would do it. It was just an idiot rule of the establishment. Although they were too ignorant to know it, it was a good thing those kinds of people were never given access to sensitive information and were left to wallow in low-level positions of no great significant importance.

"I see what you mean," Crane said. "I've seen many agency people who were one hundred percent right, back down from a lowly GS-4 just because he was from NSA."

Stan nodded. "And they accept that as routine. Some don't want to believe there's a language that's not their language. You seem to have a pretty good idea what we'll be up against. I don't want to be alone in this fight. Why do you think you're here?"

"If I weren't here, the army would have made my life miserable or put me in jail."

"That's not the real reason and you know it."

Crane had an idea what Stan was getting at but he wasn't sure. He looked to Stan. "Can you tell me why am I here?"

Stan turned and looked at Crane out of those black careful eyes. “There are some things people can no accept or understand,” he said. “A little knowledge makes some content, and some are not content with all knowledge.”

“I’ve noticed that.” Breed replied. “Most people in the military only want to know enough to get along from day to day. And some only want to know only enough to progress in their particular field.”

“That’s true.” Stan raised a finger. “However, there will always be a few who are not content with all knowledge. They want to reach out farther, and still farther.” He stared at Breed. “I believe you are one of those few. Tell me the reason you’re here.”

Stunned by what Stan had told him, Crane didn’t answer right away. When he did, he replied, “I don’t really know. Maybe it’s just the way I am.”

“Which way are you?”

“I have always fought for the little guy.”

“Maybe you hate the big guy.”

“That could be it. I don’t like the big guys because of the smug attitude they get when they get away with things the little person can’t.”

“Maybe it’s just the right thing to do?”

“I guess you’re right. I don’t know why, but I have always tried to do the right thing.”

Stan shot him a conspiratorial look. “Me too. Maybe it’s a disease. Maybe it’s some unknown force we can’t control.”

“Sometimes I wonder if it’s worth it.” Crane made a helpless gesture. “Usually, when I do the right thing, people act like they hate me and won't lift a finger to help."

"And you'll never get any thanks. Knowing the ingenuity of men when it comes to blowing each other up, do you think going home is the right thing to do?"

Crane knew going home wasn't the right thing to do. Inside, he laughed at his sudden change in plans. Staring into the flowing water, he softly said, "No."

"So, you're not taking the E-Brite and going home?"

Crane wanted to go home. But some unknown force, he couldn't control, seemed to be guiding him. And he was beginning to feel Stan could be a real friend.

"I can't go home," he said. "Some things are not about money."

Stan lifted his bottle of beer in a toasting gesture. "Welcome aboard."

Crane lifted his bottle. Together, they clinked the heavy brown bottles, took a sip of beer, leaned back on their elbows, and stared across the river.

"Sometimes when I do things like this," Stan said, "I feel like I have the brain power of a gnat. And this is one of those times. But this time it won't be the freedom of the little man we'll have to fight for. This time it will be a fight for the existence of man."

Crane felt his brain power was inadequate, too. The magnitude of teaming up with Stan and trying to do such an enormous task made him feel he had to be insane. But like every difficult thing he had ever tired, this task was not beyond hope.

He reached out and offered his hand in friendship. "When do we start?"

Grasping Crane's hand in a firm grip, Stan smiled. "First, we have to find Neal. He knows where the real E-Brite is."

Crane looked at the fake E-Brite in his hand. "What?"

"His girlfriend, Piper, should know where he is."

Crane's hart jumped with excitement. "Neal was alive and so was Piper. Where is she?"

"The last time I talked to Neal, he said she would find us. Until then, you can go back to the base and play army."

Crane' felt his brow go up in surprise, but he immediately regained his composure. Although he would rather look for Piper and Neal than go back to the base, he sarcastically replied, "Nothing would please me more."

CHAPTER 21

After meeting with Stan, Crane had been so exhausted that he just wasn't in the mood to go back to the base and put up with army ignorance that would make it almost impossible for him to rest. He decided to get a hotel room and go back to the base the next day.

When he awoke in the hotel room, it was night, but the reflection of a light from the outside kept the room dimly lighted. He scanned the room. The walls were dark, but he could make out the dark figure of a woman sitting on chair in the corner. For a moment, he lay absolutely still. No one had ever snuck up on him before. He didn't know if he were afraid or in a state of disbelief.

As the idea that the woman had managed to get into the room without him hearing her, percolated through the fog in his brain, the woman spoke. "I see you're awake, Crane." Her voice was soft and low, almost a whisper.

Crane jumped up, ready to defend himself.

"She held up her hand. Don't get excited, Crane. Stan sent me. He wants to meet with you."

"Why didn't he come here?"

"He is being followed. He didn't want to take a chance and get caught."

"What does he want?"

I only get paid to deliver the message. "You'll have to ask him." She stood and turned to leave. "Are you coming?"

Outside, they walked to the outskirts of Chitose and waded through a field of tall grass. When they were at a line of small trees that looked like a good place for an ambush Crane slowed but kept walking. After they skirted a clump of brush and walked past a few trees, he stopped.

The woman stopped, too. "What's the matter?"

"I think we've gone far enough."

A pleading look filled her face. "Please?" She pointed ahead. "It's just right after that tree."

Crane scanned the area beyond the tree. Nothing looked suspicious. "All right," he said, walked past the tree, and stopped in a small secluded clearing.

Suddenly, her hands gripped Crane's right sleeve. "All right!" she shouted into the darkness. "Here he is."

Two men leaped out of the shadows and stood in front of Crane. The tall one with the slender build and narrow face didn't seem to be a threat, but when Crane looked into the eyes of the muscular man, it was like looking to the fierce eyes of a mountain lion, all poised to leap.

"Tell us where the E-Brite is or we'll beat it out of you."

Crane was amazed that someone was going to use force to get him to tell them something when truth serums and other much better ways of getting information were available. Evidently, they were trying to scare information out of him.

In an attempt to prevent Crane from using his right hand, the woman tightened her grip on his sleeve. Then she planted her high heels firmly into the ground and leaned backwards.

Long ago Crane had learned to use his left as well as his right. Boxing, where a left is of first importance, helped a lot, but since he was a kid, he had deliberately used his left hand for many things. He could saw, hammer, eat, and do just about anything with his left that he could do with his right. And shooting was one of those things. But if he shot and killed them all, there would be a disturbance that could hinder his chances of finding Neal.

Without even thinking, his left hand came from the ground up and hit the muscular man.

The woman was so surprised that an American could use his left hand so efficiently that she lost the grip she had on Crane's sleeve, fell backwards, and hit the ground at the same time the muscular man did.

The arms on the slender man were much longer than Crane's, but the man seemed to know nothing about fighting. He took a long, clumsy swing. Crane grabbed the man's wrist and jerked him forward. When the man resisted, Crane hooked the man's ankle with his foot then released the man's hand and pushed him back. The man's feet flew up and out from under him. His rear end hit the ground so hard that he let out a painful squeal. Shocked and bewildered, he just sat there.

The muscular man rolled over, got to one knee, and swayed to his feet. Heavy bones in his face looked like a stone wall, and the skin on his hands looked like tough leather. Before Crane could react, the man slammed a solid right to Crane's head.

Crane staggered and backed away. The man charged him. Crane sidestepped and hit the man with a left hook. It knocked the man back on his heels and opened his cheek like it had been cut with a knife, but he didn't fall over. Crane stepped in for the kill, but the man sprang forward, both hands punching. Crane staggered but fired a left at close quarters. It didn't slow the man down. And the woman was trying to distract Crane by hitting him with a flimsy branch she had broken off a tree.

With every punch, Crane ducked, weaved, and swayed his shoulders. He was ripping both hands into the man's heaving belly, but he knew he couldn't hold the man off boxing. And that little branch stung. He took a long step that lowered his level. Now the man was punching air. Crane swung around the back of the man and wrapped both of his hands around his waist. Just as he had easily done to many wrestling opponents, using the strength in his legs and arching his back, in a move called the "back arch", he arched his back, thrust the man upward, and fell backwards. Not knowing how to fall, the man hit the ground head first. His neck turned sideways. Something snapped. A painful grunt and a whoosh of air flew from his mouth. He struggled to get to his feet, but fell back to the ground in a helpless heap. He was out or dead from a broken neck.

For a moment, the woman stood with her mouth agape. As if a switch had been pulled, the branch fell from her hands. It seemed that before the branch hit the ground the woman was gone. When Crane looked to where the slender man had been sitting, he was gone, too.

Crane didn't go back to the hotel. Instead, he went into an all-night bar and sat where he could watch the door, at a table near the wall. Waiting for daylight, he nursed a beer and thought about the ambush and if Piper could have set it up. He knew a beautiful woman could become habituated to using her beauty and knows that men are not only willing but eager to serve them. To get what they want, their smiles, frowns, and their graciousness can be used on all ages and all types of men. With all his heart, Crane hoped Piper hadn't done this, and he wondered how many people were after the E-Brite. But he couldn't dwell on it. He had to do what needed to be done.

When the fingers of dawn felt their way down the street, life began to stir. While the working people began to go about their business, Crane got on the bus to go back to Kuma Station and sat in the front seat. At the first stop, to his surprise, Piper got on the bus. Without the slightest hint of acknowledgment, she walked right past and sat in the seat behind him.

He wanted to jump up, sit beside her and hold her in his arms. But he couldn't risk being seen with her. At the next stop, she stood up to get off the bus. As she walked past him, she slipped and caught her balance by placing her hand on his chest. Looking at him with eyes, almost too beautiful to believe, she said, "*Gomen nasai,*" excuse me, and surreptitiously placed a note into the pocket of his suit coat.

Crane knew that in Japan whenever a person feels something should be said, but doesn't know quite what to say, they should come back with either *Sumimasen* or *Dõmo.* These words cover everything. Japanese do a lot of bowing from the waist, but it is quite formal. So, Crane bowed his head and replied, "*Dõmo,*" Think nothing of it.

After Piper got off the bus, Crane palmed the note, took out his wallet and opened it. With one hand, he secretly placed the palmed note into the wallet. Then as if the note had been there all the time, he took the note out and read it.

It read, Get off at the next stop.

He got off at the next stop, walked across the street, and waited.

Twenty minutes later, another bus pulled up and stopped. Piper got off, crossed the street, and walked right past him.

Bending over and pretending to tie his shoe, he watched her. She turned down an ally and was out of sight. Crane walked in the opposite direction, circled around, and looked to where the ally met the other street. When he turned the corner, the street was lined with restaurants, all kinds of shops, and a few bars. Here and there, bicycles rested on kickstands in front of shops that had various merchandise for sale displayed on hooks and strings. There were so many items for sale that they spilled onto the sidewalks, some items extended beyond the sidewalks and onto the street. Above, colorful banners, neon rectangular signs, and streamers lined the street. Right above Crane, one string of paper lanterns hung across the street.

A Japanese man called Aki, (Awk-ee) was on his way to his bar next to the Chitose River. Like most Japanese businessmen, he wore a fresh clean white shirt and black pants. Here and there a few Japanese people stood around or walked the street stopping to buy or just look.

As Awki walked past, he smiled at Crane and Crane smiled back.

There were only two cars parked on the side of the street. To avoid hitting people, any cars coming down the street would have to slowly crawl along and squeeze past pushcarts and people.

Searching for Piper, Crane weaved his way through the people and bicycles that interlaced the crowded sidewalk, and his eyes continued to be drawn to the flashing signs that seemed to be on every building. He passed overflowing fruit stands, and street vendors with various wares.

After he had made his way down the busy and crowded street, he spotted Piper. She was looking in a store window.

Crane zipped right past her, slowly walked past a row of bicycles, and stepped into a bar with a red sign written in *kanji*.

Inside, he took a seat at the end of the bar. When the girl behind the bar came over, he held his forefinger and thumb two inches apart and said, *"Chiisai,"* which meant small, but was Chitose slang for small beer.

The girl said, "*Chotto,*" just a minute, and turned to get the beer.

As Crane's eyes adjusted to the darkness of the bar, he hoped Piper would walk through the door. The girl brought the small bottle of beer, poured it into a glass and asked, "Would you like anything else, or would you just like to talk for a while?"

Keeping his eyes on the entrance, Crane waved his hand down. "Thank, you," he said. "I'm waiting for someone."

"Okay," the girl replied with a most cheerful voice, took a few steps to the side, and busied herself doing something on the shelf under the bar.

Crane lifted his glass to take a sip of beer, but when he looked toward the door, awe-struck, he held the glass in front of his lips.

Piper stood in the door. With the sun at her back, she looked like some kind of an angel that had just beamed down from heaven.

As if in a trance, Crane gently lowered the glass of beer onto the bar and stared at her.

Piper stepped out of the light, and like a gentle spring breeze, she waltzed toward him. When she gracefully sat next to him, he couldn't help but notice her beautifully shaped legs. Her sincere smile and her almond eyes created an aura of love Crane had never felt before. When he leaned close to her, although he wasn't touching her in any way, he felt they were one. When he looked into her eyes, the only thing he could think of to say was, "Long time, no see."

As she stared at the bruise on Crane's face, she took on a serious look. "I'm so sorry about last night. I went back to the hotel and tried to warn you, but you weren't there."

"I don't have the E-Brite. Why did they come after me?"

"Chimppeenos thought you were Neal. Somehow, they found out there is a reward for the sphere that Neal has."

"Who are these Chimppeenos?"

"They're not part of the Yakuza. You should have no more trouble from them."

One of the biggest organized Japanese crime syndicates were the *Yakuza.* They were also known as *gokudõ,* and the police called them *bõoryokudan,* which meant violent groups. Crane was glad the Chimppeenos were not part of that syndicate. What he didn't like about the Chimppeenos was that they were a wanna-be gang that only attacked helpless victims. Because they weren't very good at it, they only attacked when they could outnumber the victim. Crane recalled the day when three Green Berets who had come from Vietnam were sitting at a bar trying to get a little rest and relaxation. Two Chimppeenos came into the bar. Apparently they had never seen Americans wearing green berets, and figured the Americans wearing such silly hats were gay, or wouldn't put up much of a fight.

The two Chimppeenos went outside and gathered their forces. While ten waited outside, the two went back inside the bar, started a fight, and invited the three Green Berets outside.

Once outside, twelve Chimppeenos surrounded the Green Berets. The three Green Berets walked to the center of the street and stood back to back. The Chimppeenos attacked, but most were thrown into the air, back-fisted, karate-kicked, and physically beaten. After most of the Chimppeenos were lying in the street and on the sidewalk, a belligerent Chimppeeno continued to charge a Green Beret. After being warned to stop, and not doing so, a Green Beret lifted the Chimppeeno by one arm and slammed the arm against the cement telephone pole. The arm snapped and the remaining Chimppeenos walked, crawled or limped away. Then, the Green Berets, brushed themselves off. And, as if nothing had happened, they went back into the bar and continued drinking.

"Only three Chimppeenos came at me," Crane said. "And one was a woman. I wonder why they didn't send more?"

"There is no honor among thieves. They did not want to share the reward." She looked toward the bar entrance. "I really missed you. I wish we could be together a long time." She frowned. "But someone may be following me."

Crane gently took her hand in his. "Will it ever end?"

"Only after you find Neal, but then they'll be after you and him, too."

"Piper," he said, his tone vibrant with feeling. "I'd rather they were after me than after you."

"Thank you for caring." She looked down. For a moment, she trembled, and a single tear ran down her cheek. She took a deep breath and looked up. "Are you sure you want to find Neal?"

"I don't really have a choice."

She placed a gentle hand on his shoulder and nodded in understanding. "Maybe that's why I fell for you."

With her hand in his, Crane placed his hand on his heart. “When this thing’s over, I hope we can be together.”

Sadness filled her eyes. “It may never be over.”

“I wouldn’t say that. Even a wind-up clock has to stop sometime.”

“You may not have much faith in women’s intuition,” she said and tilted her cute head. “I haven’t much myself, but there’s one thing I know. No matter what happens or where we end up, someday we’ll be together.”

Crane wanted to believe her. But he knew better, and it caused a sharp pain to shoot through his chest and leave behind an ache. Regardless of his pain, he wanted to keep hope alive. With an upbeat attitude, he managed to smile and say, “Cheer up. We’re together now.”

She forced a smile. “I don’t know where Neal is, but one of two men who will be at Aki’s Bar tonight will know where he is.”

“That gives us time.”

With her eyes twinkling and her silky black hair flowing over her shoulder, she glanced sidewise at him. “Do you want to go somewhere private?”

Crane looked into her lovely face. “I thought you would never ask.”

He didn’t want to take his best friend’s girl and it caused a sudden pang of guilt. He let loose of her hand. “Are you sure you’re not Neal’s girl?”

"I could never be Neal's girl. He's a good friend who helped my family. Although I love Neal, he is like my brother."

Now that all guilt was gone, Crane's heart raced with anticipation. He wanted to hold her in his arms forever. The price of the *Chiisai* beer was one hundred fifty yen. He placed two hundred yen on the bar.

The girl behind the bar said, *"Dõmo,"* thank you.

Piper and he walked out into the street.

Suddenly Piper became playful. She was flouncing ahead of him.

When she stopped, she stood under a sign that read, Hotel.

As Crane walked toward her, his eyes swept the crowd on the other side of the street. Nothing seemed unusual, but he knew that didn't mean they were safe. For a moment, he thought about all that had transpired since the day Neal had placed him on the Huey.

Crane stopped next to Piper and looked to the door of the hotel. "Do you think it will be safe to go in?"

A look of mischief beamed from Piper's beautiful face. "It's elephant proof."

Crane looked at the door. It was flimsy and could be easily broken down by just about anybody. "How can this be elephant proof?"

Piper playfully opened the door and stood to the side. "Do you see any elephants in there?"

Crane looked inside. "No."

"Then it's elephant proof."

They laughed in unison and turned to enter.

As if she had been slapped, Piper stiffened.

Three men jumped in front of them.

Crane noticed a short, thick bodied man with a sickly face was a few steps behind the first man, and his eyes were straying around, looking for somebody, probably Neal.

Displaying broad and powerful shoulders and biceps bulging with muscle, the first man stood in front of Crane and blocked him. With his haggard face staring at Crane, the second man stood to the side and leaned his heavy forearm on the side of the building. Giving Crane a direct challenging look, the man blocked that avenue of escape.

The third man, of medium height and with a smooth face, gave Piper a hating stare, stepped behind her, and spread his legs in a wide blocking stance. "Going someplace?" His voice was low and threatening.

Piper's eyes widened in alarm.

Appalled, Crane wanted to cuss, but he didn't have time.

Piper dropped down to all fours and hopped under the man's spread legs. Before the man knew what was happening, using the power in her legs, she sprang to her feet. When her back drove into the man's crotch, he flew upward and off her back. Before he could land on her, Piper stepped to the side. Clunk! He fell to the sidewalk. She reared back and gave him a swift kick to the groin. The man curled into a fetal position and lay there moaning. As she took off running, she took one fleeing glance over her shoulder at Crane.

While Crane was watching her, the powerful shouldered man shoved him back against the building, and came at Crane so fast he nearly stabbed him, but Crane chopped his wrist and deflected the blade. Then he grabbed the man's wrist and jerked him forward. When the man threw his foot forward to catch his balance, Crane hooked the heel of his foot behind the man's knee, and at the same time, he pushed the man backwards. The man went down hard. The knife flew from his hands.

But he jumped back up and took a roundhouse swing at Crane. Crane ducked. The man's fist slammed into the cement side of the building. Crack! The man grabbed his broken fist and squealed in pain. Crane hit him with a powerful right cross. To Crane's surprise, the man's teeth broke under the impact. Crane's second punch to the man's stomach lifted him off his feet. Groaning in agony, the man bent over and fell to the sidewalk.

Crane knew Piper was still in danger, but before he could protect her, he had to get past the thick bodied man. But the man didn't try to stop him. As if it were a delayed reaction, he turned. He and two other men ran after Piper. Crane could tackle one of the men, but the other one would pounce on Piper.

He sprinted past the two men, ran around a crowd of people, and stopped at the side of a produce cart. Just before the men pasted the other side of the cart, Crane grabbed the side of the cart and flipped on its side. Pears, apples, and whatever else was in the cart rumbled onto the street. When the men tried to run across the apples and pears, as if they were trying to run on marbles, they tripped, tumbled to the side, and fell to the pavement.

Crane turned and ran in the direction Piper had run.

After three blocks, there was no sign of her. He hoped Stan would know where to find her.

CHAPTER 22

After Chitose had sprawled lazily in the warm sunshine and hours after the sun had blinked to black, Crane and Stan met where a street formed a T at the ally that led to Bar Eiko. When Crane asked Stan if he knew where Piper was, Stan only shrugged and said, "She's very elusive. If she weren't, she wouldn't be alive."

Even though Crane couldn't accept the fact that he may never see her again, he needed to get on with the task of finding Neal.

After laughing about being fooled by the fake E-Brite, Stan and he turned right, passed a cement telephone pole, and walked a ways down the street and stopped at the Chitose River Bridge. Just to the right, cement steps lead to Aki's Bar. About ten meters from the river and about the size of a single car garage, Aki's Bar was nestled in the stone block foundation of a wooden building. Being bigger than most bars in Chitose, it had room for tables. A smoke-laden atmosphere had a suggestive odor of cheap perfume, alcohol, and a faint hint of kerosene from kerosene stoves used in in winter. Aki wasn't there but a thin and lovely girl behind the bar looked up. Although Japanese people hardly showed emotion, she swallowed hard. With her face looking like it could have been carved from granite, she ran into the room in the back of the bar.

As Stan and Crane walked past the tables, GIs gave them a quick look, glanced at each other, and went back to drinking beer and listening to Sergeant

Berry Sadler's "The Ballad of the Green Berets" flowing from a record player fed into speakers on the wall.

Crane and Stan sat at a table along the wall and watched. A GI got up from his table, stepped to the bar, and handed the girl a record. To have up to date American music, GI's often gave girls behind the bars records they had purchased the Post Exchange. After the girl placed the arm of the record player on the record, the GI was rewarded with Zager and Evans' "In the Year Twenty-five, Twenty-five" streaming throughout the bar.

When Zager & Evans sang about their visions for the year ninety-five, ninety-five, if man is still alive, Crane wondered if the colonel got the E-Brite, would man still be alive in nineteen-sixty-nine.

With the music playing at a comfortable level, but loud enough to block or distort what Stan and Crane were talking about, a girl with a trim figure and a soft, charming face, was seeing to their wants by going to get two large Sapporo beers.

Stan leaned toward Crane and talked low. "After Neal took the E-Brite from Burke, we were going to turn it in."

Crane was surprised. "Why didn't you?"

Stan's face tightened then relaxed. "Neal and I made a deal with the colonel, but he didn't honor it. When the Russian helicopter landed to pick up the E-Brite, I watched from the trench we had dug. Right after Neal gave the colonel's men a fake E-Brite, he took off running and dove into the trench." Stan quit talking and looked up.

The girl walked toward them. The red stars on the frosty cold bottles on the Sapporo beer labels seemed to flash the beginning of a good time. After the girl set the glasses on the table and poured the beer into the glasses, she stood back and waited.

Crane figured because the bar was bigger than other bars, and Aki wasn't there, she was waiting to be paid. He reached into his pocket and turned to Stan. "I'll get it."

Stan shook his head. "They put it on a bar bill. It's just like the other bars. We only pay after we're done." He looked to the girl. "She wants you name for the bar tab."

Crane didn't want his real name to get into the Chitose grapevine. It was said that if a GI sneezed, the information grapevine between the bars was so good that in five minutes the whole town of Chitose would know the GI had sneezed.

He looked to the girl and gave her a fake name. "Michael."

The girl nodded. "Michael, row the boat ashore?"

Crane nodded.

After the girl had gone back to the bar, Crane asked Stan, "Were you ever going to give the colonel the E-Brite?"

"If he had been on the up and up, all would have ended there. But after his men got the fake E-Brite, they began firing."

"You're lucky you're not dead."

"It wasn't luck. We didn't know if we could trust the colonel. To cover ourselves, before the helicopter came, we set up a cache of mortar rounds and booby-trapped them with Claymore mines. Right after the colonel's men started firing, we blew the catch up in their faces. Somehow the blast knocked the E-Brite out of Neal's pocket. But another big problem was that the Huey had radioactive plutonium aboard. Like a dirty bomb, the explosion spread the plutonium around the area. You were with Neal when he went in. He found the E-Brite and retrieved the plutonium. Then, so I could stay alive, he faked his death."

Crane was confused. "What do you mean *you* could stay alive?"

"As long as we have an E-Brite sphere or know where one is and the colonel doesn't, he won't have us killed."

As Crane's mind raced with deductive reasoning, a sudden realization flashed in his mind. "You're one of the men who picked up Al Capone's gold vault? You should have all kinds of protection."

"We *did* have all the protection we would ever need, but everybody has been eliminated."

At first, the words failed to register in Crane's mind. When the words did, he said, "I don't see how that could have happened."

"The amount of money involved in the E-Bright is more than anyone can imagine. Our money was no match for what their money bought." A tremor of concern passed over Stan's face. "The scary part is that the colonel doesn't know just how dangerous the sphere really is."

"He might," Crane said. "He told me Burke got plutonium from the Hue University reactor and managed to have it placed it into the E-Brite sphere. He said the exotic metal for the E-Brite was made in my home town at Sharon Steel."

Stan shifted in his chair and smiled at Crane. "Do you really believe that?"

Crane thought about the process that had been used to cover up the underground nuclear event called Long Shot that had been detonated on Amchitka Island: Pre-event-written reports stated that the event was fully contained, seals were swimming in the sea, trout were jumping in the pools, Arctic blue foxes were playing in the tundra, and sea gulls were flying over the island. But what really happened was that the containment cage failed, and the explosion had not stayed underground. The uncontrolled blast shook the island like a great earthquake measuring more than 8.0 on the Richter scale and killed much of the wildlife. Then a plume of radiation vented into the air. And the permanent low-pressure system carried the radiation to Shemya where it came down in a mist of rain.

This technique of adding familiar things that were not true to a lie, caused people to believe everything on Amchitka Island was the familiar way it had always been. They did not question the false reports. The colonel had said the steel for the E-Brite sphere had been made at Sharon Steel. Sharon Steel produced specialty steel. The colonel's little nugget of familiarity validated what Crane thought he already knew. It caused him to believe a lie. The colonel was a piece of leftover army garbage that never should have been a part of the ASA.

Crane remembered the motto of the law: *Falsus in uno, falsus in omnibus.* False in one thing, false in all. He nodded to Stan. "I did get sucked into believing him, but not anymore."

"Just to give you an idea of how ignorant the colonel really is..." Stan's face twisted into a distasteful smile. "There is no way plutonium could have been placed in the sphere, and the metal for it was not made in Sharon Steel. He claims all nuclear weapons are the same, but in reality, he only wants a share of the enormous amount of money the sphere can bring."

After being given over two million dollars in counterfeit money for Capone's gold vault Crane was having second thoughts about Stan. He gave Stan a hard stare. "Enlighten me."

"The sphere is not only nuclear, it contains anti-matter."

Crane had no idea what anti-matter was. Perplexed, he rolled his hand in encouragement. "So?"

"If anti-matter comes into contact with matter, tremendous energy is released. If they had found a way to place matter into the sphere, Vietnam would no longer exist."

Extremely interested, Crane continued to roll his hand. "And?"

"And, the energy released would have been thousands of times greater than any nuclear bomb."

At first, the devastating potential of the E-Brite sphere didn't register in Crane's mind. But the saying, "All that glitters is not gold," kept running over in his mind. In the past, the gold that encased the vault had made him wonder if it had another layer or something that was worth more than the gold.

And now he knew.

The spheres had been hidden somewhere in the vault. The real value of the vault had been the spheres. He didn't know if Stan knew that one of the spheres had somehow fallen out of wherever it had been hidden in the vault and that he had picked it up and hid it in the stainless-steel chamber attached to the concrete storm culvert that led into the Shenango River. And the colonel's lie could have been a ploy to find out if Crane had a sphere and where he hid it. If the spheres were as dangerous and as powerful as Stan had indicated, Crane couldn't fully trust Stan or anyone. He couldn't tell anyone where his sphere was.

He looked at Stan with contempt. "I don't know if I can trust you."

"You should. I saved your life."

Crane didn't believe him. "Really?"

"He had your pretty face right in his sights. If I wouldn't have shot him, your brains would still be in Nam."

With sudden realization, Crane turned toward Stan. "You were the man that had the Gyropistol. Just before you shot, you yelled, 'Happy Fourth of July!' And the mini rocket cut that VC's stomach open. And then you shot that VC that was going to shoot me? You were the angel on my shoulder?"

Smiling Stan slowly nodded. "Enough said?"

While they nursed their beers, all the GIs left the bar, but two Japanese men stayed, and the

Japanese bar maid continually refilled their glasses and offered pleasant conversation. It wasn't that she was looking for a date. Japan, being a service economy, entertaining patrons was her job. And she did it very well.

At the end of the bar, the man wearing a white baseball cap apparently didn't know this. Sitting next the other man, he was enjoying a party-like atmosphere and getting soused. Usually it wasn't a big deal, but the man or the other man in the bar had to be the person who could possibly lead Stan and Crane to Neal. To get into hearing range of both men, Crane and Stan got up from the table, sat at the bar, and waited to see which man it was.

As his party-like atmosphere slowed a bit, the man with the baseball cap seemed to be having trouble staying awake. His head drooped, but he jerked it up and burped loudly. His lips slackened and his eyes bulged and caused his heavy cheeks to looked sick and flabby.

The other man, wearing some kind of ill-fitting uniform, stood up. Hugging his beer as if he were protecting it from harm, he walked past the partying man, stopped in front of Crane, and smiled a too much beer puckish smile. There was something deep within the man that caused Crane to feel a stirring of inner rebellion. Instantly, he resented the man.

As the man stood there, Crane reached over and gently placed his hand on the baseball-hatted man's shoulder. "Do you know Neal?"

The man jerked his head up. Like a trapped animal with wide eyes, he seemed to fear Neal's name. He spun around, knocked his bottle of beer off the bar, and looked at Crane in surprise. And the other man did, too. With his eyes slanting at Crane without expression, the man with the ill-fitting uniform looked slowly around. Then as if seeking safety, his eyes darted everywhere. Apparently only finding fear, with his eyes blazing, he reached behind his back and pulled out a meat cleaver.

The girl behind the bar clutched her throat and let out a gasp of fear.

With every sense alert, Crane crouched down and grabbed the metal sides of a bar stool that had been bolted to the floor. In one motion, he pulled with his arms and straightened his legs. The wood below the bolts at the bottom of the stool cracked. Wood splintered. Crane ripped the stool from the flimsy floor. Then, he lifted the bar stool high. With almost negligent ease, he swung it down on the man's hand. The clever thumped onto the floor. Crane jumped up onto the bar and held the stool, ready to swing at the man's head.

The man held up his hands in defeat. "I only joking. Neal Sapporo."

The eyes of the man with the baseball cap flew wide open with surprise. His face purpled and his eyes grew mean. "Shut your big mouth."

Apparently, the man with the ill-fitting uniform was not supposed to tell anyone where Neal was.

Knowing Neal was thirty miles away in Sapporo, Crane and Stan no longer needed to be in the bar.

Cane looked to Stan.

Stan tilted his head toward the exit.

Crane wanted to just walk out of the bar. But he was held by suspicion that the two men may do something worse than pick up a meat cleaver, and they were blocking his exit. As a diversionary tactic, Crane directed his attention to the men, and yelled. "Here! Catch!" He tossed the stool to the man with the baseball cap and jumped up onto the bar. While the man involuntarily caught the stool and the other man bent over to pick up the meat cleaver, Stan ran out of the bar.

Still in a crouching position on the bar, Crane snatched a beer bottle off the bar and threw it like a football. It spun through the air. Clunk! The bottle hit the other man upside the head. He was dazed, but he still managed to grab the meat cleaver.

The ceiling was too low for Crane to walk down the bar. Walking in a crouching position would be too slow, too. From his crouching position, he leaned forward, somersaulted past the man, rolled off the top of the bar, and landed in an upright position. While the baseball-hatted man stood holding the stool with his mouth agape, Crane closed one eye to protect his night vision and burst from the all-night bar and ran up the cement steps. Safely standing on the Chitose River Bridge, a fierce morning sun blasted into his dark-adjusted eyes.

Although Crane and Stan now knew Neal was in Sapporo, they also knew he had been operating alone, and it was always difficult to find a lone operator. Lone operators were always elusive and immune to betrayal by inept subordinates. And to top it off, Neal was no ordinary solider. Before what Crane called "The wild days with Neal" he believed there was no possibility that John Dillinger or Al Capone had ever walked through his dump town neighborhood in Patagonia. But Neal had proven him wrong. And then there were the exaggerated stories of Neal's legendary exploits. Some people said he could actually walk on air.

If they were ever going to find Neal in Sapporo, Stan and Crane needed time to think things out. Crane didn't know when he was going to get another chance to eat or sleep. Using the old army rule: Every time you can sleep, sleep. Every time you can eat, eat. He went back to the base, ate and slept.

CHAPTER 23

The next evening, Stan and Crane stood inside the Chitose train terminal, waiting for the train to Sapporo. One thing Crane had noticed about Japan was that everything seemed to be clean. The floors of train and bus stations in the States were always covered with cigarette butts, gum, and spit. And the uncleanness gave off a feeling of sadness that only American train and bus stations have. But the Chitose train station floors were spotless. They didn't project sadness.

Outside, when people with closed umbrellas tucked under their arms walked under the lights of the station, Crane noticed that the tracks were spaced narrower than the American railroad tracks. But it wasn't important. No matter how wide or narrow the tracks were, they would still get a person to and from where they were going.

Crane reached under his suit coat, checked the 38 Super he had in his shoulder holster, and smoothed out his tie. He didn't usually carry a weapon or wear a white shirt and a tie, but things seemed to be getting serious. Wearing the white shirt and tie and sunglasses to cover his round, American eyes, and being that his hair was black, he could pass for Japanese.

In the 1930's John Dillinger discovered that the standard issue 38 Special, and the .45ACP didn't have the velocity to propel a bullet through a car windshield. When he found out that the 38 Super could not only go through a windshield and the thick metal of a car, it could also punch a hole straight through a bullet-proof vest at over forty-five meters away, the 38 Super became Crane's favorite weapon.

Crane liked the Super because it had a velocity and a bullet pressure equal to a 44 Magnum. Because the weapon had served Dillinger very well during his incredible string of bank robberies and impossible escapes, Crane had a feeling that it was a weapon that would bring him luck. And he would need luck: Neal could be extremely elusive. Once they spotted him, if they couldn't get closed enough for him to recognize them, he would believe he was being pursued by the colonel's men, and he would flee. If he did, he would almost impossible to follow.

On the train, Crane dropped into one of the plush upholstered seats and settled back for the ride. Even though it was already dark outside, the atmosphere inside the train wasn't anything like American train travel where people sit stolid in their seats and wish the trip was over. Once the train to Sapporo began moving, the Japanese reached into the overhead carry racks, took down picnic baskets, and flipped them open. Then they uncapped bottles of beverages and began to party. No use wasting an opportunity for a good time.

As the jovial mood began, Stan leaned back and closed his eyes. Crane leaned back, too. Before he closed his eyes, he spotted a Japanese man with a weird shaped head who looked to be costumed as a conductor. Crane recognized him as the man with the ill-fitting uniform and meat clever Stan and he had run into in Aki's Bar. The man kept looking around the car. His constant searching didn't bother Crane, but the dirt on his clothes and the faint odor of death, the man emanated, did. Japanese workers were precise. They cleaned up their work areas at the end of every day and washed up. A respectable Japanese man would never step out into public covered with dirt, like this man had done. Crane figured the man's name just had to be Filth.

With the knowledge that patience is the hunter's deadliest virtue, Crane waited for the man to do something out of the ordinary. And it didn't take long.

The dirty man reached behind his back, pulled out heavy duty wire cutters, and leaned over a seat. Then he reached up and cut the emergency stop cable.

"I fix," he said and smiled. When he stepped to the other side of the car, his harsh voice stopped every conversation in the car. "I takie off fish plate. Everybody die." He reached up and began to cut the emergency stop cable. If the train needed to be stopped, there would be no way a passenger could warn the engineer.

Crane yelled at him, "Hey, Filth! Don't do that."

"Why not?" Filth said with a flair that indicated he was accustomed to getting his own way.

"That cable's for emergency stops."

Filth flashed Crane a huge ear-to-ear smile. "This is emergency stop."

He cut the cable.

In that one single moment, Crane knew he was facing madness.

Filth exploded in anger. "Fook You!" In a flick of motion, he drew a throwing knife from his boot. With an underhand twist of his wrist, he threw the knife at Crane. The chrome blade blinked with a single flash of light and hissed through the air. Crane jerked out of its path so fast, he banged his head into the steel wall of the car. As the knife twanged off something next to his shoulder, pinwheels of stars danced in front of his eyes. He shook his head. The stars quit dancing.

From working on the Erie Railroad, Crane knew a fishplate was a piece of steel that held two ends of butted rails together. Somewhere up ahead, this filthy lunatic's accomplice had unbolted a fishplate. When the train's great weight ran over the loose rails they would fly apart, sending the wheels of the train onto the ground, causing the following cars to smash into the stopped cars.

Crane went to the end of the cut cable and pulled it. The train kept right on moving. He went to the other side of the car and pulled that cable, too. Still, the train kept right on moving.

The next car should have an uncut emergency brake cable. All Crane had to do was go into the next car and pull the cable.

As the train snaked around an S curve, Crane rushed toward the front door. Before he could get to it, yelling and shooing his arms at him, Filth yelled in Russian, "*Othyt', otbyt!*" Go away, and grabbed Crane by the arm.

Crane spun around. With enough force to drive his nose back up into his skull, he smacked his clinched fist into Filth's face. Filth staggered backwards, tripped over his own feet, and fell on his back. Before he could get back on his feet, Stan jumped up, lifted his foot, to smash Filth in the face, and stood over him.

Cowering, with his hands protecting his face, Filth stayed on the floor.

Crane tried the door at the front of the car. It wouldn't open. He looked past his own reflection in the glass. On the other side, someone had jammed a metal bar diagonally across the door. Crane couldn't open it. He reached for the 38 Super he had in his shoulder holster but didn't pull the gun from the holster. He wasn't sure the steel-jacketed bullets wouldn't go through the wall of the other car and possibly kill somebody. He dropped his hand from the 38 and looked down. A little man, sitting in the third seat back, held a huge bottle of beer as big as the ones Stan and he had drunk from while on the bank of the Chitose River. Crane reached around and yanked the heavy bottle from the man's hands.

"Sorry," he said to the amazed man and slammed the bottom of the bottle against the window. The window shattered into diamonds, but the bottle didn't break.

Sliding the bottle over the side of his pants, Crane wiped off the few particles of glass that had clung to the bottle, and handed the bottle back to the man. "Thanks!"

Bewildered, the man only took the bottle back and nodded.

Crane took off his jacket, placed it over the jagged glass at the bottom of the window, straddled it, crunched into a ball, and managed to slip through.

The door to the other car was unlocked. Crane opened it and rushed in only to find that those emergency brake cables had been cut, too.

It was evident that all the cables had been cut. But even if they hadn't been cut, there was not enough time to go to every car and find out. If Crane could get the cars uncoupled, the air house would break apart. The emergency air brakes would clamp on. The train would stop.

He went back through the door. Outside, he lay down, extended his body on the steel walk-plate between the two cars, stretched his hand toward the outside of the car, and grasped the cutting bar. When he tried to lift it, the constant pressure of the train pulling the cars, would not permit the coupler to release. As the train rocketed down the tracks, Crane kept jerking the bar.

From out of the dark, some kind of black uniform covered the stocky body of a man with black grease smeared on the side of his face. Believing the man was a conductor bending over to help, Crane stayed in the stretched-out position and continued to try to uncouple the cars. Before he knew what the man was really going to do, the man bent over, grabbed Crane's 38 Super from his shoulder holster, and tried to shove him away from the coupler. Crane sprang to his feet and held his ground. Starting from his knees, he slammed his fist up against the man's jaw. The man tumbled sideways. Trying to catch his balance, the man's hand with Crane's 38 Super smacked against the steel side of the car. The 38 fell from his hand, clanked once, disappeared between the couplers, and thunked onto the railroad bed below.

Crane loved that gun. Now it was gone. He wanted to cry. But he had no time for feelings. The man went to swing. Crane ducked. The momentum of the man's swing caused him to step to the left. Crane feinted a kick to his face. Avoiding Crane's foot, the man pivoted a half circle. His foot caught on the edge of the car floor. He tripped and fell between the cars. A quick loud thrump and slower thumps were familiar to Crane. When searching for Capone's vault, a man had tried to pull him off a moving hopper car. After the man had fallen, he had made the same sounds. Those familiar horrible sounds told Crane the man had not only been sucked under the moving train, the steel wheels had cut him to chunks.

Crane went back to trying to uncouple the train. When the car hit an uneven stretch in the rail, it caused slack. The coupler released. The air hose broke apart and hissed with an angry snarl. With air pressure in the line gone, all the emergency airbrakes on the cars clenched their shoes onto the wheels. This was what the Erie Railroad called the "big hold". Groaning as if in torment, the train came to a slow stop.

When Crane went back inside the car, Stan let Filth stand up.

With a look of cunning expectation, Filth asked, "Train go off track?"

No one answered.

Filth sat down and watched Crane with what seemed to be victorious merriment. It was evident that he had been drinking.

Crane went outside to see how far down the tracks the engine had pulled the other half of the train. It had stopped fifty meters ahead of the car he was standing on. A figure, carrying what seemed to be a square flashlight, stepped down from the rear of the distant car and walked toward him. Crane couldn't make out his face, but he figured someone was going to couple the cars back together and bleed the brakes off all the cars in the train so it could get moving again. If the train started again and ran through the missing fishplate, it would derail. Crane called down to the man. "A fishplate has been taken off. Call and have someone check the tracks ahead."

The man kept his head down. As if Crane were the most ludicrous person imaginable, in a harsh voice, the man replied, "What would a tit-less WAC know about a fishplate?"

Crane had almost been stuck with a knife, and he had just saved the train from going off the tracks. He was in no mood for harassment from a regular army person who was mad because he was in a hurry to get to a bar, and an ASA man was telling him what to do. Crane vehemently pointed at the man. "Do you want me to come down there and show you what a tit-less WAC can do?"

Although Crane couldn't see the man's face clearly, he could see that the man's eyes had widened at the coldness in Crane's voice.

Crane jumped down off the car.

After three effortless strides, the man was standing in front of Crane, but he turned his back to him and shined the flashlight in the area just beyond the tracks.

Crane grabbed the man's shoulder. Being wary of what the man might do, Crane gently pulled. Instead of whipping his arm around in a flying back-fisted movement and trying to take Crane's head off, the man only turned to the side.

"The train won't get going until it's bled off," Crane said. "And they'll have to check the tracks for a missing fishplate."

As if he were going to hit Crane with it, the man clinched the square flashlight in his hand and continued to speak in a harsh voice. "Japanese railroads don't bolt on fishplates. They're welded to the tracks." He turned. "Get out of my way."

Not wanting to really hurt the man, Crane threw a half-hearted punch to his arm. To avoid the punch, the man effortlessly swayed his upper body backward. Crane was about to shove the heel of his hand up into the shelf of the man's chin. He shifted his feet and braced to do it.

The man turned and faced him.

Crane abruptly stood still and stared.

The man seemed to be breathless with mirth.

It was Neal.

Somehow, he had gotten out of Vietnam, and he was holding in a laugh.

Knowing Neal was up to his old tricks, Crane broke into a huge welcoming smile. "Glad to see you're still alive. What happened to your voice?"

Seeming unfazed by being reunited with his old boyhood friend, pointing to his short-brimmed Brixton gain fedora, with a pheasant feather tucked into the black band, Neal laughed once and rubbed his neck. "They tried to choke me, but I was wearing my lucky hat and I got out of it." A cold unwelcoming feeling emanated from his body. "We don't have time for hellos." With a stone face, he pointed to a body hanging under the underpinnings of the passenger car.

Although Crane was perplexed at Neal's behavior, in horror, he stared down at the body.

"Okay, Frederick," Neal said. "There's what happens to people with big brains who don't know anything except one thing."

At first Crane thought the body was the man who had fallen off the car. But a black uniform wasn't covering this body. A canary-yellow jacket with a torn red-checkered bow tie, covered this body, and the stench the decomposing body emitted, made Crane's eyes water and his throat close.

Neal reached out, grabbed the mangled leg of the body, and began pulling the body out from beneath the car. As he pulled, the body's head twisted halfway around its neck. The odor of blood and fresh busted guts became a backdrop for broken bones bursting out through pants and shirt. As Neal dragged the limp body along the railroad ties, flesh was torn with sickening ease, and the light coming from the windows of the passenger car amplified purple pools of blood.

"Take a good look," Neal said. "Generals with chests full of unearned ribbons and wild-eyed colonels surround themselves with overweight, over-aged senators and congressmen and never see things like this." He stared at Crane, his eyes thoughtful. Then his distant feeling seemed to change. "You okay?"

After a tragedy, most grief-stricken people are spoiled by people wishing them well, and they become used to it. Crane never had time to be spoiled. He was almost used to the sight of a horrible corpse. The real life and death game had visited him before. He gave Neal a shrug. "I've seen worse."

Nodding in understanding, Neal ran the beam of the square flashlight over the mutilated body. "Man has to be the cruelest animal on earth."

"How did the body get under there?"

"Somebody jammed it there. It's slightly radioactive, most likely meant to be incentive for us to give up the E-Brite."

The death odor of the dirty man still hovered in Crane's nostrils. The dirty man must have been the person who placed the body under the train.

Neal placed what Crane had thought was a flashlight close to the radium dial of his wrist watch. "Just want to make sure this thing's not sending a false reading."

Crane realized that the square flashlight wasn't only a flashlight, it was also a Geiger counter. Then turning his eyes on Crane like he hadn't seen him before, he reached out and offered his hand in friendship. “Glad to see you. But what are you doing here?”

Gripping Neal’s stone-like hand Crane replied, “We have a man who may have something to do with the body. He jerked his head in the direction of the car. “Stan’s holding him in train.”

The mention of Stan’s name caused Neal’s eyes to light up. He jumped up onto the platform on the back of the car. Crane followed and went in. They pushed their way through the crowd of people looking to see what was happening and stopped next to Stan. He was sitting next to Filth holding him at bay.

Before Stan could say anything, Neal took one look at Filth and told Stan, “Get him up. We’ll talk outside.”

Outside, with his face twisted with fury, Neal placed his hands on his hips and stood in front of Filth.

Smiling excessively, Filth defiantly looked at him. “You can knockie me down, but you can no knockie me out.”

Neal took a hesitant step toward Filth and stopped. “For what you and your asshole friends tried to do, I should hit your dumb ass, but I don’t want waste my time doing something worthless.”

Crane looked at Filth, and then his gaze strayed to Neal. “What are you talking about?”

“There wasn’t a fishplate missing, but a track switch was thrown in the wrong direction, and the lens in the red stop light on top of the switch stand had been changed to green. We stopped only a few feet in front of a blind switch. If the train had hit that, there would be cars and people scattered all over the place. There are probably people waiting at the switch the get the E-Brite from us. Someone paid this man and his shit-dippin' friends to do what he tried to do."

"How do you know that?"

"This guy's too stupid to even think about doing anything like throwing a switch." Neal ran the Geiger counter over Filth's body. "He's not radioactive. If he were of any importance, you would have never caught him."

"I wouldn't say that," Stan said. "When we're exhausted or scared, we all slip sometimes."

Amazed, Neal looked at Stan. "You should know if we want to catch the real culprits, we have to get them quick or they'll be gone. We're not talking small town traffic cops, here. These guys are trained and armed. And they're not dumb. We have to land the first punch. We won't get a second one."

Nodding, Stan slowly gestured to the body. "Apparently, he was a worthless half-wit the CIA placed on the payroll for political reasons. Something has gone wrong."

"What did you expect?" Neal said and threw his hand into the air. "The men we were working with, put an ignorant CIA man in charge. A CIA man who thought it was okay to work like any other workers. He quits work at five, heads for home, has dinner, and watches television. And for job security, he hires people dumber than himself."

"Crane pointed to Filth. "What about him?"

Neal glanced at the body and thrust his finger at Filth. "This dirty idiot tried to wreck the train so it would look like a real CIA man got killed in the wreck." He paused as if in thought. "It's just another way to spread disinformation. If you let it mess with your head, it will take the thinking out of the equation. Then you'll react the way they want you to." He turned the Giger counter off. "Actually, they may have been trying to blame a train wreck and his death on one of us."

Filth's smutted eyes flew wide. "It would have worked," he said without the least bit of an accent. "And my friends would have gotten the E-Brite."

Filth had been acting to be ignorant. The urge to hit him and satisfy a need for savage satisfaction entered Crane's mind. But it was never wise to get angry. When a person got angry, they made mistakes. In this game, when a person made mistakes, they ended up dead. Crane let the feeling pass.

Apparently knowing Filth had been faking the accent, Neal nodded. "I thought so. Us meeting here isn't as coincidental as it seems." Apparently knowing Crane had been sent to get the E-Brite from Stan, Neal suspiciously stared at Crane. "Why would they fight us when they can make us fight ourselves?"

For a moment, Neal's suspicion caused Crane to be shocked into silence, but he knew that oppression worked much better when the enemy could turn its victims against others, instead of against their oppressors. And apparently, because Crane was completely out of his field of expertise,

Neal thought Crane was doing just that, and it would explain Neal's cold shoulder treatment.

Stan gestured to Crane. "He's not as dumb as they thought he was. He's on our side."

The suspicion faded from Neal's face. In a show of affection, he smiled and placed his arm over Crane's back. "You will never know how glad I am that he is."

Crane felt a tear well up in his eye. "We've been through too much together. I couldn't turn if I wanted to."

Changing the subject, Stan pointed to Filth. "What do we do with him?"

"Filth like that is better off going to jail," Neal said. "But we're going to let him go free."

Crane disagreed. "But he could have killed a lot of people, including us."

Neal directed his voice at Filth. "For his suicidal wrecking of the train, he was probably promised that he would have his family taken care of for life. Now that he has failed, he will be labeled the failure he is. He will be shamed forever. I wouldn't be surprised if he commits *hari cari.*"

A light breeze sent Filth's odor toward Stan. Stan wrinkled his nose and turned from the smell. "If the asshole does, I hope he takes a bath and sterilizes the sword first."

For a moment, Filth turned crimson with embarrassment. Then he squared his shoulders. "I don't have to take abuse like that."

A mischievous smile spread across Stan's face. "I'm sorry I called you an asshole. I thought you knew your name. What kind of abuse would you like to take?"

Filth slumped but didn't answer.

Stan pointed to the body of the CIA man.

Crane turned toward it. "He must have been important. But now he's dead. Does that mean we're finished, too?"

Neal gave a resigned shrug. "The men we were working with will replace him with someone more incompetent. We're in for another bird-brained performance. In fact," he added defiantly. "As long as we know where the E-Brites are, we won't be killed, but the replacement will be."

Crane stood in silence and wondered if Neal still wanted to let Filth go free so they could follow him. He gave Neal an anxious look. "What do we do until the replacement comes?"

As if he were considering something, Neal studied Filth and said, "I'm not sure."

"One thing's for sure." Stan gestured to the dead CIA man. "We don't need men like that."

"This is no time for gloom," Neal said and looked directly at Filth. "If we have to, we'll deal with the devil."

"If you let him go," Crane said, "the new man won't like it."

Neal waved his hand in a dismissive gesture. "He won't know." He reached out and grabbed Filth by the front of the shirt and spit the words into his face. "And we'll do whatever we want. I still have the sphere."

"You mean *we* have the sphere," Stan corrected. "Now we're all sons of bitches."

"The sad part about all this," Neal said, "is that even if we succeed, we'll still lose."

Crane couldn't understand how they could lose if they kept the E-Brite away from the fanatics and their insatiable lust for power. He turned toward Neal. "You lost me."

"If we keep the sphere out of the colonel and his cohort's hands, we may eliminate the extinction of man, but by doing so men will continue to cut each other open with knives. Boys will still get their legs blown off by mines. Soldiers and civilians will still bleed and die in muddy fields, and the misery in the world, caused by nice colonels like yours who live for war, will go on and on."

"He's not my colonel," Crane shot back. "All I wanted to do was get out of the Army."

"That's a nice little goal," Neal said. "But now, you, Stan, and I, have a real goal. Whether we like it or not, the sphere gives us the power to organize wars between nations. We're merchants of death who refuse to sell. If we have too, we'll dodge the military systems, as well as judges and priests armed with the law." In a gesture of unity, he extended his hand. "Are we a team?"

Crane was beginning to realize that even though the powerfully built Neal was showing an affable manner. It disguised a ferocious intelligence and unyielding love of justice that Crane had never seen before. It was no good knowing what was wrong if no one did anything about it. And if Crane did nothing about it, it wouldn't matter what his future could be. He would have none. He would be dead. Nodding, he shook Neal's callused hand.

When Crane had been with Neal when they were searching for Capone's vault, Neal's hands had been strong, but now, it was like grasping a piece of steel. With the amount of money people were willing to pay for the sphere, Crane wondered if any of them would live through the next hour.

Filth shifted his eyes about uneasily. The step on the passenger car gave out a low squeak. Crane jerked his head toward the sound. The hair on a man on the step was haloed blue by the car lights behind him. Projecting a vulture-like formality that people assume when they feel they're above your intelligence, the man looked familiar. He stepped down from the railroad car, took one look at Filth, and pulled out a gun fitted with a silencer. Thup, thup, thup, the familiar sound of the silencer gun, sent bullets toward Filth and punched right through his head. He was dead on his feet, but his body hadn't quite gotten the message. Twitching spasmodically, he hit the ground face first.

Bright purple flashes from the gun had blinded Crane. He tried to see where the man with the gun had gone, but all he could see was purple spots before his eyes. Even though the man from the car had vanished, Crane had managed to get a glimpse of him. He was the man who had shot at him in Tokyo. He looked to Neal and Stan. They weren't pursuing the man. Apparently, they had been blinded by the unusually bright purple flashes, too.

Now, the people who wanted the E-Brite were using blinding bullets. Crane could see the mission was beginning to hinge on the edge of impossible. If more people were killed, a switch that had been closed since chasing Capone's vault would fall into the open position. Crane would lose the ability to feel fear. Noting would frighten him. Nothing would hurt him. No matter what the cost, this thing called E-Brite could be a destroyer of worlds. It would have to be eliminated.

Now that they had found Neal, there were three of them. The odds should be getting better. But they would have to go back to Chitose and make their pursuers believe they had melted away.

CHAPTER 24

When the train approaching Chitose slowed, Stan jumped off. His foot caught on the ballast along the rails. He lost his balance and tumbled to a stop. As if he were gracefully stepping off the bottom step of an escalator, Neal stepped off, but had no problem.

To keep the rushing ground from tripping him, Crane leaped off with his back toward the front of the train. He landed running, stumbled, and regained his balance.

The train moved past.

Soon the brakes on the train would squeal, and it would slide into the station. If the colonel's men were there waiting to ambush Crane and his friends, they wouldn't be getting off the train.

As they walked around a corpse of trees the height of a good size bush, Crane was still amazed that the Japanese called a stand of little trees, like this, a forest. After walking past the trees, they crossed the Chitose River Bridge. Thinking how good a beer would taste, they hesitated at the top of the cement steps that led to Aki's Bar, thought better of it, then cut down a paved street, and ended up on an artery that lead to the main street. Here, they cautiously walked past a collection of buildings that had been built with unpainted wood. Above the doors to the buildings, bright colorful signs had been hand-painted with reds, blues, and yellows that revealed the buildings housed, a tailor shop for military personnel, a laundry, and a barber shop, where joyous Japanese women would stand on their tip toes and cut GIs' hair for the equivalent of an American quarter.

When Crane, Neal, and Stan cut through a short dirt alley, it was shrouded in fog. Weather-beaten, buildings lined the alleyway and looked like haggard ghosts. The odor of wood and smoke, from something cooking on a high-temperature wok, filled the night with a welcome aroma of well-prepared food.

At the end of the alley, Neal, Stan, and Crane made sure they weren't being followed and stepped into a restaurant. Inside, they took seats at a booth. Directly in front of them, a gas burner sat in the center of a white Formica table. Crane didn't know why the burner was there, but the room had an odor of meat frying and gave off a warm and friendly aura.

Before Crane could ask why the burner was in the center of the table, a Japanese girl walked up to the table. Her dark almond-shaped eyes seemed to send happiness everywhere she looked. Her long black hair smoothly flowed over her right shoulder and accented the cute tilt of her head, and her clean white-toothed smile seemed sincere.

After getting over how beautiful she was, Crane held up three fingers. "*Biiru o kudasai*, Beers, may I have?"

After Stan had ordered the food, in *Japanese*, the girl brought them a plate of raw meat, three "*ookii's,*" large bottles of Sapporo beer, and three glasses. Stan inspected the meat. Nodding that it was okay, he looked up at the girl. "*Domo arigato*," Thank you very much."

The girl bent at the knees. "*Dozo*," please. She placed the glasses on the table, poured beer into them, and smiling, she handed them all around.

Crane lifted his glass and held it. "What shall we drink to?"

Neal held his glass high and looked to Stan.

Stan lifted his glass. "Making it out of Nam alive."

They clinked glasses.

The girl smiled at the toast, left the meat on the table, and came back with a large knife, a steel wok, chopsticks, and a plate of various vegetables.

Crane had never seen a burner in the center of a table. And he had never had been brought raw meat to cook while sitting in a restaurant booth.

Taking a sip of beer, Neal noticed Crane's puzzlement. "He elbowed him in the arm. "What's the matter? Don't you want to eat?"

"Sure, but this is new to me. I want to know how you got out of Nam."

Neal smiled his familiar smile from the old days. "Nothin' to it."

"When the rope broke and you fell through the trees, I thought you had bought the farm."

"I wasn't even close to dying. When I hit the first few branches, they bent." He waved his hand down. It was nothing. I slid off those branches like I was on a padded slide. And I kept on slowing down until a big branch stopped me dead."

"How did you get down?"

"I didn't have to."

"What do you mean you didn't have to? When I looked down, there were so many NVAs, they looked like ants coming right at you."

Neal cringed a little. "I thought I was done for, but the leaves, broken branches, and whatever was on that branch made it impossible for anybody to see me from the ground." A big smile spread across his face. "I couldn't see them, but I could hear them. After they quit searching for me, they camped right under me, smoking cigarettes and cooking something. For two days, I slept right on top of them. When they finally gave up, dressed like an NVR, Stan showed up under the tree."

Remembering how Stan had saved his life, Crane lifted his finger. "It's always nice to have an angel on the shoulder. But I blew up the KY-38. How did you keep that clerk from telling the NVR where you were?"

Neal looked to Stan. "When me and Stan called for an extraction, we used fake LZ coordinates. When the Huey was close, Stan set off a smoke grenade at the fake LZ. While the NVR rushed to the fake LZ, Stan ran to where I was. I flashed a mirror. The Huey came away from the fake LZ, hovered over us and came down. The NVR rushed from the fake LZ and toward us, but we were lifted out before they got there."

Stan rubbed his hands together and limbered up his fingers. "For two days, we didn't have much to eat. I'm still get hungry thinking about it." He dribbled a small amount of peanut oil into the wok, placed the wok on the burner, and let it get hot.

"Meat first," he said, picked up chopsticks, and placed the meat into the wok. Then he placed mushrooms and onions in with the searing meat. "Mushrooms and onions tenderize the meat," he said. "But this works better." He poured a small amount of beer into the wok. It hissed. A pleasing aroma, like bread baking, rose up and hovered in the air.

After a few moments, he pushed the meat, mushrooms, and onions up onto the sides of the wok to stay warm. "It's all done quickly now." He continued to stir-fry vegetables and push them up on the sides of the wok until the wok was filled to the top. After he added spinach and covered it for a few minutes, he announced, *"Owari"* Finished. The sukiyaki was ready to eat.

"Nice work," Neal said, pushed his plate toward Stan, and looked to Crane. "He's pretty good at cooking things up."

"I thought I was pretty good at finding things," Crane replied as Stan heaped Neal's plate full. "But I never found anything like E-Brite."

Neal pulled his plate across the table, stopped it in front of himself, and gestured to Stan. "Didn't good old Stan tell you how he found the E-Brite?"

"Not really." Crane pushed his plate toward Stan.

As Stan filled Crane's plate, Neal said, "After we gave Stan and his friends Al Capone's vault, they took it to a hospital and had it X-rayed. Two E-Brite Spheres were sandwiched into a thick corner of the gold vault."

"Two spheres?" Crane excitedly blurted out.

Neal held up two fingers. "Yes, two. Twice as much trouble."

Crane pulled his full plate back and strained to control his surprise. Apparently, no one knew about the third sphere he had hid in his secret chamber in the Shenango River. To calm himself, he exhaled a deep breath, lifted a set of chopsticks off the table, and held them while he talked. "If Burke didn't get the other sphere from the Hue University reactor, how did he really get it?"

Neal let out a little laugh. "We gave it to him."

"What?"

"At first, we didn't know how much money could be had from the spheres. We figured he could give it to people who would use it for the good of man. "

"So, why didn't he?"

"The people he took it to only wanted it for the money they could get out of it. They didn't get it, but he couldn't handle the trouble it caused."

"I always wondered why we had been paid over two million dollars for a gold vault that was only worth seventy-eight thousand." Crane took a drink of beer. "And I always thought there was another layer or something worth more than the gold. But when we found out the money was counterfeit, I figure the gold was the only value the vault had."

Stan began filling his own plate, but stopped. "It doesn't matter if the spheres are more valuable than gold. They're more important than gold."

Using the chopsticks, Crane clamped a piece of meat and held it. "Just how important is it?"

"Let me try to explain." Stan took a sip of beer. "During World War II the E-Brite was like a side dish at a picnic. The Trinity test was the main course, but there was an extremely good possibility that the E-Brite would turn out to be more powerful than any atomic bomb the scientists could ever build. And that's why the scientists who took the E-Brite from the Manhattan project were afraid to use it in the Trinity test. If you remember, the scientist didn't know if the first nuclear detonation would cause an unstoppable nuclear reaction and ignite the entire planet. But they were almost positive that the E-Brite spheres would. So, they took them out of the test schedules.

"It they knew the E-Brites could destroy the world, why didn't they just destroy them?"

"They knew if science and technology advanced enough, the tremendous power of E-Brite could be harnessed. The power potential for a single harnessed marble-sized sphere of E-Brite would make it possible for an electric power station to provide power the entire East Coast for at least one hundred years."

"It is still possible to use the E-Brite for peaceful power," Neal broke in. "That's why we have to make sure it gets into the proper hands."

Crane was still in a fog about what had happened. "But how did the E-Brite get into the vault?"

Using his chopsticks, Stan took a bit of spinach, chewed it, and washed it down with long draw of beer. "A few of the scientist didn't trust the government. During World War II, the Germans sabotaged an American ship. Using its usual ineptitude, the government assigned more than one hundred agents to find out if Mussolini supporters were in with the fisherman and dockworker population on the New York waterfront and were causing strikes that were slowing and stopping shipments for the war effort. But mob-controlled, tight-lipped fishermen had control of the waterfront. Needless to say, the agent's efforts were useless."

Crane shook his chopsticks at Stan. "You mean a hundred agents couldn't do anything?"

"The way it went down," Stan said, "was that Lucky Luciano and the government struck a deal. Luciano guaranteed full assistance of his organization, and it provided intelligence to the Navy. Luciano's associate, Albert Anastasia, controlled the docks and ran Murder Incorporated. He guaranteed no dockworker strikes throughout the war. In return, the state of New York agreed to commute Luciano's prison sentence."

"And guess what?" Neal said and answered his own question. "The dockworker strikes stopped." And then he added, "The government was embarrassed that they had to recruit organized crime to help in the war effort. But it worked."

Quickly scanning the area, Neal's eyes shifted right then left. Back then," he said, "the scientists were not stupid. They needed someone they could trust to hide the E-Brite. Knowing that Luciano and Murder Incorporated were doing a perfect job of protecting the docks in New York, the scientists decided to turn to a crime figure to hide the E-Brite. They contacted someone in Al Capone's gang. It could have been his front man, Frank Nitti, or the real boss, Feliece Delucia, also known as Paul Ricca, but we don't know for sure."

"Capone was supposed to be a killer," Crane said. "How did the scientists ever get near him?"

"No matter what the newspapers printed, what the radios broadcasted, or what history has recorded, Capone was known to have some feelings for his fellow man. The scientists not only told Capone what could happen if the E-Brite got into the wrong hands, they also told him about the unbelievable peaceful value of it for the future. After that, he may have persuaded Nitti or Ricca to hide the E-Brite until the scientific community was ready for it."

Leaning back, Stan threw up his hands. "We don't know how it ended up in Capone's gold vault, but it did."

"It seems the ignorance of man never ends," Crane said. "I doubt that the human race will ever be ready for power of E-Brite."

Neal jerked his finger at Crane. "You got that right. If we let the wrong people have the E-Brite, we'll have golf-ball sized nuclear bombs going off everywhere." He took a deep breath and exhaled. "Even if a person survives the initial detonation, when the plutonium-239 decays, it gives off alpha particles, and has a radioactive half-life of twenty-four thousand years. No one will survive."

"Yes, but look on the bright side," Stan sarcastically said and grinned. "When hydrogen fusion is used in the bomb, two electron-emitting radionuclides', tritium, with a half-life of twelve years, and carbon-14, with a half-life of five thousand seven hundred thirty years, is released and that causes havoc in a person's body."

Crane knew all that. "We know radiation is dangerous," he said to change the subject and recalled the day he and his friends had given up the vault. "How did you get the E-Brite spheres out of the vault? Your partners had machine guns, and they blew up the truck we used to haul the vault."

"It's hard to believe," Stan said. "But the story about the man believing he was a descendant of Egyptian royalty and wanted to be buried in a gold vault was true. As a matter of fact, after my buddies and I dug the two E-Brite spheres out of the vault, they took the vault to the Egyptian descendant that we didn't know about, and got their money." He smiled in Crane's direction. "It wasn't like the counterfeit money they gave you and your friends."

Apparently not wanting to remember the counterfeit money, Neal looked to the ceiling.

A pain in Crane's chest renew with great vigor. After Neal, Raftery, Blondie, and himself had almost been burnt to death, were beaten, chased, forced down raging rapids, almost buried in a city dump, and lied to, they had finally gotten Al Capone's gold vault. They thought they were finally rich. But the payoff was counterfeit. With no decent jobs available, Crane enlisted in the Army, and Neal got hooked up with Special Forces. Due to the fact that Crane scored very high on the entrance tests, he was sent to the Army Security Agency.

"If you had one of the E-Brite spheres on Amchitka," Crane said, "how did you manage to get it through security?"

"Simple," Stan said. "Since it was covered with a layer of lead, I managed to get it past security by claiming I was going to use it to make fishing sinkers. Everybody thinks I had it in my pocket when the British submarine came to pick me up."

"British submarine?" Crane replied with surprise. "I was told it was a Russian sub."

"That's what the colonel wants you to believe. You've probably run into classified documents stamped "United Kingdom Eyes only."

Crane nodded. "Great Britain and the Unites States have been sharing secrets since before World War II."

"And this is another one they'll want to share."

Crane held up his hand. "Wait a minute. You just said you didn't have the E-Brite in your pocket. If you would have had it in your pocket, would you have given it to the British?"

"I couldn't give it to the men in the British submarine. I can smell a conspiracy from a hundred miles away. The men in the submarine didn't seemed to be British."

Now Crane knew why Kane had worn mountain boots, with their thick cleated soles and brass eyelets. He had been on Shemya with Stan and Neal. He looked to Stan. "So, one E-Brite is on Shemya?"

"I hope it is," Stan said. "The British submarine was going to take me to secure area under one of the Aleutian Islands, but there is so much money and power involved, I wasn't sure if the people were British, and if they were, I didn't know if I could trust them."

The Japanese girl came to the table. "Everything okay?"

Smiling, Stan nodded. "Yes, ma'am. Everything okay."

The girl turned and left.

Stan continued, "After I gave them a fake E-Brite, they pulled a Doctor Jekyll and Mister Hyde on me. Got angry, put me under armed guard. If I had given them the real E-Brite, I would be dead. After they found out the E-Brite was fake, they took me back to Anchorage, said it was all a misunderstanding and not to be afraid to contact them when I had the real E-Brite."

Crane tipped his bottle of beer over the rim of the glass, but didn't pour. He flashed Stan a sardonic smile. "I'm sure you're going to do that."

"I won't have to. They flew me to Anchorage so they could follow me, but so far, it hasn't worked."

Crane filled his glass and set the bottle on the table. "How did the British know it wasn't real?"

"It wasn't radioactive."

From outside the restaurant the voice of a child called out, "Nickel! Nickel!"

Crane turned toward the calls.

Two Japanese girls went to the door and slid it open. Outside, a skinny black and white kitten sat on the sidewalk. A little girl held out her arm, pointed to the cat, and called, "Nickel! Nickel!"

Crane realized the Japanese name for cat was *neko,* and the pronunciation sounded like nickel. The little girl was trying to get her cat to come to her. One of the Japanese girls ran into the back and came back out with pieces of dried squid and gave them to the little girl.

The little girl thanked the girl, held out the squid, and called again, "neko! neko!"

The cat came to her outstretched hand and mouthed the squid. The girl picked up her cat and hugged it. As the Japanese girl closed the door, there were smiles all around.

"That was nice," Crane said, and looked to Stan. "But I have one more thing I would like to clear up."

Stan turned back toward Crane and waved his hand in encouragement. "Go ahead."

"After the submarine picked you up, I reeled in that glass ball you had cast into the Bering Sea. The colonel said the Long Shot information in it was phony, but it looked real to me. Was it?"

At first, Stan looked a little puzzled, but his puzzlement faded. "They never quit. I couldn't be sure the right submarine was out there."

Crane knew that American Navy subs regularly entered Soviet waters around Kamchatka and the Sea of Okhotsk. They shadowed soviet ships, monitored harbors, watched missile tests, eavesdropped on conversations, and retrieved secret debris from the bottom the sea. He could understand why Stan was worried about the right submarine being there.

“So,” he said to Stan. “You used empty glass ball to signal the submarine. That way, if an impostor was out there, the E-Brite would stay safe”

“Stan lifted one finger and pointed at Crane. “You got it. But whatever was in the glass ball, you reeled in, must have been placed in it when you went in the water to save me.”

“That’s possible,” Crane said. “But why did they give me a higher security clearance after I read the Long Shot information?”

“That was designed to keep your mouth shut.”

Neal broke in. “Some of Long Shot *is* secret information. When they gave you a higher security rating, it made it easier for you to believe the Long Shot information was highly classified and cause you to keep it to yourself.” He lifted one finger. “However, nothing is more highly classified or as dangerous as E-Brite. Having spent a year on Shemya, you know, except for the mission, there’s not too much excitement there. A cloudless day is rare. If you would have gone back to the compound on that sun-filled day and told your friends a man had just committed suicide in the Bering Sea, everyone off duty would have been down there.”

Nodding in understanding, Crane looked to Neal. “Now that that’s solved, how did the other E-Brite end up in Nam?”

Neal glanced at Stan and chuckled. “We lost it there.”

“Am I missing something here,” Crane said and thoughtfully took a sip of beer. “How can you lose something so dangerous?”

“I was going to give it to the colonel.”

"You must have had a good reason."

"The colonel was supposed to be part of an elite corps that frightens anyone possessing a scrap of sanity. He is considered untouchable and beyond corruption. And we believed he was."

Stan shifted his feet under the table and leaned forward. "We really weren't expecting an ambush. But just to be safe, we only took one real sphere and one fake sphere."

"It happened so fast," Neal said, his voice rising. "I almost got blown to smithereeens. The force of the blast must have knocked the real E-Brite right out of my pocket. On that mission, you went on with me, my team members gathered all the plutonium scattered by the explosion, and I found the E-Brite in the trench, but the colonel must have sent about twenty men to get it. To keep them from seeing my other team members go back to the LZ, I had to make the colonel's people chase me away from the LZ. After I lost them, I circled back, but I almost didn't make it to the Huey before it lifted off.

"Why didn't you just throw the E-Brite into the ocean, burry it, or just hide it in some faraway place?"

"It's too valuable," Neal said. "The governments of the world will use every means necessary to find it. As long as it exists, the world will never be safe."

Stan waved his chopsticks at Crane. "If the colonel gets the E-Brite and makes the golf-sized nuclear bombs, with a single detonation, he will be able to unleash something powerful enough to blow half the earth away."

As if exhausted, Neal leaned back in the booth. "You can see why we should destroy it."

"Well, why don't we?"

"It's indestructible. It's sort of like Teflon. Once Teflon was invented, no one could find a way to make it stick to anything. Now that we have the E-Brite, except with a nuclear explosion, no one can find a way to destroy it. And if they do, it could cause the dreadful chain reaction that never stops."

Stan glanced around the restaurant and then turned his attention back to the conversation. "It wouldn't be such a big deal except for the fact that no one has been able to reproduce a single sphere."

Crane held his glass of beer to the side, leaned across the table, and talked low. "Someone had to make the first one. Where did *it* come from?"

"Nobody really knows where any of the spheres came from," Stan said and turned toward Neal. "If they did, they would try like crazy to get more."

"After what mankind did with the first atomic bomb," Neal said, "any scientist concerned about the future of the earth isn't going to offer any leads to the original location of a single sphere."

Feeling the enormity of the task at hand, Crane was sure a Special Forces agent with more experience and training than he had would be the right person for Neal and Stan to work with.

"I don't feel I'm qualified to do this," he said. "If I tag along, I'll just slow you down."

Looking astonished, Neal looked up from eating. "You're not going to slow us down." His voice was sharp. "If you live to be five hundred years old, this will always be the most important thing you ever did."

Although keeping the E-Brite out of the colonel's hands was important, Crane would rather let someone more qualified do it. Staring at the red star on the label of the bottle of Sapporo Beer, he replied, "I'll agree it's important, but I doubt it's the most important thing I'll ever do."

Neal set down his chop sticks, inhaled, and let it out. "I'll try to explain it." He leaned toward Crane. "Using E-Brite, the scientists have found a way to pack more stuff into less space. Until now, the smallest nuclear bomb has been shot from the nuclear cannon, Atomic Annie. Annie weighs over eighty-three tons, so you can see that she isn't very portable. And her yield is only a fifteen-kiloton shell that can only be shot a distance of twenty miles."

Interested, Crane encouragingly rolled his hand. "And?"

"And?" Neal nodded once and continued. "The surface area of a nuclear bomb is critical. That is why spheres are used to encase the most nuclear material into the smallest space possible. If E-Brite had been used in a cannon like Annie and fired at Hiroshima, the nuclear explosion would have blown the cannon and Japan off the face of the earth."

Crane didn't think it was possible to place any more material in anything that was full. "Either I'm ignorant or I'm missing something."

Neal reached over and placed his hand on Crane's arm. "Hang in there. If you weren't smarter than the average dummy, you wouldn't be here."

"I feel like a dummy."

"If you were, you'd be like ninety-nine percent of the people on earth. You'd sit back, let other people think for you, and you wouldn't ever know they were tricking you into doing things that were unnecessary." Neal lifted his hand from Crane's arm and waved it in the air. "You would be living the easy life of the semi-ignorant."

Crane shook his head in bewilderment.

As if searching for a way to make Crane understand, Neal dipped his head, and his forehead wrinkled. "Have you ever thrown flour into the air and lit it?"

Crane remembered his boyhood gang finding maggot-riddled flour that had been dumped out of a garbage can after a rib-protruding dog had tipped it over. When his friends and he threw the flour into the air and lit it, they were surprised at how flammable and explosive it had become. Crane nodded.

Neal picked up his bottle of beer and topped off his glass. "That's a start." He took a drink. "To make it more digestible, flour is ground to increase its surface area, but as you have discovered, it also makes it more explosive."

He bent close and looked Crane in the eye. "Are you following me?"

Awed, Crane nodded.

Waving the chopsticks as if to help him speak, Neal continued, "Nuclear research teams have applied the same principal to a metal similar to E-

Brite. They have also been able to make the nuclear fission material multi harmonic, which enables minute amounts of fission material to vibrate like tiny tuning-forks. Using this process and the similar E-Brite metal, they can create multi megaton nuclear bombs that will fit in a suitcase."

Amazed, Crane stared straight ahead. He had heard of the suitcase bombs, but he was never sure they were real. Now he knew.

For a moment, Neal turned his eyes toward the girl with the dark almond-shaped eyes, then continued, "Needless to say, if the real E-Brite ever got into the hands of ignorant people, and they duplicated it, nuclear bombs the size of ball bearing, could be shot out of a rifle or pistol. They would be a real threat to the existence of mankind."

Stan gave Crane a helpless smile. "Half-wits would end up destroying the world with E-Brite BBs shot out of BB guns."

"I understand the flour thing, but I don't see how that could be used inside a little metal sphere."

Making gestures with his hands, Neal answered, "The inside surface area of the E-Brite metal is first etched into a sponge-like structure, then crushed. This process has created the highest-ever ratio of surface volume. A teaspoon worth can hold the equivalent of eight tightly-folded football fields."

"In other words," Stan butted in, "It takes more paint to cover a rough surface than a smooth surface."

Crane finally had an idea how the E-Brite worked, but the inhuman ramifications of a nuclear bomb as big as a BB seemed too huge to comprehend. “So, you’re saying that a bomb with real E-Brite metal, the size of a BB can soak up enough multi-harmonic fission material that its nuclear detonation would make Hiroshima look like a spark?”

Neal flicked the chopsticks at Crane. “You got it.”

Nodding weakly, Stan stared at the empty wok. “It’s amazing that the power to destroy the entire world has somehow landed in our laps.”

Crane couldn’t imagine the colonel or anyone could be so indifferent to human life. “Doesn’t the colonel care about what is right or wrong?”

“Like most psychopaths from Fruityville,” Stan said and grimaced, “he knows the difference between what’s right and wrong. He just doesn't care.”

Neal placed his hand on the table, turned his palm up, and moved it while he talked. “The colonel’s only concern is for what's right for himself, and because money is involved, money rules.”

A look of concern filled Stan’s face. “Even if we eliminate this satanic sphere, the colonel might have enough information to mass reproduce it. If he does, no one will know where or when the spheres will be placed.”

Crane aggressively stabbed the end of his chopsticks into his last piece of meat. “If we get rid of the sphere and expose the colonel for what he really is, the world may have a chance.”

Neal's face took on a look of amazement. "Okay, bright boy, how do you plan on doing that?"

Tapping his temple Crane said, "Together, we should devise some sort of plan."

Stan looked up from eating and directed his attention toward Neal. "Did you mention what will happen if we get caught before we expose the colonel?"

Neal shifted in his seat and projected a posture of concern. "If we get caught, they will not only deny everything, they'll make examples out of us.

"Who's they?" Crane wanted to know.

"The government, the agency, everybody." Neal threw his hand into the air. "They'll belittle us. They'll make sure our family, friends, and the news media are informed that we're nothing but a trio of traitors with top secret clearances who went nuts over drugs or something. They'll manufacture enough evidence to back up a million lies."

Stan joined Neal's train of thought. "They'll create more than enough credible assertions to sentence us to death."

Not wanting to believe what Neal was telling him caused Crane's chest to fill with excruciating discomfort. "Does someone really have that much power?"

Neal's eyes glared with disapproval. "Have you heard of Rolling Thunder?"

Crane nodded. "It was a Vietnam bombing instigated by President Johnson."

"Actually," Neal said. "It was a political program. The United States Air Force's repeated requests to bomb the North Vietnamese airfields near Hanoi and Haiphong were met with uncompromising indignation. They remained out of bounds."

"What made those cities exempt?"

"They didn't get bombed because someone was afraid the E-Brite spheres could be there."

Crane felt resentment boil inside him. "Can they really make impossible for anyone to believe us?"

"They'll make it impossible for anyone to believe a word we say." Neal stood up. "They'll set it up as plausible denial. They'll make sure every statement is convincing." He placed his hands on the table and leaned over. "But I have a plan."

CHAPTER 25

The plan Neal had come up with while they had been at the bar eating, seemed simple. And Crane finally realized why Neal and Stan wanted him on the team. He had to arrange for the colonel to land at a remote site near Lake Shikostsu. Just in case something went wrong, Neal and Stan would lay in ambush and watch the colonel pick up the fake E-Brite from Crane. Then, while the colonel tried to reproduce an E-Brite sphere from a fake E-Brite sphere, it would give them time to get the real one into the hands of people the colonel couldn't touch. And the world would be safe.

Riding the train to get close to Lake Shikostsu without being noticed, Neal, Stan, and Crane jumped off before the train stopped at the Shikostsu Station, and weaved their way around trees and brush until they were at the lakeside.

Under a waning sun, they made their way to a far shore. Crane didn't favor the prospect of getting into the freezing water and not being warmed by the sun's rays. He looked to Stan. "Who's going in first?"

"Not I," Stan said, bent over, lifted a flat rock, and picked up a cord. He winked in Crane's direction. "Watch this."

He pulled the cord.

The cord lifted from the sand where it had been buried and plowed a line toward the water. Seven meters from shore, a raft inflated and popped up from the bottom. Pulling the raft toward shore, Stan said, "Didn't want to get our weapons wet."

"I can't have any," Crane said. "The colonel will search me."

They hopped in the raft.

Sitting in the rubber raft, Neal turned toward Stan. "This raft is a good idea, Stan. If anyone's following, we'll see them coming on the water a mile away."

As Stan pulled on the oars and the bulky raft lumbered out into the lake, Crane lifted his hand, hooded his eyes, and scanned the area. No boats floated on the surface, and no one was near the shore where they had just been. He lowered his hand and looked to Neal. "It looks like the only way we won't see anyone following us is if they're under water."

As if he were cold, Neal shuddered. "Unless our followers have a wet suit and scuba tanks, I think that's out of the question."

"If they're anything like that filthy man on the train," Stan said and pulled on the oars. "I think they'll stay out of the water because they're afraid they might get clean."

Far across the lake, they pulled onto a deserted sandy shore. About a hundred yards from shore, at a small clearing, Neal pulled fresh-cut brush off to the side. Underneath, two recently dug pits, just big enough for two men to lie down in, waited to be occupied.

Neal pointed to the pits. "From the air, the colonel will see anyone near this place. But when he flies over, he'll never see us hiding under the brush."

They both turned toward Crane. "You ready?"

Checking to make sure the fake E-Brite was in his pocket, Crane shrugged. "Let's get this thing done."

While Crane stood in the clearing, Neal and Stan lay in the pits, pulled the brush over themselves, and waited for the colonel's Huey to land.

A while later, the distant chop of the Huey's rotors, rattling the air, signaled the colonel was nearing.

After three searching passes, the Huey landed.

Hunching under the slowing whops of the blade, Crane made his way to the Huey's side door, and the colonel waved him inside. The stress of the quest must have been eating away at the colonel's very soul. A permanent scowl lined his face. His domineering demeanor and his stern face had been replaced by a frail shadow of the man he once was. But no matter how bad or weary the colonel looked, when he didn't get his way, he was prone to outbursts. He could easily burst into a violent nut house thing.

Crane would have to be on guard.

While one of the colonel's men manned an M-60 machine gun, another man with a goatee searched Crane for weapons. When he found none, the colonel said, "Check for the sphere."

"You won't have to." The goateed man pulled the fake sphere from Crane's pocket. "I have it right here."

"You didn't have to do that," Crane protested, and the man handed the colonel the fake sphere.

Apparently knowing Polaroid film fogs when it's exposed to radiation, the colonel pealed back a tiny piece of the sphere's lead covering and pulled out a Polaroid camera. Holding it at bay, he took a picture of the sphere and waited for it to develop. When the picture turned out clear, the colonel knew the sphere was a fake.

His face reddened and the veins in his neck and forehead became blue and distended. "What are you trying to pull off?"

Crane feigned fear. "I wasn't sure it was you," he whined. "I wasn't going to take any chances and have the real sphere taken from me by an imposter." He glared at the man who had taken sphere. "And anyway, I didn't give you *that* sphere."

The redness in the colonel's face subsided. "Good thinking. Now be a good boy and get the real one."

Crane hated the "good boy" tag. He tried to hide his feelings, but his face grimaced with anger.

The colonel patted him on the back. "Come on, son, go get the sphere, and we'll get out of here and send you home."

The colonel had a tremendous skill for handling people. For a moment, the thought of going home almost made Crane's heart jump with joyful anticipation. But he had to stay focused on the task at hand. He stifled his joyous feeling.

If Neal and Stan rushed the Huey, the man manning the M-60 machine gun would cut them down. Crane had to find a way to get both of the colonel's men near the pits.

Knowing diarrhea is a universal calamity, Crane reached around and held his backside with his left hand. Pleading with humorous gestures, he said, "I'll get the real one, but I don't know if someone's watching. Before I can get it, I have to go really bad. This E-Brite thing has my stomach so upset, I've had diarrhea all day."

Smiling, one of the two men pointed to Crane and said to the other man, *"Stualet?"* the *Russian* word for "toilet."

As if Crane had already gone in his pants, the colonel's nose wrinkled, and a look of disgust filled his face. "I don't want you stinking up my chopper." He pointed to the brush-covered pits. "Go over there." He gestured to the two men. "I'll man the 60. When he's done, go with him to get the sphere. And keep a sharp eye out."

Holding his rear, Crane scampered toward the brush-covered pits. Apparently not wanting to watch him take a crap, the men nonchalantly followed, but stopped just before the pits and turned their backs toward him. A tiny flash of sunlight from the brush-covered hillside glinted in Crane's eye. He swiveled his eyes to where the flash had come from. The almost concealed figure of a man was watching through binoculars.

As the men stood next to the pits, not keeping an eye on Crane, Neal and Stan shed the brush and popped up behind them. Before the shocked men could do anything, Whap! Neal and Stan simultaneously spun around and kicked them in their stomachs. With stunned looks, both men doubled up, gasped for air and helplessly tried to stop the next kick. But their efforts were useless. Too late, Neal's and Stan's flying feet swung around with amazing speed and drove the men off their feet. They fell to the ground.

The colonel desperately held the M-60

With weapons drawn, Neal and Stan were coming right at him.

Crane shouted, "They have the real E-Brite. Don't shoot!"

The colonel froze on the trigger. All he could do was look up in horror. Before he could change his mind, Stan and Neal were in the Huey. Neal's hands were a blur. When they stopped, he was holding the colonel in a death grip. While Stan relieved the pilot of his weapons, for a brief moment, fear carved ugly lines into the colonel's face.

"Come on fellows," the colonel said. "I know it's useless to fight you." His face relaxed. "The penalty for breaking security is ten thousand dollars fine, ten years in jail, both, or death."

Neal released the death grip and encouragingly rolled his hand. "And?"

"And, the prospect of a firing squad should spark your attention."

"That's right," Stan said. "The old stand-by rule for traitors would apply to you, too. When in doubt take them out."

"Come on boys," the colonel begged. "We can help each other. There's a lot of money to be made here. When you can, take what you can."

Crane couldn't believe the colonel was still trying to let them in on his deal to sell the E-Brite. "What's the matter with you?" Crane yelled. "Don't you know you can't use your ignorant military mind to control E-Brite. If you do, and Moscow and China find out, and they will, then they will believe they have been betrayed. The world will fry in a thousand nuclear explosions. The last signal from Shemya will be, 'This is not a drill!'"

The colonel took on a smug look. "The strong always survive longer than the weak. It's a plan of Nature. We'll only be killing weaklings for Mother Nature." He puffed up with self-importance. "And besides, I'm only doing what any enterprising man would do." He laughed.

Shaking a piercing finger of rebuke in the colonel's face, Crane asked, "Have you no compassion for your fellow man?"

Before the colonel could answer, Neal cut in. "It's what he does. Like a fisherman catches fish. Like a baker bakes bread. Using his limited mind, he knows nothing different."

The colonel smiled a sly smile. "Don't panic, boys. We're not doing anything new. The effort to kill, maim, debilitate, and disable large sectors of the population makes that population easier to control. It's a deep state operation. In one way or another, it has been that way since the dawn of organized society." He let out a chuckle. "There's no need to try and save the world." He smiled big and held it.

Stan's face filled with anger. "I can see why you think it's funny? People like you don't have consciences. They've had them surgically removed and replaced with cash-flow implants. E-Brite in the wrong hands is the unlimited destruction of the world?"

As if in fear, the colonel's smile vanished. He held his hand in front of his quivering face. "What do you plan to do with me?"

"Since we don't really want E-Brite bombs soaring over the oceans and turning them into seas of glass," Neal said, "we'll hold you hostage until higher authority can be summoned. Then when those really in charge find out you had no intention of turning in the E-Brite sphere, but had plans to sell it to as many countries as you could, there will be no doubt that *you* are a first-class traitor."

The colonel smiled an all-knowing smile and then projected a mean and better-than-thou posture. "You're talking to an officer of the United States Army. Stand at attention."

Crane couldn't believe the colonel was resorting to the old army ruse of intimidation he had picked up in Officer Candidate School.

Implying that Officer Candidate School was a clone of an obedience school for dogs, Stan shot back, "Don't pull your obedience school horseshit on us. We're not interested in your dog tricks."

The colonel dropped his phony obedience school posture. "You can't be on your own and unsupported. You need me. I've sent Langley down dead-end paths more than once. No one will ever believe you."

Looking at the colonel as if he were crazy, Stan said, "Don't count on it. You're betraying our country. Big secrets have a habit of finding their own way out."

Crane's eyes caught a sudden movement to his left. A little white dog had stopped a few feet from the Huey. With its ears pricked, body tensed, and curiously following movements, it held its tail straight out and sniffed. With its head low and its nose sniffing the air, the dog's eyes fixed on the Huey. Crane looked toward the bushes that had covered the pits. The man that had shot at him in Tokyo and another man were crawling toward the pits. As they crept closer, he silently gestured to Neal. Not wanting to alert the creeping men that they had been spotted, Neal only shifted his eyes toward them. But it was not enough. The man on the right lifted an AK-47. Crane rushed toward the M-60. The colonel stiff-armed him in the chest. He fell backwards into Stan, and they fell in the rear of the Huey.

As Crane tried to recover from the colonel's blow that had deprived him of breath, he looked up. The colonel stepped behind the M-60 and aimed at the advancing men. Before he could fire, his eyes filed with horror.

Whap! Whap! Whap! Echoing off the sides of the distant volcanoes, the man on the brush-covered hillside sent an uninterrupted stream of bullets straight into the colonel's body. Before the bullets punched the life out of him, as if his deformities had been targets, one bullet flew out the back of the dent in his head, and another entered his cloudy eye. As the inside of the Huey, filled with blood mist, he folded forward and slumped to his knees.

Apparently only a tracker and not a fighter, the little dog yelped once and took off running. Neal pulled out a grenade and pulled the pin. Before he could throw the grenade, the pilot squirmed out of Stan's grasp and rushed toward Neal. With the grenade clinched in his fist, Neal threw a punch to the pilot's face. The pilot's head bounced of the wall of the Huey. Neal threw the grenade between the advancing men. As Crane opened his mouth and covered his ears to protect from the concussion, spurts from the AK-47 hit the pilot, but were interrupted and stopped with the exploding grenade. Fragments took the two men out, but others, he hadn't seen before, were knocked senseless for a moment, but then they kept on advancing. Neal and Stan fired their High Standard HDM, pistols. The full metal jacket bullets easily took them out, but behind them, a line of more men moved carefully. One of them always covered the advance of the others as they leapfrogged toward the Huey.

Neal jumped behind the M-60. It seemed to be jammed.

From the lake, two divers in black wet suits, but no air tanks, stood knee deep in water. They slipped off their flippers, threw them on shore, unsheathed rifles from plastic cases, and dropped the cases. With their rifles pointed in the direction of the Huey, they ran onto shore.

On the left, three other men approached. To the right, two more armed men were running toward the Huey. With the unmistakable shape of AK-47s silhouetted against their bodies, they looked to be well-trained. They were intimating.

Neal whipped around, glanced at the dead pilot, and placed his hand on Crane's shoulder. There's too many."

"What do you want to do? Give up?"

"We can't quit just because they got nasty. We'll separate. It'll be just like the old days when the cops chased us. They won't know which of us to chase first."

Stan nodded. Neal jerked his head toward the Huey's door. Firing their weapons in every direction they could, Stan and he dove out of the Huey. In unison, they hit the ground doing forward somersaults and ended up on their feet running in different directions. As the two divers watched in amazement, at Neal and Stan's acrobatic abilities, Crane leaped out of the Huey and faked to the side. With the lifesaving knowledge that even small amounts of water are enough to stop a bullet, he redirected himself to a diagonal route toward the lake.

Thirty meters from the divers, Crane sunk to his ankles in a dry slough of soft sand. Thrown off-balance, he toppled forward, his hands imprinting in the sand. With bullets zinging over his head, he scrambled, on all fours, over the sand until he stood up, ran toward the lake, and dove into the water.

Swimming underwater for as long as he could, he searched his pockets for his puff-pack. The seven minutes of air would come in handy. But before he could get the puff-pack out of his pocket, he surfaced and gasped for air. Prolonged muzzle flashes from the M-60 in the Huey blinked in his direction. On both sides of his head, bullets plinked into the water. He went under, again. A centimeter from his face, a bullet plowed under the water leaving a line of churned water and bubbles, but the bullet lost momentum within thirty centimeters.

Crane needed to go deeper and swim further away. He surfaced-dove and took two strokes toward the center of the lake. Beneath him, the outline of a miniature submarine took shape. For a moment, he thought the excitement had caused him to run out of air, and the effects of carbon dioxide buildup in his mind were causing illusions. He swam to the surface and looked to shore. The divers put on their flippers and stepped backward into the clear water of the lake.

Crane looked down into the water. The submarine was still there. It was no illusion. Now he knew why the divers didn't have air tanks. They had come from the mini-sub. They must have been using it to search for the sphere. The light on the sub would explain the reports of UFO's at night. The divers were going to swim back to the submarine. But not if Crane got to it first.

CHAPTER 26

Treading water on the surface of Lake Shikostsu, Crane filled his lungs with as much air as he could and surface-dove to the submarine. It looked like a steel-clad version of a two-man submarine. Its nose had a transparent acrylic dome that the divers had been looking through to search for the E-Brite. Under the dome, a robotic arm hung down as if it were broken. To enable the divers to search without air tanks, the sub had to have an airlock with a water tight hatch. Crane searched for it but couldn't find it. To his left, outlines of the divers approaching told him he had better find the hatch or swim away. Instead of depleting the air in his puff-pack, he surfaced for air. Although his head gathered a little warmth from the Japanese red evening sun, the cold water and exhaustion were beginning to slow his brain. It was getting difficult to focus on finding the hatch.

He dove down again.

This time he found the hatch, entered the sub, and secured the air lock. When he went to the controls, a cheap padlock had been placed into the security holes of the steering bars. Outside the sub, the divers had arrived. They pounded on the entry hatch. Crane pulled the power thruster lever. The propellers turned, but without control, power was of no use. He needed to be able to steer the sub. It only went in a circle. He pushed the thruster lever in. Then he took out his tine lock pick and held the tension on the lock's keyway. As he pulled down on the padlock, he inserted the lock pick and pushed in the tumblers until they were lined up.

The lock opened.

He hit the thrusters and steered toward shore.

The men in the wet suits hung onto the sub for a few meters, but without air tanks they were forced to let go and surface for air.

"Sorry, fellows," Crane said. "You'll have to find another ride home."

When the sub surfaced, calm water flowed against the acrylic dome. Surging forward, the twin propellers of the sub gurgled behind, leaving the men in the wet suits shaking their fists and bobbing way off in the center of the lake.

In deep water, a ways from shore, Crane lifted the dome of the sub and locked it open. Then he climbed over the side. With the dome open, he tilted the sub sideways. Water whooshed into the sub. He held the sub at the odd angle until the whooshing stopped. While the sub slowly sank to the bottom, he swam to shore.

With his wet suit coat clinging to his back and his tie flapping at his stomach, Crane waded out of the cold water. Under the last fading rays of the sun, he sagged against the side of a blue boat, and searched the area for anyone who would be waiting in ambush.

The windows in the Shikostsu hotel were lit and sent out a yellow feeling of warmth. He wished he could go in, rent a room, stand by a heater, and dry off. But in his present situation, that wish would be the final resort of a fool. Judging by the number of people who had showed up at the chopper, there were sure to be more people waiting for him at the hotel. The train station would be watched, too.

Chitose was the home of Hokkaido's largest airport, and a third of the city's inhabitants were military personnel, belonging to, or supporting the Seventh Division of the Japanese Imperial Army of Japan's Ground Self-defense Force. And Kuma Station military base personnel living off base were there, too. Even though the larger population of Chitose would make it easier for Crane to lose people following him, about the only safe place would be back at Kuma Station military base, inside a restricted area.

Except for a faint chill, the air around the lake was motionless, a sure sign of rain. With thunderheads clustered in the distance, Crane decided to make his way to the railroad tracks, grab onto a train, and steal a ride back to Chitose.

In total darkness, with only the light from a diffused moon to guide him, he sprinted in explosive spurts over the vegetation and weaved around small trees. Thunder threatened and lighting bolts reached down from the sky. But Crane wasn't concerned.

When a searchlight made a bright sweep toward the slight drop in the land where he was standing, he became concerned real fast. He fell to the ground, flattened in sparse vegetation, and waited for the light to stop searching.

But the light didn't stop searching.

While it continued to sweep past, four figures appeared and ran toward him.

Remembering his top of the hill training, on forethought and audacity to overcome large odds, Crane reached into his pocket, took out his penlight, and turned it on. Making sure the men saw the light, he jumped up and continued running.

After what seemed miles, demanding air, his lungs cramped. Panting and sweating from exertion, he stopped at what he had been looking for: a stream. The men chasing him had not given up, and it looked like they were never going to tire.

Knowing that all warfare is based on deception, Crane reached into his wallet, took out a condom, and placed the lit penlight into it. Then he blew the condom up until it was the size of a balloon and tied the end. Now he had something like Admiral Sir Thomas John Cochrane had used way back in the 1800s when his unarmed merchant ship had been too slow to outrun the heavy gunned frigate that had gained on him all day and was guided at night by the faint glimmer of light from his ship. But as the frigate drew near, towards daybreak, it discovered that it had been chasing a tub with a lantern in it, and the merchant ship was nowhere to be seen.

The condom wasn't at tub with a lantern in it, but Crane placed it into the flowing stream. As the lighted condom was swept downstream, he hoped it would be a successful tactical deception and draw whoever was hunting him away.

With the penlight directing his pursuers to where he was not going, Crane dropped to the ground, tried to make himself part of the scenery, and studied the arca. When he was sure his pursuers were following the penlight floating down the stream, he made no more visibly disturbance than a snake or a rabbit and crawled over the ground and slithered through the grass. After the length of a football field, he stood up, took off running, and headed for the railroad tracks.

When the tracks were fifty meters away, he thought the train would be there, but it wasn't. And he couldn't hear or see it coming.

A rumble came from the east. The ground shook. This time it wasn't the threatening storm. It was one of the many earthquakes that frequented the area. Crane stood up to run. The earth jostled beneath his feet. The shock traveled across his entire body. For a moment, his cheeks and eyeballs were compressed. Then the ground weaved under his feet, buckled his knees and sent him to the ground. He looked to his right. Twenty meters from him, bathed in the illumination of a dropped spotlight, a huge man was sprawled on the ground. The light in the condom had fooled three of the men, but a fourth one had turned back and continued to follow.

As if he had Crane trapped, the man twisted his thick lips and smiled a vicious smile. The man's long black hair looked like it had enough oil in it to lubricate a train engine. The scary part was that he looked heavy and strong, really strong. He could have easily shot Crane, but he didn't. The man believing Crane knew where the E-Brite sphere was, happened to be the only reason he was still alive. The moment Crane gave up the location of the E-Brite, he would be dead. The man's only hope was to catch him alive. But this man would not hesitate to beat him within a shadow of his life.

Crane watched him. For a big man, he moved fast. He feinted to his right, stopped, and dared Crane to come near.

Crane wondered how long the man would be fast. He stood still and waited.

The man's face took on a fiendish look. He leaped forward. His huge left hand scythed around in a giant roundhouse swoop. Crane ducked under it, stepped past the man and came up behind him. As if his legs were tree trunks rooted into the ground, the man stopped solid. Then spun and faced Crane.

To Crane's surprise, the man tried the same roundhouse move again. Again, Crane ducked under the deadly arm. The man began to breathe heavy. Crane didn't know if the man was getting tired or just warming up. Crane turned to run. The man grabbed the hair on the back of Crane's head and flung him onto the ground.

Acting as if he were knocked out, Crane lay still. When the man's legs were a footstep away from him, Crane sprang to all fours and rolled into the man's legs. Surprised, the man stumbled. Falling forward, he windmilled his arms. Before he hit the ground, his giant fist passed a centimeter above Crane's head. Crane jumped to his feet. Like most big guys, this man was turning out to be a poor fighter. With his huge chest heaving and his breathing coming in labored breaths, he wobbled to his feet and held his fist low, ready to strike. His size had probably scared all his former opponents away. He wasn't used to fighting.

Usually a big man ends a fight with one punch, but the weights this man had lifted hadn't developed his finesse. Crane figured the man didn't have the adrenaline-fueled fitness a person needed to fight on the street.

Like a freight train, the big man ran right at Crane.

Crane simply sidestepped and let his fist fly into the man's stomach. Although Crane's arm felt as it were going to snap off from the impact of the heavy and overpowering force, the man bowed over. Crane kneed him in the face. The man's head snapped back, but only slightly. It felt like Crane had jammed his knee into a cement block. But the man went down on one knee and looked up as if he enjoyed it. Crane kicked him in the ribs. The man bent slightly sideways but stayed on his knee. Three times Crane danced in and out, kicking or punching the breathless man.

The earthquake gave one last rumble and was still. The light of the oncoming train beamed down the tracks. Behind it, a long necklace of railroad cars followed. Before the train picked up too much speed to grab onto, Crane had to catch it. But he would have to get around the man.

As if nothing had happened, the man got to his feet and picked up his spotlight. Crane figured it might take hours to finish the invincible man. He didn't have time to finish him. For some reason his friend Rafferty's whacky humor came to mind. "If he's bigger, you'll have an advantage. He'll be easier to see."

Crane reared back to strike the man in the face. When the man jerked his hands up to block the punch, Crane stomped on the man's foot. While the man dropped his hands and looked at his foot, Crane dashed away.

Weaving and bobbing to avoid the searchlight, Crane sprinted toward the tracks and the oncoming train. As a breeze blew dust, he ran around a chaos of boards from a shack or something that had collapsed. After he had run the fifty meters to the tracks, he jumped across them, and landed in a pile of broken bricks and dust. As the dust puffed around his feet, he stepped out of the broken bricks, dropped down, and waited for the train.

Just before the head engine of the train passed, the lumbering man dropped the spotlight, and sailed in front of the beaming light of the train. Just missing getting hit, he landed on Crane's side of the tracks.

As if a war had begun, thunder rumbled, and ice blue lightning lit up the black night. A hateful sounding wind flailed distant trees and blasted into Crane's face. For a few moments, all was dark. Then the sky cracked with twin bolts of lightning, and dark clouds seemed to unfurl and allow a slice of moonlight to brighten the land. But a gush of rain fell from the heavens and blocked out the light. As the wheels beneath the moving train zipped past, they caused the light from the dropped spotlight, coming from the other side of the tracks, to flutter as if it were a strobe light. With rain beating his body, Crane grabbed onto the grab iron on the front of a moving railroad car. The dark had caused him to underestimate the speed of the train. It was going much too fast for a person to safely grab onto. He was slammed against the side of the car so hard his arm felt as if it were going to be pulled out of its socket. Pain receptors started their furious onslaught to his brain. His grip slipped to the ends of his fingers. Ignoring the pain, he re-gripped, managed to hang on, and watch the invincible man.

The invincible man flashed Crane a sickly smile and grabbed the back grab-iron of the moving car. Three bolts of lightning flashed in a row. At the same instant, a stutter of bright blue light, from the flashes, illuminated the man just as the momentum of the train slammed him into the open space between the cars. His sickly smile vanished. Even though his fingers had a vice like grip, they were no match for the speed of the train and the whipping motion of his body. As his long, black hair flew outward, his fingers were ripped from the grab iron. He sailed under the wheels that gave out dull thuds as his body was cut into chunks and were flung out and under the car. And the train whistle wailed into the night.

Even though the rain sprayed into his face, and night wind blew cold against his body, Crane was thankful his time hopping trains on the Erie Railroad had taught him to grab onto the front of a moving railroad car, not the rear. The momentum of the pickup had slammed him to the side of the car. If he would have grabbed onto the back of the moving car, like the man had done, the momentum would have slammed him toward the opening between the cars, and ripped his fingers from the grab-irons. He would have been thrown under the wheels, too.

When the train slowed for the Chitose Station, Crane hoped off and began walking.

A ways down the tracks, a curtain of rain and cold air hit his wet clothes. As he stepped away from the tracks and limped along, weak yellow light from a row of unpainted houses, was etched between the puddles. Its weird glow caused a vision of the man's body parts being flung out from under the train to vividly flash in his mind. He dropped his chin to his chest and shook with ague. The first time it hadn't been a pleasant thing to see, and this time hadn't been, either.

When the rain threw a curtain of clouds across the night and rattled on the tin roofs of the houses, he began to run and look for shelter. After running past a few streets, the rain ceased, but the eaves on buildings and the leaves on small trees still dripped.

Before the railroad crossing in Chitose, he slowed to a walk. As he wiped the rain from his forehead, the whisper of a V-8 engine and the faint exhaust burble from twin tailpipes met his ears. Japanese cars didn't sound like that. It was like he was in a dream. He was back in the states. Just like the old days, when his friends, Neal and Rafferty, were coming in Neal's 1940 Ford. Crane shook his head to clear the thought, but the tires of a 1940 mud-spattered Ford stuttered on a hard-packed dirt alleyway and lurched to a nose-dipping stop. When Crane looked at the back of the car, dual exhaust pipes with chrome tips protruded out from under the back bumper. This was usually a sign that the engine was a souped-up V-8. For a moment, he thought it could actually be Neal and Rafferty, but this Ford was different from the Ford Neal had had in the states. Instead of having a steel body painted with a coat of gray primer, signifying it was a Hot Rod work in progress, always being made faster and better, this Ford had an almost shiny black finish, and the engine snarled as if it were new.

As Crane stood there on the wet street, he almost expected to see Neal and Rafferty sitting on the blue rolled and pleated leather seats that reflected upward and caused the white interior roof of the Ford to give off a royal blue glow.

He walked toward the Ford.

The storm rolled across the sky.

Rain pattering on the roof of the Ford, made it quite dreary-looking.

The back door flew open.

The driver stuck his head out the window.

It was Neal.

Frantically waving his hand, he yelled, "Get in!"

A fire-orange bolt of lightning ripped the black sky and was immediately followed by a bellow of thunder. Crane ran to the Ford, slid onto the front seat, and slammed the door.

Stan looked over at him. "What took you so long? We've been waiting for an hour."

"How did you know I would be on the train?"

"What else could you do?"

To Crane's astonishment, Stan was right. He was glad they were on the same wavelength.

Stan lifted one finger and ticked it toward Crane. "Great minds think alike."

Neal leaned over and gave Crane a curious look. "If we would have left anybody but you back there, they would have never made it here."

"That's right," Stan added. "There was no way you should have gotten out of the mess you were in. But one of the reasons we like you to tag along is that you have a knack for getting out of things like that."

"Thanks for the vote of confidence," Crane said, but he was still having a hard time believing he was sitting in a 1940 coup almost like the one Neal, he, and Rafferty had ridden in when they had discovered the weird key to Al Capone's vault. He couldn't help checking the floor shift to see if a clear plastic rectangular wedge from a beer tap handle that encased the word "Koehler's" and had the beer company's logo of a black eagle crest was there. But the knob screwed onto the floor shift was only a plain black ball.

"Don't get complacent," Neal said. "This thing's not as fast as our old Ford, but it has a V-8 engine that's better than anything the Japanese make."

"The mud on this thing must be glued on. The rain isn't even washing it off."

"Yeah. Neal said," That stuff's dried on. We'd have to soak it in water to get it off."

Although the Ford was not their old Ford, Crane had a fondness for it and wanted to see what it looked like without the mud. "I wish we could get it off," Crane said and surveyed the shoddy interior. "Where did you get this thing?"

Without saying a word, Neal pointed to the dashboard.

The olive drab painted dashboard and the torn and old upholstering of the car told Crane the 40 Ford was a military vehicle left over from World War II, but had a newer and more powerful engine.

Neal spun out of an alley, and plowed through a puddle. With spray from the tires hissing against the underside of the Ford, and the windshield wipers sweeping aside sheets of rain, he banged a right and drove onto the paved highway that lead to Kuma Station military base.

"We made it out this time," Neal said. "But don't stop looking over your shoulder."

"I'm not too worried," Crane said and leaned back in the thickly padded seat. "I don't think run of the mill bullets can go through the steel on this car."

Stan gave Crane a thumbs-up. "That's one reason we got it."

A light rain was falling. Except for the rolling tires of the Ford singing on the pavement, it was quiet outside. Relaxing in the seat and trying to get used to Neal driving on the left side of the road, Crane was ready to get dried off, eat a good meal, and catch some rest. "Once I get back to the base, I'll be okay."

With his hands resting lightly on the bottom curve of the steering wheel, Neal jerked his head around and looked at Crane. "No, you won't."

"Why not?"

"You're not going back."

"Wait a minute," Crane said and looked to Stan. "You told me that I was in the army and not in the Army. That I don't actually exist as being in Chitose, and if I go AWOL, the Kuma Station's military police might pick me up, but they'll be notified that I am on temporary duty."

"That's correct," Stan replied. "However, now that the colonel's dead, we believe you have been reduced to a regular agency soldier with no special treatment."

Crane slumped with disappointment. "If I don't go back, I'll be AWOL."

The Ford jolted over a set of railroad tracks, and Stan broke into loud laughter. "So what? Would you rather be dead?"

"I guess you're right," Crane said and rubbed his empty stomach." I'm hungry. How about we stop at a restaurant or a bar?"

While the windshield wipers dragged across the glass, Neal scanned the area beyond the railroad tracks. "I'd like to do just that. But if one of the two demolition specialists that are after us stops in a bar or a restaurant for ten seconds, ten minutes later, an extremely loud bomb will go off. It won't knock the place down, but if we're in there, the concussion will knock us senseless."

Crane scooted forward and rested his hand on the top of the dashboard. "Just as long as they think I know where the E-Brite is, they won't kill me."

"Maybe they won't, but they'll make you wish you were dead."

Neal turned off the main road, maneuvered the Ford around a small alley, and continued driving. "Didn't the top of the hill teach you how to identify and exploit your opponent's strengths and weaknesses?"

"They did," Crane said. "But I didn't expect to get into a mess like this. Maybe I should go back to the base."

Flashing Crane a shark-like smile, Neal said, "The colonel isn't the only person who wanted the E-Brite. Think about it. Why would the colonel send a lowly Spec/5 to find it?"

"Because I saved Stan's life?"

"Maybe, but they knew you would always come back to the safety of the base. As a back-up, officers and maybe a few enlisted men are waiting for you."

"The Colonel's dead. I'll just tell them the truth."

"He may be dead, but a central authority was never established over military operations in Southeast Asia. I don't know how far his authority extends, but I'd say it extends far enough for his cronies to do a job on you. If you go back to the base, those who were under his authority will arrange a little smearing to make you look like a fool. They'll say you're trying to pull off some sort of a dangerous crank, or pull a cruel joke on the agency.

Neal was right. But Crane didn't want to accept the fact that he could never go back to the base.

CHAPTER 27

Sitting in the 1940 black Ford, Crane realized he had two choices. He could go back to the base and be imprisoned or tortured. Or he could go with Neal and Stan. They were going to where the real E-Brite sphere had been hidden.

Crane went with them.

As Neal drove the Ford down the dark road, headlights, from traffic, coming from the opposite direction, twinkled diamond bright. Up ahead, bright-red taillights glowed soft and peaceful. When a red Nissan rushed up behind the Ford with its high beams blasting into the rearview mirror and reflecting back into Neal's eyes, the peaceful feeling vanished. Neal gripped the steering wheel so hard his knuckles turned white. Squinting into the rearview mirror, he reached up and adjusted it to cut the glare. The Nissan with the blinding high beams was almost touching the back bumper of the Ford.

The man inside the Nissan was not wearing a helmet. When behind the wheel of any vehicle, all Japanese military personnel were required to wear helmets. The man was not military. The Ford coupe dwarfed the compact Nissan, and its flimsy grill was no match for the Ford's heavy steel bumper. If Neal stomped on the brakes, the sudden stop would cause the Nissan to crash into the heavy bumper. It would break the beaming headlights and crush the radiator of the Nissan.

Neal cast a devious glance in Stan's direction. "Should I hit the brakes?"

Before Stan could answer, with one long angry blare of the horn, the Nissan shot around them. Neal relaxed his hands on the steering wheel and navigated through the congested streets until he turned onto a dirt road that had been oiled to control dust. A few streets from the building where the E-Brite had been hidden, they stopped, got out, and walked to the building. While they walked, the oiled road glistened with a reflected glow, and a lone light on a tall pole cast a crooked shadow over the rusted tin roof of an unpainted, wooden building. The building seemed to be a deserted fire-trap. It was an unlikely place to hide anything of value. About ten meters from the building, another building sat next to a Japanese flower garden planted with small trees and shrubs. Near the door of the building, two bicycles rested against the outside wall. Just in front of the bicycles, a dirty-white rooster swiveled his head searching for anything edible.

Neal stepped toward the door of the building with the rusted tin roof. "Let's go."

Stan and Crane followed.

Neal walked to the entrance of the building and slid the white-paper-windowed door to the side. Inside, the place was simple and clean. Decorated in traditional Japanese style, long rice paper scrolls, covered with stylized characters in thick red and black ink, hung on the walls. Just off to the left, slippers waited. Japanese custom dictated that guests entering homes take off their shoes and replace them with slippers. A short distance from the slippers, a group of slender Japanese women with rich black hair and dark eyes sat in a lamp-lit circle. Paper shapes representing flowers, swans, and various animals encircled them. Talking and drinking tea, they were in the process of *orgomei*, folding paper to make flowers and birds. Neal took one step toward them.

Shaking her finger at him, an older woman in a white rabbit's fur jacket got up. Waving her well-manicured hands, she shooed him back to the slippers. "Dommie, put on slipper."

Crane was amazed that no matter where the Japanese women lived or where they were, they were always extremely clean and wanted everybody else to be clean, too. But he couldn't understand why the woman was wearing a rabbit-fur jacket in the summer time.

Neal stopped and held up both hands. "We're not staying. We're here for the midnight special."

The Japanese woman's almond eyes lit up. She whispered, "You say, 'midnight special?'"

Neal nodded. "Midnight special."

The woman gave him an appraising look. How many?"

Neal held up three fingers. "Just-a-three."

As if midnight special were the correct answer to a code, the woman smiled. "Okay, Joe. Forget about slippers." She gathered against him and gestured to a rice-paper-screened door. As the women in the circle cackled with mischief, she stepped to the door, and slid it open.

Crane figured the woman in the circle thought they were there for a good time, and he didn't want them to think differently.

Neal, Stan, and Crane stepped through the small door opening and could barely fit into the little room. The woman bent down, peeled back a rug, and revealed a trapdoor. Scrunching together, they all moved back.

Neal bent down to open the trapdoor.

The women held up her hand. "*Chotto Matte!*" Wait!

She went to the wall, moved a picture, and flipped a switch. "Okay! Now you open."

Neal opened the door. A wooden club sat on the first step of steps that led down into a dark hole. Around the trapdoor frame, a fairly rudimentary but effective security system was revealed. Small rectangular contact pads on the trapdoor frame led to wires stapled along the underside of the floor.

The woman placed her hand on the rice-paper-screened door to leave. Neal bent over, picked up the wooden club, and gently held her shoulder. Apparently thinking Neal was going to hit her with the club, she stiffened in momentary surprise and let out a muffled wail. Before anyone knew with was happening, she reached under her rabbit fur jacket, and pulled out a small pistol.

Neal dropped the club. Clunk! It hit the floor. He held up one hand in a surrendering gesture. "*Chotto Matte*"! Wait! With his other hand, he reached into his pocket, pulled out a roll of Japanese yen and waved it in front of her face. "Mama-san, you stay here until we come back. If someone comes" — he pointed to the club — "hit the steps three times with that."

Smiling, the woman placed the pistol back under her rabbit-fur coat and took the money. Then she picked up the club and held up three fingers. "Three time."

Holding up three fingers, Neal nodded. "Three time."

Aggressively nodding, the women smiled. "Okay! I do."

Neal pulled out his Zippo lighter, lit it, and leapt down the stone steps two at a time. Stan was next, followed by Crane. At the bottom of the steps, they splashed across an underground stream.

Crane peered into the darkness. "Is this some kind of cave?"

Stan gasped triumphantly. "It's not a cave. Its shape is too regular. It's a tunnel.

A few steps from the stream, Neal reached over his head, worked his hand into an opening, and pulled out an oil-coated AK-47. The oil helped keep rust off the rifle, but the AK 47 was a very reliable weapon, it was known to fire with sand in the chamber. After checking the action and making sure it was loaded, he continued down the tunnel.

From behind them, three sharp raps from the woman's club slapped the air and continued down the length of the tunnel.

Neal turned around. "Somebody must have followed us. Let's get out. We'll have to come back later."

They turned around, splashed through the stream, and, taking two steps at a time, they leapt up the steps and stopped at the top. As quietly as he could, Neal closed the trapdoor and pulled the rug back over it. Then he turned to Crane and Stan. "Follow my lead," he commanded. "Pretend we've just finished with a good time."

So the women sitting in the circle wouldn't see it, Neal held the AK-47 on his side, and with his other hand, he pretended to be zipping up his fly.

The woman dropped the club and slid the rice-paper-screened door open. The other Japanese women were sloped forward sitting on the floor around the pile of *orgomei.* When they turned their attention to the open door, Crane, Stan, and Neal flashed huge smiles at them. Hiding their faces, they giggled like school girls.

Walking backwards to conceal the AK-47, Neal smiled, repeatedly, bowed, and said, "*Domo arigato,*" thank you, in Japanese.

Crane and Stan did the same, and they made their way to the door that led outside.

Outside, the dirty-white rooster was still swiveling his head looking for something to eat. Neal slung the AK-47 over his shoulder and breathed a sigh of relief. "Maybe it was a false alarm. Check around. If everything's all right, we'll go back in."

Before they could separate and search the area, the unmistakable report of an M-14 rifle spitting fire met Crane's ears. A bullet hissed past Stan's head.

They dropped to the ground. The dirty-white rooster squawked once and took off running. Two men ran around the side of the building. All around, bullets sung through the air.

Neal unslung the AK-47 and turned toward to where the men had run. One of the men crouched behind a stack of firewood. Neal turned the AK-47 around and hosed him with lead. With blood puffing from his head, the man slumped across the pile of wood. For a moment, everything was still and quiet. As Crane scanned the area looking for the other man, the wood pile gave out one clunk. The dead man on the top of the pile slanted to the side. The wood pile toppled over and revealed the other man. His bloodied face was twisted with rage.

Neal sprang to his feet, stood against the wall of the building, and shot at the man. The bullet hit a kerosene fuel tank. A jet of kerosene spurted from the hole and splashed onto the side of the building. As the odor of kerosene filled the air, Crane was glad the tank wasn't filled with gas. Kerosene had a lower flash point, but once ignited, it would burn quickly, and a long time.

The man gave Neal a cold smile. Neal tried to fire again. The ammo wouldn't fire. Apparently it had sat too long in the dampness under the house. The man reached behind his back. Neal yelled to Crane, "Get outta there!" and took off running. Before Crane knew what was happening, a glimmering blade whipped past his head.

The man reached behind his back again. "I get you this time," he said with a malicious smile.

Although it wouldn't stop the knife, Crane shielded his face with his arm

Farh oomph! Fuel from the fuel tank ignited. Fire engulfed the side of the building and crawled under the tin roof. The man with the knife vanished somewhere behind the flames. Instant and intense heat blasting into Crane's face caused him to flinch and turn away. Screams of Japanese women pierced the freshly fire-lit night. The outside of the exit door on the house was engulfed in bright orange flames. If the women couldn't get out, they would burn to death. If Crane could get to a window, and if the window was as old and flimsy as the rest of house, he might be able to break the window frame and get them out.

He took one step. A long and continuous stream of machine gun fire filled the air. He crouched down. The machine gun fell silent. In its place was only ringing in his ears. Whomever was firing the weapon had not been trained properly. He should have squeezed the trigger and let off a few rounds. That was how a trained person shot any automatic weapon. If the person didn't take his finger off the trigger and use short, controlled bursts, even half of a two-hundred-round belt of ammunition would go very fast.

Hoping it would take the man a few seconds to reload, Crane dropped to the ground, crawled around the corner of the house, and looked for the knife-throwing man.

In the brief time, it had taken Crane to crawl to cover, the blaze had grown astonishingly fast. He didn't see the man. But when he looked up at the window, a sea of soot and fumes rolled from under the eaves of the roof. Right next to his head, veins of red fire made their way down the side of the building. Smoke growing thicker by the second, billowed toward him, and caused rawness to burn in his throat. In a few seconds, the fire would flare and fry him where he lay, and it would be impossible to break out the window frame.

Attempting to draw a deep breath of air before he broke the window frame, he found the air was devoid of oxygen. Like instant sunburn, searing heat from yellow flames, dancing at him in random leaps, painfully seared his face. He could not breathe. On his hands and knees, he scrambled away from the heat. When he looked back at the house and took in a few breaths of good air, red and menacing, thick tongues of blue and orange fire licked angrily, occasionally bursting fifteen meters into the air, fully engulfing the structure and sending gray smoke into the night sky.

Illuminated by the light of the rapidly forming fireball, Crane took off his suit coat and wrapped it around his fist. Then, staying low, he ran to the house and crashed his coat-wrapped fist through the window.

The glass broke easily, taking with it the two pieces of wood that separated the two-paned window. Clouds of smoke poured from within. No one could see through that smoke. Crane thought it was useless. But for a moment, the smoke cleared. With smoke billowing behind them, the wild-eyed, terrified women rushed to the window, but the opening was too small for them to get out. The white rabbit fur on the lady's coat was beginning to smolder. Any second, it would ignite.

Crane gripped the bottom of the window frame and pulled. To his surprise, the whole bottom of the window frame and the bottom boards, below it, let lose so easily that he fell backwards, skidded across the ground, and stopped with the window and the boards on top of him. The women jumped out of the opening and rushed to safety.

Crane stood up. As the boards fell from his body, he looked toward the fire. Silhouetted against the orange flames, the knife throwing man stood in front of him. Although the man's eyes were cold and gray, his face reflected the orange light of the growing fire, and caused him to look like some sort of a devil. Crane hadn't noticed it before, but the man was taller than he was. All the guards were taller than short Japanese men. The guards were not Japanese. The man's cold gray eyes warmed a little. With a jerk of his head, the man gestured to the other side of the house, then lifted five fingers. His long, dirty fingernails and skin were caked with unimaginable grime. He must have been trying to save the Japanese women. He pointed away from the house and into the darkness. Apparently impressed or thankful that Crane had saved the Japanese women, the man was giving him five seconds to run away.

For a moment, Crane stared in wonder at the huge fireball.

As if he were on the verge of crying, the man jerked his five opened fingers toward Crane. "Go!"

Crane stopped his stare and broke into a fear-driven sprint. As he ran down the street, gun shots rang out behind him. The real sound of a bullet passing close to a person's head is just a little sizzle and a stream of agitated air. It is instantaneously followed by the sharp report of the rifle the bullet had come from. And that had just happened. Crane hoped they hadn't shot Stan or Neal.

The light of the fire caused the silver keys in the ignition of a black Honda motorcycle, parked on the side of the street, to blink orange. Crane stopped, threw his leg over the seat, turned the ignition key, and jumped on the kick starter. The engine sputtered but did not start. He reached under the side of the fuel tank and turned the fuel valve on. He jumped on the kick starter again. The engine roared to lifc. He pulled the clutch in and jammed his left foot down. The transmission clicked into first gear. He revved the engine and let out the clutch. In his excitement, he had given the engine too much fuel and had let out the clutch too fast. This Honda wasn't his old belt-driven, one-speed Wizzer motorbike he had when he was a kid. This was a gear and chain driven motorcycle. It had power. The front wheel came up higher than his head. To keep from being forced over backwards and having the motorcycle land on him, he slammed his feet down on the ground. The back wheel shot forward and the front end of the motorcycle flipped over backwards. He couldn't hold it. The handle bar grips flew out of his hands. The motorcycle fell to the ground and bent the handle bars into a half pretzel shape.

If he could manage to upright the motorcycle, he may still be able to steer it. He bent over and grabbed the side of the motorcycle. A metallic click sounded to his left. He looked toward the sound. A man with a white helmet and an official looking uniform aimed some sort of a machine gun in his direction and pulled the trigger.

Hammering sounds banged into the night. A stream of bullets sputtered from the barrel. A single shot zinged past Crane's left arm. One bullet thunked into the gas tank, but it didn't ignite. Crane figured he should be filled full of holes, but the man must have been inexperienced. Unable to control the weapon, its barrel had tugged upward, sending most of the deadly lead into the night sky. As if the weapon had malfunctioned, the man lowered it and looked at it. A rope-like stream of gas spewed out of the hole in the tank. It looked as if the gas wasn't going to ignite. Crane estimated that there was still enough gas in the tank to ride the length of a football field. He lifted the motorcycle to an upright position. Another shot zinged through the air. He felt a swoosh of air from a bullet that flew past his knee. Ping! The bullet struck the frame of the motorcycle. A bright orange spark flew sideways and hit the gas-soaked engine. The motorcycle burst into flames. Crane took one last fleeting look at the motorcycle. With the promise of a swift and effortless escape gone, he took a few cautious steps down the street and stopped.

Like a reincarnated primeval giant, a huge man with a red beard, towering five inches over six feet and weighing more than two hundred fifty pounds, appeared from nowhere and stood directly in front of Crane.

Just as the man reached out to grab Crane, a bullet smashed through the man's teeth. Although he was a gigantic man, from the surprised look of horror on his face, it was apparent that he had discovered that the lead was bad tasting and indigestible.

As the man grabbed his mouth and folded to the ground, Crane turned left and sprinted across an open field.

At one point, it felt as if he had stepped into a bottomless pit. When his foot bottomed out, too late, he realized he had stepped into a hole. He tripped forward, caught himself with his hands, but twisted his knee. He struggled to his feet and limped along until he stopped at the base of a tall stone wall. Here, breath by ragged breath, he pulled himself to the top. As his heart pounded, he lay flat, listened, and tried to keep his breathing silent. The only sound was the wind. It seemed desolate and lifeless, until, as if they were out for an afternoon stroll, Neal and Stan came walking along the wall. Although they acted as if nothing had happened, their bedraggled figures showed that they had flirted with death and had almost lost.

Crane whispered down to them. "When we going back?"

Neal and Stan turned with a jolt and looked up.

Crane smiled down at them.

"This is not like the States," Neal said, "where people wait for weeks for an insurance adjuster to come and look at the burnt-down house. The Japanese are industrious. Sometimes they have the place cleaned up and another house started the next day."

Stan shook his head. "We won't be going back there until the place cools off. Come on down."

Getting ready to jump off the wall, Crane let his legs slip over the side, and a strange low-frequency thrum filled the air. He looked toward the sound. On the moon-dazzled outskirts of town, a dark helicopter descended toward the open field. It didn't have the familiar whop-whop sound of the blades of a Huey. For a helicopter, it was quiet. Crane had no idea what kind of helicopter it was. True to form, many things in the ASA ran independently. No one had a complete picture of any operation. Everything of importance was always based on a need to know. But he did know that he was grateful that Neal had gotten some help.

Crane dropped and hit the ground. Pain exploded in his knee.

With concern, Neal looked to him. "Can you run?"

Crane massaged his knee. "I'm not sure."

"Get sure. Our ride's here."

The ride in the covert helicopter was silent and uneventful. No one manning the chopper talked. Crane figured everyone had been recruited unofficially for a mission too secret to be on any books. By keeping quiet there were fewer chances of anyone rooting out the hidden identities of the true puppet masters of the operation.

CHAPTER 28

When Crane, Stan, and Neal rode in a cab to come back to get the E-Brite at the burned down house, they wondered if the Ford would still be there. It was. But when they got out of the cab, a few streets away from the Ford, all that remained of the burned down house was one slow tendril of smoke curling from one blackened timber next to a toppled chimney that was half-buried in a smoldering ash pile, hissing in the rain. Even the dirty-white rooster was gone.

With a hangdog, hopeless look, Neal turned to Stan. "Now what?"

"Don't forget," Stan said, "in the wrong hands, there is a chance the E-Brite could cause an unstoppable nuclear reaction and ignite the world."

A spasm of irritation crossed Neal's face. "The scientists that took it were always afraid it would get into the wrong hands."

Crane raised an eyebrow. "I guess it would be nice to use the E-Brite to provide enough power for every building on earth."

"That great dream is still possible," Stan said with hope in his voice. "That's why we have to sift through the ashes, find it, and make sure it gets into the proper hands."

Crane eyed Stan suspiciously. "And just where are the proper hands?"

Stan's mouth curved into an exaggerated tooth-filled smile. "Shemya."

Shemya could be the loneliest place on earth. Crane froze in astonishment. "What?"

"Remember those secret tunnels that were supposed to be dug by the Japanese during World War II?"

Crane stared at Stan, his eyed half-lidded. "I was told there were no such tunnels."

A faint smile crossed Stan's face. "Naturally. You didn't have a need to know."

"If there were tunnels, earthquakes would have caused them to cave in."

"All tunnels in Alaska had to be earthquake proof." To emphasize the expanse of the tunnels, Stan opened his arms. "The steel reinforced walls, ceilings, and floors are at least four-foot thick. "It's almost an underground city."

"That must have been where Boozer went when he couldn't be found."

Neal fixed Crane with a questioning gaze. "Who's Boozer?"

Compassion filled Stan's face. "The longest living resident of Shemya."

Even though it would be interesting to see the covert facility buried beneath the tundra of Shemya that now occupied what had once been secret tunnels and bomb shelters during World War II, Crane didn't want to go back to there. A wave of gloom resonated through his body, but the thought of the malamute husky panting with his tongue lolling and his tail wagging brightened his spirits.

He took a step toward the ashes. "Let's get this thing dug out."

Neal and Stan laughed.

"What's so funny?"

Looking around, Stan opened his arms and turned his palms up. "That car that passed us, got here first. And the Ford is still where we parked it. They're out there waiting. Don't you know we're being watched?"

It made sense. With a prize, as important as E-Brite, someone would surely be watching and waiting until they dug it out. Then those someone's would simply take it from their dead hands.

Crane shrugged. "What do we do now?"

Neal looked surprised at Crane's question. "Why can't you panic in a flood?"

Crane nodded. "Because I would be too busy swimming."

"That's right," Neal said and looked toward the ashes. "We go to keep right on swimming. Act like a Vietnamese moved in next door and ate your dog. Look like you're disappointed. We'll pretend the E-Brite isn't here and walk away."

Stan placed his hands in his pockets and faked a hangdog, hopeless look. "They'll split forces and keep following us, but they'll never catch that Ford. After we ditch them and come back, there will be fewer of them to deal with. And we can set up a few surprises."

Crane hoped Neal's surprises were nightingale devices, A CIA-developed diversionary device that had continuing explosions that sounded like a firefight. He turned to Neal. "Where did you get nightingale devices?"

"I didn't. But we'll make something just a good."

Now, Crane knew Neal was talking about flash simulators. "But we don't have scales."

"Neal smiled. "We won't need them."

They ran down the street and jumped into the mud-spattered Ford coupe. With a rooster tail of gravel and dirt shooting out from the back tires, and the red sergeant-striped taillights blazing bright, they spun around in a whirl of dust and sped away.

A few miles down the road, like some kind of haggard ghost, a black Nissan pickup with a missing muffler thundered past and pulled right in front of the Ford. Neal jerked the steering wheel and just missed the Nissan. "Sonumbitch," he cussed. They must think we have the E-Brite. Those amateurs are coming after us."

He hunched his muscular back and hit the gas. The wheels on the right side of the Ford blasted along the side of the road, and like smoke, dust trailed behind them.

This was a side of Neal Crane had seen before. It reminded him of the wild days they had spent together chasing Al Capone's vault. Looking in every direction, without moving his head, Neal found an opening, swung the car past three lumbering trucks, did a complete U-turn, and started back the way they had come. But the Nissan was behind them, again.

Looking in the rearview mirror, Neal cussed. "So, you think you're gonna get on my ass again?"

He raced way ahead of the Nissan and pulled the Ford off to the side of the road.

"What did you stop here for," Stan whined. "Were like sittin' ducks."

Keeping an eye on the rearview mirror, Neal placed his hand on the door handle. "Don't worry about it. I'm going to take care of that tin car. We'll be rich and live forever, or die trying. Take over the wheel."

Neal jumped out of the Ford.

Stan slid behind the steering wheel.

Neal raced to the edge of the road, stopped, and picked up a good-sized throwing rock. As the Nissan slowed, he sprang from the front of the Ford and threw the rock. It flew through the air and crashed through the windshield of the Nissan.

Suddenly shocked, the man driving jerked his hands from the wheel and turned sideways.

The wheels on the Nissan locked up, skidded past the Ford, and its right side slipped into a ditch, causing the wheels on the left side to spin in the air.

Neal brushed his hands together and jumped back into the Ford. "See? Nothin' to it."

Stomping on the gas, Stan shook his head, and they took off down the road.

Just before they were at the Chitose River Bridge, a shot rang out. An olive drab duce-and-a half truck with a white star on its door came up from behind and rammed the rear bumper of the Ford. At the same time, another shot rang out, and Crane was knocked backwards by another ram from the duce-and-a-half.

The bumpers on the Ford were no match for the M35 two and one-half ton cargo truck with the nickname duce-and-a-half. Although the huge truck had been initially used by the United States Army and many nations around the world, Crane had no idea where the huge truck had come from. And it was coming at them, again.

He wedged his feet up against the dashboard, and the duce-and-a-half rammed them, again. The impact snapped their heads back against the seats. Stan battled with the steering wheel, but the Ford, fishtailed out of control. It smashed through the pipe railing, and skidded down the steep bank, and splashed into the Chitose River below. A cliff of water surged up out of the river and blasted into and over the newly cracked windshield. The Ford rolled, landed on its passenger side, and caused Crane to slam his nose into the dashboard.

Seemingly completely unscathed, Neal looked out the window. Water was flowing past the it. He grinned at Crane. "I guess you got your wish. The car's soaking to get the mud off." His grin faded. "You okay?"

Seeing stars from his nose hitting the dashboard, and not wanting Neal to know he was in pain, Crane moved his arms and lied. "Yeah?"

Neal nodded and he and Stan scrambled out the opened door.

Crane's tried to follow them, but his left foot was numb. He wondered if he had been shot. At first, because the shock to the central nervous system is too great, a gunshot usually doesn't hurt, pain comes later. But the pain in his nose had been instant. When he had been a light-heavyweight boxer, his nose had been broken a couple of times. Each time, the pain had sent him into an adrenaline induced rage that created so much strength that he had easily overwhelmed his opponents.

With water rushing into the Ford's window, Crane looked at his foot. It was caught in a crease that had been created when bottom of the car had hit something in the river. It was as if his foot were in the steel jaws of a vice. If he couldn't get free and Neal or Stan didn't come back to check on him, he would drown.

Still in great pain from his broken nose, he lifted his right foot. With the strength of the adrenaline rush, he pushed on the steel floor. The crease opened. He pulled his foot free, and just as the water was up to his neck, he slid out the door and stood in waist-deep water.

Attracted by one of the Ford's slanted headlights, thrusting a narrow beam of yellow light into the black sky, people up on the bridge were gathering and pointing to the Ford. Across the river, GIs, holding bottles of beer, poured out of Aki's Bar, stood at the edge of the river, and watched. Neal was at the opened trunk. He reached in, took out a leather bag, and placed it in his shirt. "Let those people gawk. We're outta here."

With their clothes dripping with water, they sloshed along the river until the people on the bridge were out of sight. After they shook off as much water as they could, they walked up the bank and onto a street where they slunk in the shadows until they walked into a grapy-dark alley and stopped next to a 1950 black Buick. Crane couldn't help but notice that the alley was so narrow that only one side of the Buick's doors had room to open.

Instead of the usual three chrome holes running alongside of the hood that gave the Buick the street name "Three-holer" this Buick had four holes. Just above the center of the heavy front bumper, nine short, fat pieces of chrome steel formed the grill and resembled the inverted dull fangs of a sleeping mouth. The thick steel body reminded Crane of a tank. A wreck with a small Japanese car would do little damage to the Buick.

The familiar Buick being parked in the alley took Crane by complete surprise. "This is Sergeant Gunkle's car," he said. "He calls it, The Tank."

Neal smiled. "Do you think he will mind if we borrow it.?"

Stan laughed low and hard. "You have a better idea?"

Crane placed his hand on the door handle. "No, but it's locked."

Neal pushed on the little side vent window. It opened. He reached inside and pulled the door handle. The door opened.

Crane had hotwired many cars, and Neal knew how to do it, too. "Do you want to hotwire it?"

"First, I'll look for the key." Neal turned to Crane and pointed into the dark alley. "Go in there and watch no one sneaks up on us from behind."

Crane ran into the darkness, and with measured patience, he watched from a dark doorway. Neal pulled the keys out from under the seat and held them up for Crane to see. Then he went to the trunk and opened it. Just after he dropped the leather bag, he had taken from the Ford, into the trunk, Stan rushed around the car, bent over and grabbed a tire iron.

Wondering why Stan was is such a big hurry to grab a tire iron, Crane walked toward the Buick, but when the sound of a racing motor met his ears, he stopped to look to where the sound was coming from. Out on the street, the black Nissan pickup with the missing muffler raced toward the entrance to the ally. With the cracked windshield completely broken out, it skidded to a stop, and blocked the Buick.

Out on the street, the hood of a car cruising past the Nissan caught the dim neon reflection of a bar sign, but it kept on going. As aromas from something frying in a smoking wok wafted into the night, three men jumped out of the Nissan. While one man with a stringy mustache and slanted eyes ran from the Nissan as if he had to go to the bathroom, the two other men walked to the entrance of the ally and stopped.

While both men watched Neal step into view, off to the left, Stan lifted the tire iron, took aim at the man with a bull neck, reared back, and flung the tire iron like a tomahawk. The bull-necked man was too surprised to instantly react. As the tire iron tumbled toward him, he stared in disbelief. At the last instant, to avoid being hit, he lifted his arm in a blocking motion and turned to the side. But he was too late. Thunk! The tire iron crashed into the side of his chest. His ribs cracked. Whoosh! The breath was knocked from his lungs. His knees buckled but he didn't fall. Wheezing a moan of shock, he straightened. Then he inhaled a great chest-expanding breath and blasted out, "Nobody does that to me." He took one a step and fell to the ground.

His partner, a hawk face man with a serious look, jerked his finger at Neal. "You die." Whipping a knife blade around, he lunged toward Neal.

Neal executed a loop kick. It clipped Hawk Face's legs out from under him. He went down so hard that the knife fell from his hand, but he rolled and sprang to his feet. Before he knew what was happening, Neal was all over him, pummeling him back against the wall until his knees sagged and he fell to the ground in a lifeless heap.

The door to the doorway, Crane was standing in, opened. With background noise of people inside yakking like maniacs, a girl with a beautiful face and body to match looked at him. With her moist, brown eyes gleaming, she asked, "Do you want to come in?"

The girl's friendliness and fragrant and soft hair caused Crane to have a moment of gaping wonder. But his gaping wonder was interrupted by the sudden movement of a Toyota pickup with a flat tire wobbling into view. He craned around the doorway to see what the Toyota was going to do.

A green beer bottle arced out of nowhere and crashed into the side of his head. He should have been knocked out or felt an enormous amount of pain, but for some reason, he felt no pain. For a moment, he bowed his head in genuine befuddlement and looked at the man who had hit him. A stringy mustache under a pointed nose that set between two almond shaped eyes stared back at him. Now, Crane knew where the third man had gone. The man lifted the jagged end of the broken beer bottle. Before he could slash Crane's face, Crane jerked out of his befuddlement, reached up with both hands, and grabbed the man's wrist.

The man fought to free his wrist and was tremendously strong, but Crane had the advantage of two hands on one.

Keeping the sharp shards of glass on the beer bottle away from his face, Crane held the man's arm two feet away from the edge of the doorway. "Drop it!"

The man appeared to give up the struggle. When Crane relaxed his grip. the man reached up with his other hand and grabbed Crane's hair and yanked down. This time, Crane felt pain. As if were a delayed reaction, the place on his head, where the beer bottle had broken, flared up with pain so great it was causing him to black out. He reared back, lifted the man's arm, and slammed it against the hard edge of the doorframe.

Crack! The man's arm snapped. He screamed in pain and dropped to his knees.

The broken beer bottle fell from his hand.

Thinking it was the end of the man's threat, Crane leaned against the wall and tried to regain his senses.

The man reached down and grabbed a small dive knife that was strapped to his leg.

As the blade flashed in the dim purple light, Crane cussed at the man. "Do I have to break your other arm?"

The man sprang to his feet. With his broken arm dangling, he prepared to plunge the knife into Crane's throat. Crane simply kicked the man in the stomach. The man gasped and bent over, but still held the knife. Crane kicked the knife from the man's hand. In a blind rage, the man came at Crane. Crane tried to turn to the side to avoid the man, but he tumbled into Crane. They both fell to the ground. Clutching each other for control, they rolled over three times and stopped. The man went limp. For a second Crane lay paralyzed underneath his adversary, who had ended up on top of him and was drenching him with his blood.

Crane rolled to the side. The man's limp body slid off, revealing that the sharp shard of the broken beer bottle had plunged deep into his side.

Smiling, Neal looked down at Crane. "Never a dull moment with a sharp beer bottle." He reached down and helped Crane to his feet. "Let's get outta here."

Shifting uncomfortably on his feet, Crane said, "But they got us blocked in."

Neal busted him on the shoulder. "They *think* they got us blocked in. Get in the car."

"I need something," Crane said, and staying low, and risking furtive glances he took the dead man's pants and shirt off and placed them under his arm.

Then they piled into the Buick.

Neal turned the ignition key. The powerful motor roared to life. He put the shifting lever into reverse. The transmission grumbled in to gear. He gunned the engine, and let out the clutch. The back wheels rolled in a haze of blue smoke. Bam! The huge steel bumper of the Buick plowed into the Nissan. Crane's head was slammed against the back of the seat. As the thin metal on the Nissan crumpled like tinfoil, it was easily pushed out of the way. Neal shifted into low and the took off down the street.

After they made their way through streets, clogged with cars struggling to make some progress, and through a maze of twists and turns, Neal stopped the Buick between two bars. Like a jack-in-the-box, he leaped out of the car, opened the trunk, and grabbed the leather bag. "We'll need this," he said with a big smile on his face and tucked the bag into his shirt.

Crane and Stan got out. They all stepped to the other side of the street and hailed a cab.

Three cab rides later, Crane was so confused he didn't know where he was or where he had been, but they had lost the men who had been following them.

CHAPTER 29

It was a given that dangerous people would be watching the ashes of the house where the E-Brite had been buried. If Crane, Neal, and Stan were going to dig it out, they would have to create an illusion of rifle fire and smoke that would signal an attack was being launched against the people watching.

By placing flash simulators, a meter off the ground, firing could be faked. Not having scales, and while Stan kept a sharp look out, Crane and Neal measured everything with the four-six-one spoon method: Four teaspoons of black powder would create the smoke. Six table spoons of aluminum powder would create the flash, and a teaspoon of iron fillings would create a red flame. To give the illusion of different guns firing, slightly different quantities of the mixtures were used.

When they were done mixing, Neal looked to Crane. "You ready to get the E-Brite?"

Crane held up the shirt and pants he had taken from the dead man. "Not yet. I want to make one more thing."

Smiling, Neal nodded in understanding. "That gets them every time."

Crane gathered leaves, grass, and anything he could find to fill the shirt and pants and constructed a dummy. Then he quietly slipped into the area a ways from the burn site. While Neal and Stan set up the flash simulators, Crane placed his dummy and a long stick where they would be most beneficial: in a tree. Then he tied a cord around the dummy's mid-section, ran the cord down the tree, across the ground, and hid the end of it under a bush.

Back at the burn site, the three remaining guards must have been lulled into a false sense of security. The guard who had thrown the knife at Crane was sleeping. The other two guards were bent over scooping out shovelfuls of ashes, apparently searching for the E-Brite.

Although Crane had killed a few VC, he wasn't the hardened veterans like Neal or Stan. At first, because the knife-throwing guard had given him five seconds to run away, he thought maybe he could just knock him out, tie, and gag him. But when Neal and Stan easily dispatched the other two guards, the knife-throwing guard in front of Crane woke up and reached for his rifle. Before he could grab it, Crane kicked it to the side. The guard reached behind his back for his knife.

There was no way he was going to slime his way out of it. Knocking the guard's knife away, he faked one way and went another. Then he ducked under the man's arm, came up behind him, threw his arm around the man's neck, and grabbed his own opposite shoulder. He could have cut the man's life short with the elbow under the chin choke, but he only held it until the man blacked out.

Then, as a precaution, they stripped the guards of their uniforms and slipped into them.

Crane wasn't sure if putting on the uniform of another country would make him be considered a spy, but contrary to popular belief, as long as they are discarded before opening fire, the wearing of enemy uniforms was not prohibited by international law or Article Twenty-Three of the Geneva Convention. But if the wrong people caught them, it wouldn't matter. They could be branded as spies, and without notifying the United States, they would be killed.

While Crane pretended to be a guard on watch, Neal and Stan began digging out the site.

After a few minutes of making little progress, Neal stopped digging and leaned back. "The Winter Olympics are coming to Sapporo in 1970. At this rate, we'll still be here. Let's do this the easy way."

A big smile spread across Stan's face. "Excellent idea." He stopped digging and wiped his forehead with the sleeve of his uniform jacket. "If we do it, we'll have to be quick."

Neal lifted his shovel and stabbed it into the ashes. "It's better than digging our lives away."

Crane pointed to the house with the flower garden. The dirty-white rooster had returned. As if it were suffering from shell shock, it was cautiously swiveling his head but wasn't searching for something to eat. "What about the people in that house?"

Stan smiled a mischievous smile. "Ever yell fire in a Japanese movie house?"

Crane remembered GI's yelling fire in a theater. Because flammable materials used to build movie houses went up quickly, Japanese people would empty a movie house in what seemed seconds.

Right before Neal set the charges, Stan and Crane ran around the Japanese house yelling fire. No one came out. Apparently, no one was home, or the house had been evacuated.

Just before they rounded the house, a colossal explosion of soil, ashes, and rocks formed into a cloud of dust. As if it were an afterthought, the house shook, slanted to one side, and fell over.

Fleeing the destruction, and with its tail feathers smoking, the dirty-white rooster flapped its wings and rose to a height of ten meters. When it landed, it kept on flapping and ran out of sight.

With the smell of cordite from the explosion filling the air, and his ears ringing, Crane waved the dust from his face and looked to Neal. With his ash-caked hand, Neal pointed through the cloud of dust. At the bottom of a huge hole, the tunnel entrance was clear. He took off toward the tunnel. "Watch my back." He hopped into the hole and vanished into the darkness.

With sirens tearing the night in half, a Japanese police car roared onto the scene. As if the people who had caused the explosion were escaping, Stan and Crane frantically pointed away from the site. The Japanese police slowed, nodded, and took off in the direction Stan and Crane were pointing.

People dressed like soldiers came out of nowhere. Stan hit the timer and set off the flash simulators.

The soldiers hit the ground.

Neal came running up out of the hole and joined Stan and Crane sprinting down the oil-soaked road.

Another Japanese police car spun around the corner and wailed its siren. It was right behind them. A blue Nissan, with its engine running, sat along the street. Neal opened the door, but blood on the steering wheel caused him to hesitate. Crane reached for the door handle on the driver's side. A body was crumpled in the backseat. The sight of the dead body caused Crane to realize that whoever was after the E-Brite knew Neal had it, and they would kill to get it.

The police car stopped. Two men jumped out. A fusillade of gunfire tore through the air. Electrical sparks from overhead power lines crackled angrily. Recognizing the distinctive chugging booms as a Browning M2, an exceptionally good weapon for ripping apart anything unlucky enough to appear in its sights, Crane dove to the ground.

The rasp of a Kawasaki motorcycle, starting up, echoed through the night. One of the men who had jumped out of the police car was on the Kawasaki, coming straight at Crane. The man reached for his gun. Before he could get it out of its holster, he cried out in pain. The middle section of his ear had been blown clean off. He took his hand off the handlebars and grabbed his ear. The front wheel cocked sideways. The back of the motorcycle kicked like a bucking bull and sent the man flying through the air. Crack! He landed against the side of a wooden building, bounced off, and hit the ground. He moaned once and curled into a broken hump.

Stunned silence followed.

Then, as if it were a delayed reaction, one of the Japanese policemen screamed in horror. A series of thunks from another fusillade of erupting gunfire not only cut off his screams, they caused pieces of his body to splatter onto the doors of the Nissan. Whoever wanted the E-Brite didn't care who they had to go through to get it. Crane knew he had to get rid of the man firing the Browning. He ran for the tree with the dummy, but he lost his footing and fell forward. Although he caught himself with his hands, pain jolted up his left knee. Knowing the weakest were always picked off first, he did his best to hide his hobble. But it didn't matter. They were surrounded. There was nowhere to run. But if he could get rid of the Browning that kept firing at them, they would have a fighting chance. He crawled to the bush where he had left the cord. He yanked it once. A flash simulator went off. It looked like the flash of a rifle. The stick Crane had placed next to the dummy looked like a man in the tree had just fired. The Browning let lose. Crane pulled the cord. The Dummy moved but did not fall.

The man with the Browning worked his way forward to where he could see the dummy. Crouching in front of the tree, he aimed and fired a burst of machine-gun fire. A bullet clipped a small branch from the tree above Crane's head. Just at the branch dropped onto his shoulder, Crane pulled the cord. With limbs flailing, the dummy tumbled from the tree. The man went over to the dummy and looked down. Before he realized his target had been a dummy with a stick instead of a rifle, Crane sprang from the bush and was going to take the man out from behind.

But Crane wasn't fast enough.

The man turned toward him. Crane kicked the Browning. It flew out of the man's hands and into the darkness. Enraged, the man charged Crane, but his head ended up under Crane's armpit. Reaching for the top of the man's right shoulder, Crane slammed his right forearm across the man's jaw and grabbed the forearm of his own left arm, trapping the man's head. With his left hand on the man's shoulder and his right hand on his own forearm, Crane lifted his forearm up. The move securely trapped and cocked the man's head to the side. Using this Chinese headlock, Crane threw both of his feet back. The sudden pressure and the entire weight of his body caused the man's neck to snap.

Although the man wouldn't be firing the Browning anymore, they were still surrounded. Crane figured there was no use dying without trying to stay alive. He looked for the Browning but couldn't find it. He was ready to make a run for it and let the bullets land where they may.

Before he took a step, a tremor shook underfoot, accompanied by a sonorous roar. Trying to keep their balance during the earthquake, the pursuers swayed just long enough for Crane, Stan, and Neal to take off running. Beyond the cover of the little bushes there was an open meadow. Out in the open they would easily be picked off. A fresh rattle of gunfire tore into the bushes to their left, then to their right. The earthquake was spoiling their aims.

Crane took a step toward the bushes to his left, but stopped. Jumbles of concertina wire had apparently been placed there to prevent anyone from seeking concealment.

He turned to run.

His knee buckled.

He fell to the ground.

Neal and Stan dropped down next to him.

A low-frequency thrum filled the air. The light from a helicopter flicked on then off. They knew where it would pick them up.

Neal rolled over and screamed at Crane, "When I tell you, get up, get up and run your ass off."

Crane glanced back to where they had been. Three men were moving in a protective leapfrog formation. Two men took up positions to cover the third man as he overtook them. Then the rearmost man repeated the cycle. They would be on them, and quick.

Crane would have to get up and run fast, but he needed something to keep his knee from buckling. Right now, a brace would be nice. He reached up and grabbed the top of his shoulder. The adrenaline rush gave him terrific strength. He tore the sleeve off his uniform, frantically wrapped it around his knee, and tied the ends of the sleeve into a knot.

For a moment, a terrible grinding assaulted his ears. Then like the slight pause that occurs before a nuclear detonation and feels like God is sighing, both the miniguns on the chopper let loose.

As brass jackets from spent minigun rounds poured out of the guns and into the air, dirt, grass, sticks, and anything in the bullet's path puffed and flicked into the air. All rifle fire behind Crane stopped or their sounds were drowned out by the whir of the chopper's miniguns. And those leapfrogging men were out of sight.

Neal yelled, "Get up!"

Crane grunted with effort and jumped up. His leg almost gave out. He stumbled, but the sleeve, he had ripped off the uniform, held the knee in place. As fleet-footed as an Olympic runner, with two good knees, he took off running.

When they reached the chopper, it was already taking off, but they managed to dive into the open door. As the chopper skimmed past a ridgeline, Crane looked at the man to his left. In muted lights that glimmered green, the man's rangy features, a shaved head, and a boxer's pug nose, seemed out of place. No one would believe intelligence was hidden behind that exterior. He was manning an infrared screen. On it, the figures of the men who had been shooting at them scampered about.

The man looked to Neal. "Looks like people who drink champagne and pat each other on the back sent you to fix their fuckups."

Neal nodded.

"We only killed a few," the man went on. "They'll hide the bodies. The public will never know."

"What about the Japanese police, they'll sure to be missed."

"Those weren't Japanese police, and those weren't Japanese guards."

"How will they hide what happened to the house?"

"They'll just chalk it up to earthquake damage caused by an exploding gas tank or something else. No one will be alerted."

Crane wondered about the Japanese people that lived people in the house that had fallen over during the explosion. They had probably lived there for decades. If they were like most people, they preferred the illusionary comfort of the familiar. They would have a hard time adjusting to having their home destroyed.

He turned toward the man. "What will the people in the house say when they come back and see their house fell down?"

"There's an unlimited about of money in this thing. Before you got there, that house, and a few more were bought for an exorbitant amount of money." He gave Crane a compassionate smile. "Those people are better off now than they have ever have been."

Crane was glad for the people, but when he looked away from the man something didn't seem right. He swung his eyes swung back to the man. "If the houses were bought, did that mean somebody else knew where the E-Brite was?"

For a moment, the man's green eyes studied Crane. "Intelligence knew the E-Brite was in the area, but didn't know exactly where."

The chopper banked abruptly and swung toward the Chitose Airport. Trying to estimate how far he would have to walk or run with his injured knee, Crane looked toward the airport. He was glad he wouldn't have to walk to it. Bathed in light, the tall control tower pierced a cloudy sky. But the chopper didn't land there. It landed in a dark area way beyond the airport.

Crane reached down and rubbed his aching knee. "Are we going have to walk to the airport?"

The man with the rangy features cleared his throat. "We can't be seen in a public airport. And we're not going to fly you to Shemya in this thing. You're going to have to rough it."

A stabbing pain entered Crane's chest. For a moment, he couldn't breathe. He gasped and looked at the man. "Did you say Shemya?"

The man didn't answer. He only smiled.

The strange, covert chopper landed, and true to form, before they took a few steps on the ground, the chopper was gone. Hoping the man hadn't said, "Shemya," Crane limped a few steps toward the airport.

Then another helicopter dove toward them. Expecting gun fire, Crane dropped down.

Neal laughed out loud.

Crane looked up. "What's so funny?"

"Our ride's here."

For a moment, Crane wondered why they hadn't used the chopper to go to Lake Shikostsu instead of taking the train. But then he realized that the fewer people that knew about the E-Brite the better it would be to keep it secret. When they had taken the train instead of the chopper, it had reduced the impact of their movements and restricted information about the reason for them being where they were.

With the dipping blades of the helicopter cutting the air and creating a deafening chop, grass and soil blasted upward. The chopper was a standard issue Huey. Just as long as it wasn't going to Shemya, Crane didn't mind that sort of roughing it.

Still hoping the man hadn't said Shemya, he turned to Neal. "Did that man say, "Shemya?"

Neal smiled. "You heard right."

When Crane had been sent Shemya, he had gone through Oakland, California for the first time. Wearing his fresh uniform, he had walked through the airport and drew resentful stares from people he didn't know. When antiwar protestors spit on him, surprised and afraid, he hurried past people who made chicken squawks behind him. When flying, a military paid for flight, the soldiers had to wear their uniforms. But right after they got off the plane, to avoid being spit on and called baby killers, most soldiers immediately ran into a restroom, took off their uniforms, and changed into civilian clothes. But the problem was that although soldiers wore civilian clothes, their haircuts and clean-shaven faces told the world that they were in the military.

Crane was glad he wasn't going through Oakland for a third time. And he was glad he wouldn't be tempted to wrap his belt around a protester's neck and draw attention to himself, again. But he wasn't too keen on going back to Shemya.

CHAPTER 30

After Crane, Neal, and Stan cleaned up and changed into army uniforms they were given fake orders. Under the Army Security's fictional MOS, Military Occupational Specialty, of "General Duties," they were on their way to Anchorage and then onto Shemya.

When they landed in Anchorage, Crane realized he could be sitting on his porch. People would be walking up to him and giving him money. It would be a lot better and easier than going back to Shemya. And he could easily make it home in two days. Sitting in the airport terminal, he turned to Neal and Stan. "You have the E-Brite now. You are more qualified at this sort of thing than I am, and you have people helping you. How about I catch a plane and go home?"

Neal and Stan hesitated, then looked at each other and laughed.

"I don't think it's funny," Crane said. "I hate Shemya."

Stan placed his hand on Crane's back. "We'd like you to go home and get on with your life. But you have that uncanny ability to sniff things out others can't. We not only need you to help us live through this thing, we need you to help make the whole machine work."

"And besides" — Neal reached up and rubbed his ear — "I think you'll enjoy going back to Shemya. The people there have special mission for you."

"What mission?"

"We don't know. We may never know. But you'll know."

"So, the old need to know strikes again," Crane said and recalled the single pine tree on Shemya that Boozer had peed on and killed. "What will we be doing? Cutting down trees in Shemya National Forest?"

Neal grinned. "I'd say you'll be doing something more interesting."

Stan nodded in agreement. "Whatever it is, let's ride it to the end, together."

Accepting the inevitable, Crane shrugged. "We went this far. Might as well go all the way."

Nodding expressionlessly, Neal pointed out, "To keep our anonymities, we can't arrive like regular arrivals do. We'll take a Reeve Aleutian Douglas DC-6B to the island."

When weather permitted, two or three times a week a Reeve Aleutian Douglas DC-6B delivered mail and supplies to Shemya. Isolated island life, far from sunlight, women, and civilization, caused Shemya residents to be hungry for news of the outside world. If the weather were halfway decent, a herd of island people would huddle in the cold just to greet the scheduled planes. The weather on Shemya changed so quickly that no one knew when a herd of people would be waiting. This made the chance of someone preventing them from getting the second E-Brite too great. Crane, Neal, and Stan didn't need anyone greeting them they didn't know. Their Douglas DC-6B was going to land in darkness.

Once over Shemya, for a reason unknown to them, or as a joke, the pilot opened the address system and let them monitor his conversation with the control tower. "Flight 059 requesting permission to land."

The response was immediate: "Flight 059. Permission to land, denied. Fierce crosswinds on runway."

Winds on Shemya were rarely under thirty-five miles per hour. Sometimes they reached one hundred thirty-nine miles an hour.

There was no way the plane could land in hurricane force winds on the tiny island. Although the plane had a range of three thousand, nine hundred eighty-three nautical miles and cruised at three hundred fifteen miles per hour, flying the eighteen hundred miles back to Anchorage was out of the question. The pilot would try and land on Adak. If the wind were fierce there, he would have to try to fly to Amchitka and land there. But no matter where he was forced to land, it would be awhile.

Crane looked out the window and searched the Island to see if the three, tall communication linking towers, called White Alice, could be seen. But everything was blocked with darkness and a driving snow. He leaned back and decided to get some sleep.

Right after he drifted off, the familiar feeling in his ears and stomach, when a plane descends to land, awoke him. Thinking he could have slept the entire way to Adak, he looked out the window. The island seemed to fly up toward the plane. He braced for a crash. Wheels thumped on the runway. Then prop wash was blowing away a powdery blanket of snow that covered the air strip.

The one-hundred-foot-long Douglas DC-6B lift master could carry a little over twenty-eight thousand pounds of cargo, and four Pratt and Whitney R-2800 Ca15 Double Wasp radical engines, powered the Hamilton Standard 43E60 "hydromantic" and had constant-speed props with auto feather and reverse thrust. If the plane slid off the runway dropped over the edge and crashed into the rocks below, an enormous amount of supplies and material would rush forward and crush them all. Crane was thankful the plane had the reverse thrust that enabled the pilot to reverse the propellers and slow the plane just before it was about to go over the edge.

When the plane turned around and stopped, it was in front of the hanger.

The pilot spoke into the microphone, “Flight 059 requesting permission to land.”

The control tower radioed, back, “Negative, Flight 059.”

Speaking into the microphone, the pilot’s voice had a mischievous tone. “If you can’t give me permission to land, could you please turn on the hanger lights so I can pull in?”

To Crane’s surprise, the pilot had not flown to Adak. He had landed on the pot-holed, humped up, unmaintained, World War II runway. There were no crosswinds there.

Looking out the window and watching the fierce wind and blowing snow, Crane again experienced the desolate and lifeless atmosphere of Shemya. But there was no herd of people to greet them.

The copilot stood up and began to open the door. The wind slammed it open. It sprang back and closed wildly.

While the copilot went back to the front of the plane, Crane sat there and listened to threats of fines and imprisonment from the irate tower controller until the pilot chuckled and replied, "Vic Morrow, stamp pad ink frozen."

In a submissive voice, the tower controller respectfully replied, "Pull into hanger number three."

As quickly as the wind had come up, it died down. While the plane was pulling into the hanger, Crane looked out the window. The snow had stopped. In the distance, a few weak lights, struggling to blink into the night, came from windows of wind-swept Quonset huts huddled under a couple of inches of white snow.

Inside the hanger, they descended the portable steps that had been pulled up to the Douglas DC-6B lift master. With his knee shooting pain up his thigh, Crane hobbled his way down the steps. Half way down, his eyes were drawn to a large sign on the closed hanger doors. It advised,

Do Not Open Doors
At Wind Speeds Greater
Than 55 MPH

At the bottom of the steps, a man with what seemed to be a laser pistol strapped to his leg briskly walked toward them. His face looked grizzled and old, and his dark eyes showed no amusement. He noticed Crane's gaze and gave him a conspiratorial wink. "Never can be too careful." He tapped the pistol.

Crane wondered how he had spent a year on Shemya and had never seen one of these advanced weapons. He extrapolated the answer to himself: Weapons of that magnitude were not within his compartmentalized area of need to know.

Mesmerized, he looked far off to the left. The familiar sight of the C-135 aircraft, called Rivet Ball, met his eyes. Beneath the windows, perched on top of its fat black nose, white shark teeth extended halfway up the nose and were accented by a single yellow glass eye that looked like a cat's eye. The plane reminded Crane of the first American volunteer group of the Chinese Air Force, nicknamed the Flying Tigers. But the Rivet Ball was much more than the single engine P-40 fighter. Being the heaviest and most expensive aircraft, the Air Force had, Rivet Ball carried a radar system that weighed over thirty-five thousand pounds and cost over thirty-five million dollars. It was a one-of-kind aircraft.

A thick lead bulkhead on both ends of the high radiation-generating radar compartment shielded the forward and aft crew areas from the health hazard of exposure. With a mission of monitoring and keeping track of the ballistic missile testing and the activities of the Soviet Strategic Rocket Forces on the Kamchatka Peninsula, the powerful system could track something as small as a license plate from a distance of three hundred miles. The radiation emitted from the radar could cause steam to rise off the surface of the Bering Sea. The highly secretive nature of the extraterrestrial system made it impossible for the citizens of the United States to know just how well they were being protected from Russian missile strikes.

Russian intercontinental ballistic missiles, ICBMs, were guided missiles with a minimum range of three thousand, four hundred miles. And were primarily designed for nuclear weapons delivery of one or more thermonuclear warheads to the targeted Klyuchi/Kura Test Range on the Kamchatka, Peninsula, the Pacific Ocean, and elsewhere. Each year, eight million salmon migrated to the biggest sockeye salmon lake in the world that was located in Kamchatka. Kamchatka also had the largest Stellar and Golden Eagles in the world. Crane always loved hawks and eagles. Although the public was told that exploding missiles were only a few of the three hundred volcanoes erupting on Kamchatka, Crane often wonder how many eagles had been killed by wayward missiles.

Rivet Ball missions were flown on an alert basis. Crew members referred to as "Spooks" or "Secret Squirrels" consisted of three linguists, a Morse code specialist, and a maintenance technician. To be ready to jump on the aircraft and fly whenever the word came down, they lived in the hangar behind doors marked "SS" and didn't drink alcohol unless there was a weather stand down.

A bulky man with little eyes driving an electric-powered red golf cart sidled past the man with the lazar pistol and stopped in front of Crane. "Hop in, gentleman."

"Wait!" The man with the lazar pistol extended his opened hand. "Get in, but first, give me your weapons."

Neal's forehead wrinkled in puzzlement. "Is it really necessary?"

Nodding, the man replied, "It's not that we don't trust you. There's millions of dollars' worth of equipment on the island. One stray bullet could be very costly."

Although Crane didn't like the look of the man's little eyes, Neal, Stan, and he reluctantly handed over their pistols and slid into the cart. Before the man pushed the pedal to start the cart, a small rectangular slab of the cement floor heaved open and revealed a ramp that gently slanted deep into the ground. The cart swung past the man with the lazar pistol and descended down the ramp. Pencil-thin, red and green beams of light, Crane figured were security sensors, crisscrossed the path of the cart. At the bottom, the cart turned to the left and entered a cavernous room with a domed ceiling. Shemya always had construction going on. Now Crane knew why.

Although the room was impressive, Crane was more impressed when Boozer came around a piece of equipment wagging his tail.

Unable to hold in his joy, Crane called out, "Boozer!"

The Husky dog let out a joyous whine and leaped onto Crane's lap. Snuffling and wiggling his massive body against Crane's sides and chest,

Boozer demonstrated the joy of being reunited with his friend. As Boozed continued to move and rapidly wag his tail and nuzzle, Crane gently tried to stroke the white and black fur on Boozer's head, but he wouldn't be still.

Looking toward Stan, a huge smile spread across Neal's face. "Boozer seems to recognize him."

A middle aged-man wearing an olive drab parka with the fur-lined hood over his head came from around a hall and walked toward the cart. When he stopped in front of the cart, his parka flared open and revealed hips enormous with weaponry and paraphernalia, including flashlights, a small walkie-talkie, and silver handcuffs. With an all business look on his leathery face staring from inside the hood of the parka, he coolly observed Neal and Stan. "Sorry, gentleman," he said and slipped the hood from his head. "You won't be coming on this one."

Boozer jumped off the cart and looked at the man. Then he jumped back on the cart and sat next to Crane.

The man glanced at Boozer, turned toward Crane, and extended his hand in friendship. "We've been waiting for you."

Perplexed at Neal and Stan getting cut off, Crane got off the cart. While he shook the man's hand, Boozer jumped off the cart and stood by Crane's side. "Are you sure you have the right person?"

The man laughed. "We've been watching you since you left the rock. You *are* the right man."

Puzzled, Crane turned and faced Stan and Neal.

The man noticed his puzzlement. "There is a good chance you have been followed. Neal and Stan are going to create a diversion. They're going to carry the fake E-Brite off the island."

Sometimes to ensure total concentration of a secret task, depending on the complexity of the mission, isolation could last more than a month. He didn't want to be with total strangers for that long of a time. Hoping he could persuade the man to let Stan and Neal tag along, he said, "They'll be looking for three people. It might not work."

"No problem," the man said. "Your Vietnam buddy, Kane, is taking your place."

Having a Special Forces man like Kane taking his place, made Crane think of the old marching cadence mantra *I wanna be an Airborne Ranger. I wanna live a life of danger* that ASA men had changed to, *I wanna be a Chairborne Ranger. The hell with that life of danger.* He shrugged. "Kane might as well take my place. I took his place once."

Holding the E-Brite, Neal extended his hand toward Crane. "This is yours now."

As Boozer stood on his hind legs and placed his head next to Crane's neck and snuggled, Crane opened his hand.

Neal placed the golf-ball-size sphere of silver E-Brite into Crane's palm and closed Crane's fingers around it. "This is the real thing. Watch yourself."

Stan lifted his hand to deliver a comradely poke in Crane's shoulder. Before he could do it, Boozer growled. Stan dropped his hand and advised, "Do what Neal says."

As Stan and Neal were whisked away in the red cart, Crane realized he could only go on and await developments.

The man turned his back to Crane, and started walking at a brisk pace. Before Crane could take a single step, the man wheeled his arm and talked over his shoulder. "Follow me."

Struggling to keep up, Crane ignored his painful knee and followed the man to what looked to be a latrine door.

The man pointed to Boozer. "Sorry, pal. You can't come this time."

As if he had just wanted to check that Crane was okay, Boozer nuzzled Crane's side for a moment, then turned and went on his merry way.

The man opened the door. He and Crane stepped inside. It was a latrine. From the quick pace of the man Crane figured he had to go to the bathroom. The man opened the door to a stall. To give him some privacy, Crane turned his back.

"Come here," the man said from inside the stall.

Wondering if the man was gay or something, Crane hesitated.

"Come on," the man said with impatience in his voice. "We won't be in here long."

Crane turned and squeezed into the stall. The man took the lid off toilet tank. Making sure the edge of the lid made contact with a brass pipe on the back of the wall, he leaned the lid against the pipe.

With the commode lid down, he sat on the commode.

"Sit on my lap," he said. "This thing only works when everyone in the stall is sitting down and have their feet off the floor. Crane sat on his lap. He and the man lifted their feet. A low hidden door slid open, and the floor and the commode rotated around and took them through the opening in the wall. When they stopped, the man placed the lid back on the tank. After they stood up, the commode rotated into the latrine stall, and the hidden door slid shut. Now Crane knew why people were watched when they sat on the toilet at the top of the hill.

When Crane turned away from the wall, they were in a small concrete reinforced room, with one metal door that didn't have handles.

"Crane looked at the door. "Now what?"

"We wait, but don't make a sound. If you do, the ten-minute cycle will start all over again."

After ten minutes of silence, the door opened.

They walked through the doorway and paused. Angular and intersecting passageways, like funhouse corridors, met Crane's eyes. Then the man led Crane through the passageways and into a hall with empty rooms on each side. At the third room, at the edge of a pool of light cast by a red bulb, a huge master sergeant with a red face and ribbons on his chest, stood guarding a door.

When Crane and the man were within few meters of the sergeant, he cracked to attention. The man nodded to the sergeant, and looked to Crane. "The fewer people we involve, the better. This is where I leave you." He abruptly turned on his heal, and walked away.

Before Crane could say good-by or hello, under the glow of the red light, the sergeant placed his hand on the handle of the thick door, turned the handle, and pushed.

As the thick door swung back, Crane noticed that it was coated with a layer of Teflon that dampened vibrations that made eavesdropping from outside impossible.

Crane limped into the windowless room.

Staying outside, the sergeant closed the door.

Standing alone in a vast chamber with a ceiling that rose over thirty feet, Crane felt small and insignificant. Cone-shaped spikes lined the walls, ceiling, and floor. At first Crane thought the spikes were solid plastic. But when he squeezed one of the spikes, he found that they were foam-rubber. Then he knew he was in an anechoic chamber that would absorb electromagnetic radio-frequency waves from sophisticated electronics and other sources.

Above the foam floor of cones, a large platform supported with steel stilts, stood in the center of the room. On the platform, metal cabinets formed a U around several racks of strange equipment. In the center of the platform, cabinets and racks contained gray modules that were linked together with several yards of shiny orange cable. On each rack, coffee cups set next to thin corporals who were pounding away at keyboards. The way their foreheads were creased, Crane figured they were taking very high-speed Morse code. At one time he wondered why people manually took Morse code when there were machines that could take it. The answer was that people who keyed Morse code had certain rhythms and characteristics like no other, and that by manually taking the code, the person intercepting the code developed "an ear" for the person sending the code. Whatever secret frequency the person was transmitting on, manually Morse code takers could find it.

Off to the left, the click of teletype machines invaded a purple haze of light, where a muscular Specialist Five with a pencil clinched between his teeth was working below purple and blue lights displayed on various dials and power meters. In front of his face, an array of white dials, marked FREQUECY, stood out above a monitor. Keyboards, cabled in sequence to transmitter cabinets were about the only equipment Crane recognized.

Off to his right, a door opened. Crane zigzagged around the foam cones and walked into another room. Inside, it was as if an electronic wizard's paradise had been built in an invulnerable fortress. No pictures decorated the walls, and no unnecessary furniture cluttered the room. It was like no other room he had ever seen. The walls had to be five feet thick and insulated against any form of electronic intrusion or attack.

A blue suited man, seated and huddled over, typed on a keyboard at a battleship-gray console that stretched the entire length of one side of the room. In front of him, a four-foot-wide television screen showed what the man was typing. Crane had used typewriters and keyboards on teletype machines and radar monitors, but he never had used one so big that would display text and images on a screen like this one was doing. It was new to him.

The man made a small sound of exasperation. Typing rapidly, he huddled deeper over his keyboard. Below the screen, little rectangular windows with white numbers, used to pilot black tuning knobs, were mounted in convenient places on R-390 radio receivers. Switches, buttons, gauges, and white, yellow, green, and red indicator lights, dotted other metal-encased equipment. At the far end of the console, radar monitors sat all dark and silent. Other than that, the only thing that could be considered not advanced or new was the quiet whir of a distant combination heater/air conditioning unit used to keep equipment at an optimum sixty-five-degree operating temperature.

When Crane looked up there was a second level, sort of like a balcony, it consisted of a small room with thick glass windows that overlooked banks of gray mainframes, the size of refrigerators. The three men watching out the windows were encased in what seemed to be a main data center.

Off to Crane's left, a door to a small room was open. Inside, a man captivated by a green glowing monitor screen, connected by wires to a plethora of other equipment, was perched on the edge of his seat. While his unmoving eyes watched white images leap across the screen, his bushy, gray hair framed a pale complexion, and his gold rimmed glasses rested halfway down his long nose. Crane would have guessed the man hadn't been in the sun for months. This much dedication revealed that the man was not an ordinary soldier. Crane's first impression of him was that his expertise would be far ahead of any soldier.

"Interesting," the man said and straightened from his hunched position over the screen. Arching his neck and looking at Crane over his glasses, he waved Crane into the room. "Come on in and close the door."

Crane stepped into the room.

The man held out his hand. "Close the door."

He wanted the E-Brite.

Crane closed the door but hesitated.

The man smiled. "It's all right. I'm the professor."

Without Neal and Stan next to him, Crane wasn't sure he could trust anyone. He reached into his pocket, held the golf-ball-size E-Brite sphere, and walked to the desk. "How do I know I can trust you?"

Turning from the screen, the professor swiveled his chair and faced Crane. "How do I know I can I trust *you*?"

"Because I have the E-Brite and you don't."

"*Touché,* but is it the real article?"

"You tell me."

"I won't tell you. You can check it yourself." The professor pointed to a small shelf under a silver machine. "Set the E-Brite sphere under the scanner."

Still wary of a trap, Crane reluctantly set the silver sphere on the shelf.

The professor reached around the back of the machine and flipped a switch. "This will only take a few seconds."

The machine hummed to a high pitch. Crane moved back.

The professor leaned back in his chair. "Relax, it won't hurt you. I'll show you how it works." He leaned over, reached to the side of the machine, and turned what looked to be a rheostat. "As you are well aware, every day, millions of cosmic, muon particles constantly bombard the earth."

"You lost me," Crane said. "What are muons?"

The professor gave him a conspiratorial wink. "At least you ask. It shows you're honest. These dummies around here just nod in stupidity." He pursed his lips in a businesslike manner. "Muons are cosmic particles. Heavier atoms, in dense elements, like plutonium and uranium deflect these particles more than the lighter atoms."

Crane had an idea what the professor what talking about but he wasn't sure. His confusion must have shown in his face.

The professor turned his attention toward the sphere. "Because the heavier radioactive atoms deflect the muon particles more than lighter atoms, hidden nuclear material is easy to find. Earlier this year, we scanned a packing crate. In only a few seconds, we knew there was nuclear material inside." He tapped the machine. "This machine is more reliable than the old x-rays scanners that couldn't see through steel or lead."

The buzzing of the machine slowed to a dull whirl then stopped. Bright eyed, the professor made a theatrical gesture to the machine. “Your E-Brite is radioactive. You may have it back.”

Crane took a step back. “If it’s radioactive, I don’t want back.”

“No need to worry. All the radiation is contained inside the sphere.”

Crane stepped forward, reached under the scanner, picked up the E-Brite sphere, and put it back into his pocket.”

Without missing a beat, the professor turned, pressed the keyboard, and faced the screen. An image of something similar to the E-Brite sphere appeared. “The last time I had an E-Brite, I examined it at the molecular level. I found cementite nanowires, carbon nanotubes, and an unknown element within it. I am almost positive that the unknown element gives the metal its high resilience and toughness. The E-Brite metal is similar, but much superior to the metal obtained from the Roswell incident that has been incorporated in satellite wars and is a very effective material for laser beam space shields.”

Mentioning the Roswell incident and laser beam space shields as if they were common knowledge caused Crane to wonder if the professor was some kind of nut house thing. But then he remembered the weird writing on Al Capone’s vault. If the professor weren’t crazy, the writing could have been some kind of alien writing.

“We don’t really know where the E-Brite came from,” the professor said. “It could have been one of the powerful crystals used in Atlantis. Being that Vietnam is in proximity to Yonanuni, Japan, the spheres may have come from the underwater structures of the Land of Mu. About twelve thousand years ago, Mu had sixty-four million inhabitants, and many believed they were ready for the power of crystals, but mankind never evolved enough to handle them. Their ignorant use of the crystals destroyed the Land of Mu, and later on, Atlantis, too."

The professor leaned back, took off his red bowtie, and set it on the table.

"Recent evidence suggests the power of E-Brite was the heat source that enabled many people to survive the Ice Age. The problem was that the free energy caused the people to believe the E-Brite energy would last forever, and they became complacent. As near as we can figure, a magnetic pulse from a sun flare wiped out their systems that converted it to friendly energy. The big problem was that no one had retained the knowledge to rebuild them." Peering over his glasses, the professor stared at Crane. "Sometimes an E-Brite sphere surfaces and we have to deal with it. Compared to E-Brite, alloy steel is soft and pliable." He pointed to the screen. "Look at the E-Brite I had before. You can see that it is much harder than diamonds. It is very dense."

He hit the keyboard. The image of the E-Brite enlarged. "Ahh, yes," he said and leaned back in his chair. "Usually the denser the metal, the better it retains heat. But due to the fact that E-Brite resists heat, sudden variations in temperature does not affect it."

Crane figured the heat resisting property was the reason the E-Brite hadn't detonate in the explosion in Nam. "So… that's why it didn't erase Vietnam from the face of the earth?"

For a moment, the professor's eyes rested on Crane. "If it had detonated, Vietnam, Cambodia, and part of China would be gone," he said with a little annoyance in his voice. "We don't want anything like that to happen. We have to move it to a safe place."

"What is a safe place?"

The professor reached up and pushed his glasses up. "We had planned to store it at Fort Knox."

"What?"

The professor sighed. "Although Fort Knox is a proving ground for tanks, artillery, and all kinds of armored equipment, the E-Brite will not be safe there."

Crane frowned in disbelief. "Fort Knox is a one hundred seventy-seven square mile facility," he said. "Military personnel cross train with tanks infantry, and all kinds of war machines. I have heard that gold, nerve gas, narcotics, biological agents, and Roswell aliens have been stored there with no problems."

The professor waved his hand down. "It doesn't matter. Security has been infiltrated. An enormous amount of money is permitting the bad guys to use the facility as their own personal safety deposit box." He leaned his face close to the screen. The blue glow from it, bathed his face. "This E-Brite could open a gigantic new field of industry and a source of limitless wealth." He arched his brows and turned toward Crane. "Or" – he held up one finger – "it could destroy the entire earth." He folded his finger and let his arm fall to his side. "With the capability to begin a nuclear fission reaction, E-Brite could destroy the universe, too." He directed his attention back to the screen. "The damn thing is too valuable and too dangerous to be put in Fort Knox or any other so-called government secured facility."

He held out his hand. "May I hold the E-Brite?"

Crane began to pull the E-Brite from his pocket. "Do I have a choice?"

"Does mankind have a choice?"

Crane shook his head and gave him the E-Brite.

The professor nodded. "Thank you." Turning the sphere with his fingers, he examined it. Then he pressed a few keys on the keyboard. Before a new image came up, the door behind him opened. Two men with long white lab coats entered the room. One rail thin man stood six feet tall. The other was short and squat.

The professor gestured to them. "These are my assistants."

The assistants nodded.

"They'll do some preliminary scans on what I have entered it into the computers and get the results back to us." He stood up. "It may take a while." He held out the E-Brite sphere. "Take this until we know if it's real." Crane took the E-Brite, but he was amazed that the professor had said, "I have entered it into the computers." Crane had run

Univac computers that took up a whole wall and had hundreds of flashing lights and had to be programed with perforated paper tapes. The computers the professor was using, were way beyond anything Crane had ever used or seen.

The professor stood up and turned toward Crane. “Have you eaten?”

Crane had been so caught up in getting the E-Brite to Shemya that he hadn’t realized he hadn’t eaten for two days.

“That sounds like a good idea.”

The professor gave him a mischievous grin. “They’re not having pineapple today.”

The word “pineapple” brought back memories of Crane’s tour of Shemya, when for over two months, just about everything served, contained pineapple. He had learned to put up with it, but when a Private Steele got the bright idea to eat only breakfast, because he believed there would be no pineapple served then. To his great surprise, the cooks had gotten together, made a pineapple-filled pancake as big as a garbage can lid, and served it to him.

CHAPTER 31

The Professor didn't lead Crane to the regular mess hall where the pineapple pancake had been served. They went through the door behind the professor's chair, walked down a short hall, and entered a small mess hall with six tables and a single door to the kitchen.

A man in white pants and white jacket came out and stood before the professor. "Are you here for breakfast?"

The professor looked to Crane. "Will breakfast be okay?"

Crane wasn't too keen on eating powdered eggs and drinking powdered milk that he had eaten for the year he had been on the rock. But he was hungry. He sighed. "Breakfast will be fine."

In a few minutes, the man wheeled in a cart with covered plates and placed them in front of Crane and the professor.

Expecting the worse, Crane lifted the metal cover. On the warm plate, real eggs, real ham, and home fries beamed back at him. He lifted the glass of milk and took a sip. It was real milk.

Holding his fork in his hand, the professor winked at Crane. "Knowledge has its privileges."

Crane was amazed that during his year-long Shemya tour, real food, had been right under his feet.

Back in the room, while Crane stood at his side, the professor sat in the weird nest of equipment and peered at a screen.

"Is it the real E-Brite?" Crane asked.

The professor gave no sign of acknowledgment. He was in a world of his own.

After a few minutes, he twisted toward Crane, closed one eye, and stared at him. "*If* the dummies working for me have done the microscopic analysis of your E-Brite correctly, it reveals an unusually dense atomic structure. It has macromolecular structures of unidentifiably atoms fitted tightly together like a thousand locks. I have never seen anything like it." He pointed to the screen. "Look at this. It has some chemical reactions but they require a set amount of energy to get them started."

Crane persisted. "Is it the real E-Brite?"

Still in his own world, the professor didn't answer. He continued thinking out loud. "The E-Brite will remain a mystery to modern physics for a long time." He raised one finger. "However, dependent on the volume or mass of the bomb a person is trying to detonate, the pattern can be constituently controlled." With a look of realization, he leaned back. "That's why everybody and his cousin want this."

He pushed his chair away from the weird nest of equipment and stood up. "From the information we have, it seems real. Now we have to take a ride."

"Where are we going?"

The professor opened his mouth to speak. Bam! The sudden sound of the door being forcefully opened, interrupted him.

A voice shouted from the door. "No, Professor!"

The professor's two assistants and two massive men in black suits with coffee cups in their hands came through the door.

When the four men stopped next to the professor, he turned toward the two massive men and smiled. "Hi, Yates. Hi, Chick. Coffee break already?"

Although Yates was massive, he had no color to him. Being shabbily dressed seemed to fit his rough, strong body. As if the professor were not there, Yates lifted his cup, sipped coffee, and through his cold gray eyes, he slowly watched Crane over the cup's rim.

Chick smiled and the scar on the side of face touched his ear and resembled a grotesque closed mouth. When Crane's eyes followed the scar, as if Chick were suddenly aware of the hideous way the scar made his face look, his smile vanished and caused his massive body to look more menacing than before. "Coffee break is anytime we want one."

The rail thin assistant shook his head and pointed to Crane. "Professor, he doesn't have the need to know."

The professor's face hardened. "This man has a unique skill. I need him to come to the pen."

The rail thin assistant took an aggressive stance. "But he doesn't have a need to know."

The squat assistant chimed in. "We've spent a lot of money on this thing. Strict security is a must."

The professor made a face. "Money only buys so much trust." He gestured to Crane. "I trust this man."

Searching for a response from the two assistants, Crane turned his head and looked at them.

In unison, they both shook their heads.

"What do you mean, No?" The professor said and threw his hand up. "He brought the E-Brite to us, didn't he?"

"That doesn't matter," the rail thin man said, anger rising in his voice. "He's not going into that sensitive area."

The professor leaned back and placed his feet on the desk. "If he doesn't go, I don't go."

While Chick and Yates defiantly crossed their arms across their chests, the squat assistant gave Crane a squinty-eyed look, turned on his heel, and briskly walked out the door.

As if on cue, the rail thin assistant stepped back.

Yates turned toward the door. "I'll be right back." He left.

Chick walked up to the professor and stood next to Crane.

The professor stared hard at Chick. "Can I help you?"

Chick nodded politely and held out his hand. "I'll take the E-Brite, now!"

Somehow, security had been breached. Panic splashed through Crane's body. When it came to money, nothing could be certain. From tracking Russians missiles, he knew they weren't very accurate. To make up for this they created bigger and bigger nuclear bombs. That way if the missile came close, it still wiped out its target. If these men sold the E-Brite to the Russians, they would use it in their inaccurate missiles. It could be the end of the world. Crane would die in its destruction.

Crane figured he had two options. Try and stop them now and maybe die now, or let them go and die later. If the men had gone through training like he had at the top of the hill, they would know just about everything he was going to do. The only chance he had was to use something they weren't familiar with. He decided to try a wrestling move he had used while at the top of the hill, when he threw off multiple opponents and became King of the Mat.

Although Chick was big and heavy, Crane figured he could use leverage to maneuver the man's weak spots: his ankles, wrists, and lack of speed. The rail thin assistant looked as if he would not fight, and if he did, his rail thin body would just about break in half. That would be one less to disable. Until Yates or the squat assistant came back, it would be two against one. Crane didn't want to fight all four. He had to make his moves, and fast.

Chick pulled a long, pointed steel rod from a hole in an R-390 receiver and pointed it at Crane. "Let's make this easy."

Apparently, Chick didn't want the sound of a gunshot to bring anyone to the room. Pushing off his uninjured leg, Crane lunged forward and entered Chick's guard. Now the rod was too long to stab him. He whipped his arm around Chick's arm and clamped him in a wrestling whizzer position. Before Chick could react, Crane did a back step and hip-threw him twenty feet across the room. Chick landed on his back. The rod fell from his hand. He moaned in pain.

The rail thin assistant lunged for Crane. Ignoring the pain in his knee, Crane ducked under the assistant's arms, did a double-leg-drop, picked him up, and slammed him down back-first onto the hard floor. The assistant's breath whooshed from his lungs and he went limp.

He was out.

Crane figured he was safe, but Chick was shaking his head, trying to shake off the shocking surprise of being thrown so far by a smaller man.

For a moment, the professor only sat there with his mouth agape. Then, as if he had just woken up, he jumped up. "Let's go."

Crane grabbed the chair and followed him out the door. In the hall, he slammed the door and jammed the back of the chair under the door handle. Before he took a step, Chick jerked on the door. The wheels on the bottom of the chair wouldn't give the chair enough traction to hold the door closed for long.

Down the hall, the professor excitedly waved his arm in encouragement. "Come on!"

At an intersection in the hall, the professor turned right and disappeared.

Moving as fast as he could, Crane hobbled after him. Behind Crane, the door opened with a tremendous bang and sent the chair crashing into the wall. It bounced back and headed for the now open door. Chick leaped out of the room and kicked the chair. It went flying down the hall.

Jerking his finger at Crane, Chick yelled, "You're not going anywhere."

Crane stopped at the hall intersection and made a quick right. The professor opened a metal door and held it open. "Hurry up!"

Chick was right behind Crane. If the professor held the door open for him, the massive Chick would surely make it through the door, too.

Crane yelled at the professor. "Don't let him in! Close the door."

With eyes wide with fright, the professor stepped inside and slammed the door. Crane turned and faced Chick. Standing with his arms out and his legs spread into a wide base, he attempted to stop Crane. Crane took a step to the right, but immediately stopped as if he were going to change direction. Chick anticipated Crane's change in direction and shifted his weight to that side. Only Crane didn't change direction. He continued to move in his original direction. In one movement, he lowered his level, pushed off his left foot, and did a long step. Ducking under Chick's outstretched arm, he swished right past Chick's legs, came up behind him, and bad knee and all, he immediately took off running.

After limping around a maze of halls and false exits, Crane stopped a hallway that could be a way out.

Poorly lit by low-wattage bare bulbs, about thirty feet apart, the hallway looked to be a natural fissure, more like a cave. Then it occurred to him that the many earthquakes he had been through while on Shemya may have not been earthquakes but controlled explosions to blast out tunnels. As he walked on, the walls of the hallway seemed to have been hewn out of the rock by some sort of advanced tool. Farther on, the hallway had perfectly smooth and straight walls that ran beneath a curved ceiling.

When he came to a place in the hall that had light bulbs that must have been strung along the hall to provide construction workers light, he stopped at a plywood door. He opened it and stepped into a huge room. A superstructure's geometric network of cross-beams silhouetted against the darkness of the room. As he approached, the superstructure seemed to soar up into the heavens. It was nothing like the four-story-high climbing wall he had practiced scaling and rappelling from at the top of the hill. There were no safety rails, no footpaths. Those with faint of heart would never cross it. It could be a way to ditch Chick.

Carefully Crane began a long climb up a slanted beam. When he got to the top, he stood up and looked across the length of the structure. The only way to walk across would be to keep his balance and step from one beam to another. From balancing on the top of the Clark Street Bridge in his home town when he had been a kid swimming in the river, walking across the eight-inch beam that stretched across the chasm would be a feat in which he would be adept.

A stripe of white light beamed from the opened plywood door.

Chick entered and looked up.

Crane would have loved to lure Chick up onto the beam and play a game of balance he couldn't win.

Crane waved to Chick. "Come on up."

To Crane's surprise, Chick did come up.

Crane scampered across the bean, but to Crane's disbelief Chick had no difficulty following him. Off to the left, a cable similar to unelectrified grounding cable at the very top of the high-tension tower where he and his childhood friends used go hand over hand in a contest to see who could go out the farthest, was right in front of him. This cable wasn't on a high tower, but a dark chasm waited below. Falling into it would be instant and guaranteed death.

Just as Chick reached out to grab Crane and fling him off the beam, Crane grabbed the cable and began going hand-over-hand. When he looked back, Chick grabbed the cable. Matching Crane's hand-over-hand moves, he came toward Crane. When Chick was right next to Crane, he kicked at him. Crane swung away from the kicks and frantically moved along the cable. Chick followed. Crane's hand strength was beginning to fade. But Chick was slowing. Crane hoped Chick's hand strength was fading, too.

Apparently trying to rest his hands and go back, Chick stopped and just hung there. Crane's hands were tired, too. He couldn't hold on much longer, but unlike the heavy Chick, who could not swing his feet over the cable, Crane simply swung his feet onto the cable, threw the back of his knees over the cable, hung down, released his grip on the cable, and waited for his hands to recover. Seeing this, Chick started back. But the strength in his hands had not recovered enough to go back.

But he kept on trying.

Just when he was a few meters from the beam, he stopped. Infuriated that he had been outwitted, he turned his agony-filled face toward Crane and yelled, "You rotten bastard."

His fingers stretched and hung away from the cable. When his fingertips were barely gripping the cable, they slipped off. Chick fell into the dark abyss and was gone.

With his hands rested, Crane easily made back it across the cable, walked across the beam, and climbed down.

On the other side of the room, he opened another plywood door.

It led to a hallway with more construction lights. As footsteps echoed down the hallway getting close, he managed to unscrewed three of the bulbs. Then he flattened against a stone wall, slid into the deep shadows of a doorway, and watched.

Yates entered the turn to the hallway where Crane was and stopped.

Crane knew Yates would see him. He took three steel ball bearing from his pocket and hoped it would work. As Yates neared, Crane stood in the center of the hall, juggling the three ball bearings. While the bearings continually flew into the air, he made a goofy face and talked like a carnival barker. "Step right up, young man. See the jugglers and the clowns, see the freaks, and shake hands with the baby elephants."

Amazed, Yates stopped a few feet in front of Crane. A complete look of bewilderment filled his face. "What the hell?"

Before Yates could react, with incredible speed, Crane caught the bearings, and one at a time, he threw them at Yate's face. The last one he threw hit Yates in the eye. He yelped in pain and grabbed his eye. Shouting a fine flow of profanity, he staggered. Then, pawing at the air, he bent over. Crane lifted his foot and pushed on Yate's rear. Yate's head slammed into the rock wall. His head cracked with a satisfying crunch of teeth and bone. Out cold, his body collapsed limply and sagged to the floor.

Wondering if someone could have set a trap, Crane flattened himself against the wall, took out his small stainless-steel mirror, and held it so he could see around the turn in the hall. The hall was void of any activity.

He cautiously leaned his head out and checked all three hallways and took another look.

Still, no activity.

He broke into a limping sprint.

When he made it back to the metal door, the professor was holding it open, but heavy breathing slipped up behind Crane. Even with a bad eye, Yates had somehow followed him. Crane swung around, lifted his foot, and whapped Yates in the face. Instantly, pain erupted in Crane's knee, but a snap came from Yate's jaw. Blood spurted from his mouth. But he managed to lift his leg and kick back. Crane ducked and dropped to the floor. In an effort to sweep Yate's legs out from under him, Crane whipped his leg around. But Yates only jumped over Crane's leg. Crane looked up. Yates reared back to kick Crane in the head. A green metal toolbox arced out of nowhere. Clunk! It hit Yates in the side of the head. Flap! He landed on his back. Klunk! His head slammed onto the cement floor.

Whipping his arm around, the professor encouraged Crane to, "Come on!"

Crane didn't know where he was going, but he slipped past the professor and entered. The professor locked the door behind them, and Crane was glad the professor had thrown the green toolbox.

CHAPTER 32

Under Shemya Island, with the steel door securely locked behind them, Crane surveyed what was in front of him. A cavernous concrete chamber with a roof, three times higher than the hall, stretched outward into a vast room the length of a small ship. Two rows of what looked to be earthquake proof, steel-reinforced concrete pillars, supported the ceiling. Beyond that, a dock extended into a pool of calm blue water that slowly heaved as if it were breathing.

The professor reached into a square opening in the concrete wall and pulled out a flashlight. He turned it on, cast the light around, and stopped the beam on a red lever.

The chamber wasn't reading-light-lit, but everything could be seen. Crane turned toward the professor. "Why are you using a flashlight?"

"It's a security maneuver. If I pull the switch without the light on, it won't come up."

Crane didn't know what the professor was talking about. "What won't come up?

The professor pulled the switch. "You'll see."

As Crane stood there, watching the water, he was amazed that just about everyone on Shemya Island didn't know about the boarding chamber beneath its surface. As he watched the water, it slowly churned and sent a layer of fog across the surface. When a bullet-nosed submarine surfaced, water flowed from its deck, rushed over its sides, and sent waves to the dock. And Crane couldn't help but notice that the sub was covered with anechoic tiles. These synthetic polymer tiles contained thousands of tiny voids that attenuated the sounds emitted from the sub, and reduced the range at which it could be detected by passive sonar. Now Crane knew why the sub hadn't been detected, and he knew how Shemya Stan had survived the day he had been casting the glass ball into the Bering Sea and swam out to deep water: The small submarine had come from this chamber and picked him up.

Although sparsely populated, the Aleutian Islands and the Kamchatka Peninsula were "target rich" environments for the military forces of both the United States and Russia. Based on the Kamchatka Peninsula, Soviet long-range reconnaissance aircraft, TU-95s and TU-16s made passes around the gray skies of Alaska and Shemya, but American intelligence had a more immediate concern: Soviet submarines were using the deep trench south of Shemya as a natural highway between Kamchatka and the west coast of the United States.

Normally this would not be a problem, but thermal bands in the trench acted as shields against sonar detection. To prevent Soviet submarines from arriving at California's back door armed with nuclear warheads, United States submarines patrolled the areas.

After the bullet-nosed submarine's hatch opened, a man pulled himself onto the deck, stood at attention, and saluted. The professor saluted back, turned, and saluted the American flag at the end of the dock.

Crane and the professor stepped onto the narrow gangway that led to the hull. As they ducked under the tent over the after-escape hatch on the submarine, a voice, from a public-address system, traveled across the blue water and echoed throughout the chamber, "Professor and guest arriving."

Lowering himself down the ladder to the hatchway at the bottom of the escape trunk, Crane wondered if he were taking his last taste of real air. Inside the sub, a sharp electric-ozone odor told him there was a lot of advanced equipment on board. Light-emitting diode lighting bathed the cave-like interior of the submarine in a soft glow of red light.

As if giving a tour, the professor began, "This is NR 1, one of the most secretive vessels in the undersea force. It is a sample of an upcoming generation of attack submarines that are smaller, faster, and deadlier than anything on earth. It can dive deeper than any other submarine. When it's on the ocean floor, it can roll on wheels." He gestured to a thick window in the side of the sub. "And powerful lights reveal what's below."

As the sub submerged and got under way, Crane peered out the window. The strong light revealed a retractable arm with a claw that could grab objects on the ocean floor.

"This thing has unmatched capabilities," the professor said. "Without cutting into them, crews can place rubber-coated induction tap devices over communication cables and record the signals from its electrical fields. When necessary, they sneak spies onto any shore."

From the size of the sub, Crane doubted that it could hold enough fuel to go long distances. "Sneak spies onto any shore?" he questioned. "What makes it go?"

"It has a custom-built miniature nuclear reactor that can pound out enough power to send this one hundred forty-foot glorified rowboat down to three thousand feet. About the only thing not high-tech is the chlorate candles. When lit, they produce enough oxygen for a ten-man crew to stay at sea for a month or more."

The sub slowly moved through the water, but when Crane felt the push and pull of the ocean's currents, he felt sick.

The professor smiled an all-knowing smile. "Everyone gets sick," he said. "It isn't a matter of whether you are going to throw up, it's when."

Even though the sub seemed to smooth out, Crane still felt sick, but he knew sea sickness was mostly in a person's head. He told himself to quit being a crybaby and immediately felt better.

The professor turned to Crane. "They can't follow us now."

Crane remembered all the monitoring equipment he had seen just hours ago. "What's going to stop somebody from intercepting your messages and find out where we went?"

"That's not likely. We placed instruments on telephone lines, transmitters, and receivers that tell us whether bugs have been placed and if we have been intercepted. If we have been bugged or intercepted, we have hardware that misdirects those signals to other frequencies. We can jam all radio broadcasts, including missile control transmissions. We can override jamming with laser beams. We can leak so much false information that we can keep them busy for months or years. We keep secrets and divert the flow of accurate information every chance we can."

As they traveled under the frigid water, Crane remembered the story of why the closest island to Shemya was called Hammerhead. During World War II, soldiers stationed on Shemya strung lights onto the eight-hundred-foot-long island. During air raids, all the lights on Shemya were turned off, and the lights on Hammerhead were turned on. While soldiers on Shemya sat in chairs drinking beer, with great amusement, they watched the Japanese planes hammered Hammerhead with bombs.

From the amount of time it had taken for the sub to get to where it had stopped, Crane knew they couldn't be near Hammerhead Island. Hammerhead was too close. And it couldn't be the island next to Hammerhead, Nizki Island. It had to be Alaid Island. Alaid Island was not very inhabitable. Williwaws from the Bering Sea constantly pounded its shores and eventually destroyed any building not made of steel-reinforce concrete. Any major building on the surface of Alaid would be almost impossible to erect, but under the island would be a perfect place for any clandestine construction. When not frozen, three small ponds on the surface would be a place where, under the constant shroud of fog, secret and experimental craft could surface in calm water for a brief time.

Once outside the submarine, they were not on Alaid Island. They were under it, standing on a dock. Under the dim orange light coming from strange overhead lights, Crane surveyed a manmade underground cavern. At the beginning of a pier, a gray-painted submarine lay tied up. It looked as if it had enough firepower to level the cities of any adversary.

The professor tugged at Crane's elbow. "This sub is special and falls under restricted compartmented information, but you're here now, so it doesn't matter." He pointed to the submarine. "That's a strategic ballistic missile submarine."

It was evident that in unknown locations, such as this, the submarines were powerful deterrents to any country foolish enough to think they could win a surprise nuclear attack against the United States. Although Crane figure that he had lived this long was a miracle, the fact that he was standing in one of the most kept secret places of the world overwhelmed him.

The professor looked to Crane. The crow's feet at the corner of his eyes crinkled as he smiled. "Impressive, isn't it?"

Crane nodded in awe.

Tied up next to the strategic ballistic missile submarine was another smaller sub. The professor continued, "That is a fast attack submarine. They spy on enemies in shallow harbors, drop off spies, tap underwater cables, and covertly sink enemy ships."

"Did anyone ever get a medal for risking their lives?"

"Did you?"

Crane let out an uncontrolled laugh. Although many ASA units had earned Presidential Unit Citations, Meritorious Unit Citations, and Foreign Citations, due to security reasons, they could not be placed in personnel's military records. When General Westmoreland visited a hospital to pin a Purple Heart on the pillow of a wounded soldier, and told him he would like to submit him for the Medal of Honor, Westmoreland told the soldier he was sorry, but the classified mission location made it highly unlikely. Although the soldier had risked his life, that blue ribbon would never be placed around his neck. Even though everyone knew it was an injustice, the man said he wasn't fighting for medals. He was fighting for comrades and the country.

"No, I didn't get any medals for risking my life," Crane belligerently replied and faked being excited. "But I got a good conduct medal."

"The president knew what you did or had a pretty good idea. But no president has ever had knowledge of these subs or of the E-Brite."

Crane shrugged. "I know. The president doesn't have the need to know."

"That's right. Presidents come and go, but the defense of our country goes on for years and years. As you have found out today, with something as important as E-Brite, not too many people can be trusted."

As the professor stepped away from the dock, Crane blinked away the glare of a shiny door guarded by three mean-faced men who looked to be escaped prisoners. His heart thudded in his throat. These men reminded him of the men who had trapped Neal, Rafferty, and him in an apartment house and tried to burn them to death. Although those men were long dead, just the thought of those men left a cold dread in Crane's chest.

When the men saw the professor, their mean facial expressions softened. Crane's fears subsided. Smiling, the men almost fell over themselves opening the door.

With reflecting beams of orange and blue light dancing all around them, Crane and the professor stepped into a ten-meter-high, round tunnel that seemed to have been bored into the rock. As his breath came in clouds of vapor, Crane didn't know if the substance on the sides of the tunnel were bioluminescent algae, fungi, or various bacteria emitting the light, but whatever it was, it was a natural source of colorful indoor lighting that gave the ice a translucent glow.

When they came to the end of the tunnel, Crane was stunned by what he saw before him. A domed roof stretched far above. Across the floor, equipment wound around in a circle. In the center, more equipment with crazy sequences of numbers and letters, flashed with blue and orange lights.

Standing in front of a tremendous bank of huge supercomputers, Crane stood in awe.

"The professor noticed Crane's amazement. "Those control all our military nuclear operations and regulate the fail-safe mechanisms that prevent errors and unintentional firings."

Underground is usually fifty-five degrees, and most equipment worked best at sixty-five degrees. Crane wondered why the tunnel was so cold. "Heat is available," he said. "Why all the ice?"

"The ancient people that originally built this place could not stand heat. It was difficult for them to come into an area above twenty degrees."

Crane didn't know what the professor was talking about. He figured the advanced equipment needed to be cold to operate at maxim efficiency. It was just another thing he didn't have the need to know.

They walked a few steps, and another door with a guard standing in front of it, blocked their way.

Crane had seen guards like this before. They always stood rigid and didn't have the casual attentiveness of someone babysitting civilians.

Despite his threatening display, the guard smiled and waved them forward.

The professor stepped toward the door.

The guard's smile vanished. He stopped the professor. "This is a restricted area. You may enter, but your friend has to have authority to enter."

The professor waved his hand to the side. "This comes under the sanction of a national emergency. We cannot wait for credentials of authority."

As if deciding what to do, the guard's eyebrows arched higher and higher. Then he said, "Ooo-kaay."

The professor turned toward Crane. "Let's go see the real secret." He tossed the guard a salute.

The guard nodded and seemed to reluctantly open the steel door.

They entered.

Inside, resembled a miniature repair shop. Bays, filled with parts, surrounded a machine shop office. Off to the left, a welding bay flashed with the shielded flashing of arc welding.

Crane and the professor walked to the center of a parts bay and stopped. The professor took a part from the shelf and placed it on the shelf below it. A barely audible squeak came from under the rack. The professor reached around the back of the rack column and intermittently pressed something and sent a string of Morse cope ciphers. The rack moved back and to the right. Another door met Crane's eyes.

"Reminds me of a fun house," Crane remarked in undisguised befuddlement. "What did they do, have a sale on doors?"

"Seems more like a mad house. As you have noticed, we keep things decentralized for security reasons."

The door opened automatically only to reveal a small room with another door.

The professor turned to Crane and smiled. "After a while, they'll grow on you."

The professor closed the door, reached up, and pushed a cement block. It turned sideways and revealed an aluminum box with gas masks in plastic bags. He reached over, picked up a mask and handed it to Crane. "You'll need this. Put it on."

After they donned and cleared the masks, the professor pushed open the new door, and they entered a small room filled with gas. Crane caught the faint sweet odor of nitrous oxide, laughing gas. Whomever came through the room without a mask would slip into a euphoric state and be asleep before they could get to the next door.

The professor opened another door that led to another room. Then he closed the door behind them. As a hissing sound filled the room, they waited for the gas that had escaped from the main room to be sucked out.

When they finally quit going through doors and chambers Crane felt like a rat in a maze, but they were in the main room. The professor looked to Crane. “It took a lot of circus tricks but we’re here.”

Communications equipment, Crane had never dreamed existed, graced the sides of the room. Computers, twenty feet long, with tiny, round flashing lights, were a backdrop for printers, tape recorders, radar screens, TV screens, and paper grafts with continuing rolls of white paper slowly being scratched on by needles of black, red, green, and blue ink.

Off to the side, as if orphaned, radio receivers and transmitters sat next to radar scopes. Some of the dials indicated the receivers were very low frequencies and others very high frequencies. It looked as if the receivers and transmitters could receive or transmit on every frequency of the world. And he knew one of them almost did: The Tricor III Wideband Receiver/Recorder. It had a price tag of a million dollars and recorded the full range of radio waves twenty-four hours a day. After being recorded the two-foot across wide-band spools of three-inch wide tapes, were sent back to NSA, where whole rooms full of R-390 radios could search for missing parts of high priority messages. Producing an extremely wide range of frequencies, searches could be accomplished as if the messages were being transmitted on live airways. But this Tricor receiver/recorder was not in use. Next to it a larger version of the Tricor had an eight-inch wide tape with a three-foot-wide spool. Like the smaller Tricor, this Tricor was also encased in glass and all supporting braces were also breakable glass. In the event of a security breach or attack, the glass could be easily broken and all the insides damaged very quickly. However, even though this Tricor, was advanced way beyond Crane's expectations, it was not being used. Apparently a better more efficient receiver/recorder had been developed.

Three men in the three-piece suits extended their hands in friendship. Pimples covered one man's face who appeared to be a large Asian and had a huge head with flat, menacing features. Unnatural bright-white teeth flashed from a bronze-faced man, and the receding hairline of the third man seemed to make him look older than he really was. Before Crane could shake their hands, in unison, they flashed him a smug smile, turned and stepped away.

"Glad you could make it," the pimple-faced man said while walking. "Follow us."

The professor and Crane followed the men into another room. Inside, coffee mugs hung from hooks on a shelf attached to a light-green wall.

Compared to what Crane had just seen, a coffee pot sitting on top of a hotplate secured to the shelf seemed so far out of place that it looked to be antique. Crane, the professor, and the other three men sat down at a white Formica table.

Crane had a pretty good idea how the Russians thought and how they reacted. He had tracked their missiles long enough to be able to recognize them by the sound of their telemetry. He figured that was why the men had taken him into the communications section.

"I don't know what you need me for," he said. "Anyone can pick out missile signals."

The three men shook their heads in unison.

"We know that," Pimple Face said, "but that's not why you're here."

Crane was dumbfounded. "You made me go through your circus tricks just to get here, and now you say you don't need me?"

Holding his coffee cup in both hands, the professor looked to the man with the bronze face.

Bronze Face nodded.

Staring at Crane, the professor's face brightened. "Now that we know it's really you, we need to ask you a question."

"What do you mean you know it's really me. By now you have my fingerprints."

"We tried confirming your identity with your fingerprints,' the professor said. "But they came up blocked."

"What do you mean, blocked?"

"Not known, restricted. Usually that means prints belong to US intelligence or Special Forces."

Gesturing to the classified equipment around him, Crane waved his hand in an ark. "With all the security around here, that shouldn't matter."

"That's what we thought, but past or present, it doesn't matter. Spooks always cover each other's identities.

"Why all the suspense?" Crane wanted to know. "I could be sitting on my porch collecting money. Ask me what you want to ask me and get it over with."

The man with the receding hairline turned his palm up. "I'm sure you don't' have to be told how dangerous and valuable the E-Brite spheres are."

"Spheres?" Crane questioned as if were surprised. "Are there more than one?"

Receding Hairline held up three fingers. "There are three."

Taking a Zippo lighter out of his pocked, Bronze Face said, "What we want to know is where the other two E-Brite spheres are."

"What is this, exchange stupidities day?" Crane asked. "How should I know?"

Receding Hairline leaned across the table and talked directly into Crane's face. "We know about you and Capone's gold vault. In addition to other things that this place is, it is an advanced, just about futuristic, nuclear storage facility. For the safety of the world, those E-Brite spheres belong here."

An irritating tapping sound met Crane's ears. He looked toward the sound. Bronze Face was tapping the Zippo lighter on the hard surface of the Formica table. He didn't speak. He only stared at Crane, waiting.

Crane turned his head away from him and thought about the vault. It had almost made him wealthy twice, but each time, he didn't get any real money. The first time, Blondie, the gangster, had cheated him and his two friends, Neal and Rafferty, out of the vault. The second time, Blondie came back and they had managed to get the vault and two million dollars for it. But before they had a chance to divide all the money, the people that were after it were too close. While Crane took two hundred thousand and ran a diversion with dummies dressed as Neal and Rafferty in the back seat of Blondie's Oldsmobile, Neal and Rafferty were going to hide the money and get back to Crane within a week. Crane didn't get caught, but when Neal and Rafferty came back, they had discovered the money was counterfeit. Blondie tried not to go back to a life of crime, but he was shot the first day trying to save a man's life.

A dull pain filled Crane's chest. He didn't really want to bring up the vault. The third E-Brite sphere, the neatly stacked and banded counterfeit two hundred thousand dollars, and Crane's meager savings, were still hidden in his stainless-steel chamber attached to the storm culvert in the Shenango River. If he gave that sphere to the men and they had the other two, they would have no reason to keep him alive. Dead, he would pose no security risk. They would have to kill him.

The tapping stopped.

Crane looked toward Bronze Face.

He said nothing, but Crane figured Bronze Face was a direct-action man. The type that would bull right in and keep crowding until he caused Crane to act without thinking.

"I'm not the only one who knows about the vault." Crane said and gestured to the door that led to the room with all the sophisticated equipment." What about Neal and Rafferty? With all your machines and scanners, why didn't anyone go after Neal and Rafferty?"

With his face flushed with anger, Receding Hairline recoiled as if he had been slapped. "That's our business."

Crane raised his voice. "That's just great. I thought I was done with that vault and the trouble it brings."

Without cracking a smile, the professor said, "It does seem to have a constant state of resiliency."

"I always thought something about the vault made it more valuable than gold," Crane said. "Especially when it was worth only eight hundred forty thousand dollars and we were given two million."

"Your suspicions were correct," the professor said. "When Stan was with the men who picked up Capone's gold vault, it only contained two spheres. There were three."

As if accusing Crane of something, Receding Hairline vigorously shook his finger at Crane. "It wasn't in the lining of the vault, but there were three indentations where the three E-Brite spheres had been taken out. Maybe you picked one up by mistake."

Apparently trying to agitate Crane, again, Bronze Face began tapping the Zippo lighter on the Formica table.

This time, Crane didn't look at him. The first time Crane and his friends had gone into the mine and found the vault, a trapdoor had opened in front of the vault. A skeleton, blanketed with a three-piece suit, a white fedora on the skull, and a rusty gun in its hand, was in the pit. When they came back the second time, the skeleton was gone.

While Bronze Face continued to tap the Zippo lighter, Crane ignored the irritating noise and offered an explanation. "Maybe the third E-Brite was in the mine with Capone's skeleton."

Pimple Face jerked his finger at Bronze Face.

Bronze Face's face tightened.

He quit tapping the Zippo, but Pimple Face seemed to be growing angry. "We took the skeleton out," he said. "The E-Brite wasn't in the mine with Capone's skeleton."

Another mystery solved. Crane had always wondered where the skeleton had gone and if it had been Al Capone. The men were beginning to project a feeling that made him feel trapped. He wanted to get away from them. He figured if he could send them someplace to look for the sphere, they would let him go home.

"About the only place the other spheres could be," Crane said and paused, "are in one or both of the cars sitting at the bottom of the Shenango River."

Pimple Face extended his large, veined hand and let if flop on the table. "Why would you say that?"

"When we were chased, for about an hour, the vault had been left at the top of Myers Hill. In that time, Blondie used his Oldsmobile, and Neal used an orange truck. Together they pushed a 1957 Ford, and the thugs in it, off the bridge in Sharpsville. If the thugs took the spheres, they could be in twenty feet of water at the bottom of the bridge. Or, they could be in the 1958 Chevy, Blondie forced down Myers Hill into fifteen feet of water."

Receding Hairline cocked his head with interest. "You think the E-Brites are still there."

"The river floods just about every year. Flood waters may have washed the cars and the E-Brites away."

"We've already checked that out," the professor said, impatience rising in his voice. "The river in Sharon had been dredged to stop floods until the new Shenango Dam could be built. They didn't find any cars."

Grinning, Crane looked at Bronze Face. "They didn't find them because they didn't dredge where the cars went in."

Bronze Face turned toward Crane, his green eyes flat and cold. He opened his mouth to speak, but the professor interrupted.

"That's another reason we need you," he said with a rising hint of exasperation. "As a kid, you and your buddies swam in and had boats on that river for years. You know every drop off and current from Sharpsville to downtown Sharon. If the current moved the cars, you would have a pretty good idea where they would be."

He was right about that. With no floods, and if no one had found the cars, they should be just about where they had gone in over four years ago. But Crane wasn't too keen on diving into dark water with dead bodies in the cars.

"Why don't you just get the police to pull the cars out?"

Pimple Face let out a disgusted breath of air. "Do we have to keep reminding you just how dangerous and valuable the spheres are? The E-Brite project is covert."

Crane looked around. From the strained faces and their nervy eyes, it was clear that the men sitting around the table had something other than searching the Shenango River in mind but were reluctant to tell him what it was."

"What do you really want?"

A leaden silence greeted his words.

The professor came forward. "Of course, you are familiar with MAD?"

Wanting to keep the men thinking his intelligence level was below theirs, Crane lied. "I'm not sure."

"Besides being a good magazine" — the professor grinned — "MAD is an acronym for a national security policy called Mutual Assured Destruction. If used, it would mean a full-scale use of high-yield nuclear bombs."

Pimple Face gave Crane an unctuous smile. "Do you realize what that means?"

Crane knew what would happen, but he feigned ignorance and shook his head.

With his eyes gleaming maliciously, Pimple Face leaned over the table and looked directly at Crane. "With Russia and the United States both using full scale nuclear bombs, it would cause complete annihilation of both countries and maybe the entire world. With both countries bombing themselves out of existence, there would be no victory or armistice. Presuming neither side considers self-destruction an acceptable outcome, it becomes a deterrence." He lips curled with wicked pleasure. "Are you following me?"

Crane nodded.

Pimple Face grunted and continued. "It's an effective form of Nash equilibrium, where neither side, once armed, has any rational incentive to initiate a conflict or to disarm the other." With a satisfied smile on his face, he leaned back.

The professor's face screwed up into a grimace of acute discomfort. "The nation's defense is at stake, Crane. If Russia gets just one E-Brite and reproduces it in a size as big as a BB, there will be no way the United States can retaliate. BB size E-Brite spheres could be placed anywhere. And their BB size would make it impossible for them to be found. Strategically placed BB size E-Brite spheres could destroy all our missile sites, airports, and cities. Russia would have the upper hand. The effectiveness of Nash equilibrium would vanish."

Without thinking, Crane blurted out, "But Russia doesn't have the spheres."

Again, Bronze Face began tapping the Zippo lighter on the Formica table.

With sudden realization showing in their faces, Pimple Face and Receding Hairline jerked their heads in Crane's direction. Too late, Crane knew he had made a mistake. If he knew the Russians didn't have the spheres, then he had just told them that he knew where they were. He hoped they hadn't caught his mistake.

Trying to keep the conversation going and maybe smooth over the mistake, Crane quickly said, "You have one of the spheres, the other ones are probably protected by the highest security. You won't find out where they are."

With Bronze Face excessively tapping his Zippo lighter on the table, the professor said, "No matter how honest people are, the amount of money other people will pay for the E-Brite spheres is more than enough to buy out or bribe anyone who knows where they are, and that includes local police forces, and all the judges, too."

As if agitated by Bronze Face's tapping, Receding Hairline lifted one finger and pointed to Bronze Face. The tapping stopped.

"We have to keep this thing low key," Receding Hairline said. "We must get the E-Brite and get out. We'll leave the finding of the cars to the police or some unsuspecting fisherman."

Feeling the men hadn't caught his slip, Crane lit up with excitement. "So, that means I'm going home?"

The professor seemed to share his excitement. "Keep in mind," he said. "The more good something can do, the more evil it can produce. We must keep it out of the wrong hands."

"I realize that," Crane said.

"I must warn you," the professor said and jerked his finger toward Crane. "We are working on a time thing here. It will be only a matter of time before the people after the E-Brite discover Kane is not you. Under your directions, we'll be diving in the Shenango River, just as soon as we can get you out of here."

Although Crane still wasn't out of danger, he felt relieved. He was going home. After he got there, he was going to get his knee fixed.

The professor stood up. "We better get started now. By the time we get through all the doors and chambers, we'll be ready for the old folk's home."

Crane sighed with relief, but it was premature. Just when the stress of knowing where one of the spheres had been hidden subsided, sitting across the table, Bronze Face gave Crane a menacing look. "All right, we're tired of being nice." Whack! He slapped the Zippo lighter down on the table.

Shaking a piercing finger of rebuke into Crane's face, Receding Hairline said, "Since you know the Russians don't have the other spheres that means you know where they are. And *you're* not telling us."

With a trapped feeling, Crane raised his voice. "Sorry, I just don't know."

Receding Hairline calmly continued. "If you take us to the E-Brite, it will mean a great profit for you."

Crane merely looked at him. "A great profit would be nice, but I just can't help you."

Bronze Face wasn't shouting, but his voice had a raw edge. "You know bridges and high ledges were made for people who don't want to cooperate?"

Crane didn't think they would push him off a bridge or high ledge. But he didn't know if they were going to use pain inducing pressure points and angles of twist that would cause not only physical pain but mental pain. And he didn't like the idea of being filleted by a like a fresh caught fish, and he wasn't sure if they were going to inject him with mind altering drugs and force him to tell them where his sphere was, but he would have to take that chance. Maybe the drugs wouldn't work on him. After all, he wasn't what was considered a normal person. He didn't know if it were because of being exposed to radiation or his Indian heritage, but what had always worked on others, usually didn't work on him.

Thinking about how he had saved Stan's life, he shrugged. "Do anything you want. Just because I saved a man's life, you think I know where the other E-Brites are. I don't."

Bronze Face stood up and stared at Crane. His unblinking gaze showed that he was a man who expected to be feared and had done many things to justify the fear. "Okay, Johnny Boy, you want to do this the easy way?"

People like Bronze Face often used incorrect names of the people they were grilling to add to their sense of discomfort. Bronze Face calling

Crane, Johnny Boy, didn't bother Crane. Although he was out-numbered and there was definitely no escaping where he was, but he had a plan.

He looked directly into Bronze Face's eyes. "I'll do anything you want."

But if he could prevent it, Crane wasn't going to do anything Bronze Face wanted him to do.

When certain parts of the brain are switched off and only the deepest, most primitive sections continue to function to keep the person alive, it becomes a defense mechanism that allows the brain or body to heal itself in a coma. It's like the brain has been switched to a standby mode, and nothing that is not essential to keep the person alive functions. Crane needed to get into that state. If he could, they would never make him reveal where he had hidden his E-Brite sphere.

CHAPTER 33

Still in the secret complex under Alaid Island, Crane was escorted from the room with the coffee pot and the Formica table to another room. Before he got there, he began to go to another part of his mind. He was going back to the place he had been in one of his Indian vision quests. Deep in the forest, and for three days, he had stayed in a four by four enclosure with no clothes, no food, and no water. At that time, a red-tailed hawk had stood guard. Crane's entire being had been protected by a powerful force, which permitted his mind and spirit to go to another place. In this state, he had willed a bear, snakes, and yellow jackets away from the enclosure.

He didn't know if the place he had gone to was real or only a product of his mind, but he hoped he could get into that same state so he could will away or neutralize the effects of the truth serum or whatever they were going to inject into his blood stream.

When he walked into the room, he was almost in another part of his mind. He could scarcely walk or talk. Bright and blinding lights, he had never seen before, illuminated pale cinder block walls, a white tile floor, and a gurney with a white sheet that had been prepared for him. Off to the right, a tall cabinet, with various sizes of hypodermic needles and vials of various chemicals, gave the room an antiseptic ambience. But the room was beginning to blur. All his attention was being transferred to another place, another time.

Receding Hairline helped Crane take off his shirt and told him to lie down on the gurney. To make sure he still had the E-Brite sphere, Crane brushed his hand across his pocket. The E-Brite was still there, but he thought it was strange that the no one had not taken it from his pocket. Then the bright blinding light turned pink. Being that the color pink is known to give people a calming effect for approximately twenty minutes, Crane figured they were using the color of pink to lower his defenses.

On the gurney, he caught a glimpse of movement on top of the cabinet. A vision of a red-tailed hawk looked down at him. He knew he was on his way. He let his mind take over. When the needle went into his vein, the first hint of delirium should have begun to fog his mind. But he was so far into his trance he didn't even feel the needle.

Later, even though his voice had sounded to him as if it were coming from somewhere outside his head, he had managed to remember what he had told them. All they had gotten out of him was a string of old Shemya jokes about being a Jeep. And although he had been rewarded with a big hangover, he knew it wasn't over. They caringly patted him on the back and laughed about it, said they were going to inject him again and cut him free. But their demeanors reminded him of the final inning of a baseball game where bases were loaded, there were two outs, and the count was three balls and two strikes. Any hit would win the game. The catcher walked to the pitcher's mound. While the crowd and the announcers debated over what the catcher was telling the picture to save the game, the catcher was only asking the pitcher what he was going to do after the game. It was an old tactic. For a few moments, it took the pitcher's mind off the game. It was something like when a person stays focused too long on a task and can't function. After he takes a break, the mental drain is relieved, and the person can come back and easily do what he couldn't do before. If the professor and his cronies were relieving his mental drain, they were definitely going inject him again. If that didn't work, they would send him home, and they would watch him. But that didn't bother him. All they would see would be him starting his plan to sit on his porch and have people hand him money.

CHAPTER 34

A short time after Crane had been injected for the second time, he awoke from a half-sleep and immediately began fearing for his sanity. In a dazed stupor, he pawed snow from his eyes and wondered where he was. But he couldn't see, and he was on the verge of losing consciousness. His head felt like a leather strap had been drawn around his temples and somebody was tightening it. Fighting to open his eyes, he battled to stay awake. His snow-dusted eye lids fluttered, then closed. They seemed to be too cold to force open. He struggled against the cold and finally got his eyes open.

With his eyes heavy with weariness, he studied his surroundings. Dark and piercing cold hovered in the thick fog, and a long wind moaned over the high waves of the sea and plowed up onto the shore. He wasn't under Alaid Island anymore.

With weakness filling every muscle in his cold body, and on the verge of hypothermia, he knew he would have to stay warm.

Sprays of snow rushed past the fur on the hood of the olive-drab parka that covered his upper body. Lying next to shore, between the wind-shelter of two huge boulders that had been polished smooth by wind, he wondered if he were still sane. He folded his arms against the cold and looked across the rough water. A stretch of black sand that ran along the shore told him he was back on Shemya Island. He checked his pocket for the E-Brite sphere. It was gone. He figured he had been placed near the beach with the hope that he would get the other sphere from its hiding place on the island. And, like Stan had done, he would somehow signal a submarine. But before he could make it to the submarine, the men that had injected him would intercept him and take the E-Brite.

Apparently, they hadn't counted on him coming out of the drug induced sleep so quickly. But it did have an upside. His knee had quit hurting. When he looked to his right, dark figures of men slogging across the white carpet of the snow-covered tundra caused him to groan with dread. The two figures were Neal and Stan. They made their way through the knee-deep tundra and began running down the beach. Pimple Face and Bronze Face were close behind. By the way Neal was running, it was apparent he had a briefcase with the second sphere of the real E-Brite in it. Stan continued to run along the shore. Apparently, not seeing Crane, he ran right past and plunged into the protective cover of the thickest tundra-covered rocks. As the wind wailed and the snow blew harder, Neal turned. Using a switchback pattern, he began running up the steep, rock-strewn hill.

When Pimple Face was close to Neal and was about to fire his weapon, Neal dropped the briefcase into an indentation behind a rock. Without the weight and wind resistance of the briefcase, Neal's speed greatly increased. He was out of range of his pursuer's pistol. Crane thought Pimple Face was going to find the briefcase. But he picked his way up the hill and stepped right over the briefcase.

At first, Crane was overjoyed. All he had to do was wait for Pimple Face to climb out of sight. Then he could climb up and get the briefcase with the second E-Brite in it and hide it. But on second thought, when the briefcase was opened it could release a catch and switch on a circuit of an explosive inside. Pimple Face didn't keep climbing. Instead, he looked back over his shoulder and saw the briefcase. He quickly made his way down the hill and picked up the briefcase. Not sure if the briefcase contained an explosive, Crane tried to make him drop the briefcase by throwing rocks at him. Three rocks rocketed through the air but only one thudded onto Pimple Face's back.

When Pimple Face turned, his eyes were wide with amazement. But when he saw that Crane was the one throwing the rocks, his face filled with malice. Then he called down to Bronze Face and jerked his finger at Crane. "Shoot that rock-throwing son-of-bitch."

Crane was almost positive Bronze Face wouldn't shoot. So, he popped up from the cover of the boulders, and threw rocks at Bronze Face, but it was useless. Pimple Face still had the briefcase.

Crane gave up, ran behind a tundra-covered rock, and waited for an explosion.

Pimple Face opened the briefcase,

It didn't explode.

Pimple Face cussed.

The E-Brite was not in the briefcase.

Neal had outwitted him.

The E-Brite was still in capable hands.

Crane decided to give Neal an even bigger head start. He continued to throw rocks at Pimple Face and Bronze Face. When the men in the hanger had said that Stan and Neal would go with Kane as a diversion, Crane had trusted them. But it had all been one gigantic lie. With each rock he threw, his anger grew. The only people in this E-Brite business that could be trusted were Stan and Neal. When Crane popped up to throw more rocks, the men were gone. He quit throwing rocks, stepped between the boulders, and leaned against the biggest one.

Without warning, Pimple Face came up behind Crane.

Crane turned to face him.

Contempt narrowed Pimple Face's eyes and brought a hard edge of brutality to his acne-pitted face. Crane was so angry that Stan and Neal had been lied to that he snapped, became a wild animal. Just getting over being drugged, he was frightened and enraged at the same time. He savagely turned and kicked Pimple Face on the right shin.

"After all they did for you," he screamed, "that's the thanks you give them." With anger-filled strength, he let his fist fly into Pimple Face's stomach. He doubled over. Crane grabbed Pimple Face's left wrist and twisted his arm straight. With a clenched fist, he reached for the sky, ready to strike down.

"How'd you like me to break your arm clean off?"

Pimple Face moaned with pain. "Please stop. We're only going to take you to the flight line. Your flight leaves in thirty minutes."

"Hey! You lyin' bastard," Crane snapped back. "Don't feed me that crap."

A shout echoed from Crane's left. Still holding Pimple Face's arm, Crane looked to where the sound had come from.

At gunpoint, Stan was being escorted across the snow-blown tundra by Bronze Face and Receding Hairline. With each step, they sunk up to their knees, into the sponge-like tundra. Now a prisoner, Stan had his hands folded atop his head. All three men were having trouble walking in the soft tundra, but they seemed to be following a faint trail, and by the looks of Stan's tattered clothes and battered body, he had given escape a valiant effort.

To be absolutely sure the real E-Brites wouldn't get into the wrong hands, as a test, Neal and Stan had always given out fake ones. Bronze Face and Receding Hairline must have realized the spheres were fake, but to get the real spheres they had set a trap for Stan and Neal. But they had only caught Stan.

They already had one of the real E-Brite spheres they had taken off of Crane. Now, if they had gotten another real E-Brite from Stan, they no longer needed to protect Stan and Neal. They had become disposable. Stan would be killed, and when they found Neal, he would be killed, too.

More than ever Crane was thankful he hadn't been forced to tell anyone where his third E-Brite sphere was hidden. He knew Bronze Face and

Receding Hairline needed to kill him, too. But as long as they suspected he knew something about the third E-Brite sphere, he would live.

He slowly lowered his clinched fist, but kept Pimple Face's arm extended. He was going to release him from his forced bent over position, but he thought of something. What if Stan and Neal had hidden the second real E-Brite sphere on the island? What if Bronze Face and Receding Hairline did not have the second real E-Brite, but they thought Stan and Neal knew where it was. Then they wouldn't be permitted to kill them. It was a win-win situation. All Crane had to do was convince Bronze Face and Receding Hairline that Neal and Stan had hidden Stan's real E-Brite on the island.

Still holding Pimple Face's arm in a breakable position, Crane shouted over the snow-swept tundra. "That's all right, Stan, I didn't tell them where we hid the real E-Brites."

Still bent over, Pimple Face looked up. Bewilderment filled his acne-filled face.

Crane released his grip.

With a backdrop of the Bering Sea, laced with dull gray foam, being pitted by a light snow-rain, Pimple Face stood up and rubbed his arm. As if it were a delayed reaction from trying so hard to get the E-Brite and being tricked out of it, he jerked his fist at Stan and yelled, "You rotten bastard!"

It was enough distraction for Stan to turn and swing at the gun in Bronze Face's hand and knock it into the tundra, but when he lifted his arm to swing, he sunk into the tundra and missed. To keep his balance, he leaned back and dropped his arm.

Without warning, Neal slowly rose up out of the snow-covered tundra and crept behind the two men.

Crane realized that Neal had button hooked them, a basic countertactic of circling back to observe your own back trail to see who was following you. Then Neal had used the old Russian soldier's camouflage trick of digging themselves into the snow, but Neal had dug himself into the tundra. He had literally disappeared. But he hadn't sprung up at the men as they had approached. He had used an old Japanese tactic where they dug positions with the firing slits pointing backwards, stayed low, and waited for the enemy to move past. After the enemy had moved past, the Japanese would pop up and shoot them from the rear.

Without the men seeing Neal behind them, Neal reached around and snatched Bronze Face's wrist. Torqueing the joint, he pulled the pistol out of his hand. Bronze Face spun around. His eyes were full of blind rage, but when he saw who had taken his weapon, his rage dissipated.

Seeing what Neal had done, Stan spun around and stabbed his thumbs into the Receding Hairline's eyes. Holding his hands over his eyes, Receding Hairline wheeled away. Stan stomped on Receding Hairline's right knee. It folded. Grabbing his knee, Receding Hairline went down into the soft tundra. When he began to rise, Stan lifted his foot and came down hard on Receding Hairline's neck. It snapped and he sprawled into a stunned heap, and stayed there. While he had been doing that, Neal had hooked one hand under Bronze Face's jaw and jammed his other hand flat against the side of his face. When Neal hesitated, Bronze Face tried to get away. Neal wrenched his jaw to the right and jerked his head down to the left. His neck broke with a cold snap. As his body sent signals to his brain that he was dead, he dropped to the ground.

While Bronze Face's dead body twitched from having its nerves severed, Pimple Face jumped up, grabbed Crane, and spun him around. "You're not going to do that to me." He reached behind his back and pulled out a chrome-plated 44 Magnum, and with both hands he pointed the huge gun at Crane.

There was no way Crane could dodge a bullet that close. He knew his life and the great quest for the E-Brite was over. He hoped there was a log cabin with a porch in some great place in the hereafter.

He grimaced for the shot of death.

But it didn't come.

Rushing through the blustery wind, the big black and white husky dog, Boozer, came barreling down the beach. In one smooth motion, Boozer jumped and viciously took a hold of Pimple Face's arm that held the Magnum. Pimple Face drew his other arm back to strike Boozer.

Boozer growled and released the arm.

Before Crane knew what was happening, the threat against Boozer aroused all the ferocity innate in all of Crane's being. He forgot all the training he had learned at the top of the hill. His mind screamed at the man. *You can kill me. But you'll never hurt Boozer.*

From deep inside, a hidden reserve of strength built up from being with Boozer for a year surged through his entire being. His hand moved so fast it became a blur. Before Pimple Face could strike Boozer, Crane batted the long barrel of the chrome Magnum down and let loose with a right cross. Pimple Face went flying across the rocky beach. While Boozer watched, all of Crane's pent up anger traveled to his fists. Like unstoppable steal hammers, they pounded Pimple Face's mid-section. Although Pimple Face still held the Magnum in his hand, being pummeled backwards, he couldn't lift it. Crane reached up and pulled Pimple Face's parka over his head. With his arm windmilling to get the parka off his head, he began to fall. His parka covered head and face became a new target. Crane sent a flurry of powerful punches into his face head and neck. Pimple Face rag dolled and dropped to the rocks. Crane bend over, grabbed the barrel of the Magnum, and turned it away from his body. Pimple Face resisted. Crane reared back and kicked him in the ribs so hard they snapped. Two broken, bloody ribs sprang out through exposed shirt on Pimple Face's chest. With lung-punctured breaths, he wheezed six times and went still. Blood spilled out the side of his mouth and stained the white snow bright red. Crane ripped the Magnum from Pimple Face's death grip, knelt down, and held the barrel of the Magnum to his head, ready to blow his brains all over the snowy shore.

Neal and Stan came up behind him. Crane looked up. Neal held two forked fingers below his eyes. The standard sniper-spotter visual code for "I see" immediately caught Crane's attention. He searched the area above the fog shrouded tundra. Nothing was in sight. Stan pointed to the Bering Sea. A barely blink of light signaled through the fog.

Neal pulled the parka away from Pimple Face's head and nudged Crane away from the fallen man. "Come on, Crane. He's dead. Our ride's here."

At first, Crane didn't move. Although he was staring at Pimple Face's huge Asian head with flat, menacing features, he only thought about the dream he had had about Piper. She had been holding a briefcase full of money and was standing in front of the Rivet Amber plane with the tiger teeth. To her left, a man with muscular arms was pointing a huge gun at her, and Boozer was leaping into the air. But Boozer hadn't saved Piper. He had just saved Crane, and Crane wondered, if any, was the significance of the briefcase filled with money.

Amazed at the dream and the results, Crane lowered the Magnum, lifted his arm and threw the Magnum into the Bering Sea. For good measure, he kicked Pimple Face's lifeless body. When he began to walk away, Boozer sniffed the body, lifted his leg, and peed in Pimple Face's contorted face.

From the foggy surface of the water, a cone of red light flared from the periscope of a submarine.

Crane took one step into the water. Neal snagged his arm and pulled him back. "Take that parka off. If you go under, it'll weigh you down."

Crane walked to the boulders, took the parka off, tossed it between the boulders, and braced himself against the raw, cold air. Neal walked up to him. "Here's a fake E-Brite." He handed him a sphere encased in a plastic case. "Hide this under your belt behind your back. We might need it."

Crane didn't have time to take a good look at the plastic case, but he couldn't help but notice a small button on the side. "What's this for?"

"It's a little insurance policy. If you have to show it to someone, push the button first."

When they were waist high in the freezing water, as if on cue, a snarling wind kicked up. One of the whiteouts, Shemya was famous for, made it almost impossible to see. But it didn't matter. The periscope of the mini-submarine could be seen. With wind snapping ice and snow against his face, Crane took one last look at Boozer. As if saying good-bye, Boozer, the greatest morale factor on Shemya since World War II, sat up and lifted one paw. Crane acknowledged the gesture with a nod and a wave of his hand. Then he slipped under the water.

CHAPTER 35

Shivering with a wool blanket wrapped around him and gratefully accepting the stabbing pain of recirculation, Crane slumped back against the accordion side door of the cramped quarters of the submarine and held a cup of hot coffee in his ice-cold hands. As his eyes adjusted to the dim illumination of the sub's interior green light, he studied the huge man to his right. Under a gold encrusted officer's cap, here was a man who did not have to be aggressive. His thick legs and his muscular arms would intimidate anyone. If that weren't enough, his powerful neck supported a skull that looked to be made of iron.

With his hand wrapped around the hilt of the sheathed knife at his hip, the man turned to Neal. "What do you think of the plan?" The man's accent revealed he was Russian.

Rubbing his hands together to keep warm, Neal looked to the Russian and then to the American. "It's a conspiracy of horseshit. You two assholes are not the people we were supposed to meet."

With a stunned look, the red-haired American flashed his freckled face toward Crane. "He may have a point there." He straightened his broad-shouldered body, and adjusted the gold Rolex on his wrist that lead to manicured fingernails buffed to a shine.

"We would have killed you a long time ago," he said in a voice quavering with emotion. "But we live in an age of deteriorating spiritual values. It is possible that each one of you have been betrayed by the devil and left information in various places. If any one of you die that information will become public, and because you disobeyed the laws of God, you will go to hell for it."

Crane eyed him sharply. Not only was the American's voice full of a type of confidence that only money could buy, his tailored suit fit like a glove, and the wink of the diamond studded gold ross, used as a stickpin, brought Crane's eyes to the man's expensive silk tie. The tie, the man's voice, and his attire were everything Crane didn't like. The man seemed narrow, bigoted, and basically mean. Putting in a pious manner, he was trying to preach so-called Christianity which Crane didn't agree with. To the man, everybody was Hell-bound but him, and their only chance of being saved was by him. The man's self-assumed righteousness bothered Crane so much that he couldn't help it. He had to make a smart remark. "Why don't cut your religious bullshit and give us a truth serum to make us tell you where the spheres are hidden?"

A flicker of irritation crossed the American's face, but he ignored Crane's sardonic remark and concentrated on Neal and Stan. "We don't know how you two people did it, but you have managed to thwart every means we have to make you tell us where you have hidden the E-Brite spheres."

Apparently, Stan and Neal had been injected with drugs to make them talk, and they had kept the information locked away in another place in their minds.

Instantly relieved, Crane arrogantly lifted his head. "If you kill us, we have made sure there is no way to control whatever damaging evidence we may leave behind."

Stan lifted one finger and ticked it toward the American. "From your past treatment of us, the way we see it, is that our knowledge of where the E-Brite spheres are, is the only thing keeping us alive."

With eyes full of loathing, the Russian silently stared at Stan. Crane had seen those kinds of eyes before. They contained a combination of cunning, hatred, and death. Men who had eyes like the Russian's had been trained to hate, and if it were to their advantage, they would not hesitate to die for their twisted cause.

"You'll never find all the places we have hidden addition information," Crane said. "It could be in faraway places. We could have hidden it under a floorboard in some flop house. Or it could be deep in a stone wall along a stretch of highway."

Crane was running a bluff, but since they didn't know how much he knew, and an evil person will suspect folks know more than they do, he figured they would believe him.

As if he were taking the bluff, the Russian listened. But suddenly his face twisted with anger, and a deep, low laugh tumbled deep in his massive chest. "That's beyond your capabilities."

"That's right," the American added. "You can't feed us that crap."

"Do you really know that?" Neal chimed in. "We may have had some of the information microscopically reduced. We could have that information hidden in the seam of a shoe, even implanted in a button on a shirt, where we reached it quickly and passed it on."

"It doesn't matter what you say or what you have done, "the American said. "Your actions are futile. If you do not give us the E-Brites, we will have you put away for a very long time."

Neal smiled at the American. "And just how do you think you are going to do that?"

"Simple. We can make up any story we want. And you have no witnesses."

Crane wanted to punch the American right in the ribs. "I wouldn't say that," he said and to get a clear shot at the ribs, he shifted on the bench and pointed to himself. "They have me" — he pointed to Neal and Stan — "and I have them."

The American's face turned ugly. "You're going to learn to look at this thing with a cynic's eye. If you say anything or have given anything to anyone, we'll say you're just people who have crossed over the mental line. Three idiots who think they're not crazy. Just uneducated soldiers who fantasized their basically routine jobs are something they are not, cloak-and-danger flakes. Any latrine lawyer knows it's just a psychosis that comes with the stress of people pretending they are someone they are not."

With hate-filled eyes, Crane stared at the manipulating American and clinched his fist.

The Russian must have felt Crane staring at him. "Do you have an anger problem?"

"Yes, I do," Crane snapped back and grinned. "I don't have enough anger for you."

The Russian lifted his hand to strike. "I should smack that grin right off your face."

Stan held up his hand. "Wait!"

The Russian lowered his hand.

Stan continued. "I suppose fanatics like you have created whackos, now and then. And you have sanctimonious loathing for people you cannot fool. But have you ever tried to create three whackos in a row and at the same time?"

Crane gave up on the rib punch and looked toward the Russian. Because he could not rattle Neal or Stan, intimidation flared from the Russian's eyes. "We have complete deniability. We can do anything we want, and no one will ever know we did it."

From their intimidating stares and how the American and Russian were threatening them, Crane knew that as long as they didn't know where the E-Brite spheres were, they were not going to make good on any of their threats. He deliberately smiled at the Russian. "You better start conditioning your pea brain to accept an alternate reality. You may think you are able to do anything you want, but you can't find the E-Brite spheres."

Turning purple with anger, the Russian rose to his feet and towered over Crane. "For that remark, I should rip your throat out."

Crane cringed for a moment. But secure with the knowledge he was untouchable, he defiantly leaned back and exposed his neck. "Go ahead."

The Russian reached for Crane's throat, but pulled back and turned toward the American. "Can't we do something with this little bastard?"

The American let out a long breath. "We've tried. He hasn't much experience out in that labyrinth called *the field.* When he was put under, his summations had a peculiar eloquence and sagacity, but we're only relatively sure he doesn't know where the spheres are."

Placing one hand on the handle of the survival knife sheathed at his side, the Russian pointed to Stan and Neal. "What about these two?"

Stan and Neal looked as if they had not been emotionally affected to any significant degree. Crane tried to look the same.

"They both have been in a river cage." the American said. "They're not built like other people. Even the Viet Cong couldn't break them."

"We're not going to tell you anything," Neal said. "The information is too classified to send by courier. It's too dangerous to be permitted outside this submarine. Now you have to play our game. We have sucked you in. Remember, we have what you desperately want, what you desperately need, but if we give it to you, you will kill us."

Crane wagged his head around. "To put in layman's language, you ain't gettin' shit."

Being told he couldn't have what he wanted triggered the Russian's anger. He turned to the American. "Telephones and radio frequencies are being monitored. If we call for help, they'll know we're after the E-Brite for ourselves. What do we do now?"

Wincing, the American placed his hand on the handle of his holstered side arm. "I think they have our number."

"Look," Stan said and glanced at the man's hand. "The professor has one E-Brite sphere. You have the technology to reproduce it or do whatever you want with it. As long as we stay alive no one will ever get the other spheres."

"Not exactly," the American snapped smugly. "The professor and everybody know the sphere you gave him is fake."

Surprised that the E-Brite was fake, Crane felt as if he had been slapped. "So what? You stinking lousy sons-of-bitches still ain't getting' it."

The Russian's eyes opened wide with alarm. Then with a condescending smile, Crane hated, he asked, "Just what do you expect us to do?"

Although the Russian acted like he didn't want an answer, Crane gave him one anyway, "Tell your so-called *everybody* that right before you killed us, we threw the spheres into the Bering Sea. The water shifts and currents are so bad that Russian and American submarines could search for a thousand years and never find something the size of a golf ball in that frigid water."

"If you let us go," Stan added, "you'll make it easy on yourselves."

"Easy on ourselves?" The American questioned, held his head aloft, and held his emaciated chest out.

Crane could tell by their arrogant postures that the two men in the submarine were extreme upper-echelon. They had not grown up poor, and he instantly held it against them. The hazards of the work they did, their sleepless nights, and their prolonged periods of anxiety, showed in their lined, hollow faces. They were top of the line strategists of covert operations. They were the controllers of clandestine activities. People above them and people below them had only vague ideas of what they did. These men figured every conceivable variation. They anticipated every likely consequence of a given operation. They were supposed to be the specialists. Even though they had been fooled, they were still the only ones who could make a deal.

The American turned toward the Russian. "If we let them go without getting all the real E-Brites, it will mean we have failed."

With his dark eyes under full arched brows squinting, the Russian smiled big. "Let's do half their plan. We'll just kill them and say the E-Brites are in the Sea."

In tortured wonder, the American asked the Russian, "What about the information they have ready to expose the whole E-Brite fiasco?"

"Money fixes everything." He looked to Crane. "We can even give them counterfeit money." He reached up and patted Crane on the back. "Can't we, Crane?"

It was the Russian's turn to be sarcastic, but Crane knew he was right. Money could fix just about anything. Even though it had been counterfeit money, it had persuaded him and his friends to give away a gold vault. He thought back to when he had walked under a neon beer sign and gone into a bar in Lowell, Massachusetts. He didn't know who the great writer was, but when he entered the bar, peering from under the bill on the baseball hat on his head, watching a baseball game on TV, Jack Kerouac had been sitting on a bar stool. During the seventh inning stretch, he stared at his glass of beer. As the sun beamed across the bar and though the beer, he said, "Liquid Gold," and took a long drink.

Crane thought of the vault as liquid gold, and just like liquid gold, all the wealth it had promised had ran through his fingers. Now he felt gold wasn't running through his fingers. He felt his life was running through his fingers.

The American nudged Crane's elbow and repeated, "Can't we, Crane?"

Crane let his face fill with a pained expression but managed a sarcastic reply. "Does that mean you're not letting us go?"

The American hooked his thumbs in the sides of his dark wool finely-tailored jacket and arrogantly leaned back. "We don't let anybody go."

While Crane's urge to punch the American in the ribs returned, Stan's hard, loud voice echoed throughout the tiny sub. "You people act like psychopaths. You know the difference between right and wrong, but you just don't care. To you, there is no such thing as law and order. You only care about what is right for yourselves."

The Russian smiled big. "The E-Brite can easily get us billions of dollars. It is well worth killing for."

The American reached up and opened a first aid box that was attached to the wall. Gentleman, before we do away with you, we're going to give you a special treat. He pulled out a hypodermic needle. "*This* truth serum always works."

"Don't you understand?" Crane asked in the same hard tone as Stan's. "What you are trying to do to is just not right."

Crane glanced at Neal and Stan. They knew Crane was going to fight.

CHAPTER 36

When the American had pulled a hypodermic needle out of the first aid box attached to the submarine's wall, Crane was surprised. He had thought Neal and Stan had already beaten the truth serum. If they were injected and could not go to another place as he had done, the Russian and the American would find out the location of the real spheres. Since Crane had been on the island with them, they would figure Crane had recent knowledge of where the spheres had been hidden. It was time to use the insurance policy. It was time to bring out the plastic case Neal had given him.

As if he had a headache, Crane touched his forked fingers to his forehead. Neal and Stan took notice. As Crane lowered his hand, giving the signal to "watch me", he pointed to himself and reached around his back. "If I give you one of the E-Brites right now,' he said to the Russian, "will you let us live?"

To make it believable, Neal shouted in Crane's face, "Don't give it to them,"

"Yeah," Stan butted in. "What the hell's the matter with you?"

Crane held up both hands in a stopping gesture. "I think it is the best thing to do." He reached around his back.

Reaching out for the fake E-Brite, the Russian held his outstretched arm in front of Neal and Stan and jerked it toward Crane. "Let's see what you got?"

The tension in the cramped quarters of the mini-submarine increased. The Russian and the American snapped their heads in Crane's direction and leaned forward with interest. As if they wanted to see Crane pull the E-Brite from behind his back, Neal and Stan moved as close as they could. But their darting eyes were looking for an opening. With the American's and the Russian's eyes fixed on Crane, Neal and Stan had the distraction they needed. Crane pushed the pre-determined timer and pulled the encased E-Brite, he had clutched in his hand, from around his back. "You sure you want me to relinquish this?"

The Russian pulled his hand back, reached down, and placed his hand on the handle of the knife sheathed at his side. "Open your damn hand before I cut it open."

Crane opened his hand. The sphere-shaped E-Brite enclosed in a clear plastic box sat in his palm. As if it would detonate at any moment, he laid it gently on the small space on the bench between the American and himself.

The Russian and the American craned their necks to see the sphere.

The American's forehead wrinkled with confusion. "That doesn't look like any E-Brite I've ever seen."

Neal held up his hands. "You have never seen a real E-Brite armed. Look close! You'll see how it's working."

Inside the case, the plastic explosive, Semtex filled the area around a small metal ring that encircled the sphere and was fastened to the case by a single gold screw. Attached to the screw, a tiny firing device was connected to a charged capacitor. An orange circle, the size on a dime, sat on top of a digital timer. A red wire ran from the one side of the capacitor through the tiny hole drilled through the head of a chrome bolt and into the sphere.

The timer indicated that detonation was three minutes away.

While they all watched, second by second, the digits ticked down.

Crane figured Stan, Neal, and he had fewer than three minutes to do something, and then turn the timer off.

As if they had touched something loathsome, the Russian and the American jerked back. The American had jerked back so fast that his tie pulled free of the diamond-studded cross. It popped off and fell to the floor. But he was too afraid to notice it.

"What the hell's the matter with you?" the American wanted to know.

"Since you are going to kill us," Neal said, "we thought it would be fitting that none of us have a long-life expectancy." He turned toward the Russian and smiled a big exaggerated smile. "It might be too much for your feeble brain to absorb, but we're all trapped."

Alarmed, the American bent over and grabbed the plastic encased sphere and shook it. "Turn this thing off!"

To add to the distraction, Crane pointed to the cross on the floor. "Don't you want your cross?"

Surprised, the American bent over. When his finger touched the cross, like a blur of solid steel, Neal's hand flashed past Crane's face and rocketed into the Russian's face.

Stan jerked to his feet, ripped the first aid cabinet off the wall, and swung it at the American.

He missed.

The door of the cabinet flew open.

Needles and vials rolled across the floor.

A spatter of blood glistened harshly on the steel wall

Neal had hit the Russian so hard his nose had been jammed flat into his face, and the blood had splattered against the wall.

The American punched Stan in the center of the chest.

Stan grabbed his chest.

His knees buckled.

He fell to the floor.

Neal turned toward the American.

Crane shot up from the bench. In one motion, he reached up with one hand and jammed the Russian's gold encrusted officer's cap over the Russian's eyes. Then he grabbed the knife from the sheath on the Russian's belt, and sank the long blade into his chest. With a rush of blood erupting over his hand, he twisted the knife. The deep-voiced Russian responded with a guttural reply. Crane withdrew the knife and dropped it on the floor. The Russian's horrible heart pumped blood out a severed artery. Like a fountain, blood squirted in front of Crane's face. He stepped back.

Next to the dying Russian, Stan lay gasping for air. His features contorted, his eyes glazed and frenzied.

The American lurched toward Stan.

Neal came at him, wild-eyed, he reached up, gripped the lapels of the American's jacket, and slammed him against the blood-spattered wall with such force that the air flew out of his lungs in one great whoosh. Holding him in place, Neal looked down at Crane. "It's him or us."

Crane scooped the Russian's knife off the floor, slammed it into the American's stomach, and turned it upward into his heart. Although the American's eyes grew white and wide, a smug better-than-thou look, Crane hated, beamed from his face. Crane's urge to punch him in the ribs returned. He let go of the knife, swung, and hit him in the ribs. A gush of blood-filled breath sprayed from his lungs and past Crane's shoulder. The American's last labored breaths were quick and fatal. Neal released his grip. The American rag dolled to the bench, slumped over, and flopped onto the floor. As if it were a last dying effort to be forgiven for his crimes against humanity, his hand fell on the cross laying on the floor.

Crane looked at the plastic encased E-Brite lying on the floor. The timer flashed sixty seconds. Trying to be calm, he grabbed Neal's shoulder and pointed to the E-Brite. "Don't you think it would be a good idea to turn that thing off?"

Stan sat on the floor and stared at the timer. "It's supposed to be fake. But in this game, it may have been switched for something real."

Neal glanced at the timer. "It's just like the E-Brite you gave to the professor. It's fake, too."

Crane's felt his mouth drop open. "What?"

A sneaky gleam emanated from Neal's eyes. "We never gave a real E-Brite to anyone."

"That can't be," Crane protested. "After they drugged me, they took the sphere that past the professor's muons cosmic particles test out of my pocket. It is radioactive."

"Sure, that one was. Neal said and broke into triumphant laughter. "I took some of the plutonium, I had gathered in Vietnam, to a very skilled Japanese man that Piper had told me about. But he had something better. He made the fake E-Brite spheres and placed a particle of Colbalt-60 in some of them. I didn't give you a radioactive one to give to the colonel because I didn't know he was smart enough to test it with Polaroid film."

Confused, Crane looked at Neal. "A radioactive one would have saved a us lot of trouble, but just what is Colbalt-60?"

"About the size of a grain of rice, it's a source of gamma rays used in radio therapy. To make it more interesting, it glows blue."

"The sphere may be radioactive, but now I think the professor always knew it was fake."

"How did you figure that out?"

"When the professor examined the E-Brite, he had said, '*If* the dummies working for me have done the microscopic analysis of your E-Brite correctly…' Then, I should have realized that even though the E-Brite I gave to the professor was radioactive but fake, he pretended it was real.

Probably arrange his assistants and the massive men to make it look like they were after him and me. Because they were after both of us, he probably figured I would trust him enough to show him where the real E-Brites were hidden."

Neal's eyes slanted toward Stan. "Makes sense."

"Sure does," Stan said. "But if Neal had had another fake E-Brite, all this trouble could have been averted."

"How's that?" Crane wanted to know.

"He would have placed it in the briefcase. When the man chased him up the hill and stopped to pick up the briefcase, he would have taken a fake E-Brite and went on his merry way."

"He would have been on his merry way after he shot me," Neal corrected. "If you remember, the only reason we are alive is because we know where the E-Brites are."

"That's true," Crane agreed. "But the plutonium you gathered in Nam has a half-life of eighty-seven, point seven years. Did you have a radiation suit and mask to pick it up?"

"You didn't know it, but each one of us had a suit. After we used the Giger counter with the little TV screen and found the plutonium, we placed in the containers and it was rendered harmless."

"I hoped you didn't get exposed." Crane grabbed the end of the American's jacket and began wiping the blood from his hands.

"We didn't." Neal smiled and looked at Crane's hands. "Don't worry about the blood. It'll come off in the ice water."

Crane stopped wiping his hands. "What ice water?"

"The water you're going back into. You're going back to shore."

Dumbfounded, Crane slumped down. "Didn't you see the whiteout out there? What do you want me to do, freeze to death?"

For a moment, Neal's face held a hint of pity, but he managed to speak with a pretense of optimism. "What's a little discomfort when you know you'll be sitting on your porch collecting money?"

"How can I go home and sit on my porch when they know I killed that man?"

"Nobody except Boozer knows you killed him," Neal said. "You were not supposed to come out of the chemical injection so soon. You have done what nobody else has ever done."

Stan eyes glistened with approval. "Your advantage will be being at the rendezvous already established." He grinned mischievously. "And besides, I don't think Boozer is going to tell anyone what happened."

Suddenly Crane felt lost and lonely. He was, again being separated from his old friend Neal. Trying to make his time with Neal last a little longer, Crane said, "I still haven't warmed up yet." He groaned at the thought of going back into the ice-cold water. "Hey, just a second. Doesn't this sub have a full complement of equipment?"

It was supposed to have compressors, rebreathers, wet and dry suits, and one submersible, robotic camera, the whole nine yards. But it doesn't."

With his head bobbing with fake sadistic laughter, Stan said, "We'll take you where it's waist deep."

"It might not work," Crane said. "I'd rather go where you go."

Neal's voice took on a tone of total authority. "I'm not going to let you base your decision on ignorance. Here's how it is going to be. Stan and I are marked men. If our escape pans out, we'll be okay, if not, they'll be after us until the day we die. You have been given an out."

Crane faced Neal and Stan. "But what about you?"

"We have a ride waiting for us at Adak." He reached under the bench, slid out a box, and opened it. The chemical smell and the claylike substance, told Crane it was filled with C4, a greasy feeling explosive that was notoriously stable. Burned, electrocuted, or shot with a bullet, it would not explode. But an intense shock wave, like the one caused by an exploring cap, would release its powerful force.

"Before we go ashore on Adak," Stan said, "we'll surface. Then we'll tune to VHF channel sixteen, the international distress frequency. We'll send a Mayday that Neal and I are in the Bering Sea and the sub is going down." We'll eventually blow this sub up and send it to the bottom. But before we do that, you'll go back to Shemya."

"Why would I want to do that?"

"We figure that when they find you and you're still where they left you, if you act like you're in a groggy state, they'll believe you never recovered from the truth serum. We'll be blamed for killing the men on Shemya, and because they'll believe that you never went after the E-Brite, like they thought you would, they'll think we have the other two E-Brites. You'll get to go home, build your porch, and do more exciting things like watching chickens peck and cows graze. You'll be out of the E-Brite picture."

Crane wanted to tell Neal what he was really going do when he got out, but at the moment there was not enough time. "I might be out of the picture, but my clothes will be wet. When they pick me up, they'll know I've been in the sub."

"We'll dry your clothes here, and put them in a waterproof bag."

Crane looked around the sub's interior. "Where are you going to get a waterproof bag?"

Stan leaned forward. "It's a body bag."

Remembering the body water that had fallen on him, Crane slumped with disappointment. "It was ice water and something like that that got me into this mess."

Apologetically looking at Crane, Stan added, "If it'll make you feel better, we'll put a towel in it."

Neal seemed stunned. "You and I have done things like this before," he said and jokingly smacked his hands over his eyes in exasperation. "You should be getting used to it by now."

"Maybe you're right. I rather bury a corpse than be one."

Neal gave Crane a thumbs up. "That's the ole Crane I know." He nudged Crane's ribs. "You want to know what we're going to do with the E-Brites?""

"Don't tell me what you're going to do with the E-Brites," Crane said. "That way, if a new truth serum is discovered, no one will ever get its location from me."

Stan's manner took on a shrewd, significant air. "Any sane person would not want a weapon like the E-Brites."

"That's true," Crane said. "But couldn't we find someone in the government to do the right thing with the E-Brite?"

Stan waved his hand in the air. "After all you have seen, do you think any bureaucratic arm of the government would be able to keep the E-Brites out of the hands of psychotics?"

Crane lifted one finger and jerked it. "You have a good point. The bureaucratic arm of the government has become a breeding ground for idiots."

Neal grinned with satisfaction. "So…it makes sense to give the E-Brites to no one. We might just drop it into the Mariana Trench. It's just down the road from Japan, and it's almost seven miles deep. At that depth, the tectonic plate subduction will eventually push the E-Brites deep into the mantle of the Earth."

Stan assuredly placed his hand of Crane's shoulder. "Let's just say we're taking it to Tinkerville. But if you really want to know what we're going to do with the E-Brites, you can base your decision on ignorance and come with us."

For a moment, Crane thought about staying with them. But he wasn't like Neal. Neal never valued the ordinary. In war, most people feel the loss of the humdrum and the security of the everyday routine. Neal could never find himself longing for a settled life. That was just the way he was. And Stan seemed to be just like Neal.

Neal and Stan would always be chasing the wild free feelings they had in combat. They were addicted to the indescribable thrill of danger, but Crane wanted no part of it. Five thousand, seven hundred and eighty-three miles away, his cabin and porch were waiting to be built.

They parted with handshakes, and Crane stepped toward the escape hatch. He was sad that Neal was staying, but Neal had always liked to be on the move. Beyond every road there were only more roads, and no man could drive over them all. Neal had known many girls, but had never been in love. Crane hoped that someday Neal would feel a vast longing, a yearning for something more, and although he would not know what he was yearning for, eventually he would come back to Patagonia and search for it. Then, the trio of Neal, Crane, and Rafferty would be together again.

"Hey, Crane," Neal said.

Wondering if Neal had somehow changed his mind, Crane turned.

Neal stood there with his famous smile that could sell toothpaste. "We'd say good-by, but you're not here."

Crane knew he would never be able to tell anyone what had happened. He shook his head in undisguised admiration. "That's right."

CHAPTER 37

When Crane popped his head above the opened hatch to leave the submarine, a frigid wind kicked up a steady blast of fine snow. It whipped at his face, and a new pain gnawed in his head. As mist and darkness made it impossible for him to see more than a few feet ahead, his thoughts spun, turned smoky, and his brain struggled to distinguish between the real and unreal. As he had done many times before, he recalled what had happened when he was five years old. Only this time it was as if a phantom movie screen had been positioned before his eyes, and he was watching it through a haze.

At first, all he could hear was a continuous murmur of talk, intersperse with laughter rising and falling. As his vision zoomed in, he realized it was the old smiling-faced neighbor setting in a metal lawn chair listening to a baseball game on a tube-type radio that set in the window of his house. Beyond the sound of the radio, Crane watched himself. He was once again five years old, standing outside in the backyard of his house in Patagonia. The unpainted and dismal ramshackle house was badly in need of repair, and the other houses around Crane's were also dirty and unkempt, and the back yards were patchworks of backyard burning dumps that sent sickening smoke curling into the air.

A slight breeze blew between the neighbors' dilapidated houses, and when a rat scrambled under a stack of broken wooden boards, a lone blue jay scolded the air. In the distance, the shrill steam whistle of the steel mill cut the day. The horn of a locomotive engine, switching cars at the Ferrona Yard, droned into the neighborhood. It was a usual day in Patagonia, until the breeze stopped.

Then all sounds stopped.

All became calm.

While Crane stood under the splendid arch of a crystal-clear blue sky, a weird feeling of peacefulness surrounded him. He looked up and to his left. No more than the height of a tall Maple tree, a dull-silver rocket ship hung horizontally in the sky. Crane was amazed at its shape. Instead of having a long, pointed end like the comic book space ships had, so they could conceivably punch through atmosphere of the earth, this space ship had a blunt end, and not a single fin had been attached to the tail end of the rocket. Instead, curved pipes, in the form of monkey bars, he had climbed on in the playground, wrapped around the rocket's tail end. On the side of the rocket, there were three dark porthole-like windows.

As he watched in awe, the rocket began to move. It didn't roar and blast off like rockets he had seen in comic books, and even though the rocket was moving, no fire was coming out the tail end. Scarcely moving in the calm sky, the rocket began to go away, not straight up, but horizontally in a slow straight line. Excited, Crane ran into his house. His mother was baking bread. Breathlessly, he pointed to the door. "There's a rocket ship outside. Get the camera and take a picture."

Puzzled, his mother glanced toward the door. "What are you talking about?"

Crane slowed his speech a bit. "There's a rocket ship outside. Get the camera and take a picture of it before it goes away."

"It only a beach comber. We don't have money for film. Go outside and play."

Crane didn't know what a beach comber was, but he ran outside and looked up. The rocket ship was still scarcely moving, but it had moved a good way. Then as mysteriously as it had appeared, it vanished.

Barefooted, with the breeze blowing through the holes in the knees of his pants, Crane stood in his back yard with his eyes fixed on the sky searching for the rocket ship. But it never reappeared. When he lowered his eyes, the blast of the locomotive engine resumed. The blue jay once again scolded the rat. After one lone peep, from the steel mill's steam whistle, cut the once calm air, the neighbor's radio began broadcasting the baseball game, again.

Everyone Crane had told about the rocket ship didn't believe him. They told him he may have dreamed it or was making it up. After a while, he quit telling people. Over the years, thoughts entered his mind that he may have indeed been dreaming, but the space ship had been so real and had made such an impression on him that no matter what anyone said, he knew he had seen it.

When incredulous greenish rays filled the air above the submarine, Crane figured the faint and eerie display of greenish rays were from the Aurora Borealis. But when the greenish rays dissipated, he knew he was seeing the rocket again. The Flying

Tiger incident between Anchorage and Tachikawa Air Force Base, revealed objects that not only had been tracked by radar, they had been sighted, and those objects could have been this rocket or similar ones.

While Crane had been watching the phantom screen, the submarine had completely surfaced, and the wind had died down. Still standing in the open hatch, he tilted his head upward. Suspended in midair, in a milky mist coming from the island the rocket was above his head. He turned and called down, "Neal, Stan, there's a rocket ship up here."

There was no answer.

Crane didn't see the alien depart the rocket, but it was on the submarine, and it was standing directly in front of him. It had its hands clasped behind his back and was staring at Crane.

At first Crane thought the alien was sitting down. But then he realized the alien's full height was half of his. The alien extended his three-fingered hand and touched his withered neck with what seemed to be a serpent's tail and smiled through a tiny toothless mouth. As springy white hair danced away from its large almond shaped eyes, its pitifully hunched shoulders sloped forward. When its head slowly turned on its thin neck, its gray skin stretched tight over its delicate, finely-boned face, and it looked up at Crane.

Crane reached out and offered his hand in friendship. The alien extended his hand. But the moment the alien's three fingers touched him they became strangely withered and dry. It seemed as if the heat from Crane's body was too hot for its delicate skin.

The alien didn't talk. He communicated by thoughts, and Crane could understand everything the alien was showing him in his mind. Crane realized that he had entered the alien's mind set used for the observation of human beings. He was in an aura where the ordinary laws of nature had been suspended or superseded.

As if in a time machine, Crane peered into one of the dark porthole type windows of the rocket. To his amazement, he was not only looking down at himself, he had somehow been transported into the rocket. Although the inside was suffused in a weird blue glow, some sort of highly reflective silver coat covered his body. His breath came out in huffs of fog. It was cold in the rocket, but the aliens wore no coats. They wore no clothes at all. Having no reproductive organs such as earth people, there was no need to cover themselves.

One of the aliens touched him on the shoulder and smiled. Although he didn't speak, "You'll be just fine," entered Crane's mind. "A tiny chip has been placed in the bone of your skull. You will never know it is there, unless we need you."

As if in a trance, Neal and Stan appeared in the rocket and gave the alien the two real spheres. The alien nodded and gave them two identical fake spheres back.

In his mind, Crane wanted to know what the alien was going to do to Neal and Stan.

Again, the alien's thoughts entered Crane's mind. "Neal and Stan will be returned to the submarine. They will have no memory of what has happened. They will throw the fake spheres into the Mariana Trench and never know the difference."

Thinking it was all some sort of nightmarish buffoonery, Crane violently shook his head. The alien didn't fade or disappear. Although Crane could feel his feet standing on the cold metal floor of the rocket, he was sure he was having withdrawal hallucinations brought on by the truth serum.

Like cold water, the frigid air inside the rocket splashed into Crane's face. As colored lights cast crazy patterns, the alien lay down on his ice-strewn bed and looked up. Like a lost child, it expectantly gazed at Crane through big almond shaped eyes.

Without uttering a single word, the alien permitted Crane to understand that the E-Brite could very easily cause a nuclear, man-made star of death, and that he needed the E-Brite spheres. They use them for stored fuel for their rocket ship. Gold was the only truly safe container for the spheres. That was why they had been stored in Capone's gold vault. After taken out of a gold container, the spheres became unstable. They would begin to disintegrate, and to keep them from falling into ignorant people's hands, the spheres would detonate after five years. Crane was five years old when the rocket had come into his back yard, but four and a half years ago, the spheres had been taken out of Capone's gold vault. In six months, the spheres would detonate.

The alien reached out and opened his hand. He wanted Crane to give him the third sphere.

Crane communicated back to the alien, "We're too far away from the Shenango River to do anything."

The alien pointed to the porthole type window.

Crane looked out.

The rocket was still stopped in midair. In the distance, the area was cloaked in fog. But right below him, the icy waters of the Bearing Sea had been replaced with cobalt blue water sparkling in a huge beam of warm sun. All around the blue water, frothy sprays of white foam creased the shore. The steep bank above the shore, was a dark and gloomy place where someone had dumped old lumber and bricks into a rank growth of weeds and grass. Off to the left, the outline of the Clark Street Bridge materialized out of the fog. Although the usual murky green water was now blue, Crane knew he was above the Shenango River. The culvert that hid the E-Brite sphere was directly below the rocket ship.

The alien communicated to Crane that he wanted him to swim down and get the third and final sphere from the storm culvert.

Mentally, Crane asked the alien why he hadn't gotten the sphere himself. The alien replied that it could not go into the water. If it did, it would be like stepping into molten metal. A water temperature above forty degrees would surly vaporize it. Now Crane knew why there was ice under Alaid Island and the tunnels were so cold. If the aliens returned, they would need the coldness of the ice to keep them alive.

Crane nodded in understanding, dove out of the cold rocket, and plunged into the familiar water of the Shenango River. The water wasn't warm, but it was much warmer than inside the rocket ship.

Without a mask, Crane felt his way to the culvert and the hidden chamber that held the sphere. Before he could open the chamber, he ran out of breath. He surfaced to let the sun warm his face and looked toward the bridge. Piper was standing on the catwalk holding the briefcase from the dream. It was still filled with money. He rubbed his eyes to make sure she wasn't an illusion.

She waved to him. "I'll wait for you."

Crane wanted to get the E-Brite, give it to the alien, run up onto the bridge, and rush into her arms.

Rejuvenated and warmer, he dove back down. This time, he swam for the bottom and picked up a small stone. Then he swam to the chamber and opened it. For a second, he felt the two hundred thousand dollars, then he removed the sphere and replaced it with the stone.

When he surfaced, somehow, he had been transported to the inside of the rocket. Before he gave the sphere to the alien, Crane mentally asked, "Why don't you share your advanced technology with the earth?"

"The people on Earth have not evolved much past the caveman. About the only difference is that they have better communicating skills and machinery. But they still fight amongst themselves and have no regard for the future."

Crane mentally agreed and handed the alien the E-Brite sphere.

When the alien nodded and smiled, Crane felt the alien's gratefulness and relief, but when he asked where the E-Brite had come from, it was as if the alien and the rocket ship had been sucked into invisibility.

Without warning, Crane was back in the icy water of the Bering Sea.

CHAPTER 38

When Crane popped his head up out of the frigid waters of the Bering Sea, he expected fierce wind to be icy cold on his face. But it was not. He should have been on the verge of hypothermia. He should have been experiencing amnesia and slurred speech. If his body temperature had dropped to ninety-one degrees, a stupor would have set in. If his body temperature had dropped to eighty-seven degrees, he would be uncontrollably shivering, and his heart could stop beating. But none of these things were happening.

In horror week, the top of the hill had flown him to an undisclosed snow-covered, deserted beach. There, he had learned to achieve what some called the "porthole effect". This was when his real self had become a passenger in his body. Back then, many hours in icy waters had caused his skin to become chafed and frozen. With his muscles aching from constant exercise and no sleep, he had learned to mentally retreat to the inner safety of his body. Once there, it was as if he were peering through a porthole, where he watched the hostile world around him. Regardless of the pain and discomfort outside of the porthole, his mind had still functioned. If he hadn't learned to retreat into the porthole, he would have allowed the physical discomforts to take over his mind. He would be dead. He had hated horror week, but now he knew it was why he was able to cope with the madness of cold water.

He took a deep shuddering breath and studied the shore. Looking through a faint sheet of fog that had settled low to ground, he could see no ruthless hunters swarming the island. A whiteout must have stopped any search activities, and wind was still scraping ice and snow along the beach.

A thick swirl of snow kicked up and sprinted toward the rocks where his parka hid. Once the swirl got there, it skirted along the shore and stopped. Then Crane noticed it. For a distance of fifty meters around him, and all the way to the shore, not only was he standing in calm water, it was as if an atmospheric god was taking a break to inhale. The blowing winds ceased. Right in front of where his parka was hidden, the whiteout had subsided, and the rocks glistened with wet.

Beyond the calm water, as if they were waiting their turn to pound his body into the surf, three kinds of waves jumped and rolled. At the edge of the calm water, gentle spilling waves that he could swim through, using quick swimming strokes, didn't look threatening. But on both sides of those waves, surging waves waited. They were the types of waves where two bowmen would have to dig their paddles into and attack them so the raft would leap over. If they didn't punch through, the waves would come crashing down on their raft and fill it up with water. Further out, in the misty distance, plunging waves threatened. They were the ones that arched and formed a tunnel like surfers rode. Plunging waves like this couldn't be punched through. The only way to handle those waves was to avoid them or body serf them to shore.

But Crane didn't have to avoid any waves. The water around him was icy, but calm.

Towing the floating body bag that held his clothes and wondering if the shore line was an illusion, he took a tentative step toward the glistening wet rocks. He waited a bit, took another step, and waded ashore. After he walked past Pimple Face's half-frozen body, the calm water roared. All three waves crashed together and sent white foam flying into the air. Fierce wind kicked up and blasted a ribbon of ice-rimed human entrails from Pimple Face's side and caused them to turn in the wind like a kite's tail.

Crane turned from the sight and leaned into the great rush of icy air. As his face went numb, he took cover between the boulders, and hunched down. Then the fierce wind stopped. When he stood upright and began to dry off, he found that the water on his body had frozen. Although he was wiping drops of ice from his body, he knew it was better than trying to get sand off from doing sugar cookie drills at the top of the hill, which was when a combination of surf torture and drills had left him with wet sand clinging to his entire body.

After he dried off and put his dry clothes on, he dug his parka out of the snow, shook it out, and put it over his now shivering body. Before he could zip up the parka, just as quickly as it had stopped another wind-whipped whiteout blasted the Island. As he struggled to stand upright in the blasting wind and snow, his boots crunched on the snow, and his open parka flapped like useless wings.

For Crane, the old Inuit proverb, "It's not the cold that kills, it's the wind," became fact, and he wondered if he would ever be warm again. He hunkered down between the shelter of the boulders, and with fumbling, clumsy fingers, he closed his parka, and zipped it up. With his teeth uncontrollably chattering, he hunched in his parka and pulled the edge of his fur-lined hood over his face.

As his face began to warm, it painfully burned.

Still shivering, he picked up the body bag and was thankful that it was big enough to contain his entire body. He stepped into the bag, lay on the ground, and curled compactly on the dry surface of the bag, but his legs felt cold. So, he used the semi-frozen towel to cover his legs and waited.

An hour later, the sound of two small Russian jets thundering overhead roared in Crane's ears. He sat up and poked his head out of the bag. The sky had cleared. Although the boulders blocked his view of the jets, from previous experiences, he knew that in an attempt to intimidate the people on the island, the jets had swept down and across the buildings. When the jets roared overhead, Crane looked up. As if they had been trying to intimidate the cold horizon and gave up, the jets peeled off in different directions and shrunk to dots. When he looked to his right, the sea before him stretched flat and empty to the horizon. Then sullen clouds filled the gray sky to sift sparse snow over the island. The fall of snow thickened and the vague horizons were blotted out, and Crane sat alone in a white and silent world.

The body bag had kept the icy wind at bay, but his feet were numb, and cold was traveling to the center of his back, and his knee was throbbing. The Alaskan winter days were only a few hours long. It would be dark soon. He wished he were home in the summertime, and he was standing on a hot blacktopped road where the heat waves shimmered and danced. If someone didn't find him, he would have to walk to one of the old, World War II Quonset huts, the hanger, or someplace warm. But if he did, and someone saw him, the professor and his cronies would know he had come out of the drug induced sleep early. His whole charade would collapse. He would be an E-Brite target again. He had to stay where they had dropped him off.

Shivering, he stayed between the shelters of the boulders, lay down, and curled into a fetal position. With wind howling over the rocks and spurts of ice and snow blanketing him, he waited.

He tried counting backwards from one thousand and back up again, but time dragged on. When he stood up and looked around, the world of Shemya had not only been whitewashed away from view, it had been swallowed by a thick, dense fog. He lay back down, and his shivering continued. He huddled into a tight ball and tried to shut out the cold.

An hour later, with his frosted breath sending icy fog into the frigid air and wind whipping fine grain like snow against his body, the scant light, from a cloud-blocked sun, faded to almost nothing.

He tried to make the time pass and forget how cold he was by thinking how it would be after they rescued him. After the wheels of the plane lifted off the runway, eventually the coldness of the Bering Sea, the Shemya snow, the Shemya fog, the Shemya desolation, and the Shemya sadness would fade away. Once he was home, the reeking vapors of death would clear away. Tree leaves, blades of green grass, flowers, gentle lakes with cattails sheltering bass, and eagles and hawks flying overhead, would be part of his world again. All would be as it had always been. The familiar light of day would shine from a fogless sky. Shemya, the E-Brite spheres, and all the trouble they had caused, would vanish as if they had been a bad dream. He would try to forget the dark and hateful betrayal of mankind. He would try to rid his heart of the innermost feelings of whatever unspeakable, evil thing it was in the souls of men. But not completely. He knew he could never forget what the promise of wealth and the power E-Brite could cause some men to become.

For hours, the snow had been dancing down, and he had stood up, beat his arms about him and stamped his feet to keep them from freezing. When he lay down to sleep, he found that nothing was warm anymore, and it was possible to be too cold to sleep.

All the thinking or daydreaming in the world wasn't going to keep him warm. He realized he had never recovered from his last swim in the Bering Sea. His shivering had gotten worse. His damp pants legs had actually frozen together. It would be a struggle to get back on his feet.

Even though his charade would collapse, he decided to get up and hobble along until he could find someplace warm. If he didn't, he would die.

Trying to prepare to meet his terrible fate, he sat up. Before he could struggle to his feet and shake off the snow, a low wind moaned. Then something making light whispering sounds, was moving through the snow. A familiar whimpering sound enter his parka-covered ears, and a rare slice of sunlight filtered through the fog and brightened an area an arm's length away. And Boozer's snow-dusted face appeared.

After a look of reorganization, Boozer barked three times. Wagging his massive tail, he came over to Crane and nuzzled his thick furry body next to him. Just the sight of Boozer warmed Crane's heart. He stood up and looked toward the Bering sea. As if in a dream, all ice and snow were gone. Off to his left, Rivet Amber with the laser eye and the shark teeth painted on the front of the fuselage stood suspended in midair. He wondered if the spy plane was using its photographic eye to film the alien and the silver rocket. If it were, it would be no problem. Rivet Amber could film in black-and-white, color, infrared, three-dimensional, and imagery techniques that were highly classified and totally unknow to others anywhere. At his side, Boozer stood on his hind legs just in front of the glass ball Crane held in his hand. And he noticed that he no longer was wearing a parka, but he wasn't cold. He was wearing black T-shirt and his old blue jeans. The purple gold pink and magenta sky which was rarely seen on Shemya had become an artist's masterpiece. But it only lasted for a moment, and Crane wondered it had been real or a result of the extreme cold and ferocious winds that scourge the island causing him to hallucinate.

The next thing he knew he was back in the wretched land of constant wind, rain, fog, and snow. Laying in the bag on the ground, he curled compactly, staring at the semi-frozen towel covering his legs cold legs. As he used his hand to stroke Boozer's back, Crane no longer felt the cold. Then, as Boozer had done in the theater, during Crane's Shemya tour, Boozer curled up at Crane's feet.

Minutes later, beams of searchlights crisscrossed and penetrated the dense night fog. They were searching for him. When boots crunched on the snow, Boozer sprang to his feet and ran down the beach, barking.

Crane squirmed inside the body bag he had been laying in. If they found the bag or the towel, his deceiving actions would be for not. He shed the body bag, picked it up, and placed the towel in it. Even though Boozer's barking was leading them toward him, the search party moved purposefully. And Boozer was walking back to him. They were getting close. The body bag had become stiff from the cold, but he managed to fold it and tuck it beneath a rock covered with tundra.

Faking a groggy state and with Boozer protectively at his side, Crane was rescued.

Everything went the way Neal had said it would go. On Crane's separation papers, the reason listed for his discharge read, "Unfulfilled enlistment commitment". But he did manage to get out of the army without arising suspicion from fellow soldiers or the railroad.

He never did get the ten-thousand-dollar Variable Re-Enlistment Bonus, and the powers to be had sent him home without pay.

Although surgery at the Walter Reed Army Medical Center had not completely repaired his knee, because his military records indicated he was not on active duty at the time of the injury, he was denied service-connected disability benefits. With no money and no disability benefits, apparently, the people who wanted the E-Brite believed that if he had somehow had the sphere, they had a slim chance that he would try to sell it.

Even if Crane had the sphere, he wouldn't have to sell it. Hardship hadn't broken him. It had strengthened him. Finally, free, he would pursue his plan to sit on his porch and have people hand him money

After the plane landed in the Youngstown, Ohio airport, the door swung outward. When the retractable stairs slid down and touched the ground, he had it all set in his mind.

After he bought the land, he would build his log cabin with the porch. In the intoxicating essence of summer, he could watch his black and white, speckled-faced border collie. Being extremely energetic and sheltered by a blue sky with slow-moving white clouds, as wooly as sheep, the collie would romp around the front yard, and it would have space to run. It would herd the swans and the ducks. Maybe, in a flurry of fur, with a few whorls of white, it would playfully chase a working largemouth bass away from the shallows. After snuffling like Boozer, the collie would know good people from bad and be somewhat reserved with strangers who would destroy the land.

His porch would have an airy room off to the side. Inside, bookshelves against the inner brick wall would be a back drop for an old assortment of comfortable furniture where, Sparky, a long-haired black cat would sit on his shoulder and purr while he sat at his typewriter.

In winter, huge windows would allow a spacious view of the fields, the woods, and the lake that meant so much to him. What he would see was what others would pay to see and use: An ever-changing landscape of sanctuary. In the warm days of summer, cattails would populate shallow water. Balanced on green, glassy water, wild mallard ducks would propel themselves gently around the curve of the bank.

Surfacing-feeding fish would jump and splash, defying fisherman to catch them. In the fall, orange, red, yellow, and golden trees would reflect across still water and imitate beautiful Bob Ross paintings. Canadian geese would fly over in huge V formations always followed by one straggling goose, honking behind.

When the golden dust of twilight settled, and the geese had water-skied across the water, making long white lines, sunsets would turn orange then red. In the final magenta twilight before nightfall, the water would radiate with purple shimmering colors until the night blinked to a peaceful black.

Then a night sky would brighten with stars and send down moonlight to dance on the water, and he would leaf slowly through his treasure trove of mental images of Piper.

The final problem was that Crane discovered that he may have been given ketamine, a drug that produced what doctors called a "dissociative reaction," an almost an out-of-body experience that gave users the feeling they were in two places at once, watching themselves from a distance. And it caused him to not be absolutely sure that the alien encounter, and Piper standing on the bridge was not just a hallucination from the truth serum, the cold water, or a dream. At first, he figured it didn't really matter. Even if the E-Brite wasn't fake, it would be in the deepest part of the oceans of the world, and subduction would take place. One tectonic plate would move under another tectonic plate. As the plates converged, the two E-Brites would sink into the mantle of the earth and never be found.

Even though the world was safe, Crane still needed to know if the encounter had been a hallucination or a dream. He went to the Shenango River, swam down to the chamber, and opened it. The sphere was gone, but the stone he had taken off the bottom of the river had taken its place. The E-Brite threat was no more. As if guided by a ghost hand, he reached back into the chamber and gathered a few bills from the now jumbled stack of two hundred thousand dollars.

When he surfaced, and examined the money, it didn't have the feel or markings of counterfeit money. Maybe that was what the briefcase full of money Piper had been holding in his dream was all about. The money could be real.

With his heart jumping with anticipation, he looked toward the bridge. An old battered 1940 Ford coup with duel exhaust pipes thundered across the bridge. Behind the wheel, Neal excitedly waved his hands as he talked. The red-headed man next to him acted as if he weren't paying attention to a thing the driver was saying. He was smiling a toothy grin that habitually flashed from his freckled face. It had to be Crane's old friend, Rafferty Alnut. Neal had come back. The escape plan had worked, and Rafferty was still alive.

Neal stopped the Ford.

The door opened.

Rafferty stepped out. Being the half-wit, he had always been, as if he were stepping to unheard music, he began merrily bobbing his red-headed head and lifting his knees as he marched across the catwalk. His crazy antics would do a lot to wipe out bitter memories of people who have lost their respect for humanity. He made Crane feel humble.

Piper stepped out.

Not only did Crane fall in love again, he felt he was in a place with people who were abnormally happy to see him alive and in their presence.

With the E-Brite threat eliminated, old friends back together, and Piper at his side, Crane would share a special place the E-Brites would never destroy. He had learned too much to believe that anybody could be harbored from the everlasting universe of human hurt at human hands, but his plan would make a better world for the people who would walk up to his porch and pay to use his fishing lake. It wouldn't be the cockamamie plan Sergeant Gillette said it would be.

THE END

DOUBLE DRAGON NOVELS BY RONALD K. MYERS

Action/Adventure/Mystery
DILLINGER'S DECEPTION
IMPOSSIBLE GOLD

Military Espionage/Action Adventure/Thriller.
ALMOST FREE

Humorous/Historical Fiction/Action Adventure
I'M GONNA CUT YOUR EARS OFF
FREE RIDE

Futuristic
STAY ON THE BLUE GRASS
THE ORANGE TURN
PYGMY WARS

CPSIA information can be obtained
at www.ICGtesting.com
Printed in the USA
LVHW040232121121
702953LV00008B/588

9 781786 955180